SUNRISE

Janice, Sue
Shared in a

Remember the Old Woman and Shoe?
Playing under the Big Oaks and quilting?

Walk in the Son shine

Enjoy —
Cheryl

Written and Illustrated by
Cheryl Gore Pollard

Sunrise
©2013 By Cheryl Gore Pollard
All rights reserved.

Published by Dogtrot Publishers
w/CreateSpace.com
978-1483970462
ISBN-10: 1483970469
Also available in eBook publication

All rights reserved. No part may be reproduced without written permission from the author/illustrator.

This is a work of fiction. Characters are drawn from the imagination of the author. This book or parts thereof may not be reproduced in any form, stored in a retrieval system, or transmitted in any form by any means without prior written permission of the authors, except as provided by United States of America copyright law.

Cover Photo and Interior Illustrations: Cheryl Gore Pollard
Cover Graphics: Elizabeth E. Little, hyliian.deviantart.com
Interior Formatting: Ellen C. Maze, The Author's Mentor,
www.theauthorsmentor.com

The following is a work of fiction. Names, characters, places, and incidents are fictitious or used fictitiously. Any resemblance to real persons, living or dead, to factual events or to businesses is coincidental and unintentional.

PRINTED IN THE UNITED STATES OF AMERICA

Sunrise is for my husband, Jimmy

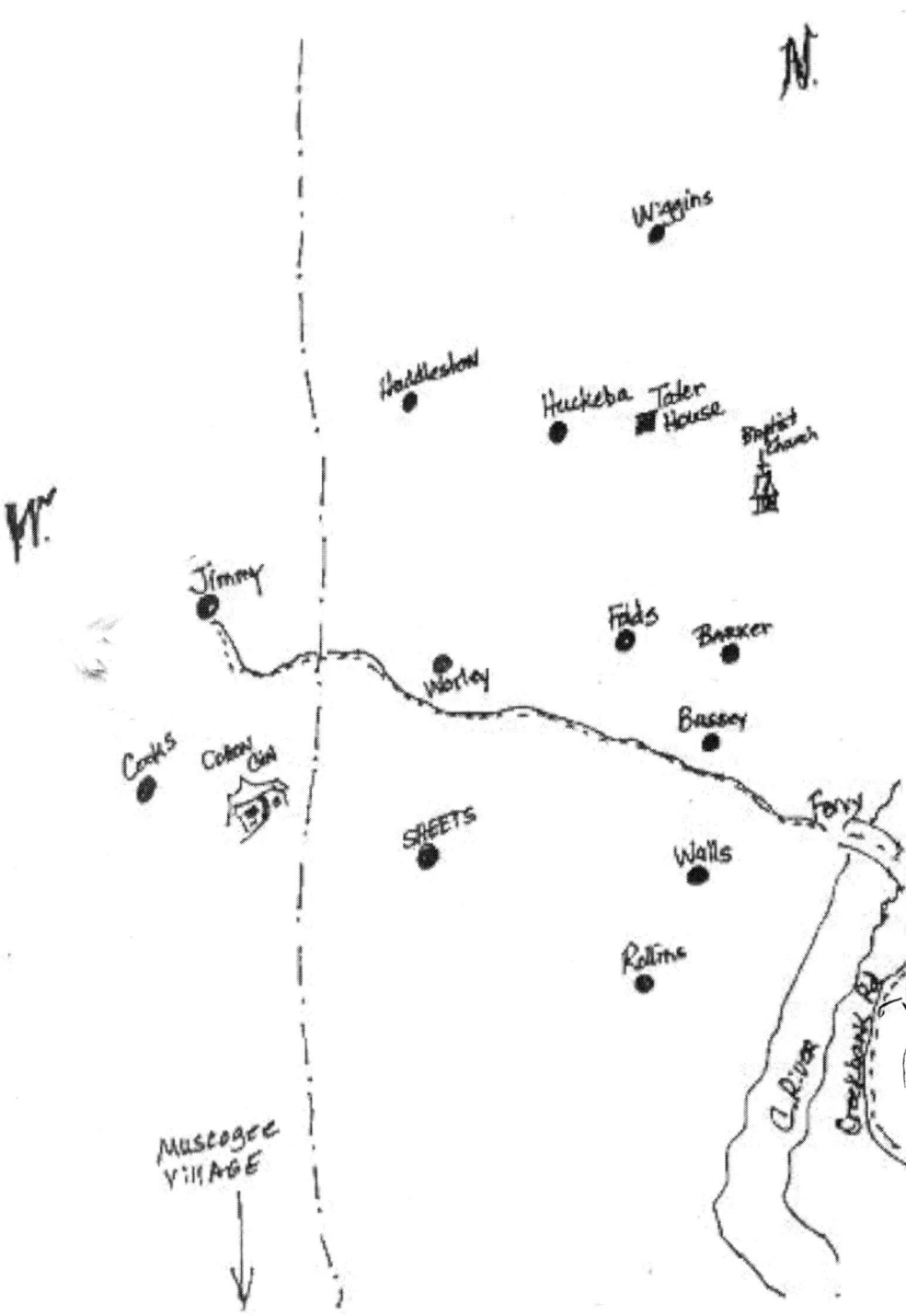

INTRODUCTION

Sunrise is written to remind us to walk with Jesus, the Light. God gave us, from the very beginning of Creation, light to take away darkness. With the coming of light, many of our fears, insecurities, and apprehensions are banished. Isaiah 2, verse 5 prophesizes: O house of Jacob, come ye, and let us walk in the light of the Lord.

And we know, according to John 8:12, Jesus spoke and acclaimed to us that He is the light of the world; he that follows Him shall not walk in darkness; but shall have the light of life. "Light of Life" – what wonderful words!

Sometimes we enter Darkness and become afraid. Without assurances of greater things to come, we often get 'stuck' there and find it hard to experience true happiness, share love, and freely walk as a child of God. Darkness, supposedly, holds evil spirits, monsters that live in our closets or under our beds, and pushes our imaginations to the limit. Fear lives in Darkness and threatens to overtake us. Then comes Light! He's with us even in Darkness!

Darkness cannot live where Light abounds and that is a wonderful promise. We can see in the light and not stumble; we can find our way in the light, and we know that we are not plagued by spirits or monsters. Each time we enter Darkness, whether through true night or emotional or psychological Darkness, God is with us and His Light will surely overcome Darkness. With God comes Light to help us follow the good and true path. Be assured: Light will come and banish Darkness; Light will envelop us and keep us safe. Against the purity of faith darkness cannot prevail.

Continue walking in His light,
~Cheryl Gore Pollard

ACKNOWLEDGEMENTS . . .

My sister, Jan, midnight e-mailer and fellow insomniac, for the memories and fun things she remembered and shared for the book.

My sister, Denise, who read, and read, and read and provided support and wonderful insight.

My husband, Jimmy, who had to fend for himself while I sat at the computer.

My grandchildren: Hayden (who expects a 'trilogy'), Greer (my future illustrator), Greyson (lover of outdoors and 'old' stories), Rilyn, Carly, and Ellie (future historians).

My parents, Charles and Dara Gore, for all my cherished memories.

My brothers, Eddie and Bruce, for their humor and fun.

All Boot Campers, at Beeson School of Theology in Birmingham, Alabama- especially Becky, Denise, and Ellen, for their inspiration and encouragement.

. . . . . And from Denise. . . .

For all those who were – and are – a part of our childhood. Many instances written about in *Sunrise* are actual events and happened with friends and/or family. Cheryl has taken liberties and modified or changed names, times, and places, spelling and grammar. If the reading seems too bizarre or strange to be a true happening; it probably did really happen! She's added to some things, and omitted some, embellished some, and played with others to, hopefully, make the story more entertaining. If you're reading this and think, "Oh! I remember that—but it didn't happen that way," it's because she either chose to change it or she simply wrote it the way <u>she</u> remembered it. Hope you enjoy.

~ Denise, editor

ONE

Outside the world was soft and quiet. March had indeed entered like a lion, but now was humble as a sleeping lamb. A blanket of snow covered the nearby forest and created false fullness on the bare branches of the hardwoods. Pines, weighed down by frozen wetness, bowed their heads as if in supplication to the power of millions of tiny flakes. There was no wind, no songs from birds: just deafening silence.

Inside, the log dwelling was warmth filled with soft sound; the erratic crackling and popping of logs smoldering in the rock fireplace. Lizzie listened so hard her ears seemed to ring. Her six-year old sister, Beth, lay still and warm as one of the field mice burrowed deep in the winter bed of grass hidden beneath a covering of early March snow. Beth dreamed, snug beside her, not making a sound, sleeping deeply and contentedly in their cot made by Bulger when they'd first arrived. Their homemade bed fit next to the wall in the kitchen, the warmest place in the two-room house. Bulger's and Miss Claudie's bedroom was separate, directly across the open dogtrot-hallway that separated the two rooms.

Lizzie, however, found herself at a loss for sleep. She was lost in memories that still filled her with fear and cold that warmth from the fire could not replace.

She remembered the wagon train and the people who were so loving and kind who joined them on their trip to Georgia. The Gores, Huddlestons, Huckebas, Walls, Worleys, Rollins, Sheppards, Wiggins, Rogers, Cooks, Barkers, and, of course, Jimmy, the boy who traveled on his own. When a fever struck the train and many children became very sick--or worse, died, Mamma persuaded Papa to leave the train and continue on to here: Heard County, Georgia, on their own. The fever didn't invade their wagon and everything went well until they tried to ford the Chattahoochee River. Unknown to Papa, the river had quickly filled with recent rain and snow run-off, and as they tried to ford it the powerful water demolished their wagon in the dirty deluge. Papa and Mamma drowned and Bulger and his wife, Miss Claudie, found them on the banks of the river and gave them a proper funeral in a lovely glade in a patch of pines. Bulger recovered Pa's knife and flint and Miss Claudie discovered a cloth pouch Mamma had pinned to her slip. Safe inside was all the money they'd saved to start their new lives. Bulger put it away safely, waiting to pass it on to the children.

Lizzie, Beth, and her older brother, Eli, heard the terrible news of their parents' deaths from Bulger. Thank goodness he brought them here to his and his wife's cabin. Not a day passed that Lizzie didn't think of Papa and Mamma. She knew she and her brother and sister had been blessed to escape the anger of the river, and blessed even more to have become part of Bulger and Miss Claudie's family. With no children of their own, they had become the children the couple had always wished for.

Lizzie quietly turned onto her side, bent her arm up to her pillow and rested her head in its crook. She stared into the sleepy fire. Bulger said that he expected this sudden March snow to be the last of winter's bad weather and the added moisture would be good for the soil and help keep the well from going dry later in the summer.

It sure was quiet. She sighed and quietly slipped out of bed, careful not to awaken Beth. She moved to the window and spread back the curtain and gazed outside. It was beautiful. The beauty was marred only by Papa and Mamma not being here to share it. A sudden fearful second thought struck: The Indians. She'd met several who lived nearby who were good, kind, and helpful. But she'd heard rumors of another group who had broken off their Muscogee-village and gone wild. They hid and stole; threatened and plundered. She could only hope her family was safe here—away from the dangerous group of Indians.

She breathed deeply and released the curtain, letting it fall back into place. Added to her restlessness, too, was the concern for the others on the train: where were they now? Had they reached their settlements safely? And Jimmy . . . she wondered where he was and how he was faring. When she turned to return to bed, she was startled to see Miss Claudie standing, framed in the doorway, watching.

"Oh, Miss Claudie, you almost scared me to death!" Lizzie exclaimed as she grabbed her hand to her chest. She moved to the table and sat in a chair handcrafted by Bulger, and Miss Claudie tiptoed across the room and gently lowered herself into her small rocking chair. Miss Claudie was a tiny woman who always wore a smile. Tonight Lizzie noticed her face looked drawn and her gray hair hung to her waist. Lizzie rarely saw Miss Claudie's hair down, she usually wore it twisted in a bun and pinned at the base of her neck. "Something bothering ya, child?" she asked.

"No, not really, Miss Claudie," Lizzie's voice came out in a whispery croak. "Just having a hard time sleeping."

Miss Claudie leaned back in her chair and slowly rocked. She folded her hands across her lap and nodded her head as she looked into the low fire. "Thought as much," she mumbled. "The hurt is still there, ain't it?" she said, meeting Lizzie's eyes.

With that, Lizzie broke. She jumped from her chair and kneeled on the bare wood floor in front of Miss Claudie and folded her arms into Miss Claudie's lap. Miss Claudie gently placed her hands on each side of Lizzie's face and whispered, "It will be all right, Lizzie, sunrise's comin' 'fore long and the dark'll be all gone. When those bright sunbeams flash over the horizon they always overcome the night—the darkness can't stay where there's light—dark never wins." She said with such conviction that Lizzie felt Miss Claudie's words filling her with comfort. In a softer, faint voice, Miss Claudie confirmed, "Sunrise is comin' 'fore long," and she tenderly pressed Lizzie's head down onto her lap and gently caressed her hair.

Miss Claudie sat until Lizzie finally fell asleep. Neither stirred until Lizzie opened her eyes and they immediately shifted to the window where the sun was just rising over the top of the barn: sunlight sparkling and shimmering, bouncing off the whiteness of the snow. Sunrise had indeed arrived.

TWO

Lizzie pulled herself to her feet and reached to hold onto Miss Claudie's arms and help her up, too. "Whoo, girl, 'most got myself all cricked up settin' there with ya. But ya looked so peaceful, sleepin' and dreamin'. Warn't the bad dreams either, was it?" she asked with a grin as she hobbled and hopped across the floor trying to get the kinks out of her bones.

"Not at all," Lizzie responded. "I was dreaming about sunrises; new days and the light. I think I need to get away from the dark things that happened during our disastrous fording the river and look forward to each new sunrise and find goodness in the light." She took a deep breath. "And I will, too. I'll change my prayers and ask for a change of mind instead of asking for everything to change for my wishes. From now own, I'm walking each day in the sunlight." She propped her hands on her hips and turned to the peg on the wall next to her and Beth's bed where she had hung her clothing the night before. "I'm getting dressed and getting in enough wood to cook us up a fine breakfast and make that fireplace sing! Bulger won't know what to think about that, now, will he?" Lizzie had her dress, boots, and coat on in no time and quick as a wink was outside at the woodpile and whizzed right back inside with a double armload of firewood. Just as she finished brushing lingering snowflakes off her coat, Miss Claudie returned from her bedroom dressed—and her hair pinned in its perfect little bun. "Ain't today the day Eli said he'd come by?" She asked as she tossed firewood through the door of the big green and white enameled cookstove.

Lizzie threw her arms up and gasped. "Oh, lordy, I plumb forgot!" she exclaimed. "Wake up, Beth! Eli's coming and I just can't hardly wait! Today's breakfast will be extra special, won't it, Miss Claudie?"

Miss Claudie smiled a knowing little grin. "Yes, Lizzie. Today it will be a special time."

"What's all this clanking and knocking around in here?" asked Bulger as he quick-footed into the kitchen in his sock feet, pulling his overall galluses over his shoulders. "Whew, it sure is cold comin' 'cross the 'trot. I'm glad to see ya'll have the cookstove warming. Here, let me freshen up the fireplace some." With that, he tossed wood in the fireplace until it was heaped high and the flames seemed to be trying to leap out of the top of the chimney. "Now, that ought to do it," he said with a satisfying grin. "Gotta get my boots from back of the stove on while they're still warm and see to the milking." He pulled his heavy boots over his socks and moved to get the milk bucket hanging from a nail near the sink.

"Here," Miss Claudie said, "dip some water from the warmer here on the stove and use it to wash Bossie's udder. I'm sure it will make her feel better on a morning like this."

Bulger carried the bucket to the warmer on the side of the stove and dipped hot water into the bucket. He gathered his coat from the peg beside the door. "Be back in a jiffy," he said as he headed out the door.

"Did I hear somebody say Eli's coming today?" asked Beth as she jumped out of bed. "Is he comin', for real?" she repeated as she pulled the covers neatly over the cot. She stripped off her nightgown and tucked it under her pillow and grabbed her dress and apron from the foot of the bed. She pulled both over her head and scooted to Miss Claudie. "Please button me up so I can gather some eggs for breakfast." She bounced from one foot to the other as Miss Claudie tried to hold her down long enough to get her buttoned. Beth pulled on her stockings and boots and snatched the woven oak basket from beside the wall cupboard.

"Don't forget your coat!" Miss Claudie admonished as she

took Beth's coat from a peg behind the door and held it out. Beth shot her arms in and ran outside, slamming the door.

"Oh, my lord, that girl," she chuckled and shook her head. Dusting her hands on her apron, she looked to Lizzie. "Get that biggest black skillet out and start the bacon, Lizzie. I'll put on a pot of water for coffee and another for grits and then get started on biscuits while the water comes to a boil."

Lizzie got fatback sizzling while Miss Claudie lifted her large white earthenware biscuit bowl from a shelf in the cupboard. She removed the sifter and walked over to a ten-pound bag of flour resting next to the wall beside the cupboard and opened its top. She scooped the sifter full of flour and returned to the bowl. As she turned the red handle of the sifter, flour wisped down like a powdery waterfall and piled into a soft, white peak. She set the sifter aside and doodled out a round crater in the middle of the flour and moved to a large, tin lard can sitting beside the cupboard and removed the lid. With her free hand, she scooped a handful of the greasy lard and quickly popped the lid back and scooted over to the flour bowl, careful not to drip grease on the floor. She plopped the lard in the middle of the soft crater and spread the leftover grease sticking to her hand over the bottom of the darkened, flat, biscuit pan before she wiped the rest away on a dishtowel.

Just then, Bulger came bustling in with a pail full of warm, frothy milk. "Get that strained. I'm about ready for it to make up the biscuits," Miss Claudie instructed Bulger, and moved to check the water on the stove.

Bulger placed the milk bucket on the side of the sink and removed the strainer from a nail hanging above the water pump handle. "Now, where's that sweet milk pitcher?" he asked, twisting his head to look over his shoulder.

"Here ya go," Lizzie said as she placed the large brown pottery pitcher next to the bucket and returned to the stove to watch over the frying meat.

Bulger placed the strainer over the mouth of the pitcher and slowly poured the milk through so any trash that happened to land in the milk during milking was caught. Miss Claudie added coffee grounds to the water to boil and grits to cook in another pot.

"Don't forget to add a big spoon of butter in the grits, too," reminded Lizzie, and Miss Claudie promptly stirred the gold flavors in.

She peeped in at the bacon and asked, "You think you'll have enough drippin's for sawmill gravy?"

"Sure," Lizzie noted. "And I'll get another skillet for the eggs. When Beth gets back it will be ready. As on cue, the door burst open and Beth rushed in holding the egg basket high.

"Just look at these eggs," she said as she plopped the basket on the table and shucked off her coat and hung it back on its peg.

"Be alert there, girl, you'll have scrambled eggs before they hit the skillet if ya not careful!" Miss Claudie said. "Go ahead and get that yellow bowl down and crack them eggs in it. Lizzie has a skillet 'most ready for them. How ya comin' with the sweet milk, Bulger?" she asked turning her head away from Beth.

"Ready right now," he said as he placed the pitcher on the table beside the waiting flour bowl. "That finishes up my part of makin' breakfast," he chuckled as he moved to the hearth and lowered himself into his rocker beside the fireplace.

Miss Claudie poured sweet milk over the flour and kneaded it until it was just right. She rubbed her hands together over the bowl to remove all the sticky dough from her fingers, then dusted fresh flour over her hands and pinched off just enough dough for a perfect biscuit. Gently she rolled the dough in her hands and before Bulger could swat a fly, the biscuit pan was full. She folded her fingers into a loose fist and gently pressed the top of each biscuit to flatten it a bit, leaving neat furrows across the tops.

Lizzie watched Miss Claudie's hands move, and her mind moved back to another kitchen: theirs in Hooverville where Mamma made her biscuits. She didn't make furrows on the tops of her biscuits like Miss Claudie. Lizzie could picture Mamma finishing her bread pan. Each mound of dough had Mamma's thumbprint left on top where it was imprinted as she placed the biscuit on the pan. She quickly snapped out of her reverie when Miss Claudie called, "Lizzie, get that oven door open. Biscuits are made. Only a few minutes now and breakfast will be ready.

Beth, better get that table set while Lizzie and I finish up."

Beth had the table set and Lizzie was pouring up the gravy when they heard heavy thudding outside on the porch.

"Eli!" Beth shrieked, and ran to fling open the door. She grabbed him around the waist and hugged him tight.

"Land sakes, child," Miss Claudie said as she moved to the door. "Let that boy loose so he can come in and get warm."

Beth stepped back, but continued touching Eli softly as Miss Claudie shut the door. "Get that damp coat off and let me hang it here on the back of a chair behind the stove to dry out," she commanded. Eli quickly handed her his coat and she reached and held him at arm's length. "Ya must have growed a foot since ya been here last," she said, beaming up at him. "Am I too old for a hug?"

Eli reached and grasped her by her tiny waist and lifted her off the floor as he swung her around.

"Whoo, now Eli, put me down, ya making me dizzy," she laughed.

Eli put her feet back on the floor and reached to put his arm around Beth and gave her a tight hug. He sniffed. "I smelled that bacon and biscuits halfway here and my stomach told my feet to get to moving. I haven't had decent vittles since I've been working on the house at my place. Is breakfast ready yet?" he asked.

"Just 'bout," Bulger said as he stood and prodded Eli on the shoulder good-naturedly. He was proud to see Eli, too. And mighty glad he was home, if only for a day's visit.

Lizzie was mutely standing in front of the stove holding a fork—still having a hot slice of bacon skewered to it---feeling the love and affection that radiated from her new family as she watched sweet tenderness being shared. She felt a twinge of hurt that the siblings shared this moment with Bulger and Miss Claudie instead of Papa and Mamma, but quickly pressed the feeling away. She remembered her talk with Miss Claudie the night before and was determined to find joy and gladness instead of sorrow and darkness. At that moment, Eli turned and looked right into her eyes. He opened his arms and straightaway she dropped the bacon on the platter and flew into them. "It seems like forever since you left to set up your place," she whispered in his ear. He squeezed her tighter and whispered back.

"I know. It's been mighty lonely out there." He pulled back and slowly let her hand go. He grinned from ear to ear and asked as he slapped his hands together, "Breakfast about ready? I'm starving. I haven't had a good meal since I was here last and my belly is hollering for Miss Claudie's biscuits and sawmill gravy." He dropped his arms and patted his stomach.

"And my eggs," Beth exclaimed. "I gathered them fresh this morning. Come on and sit. I've got it all set!" she said as she gestured toward the nicely set table.

Eli and Bulger sat and pulled their knees under the table. Beth poured milk for her and Lizzie, and Miss Claudie filled coffee cups for Eli, Bulger, and herself. Lizzie put the bacon on the table and got biscuits out of the oven and quickly buttered half of them. Miss Claudie poured gravy in a bowl and set it out, too. "Now grits with another big spoon of Bossie's butter on top." She said and placed the aged brown bowl of grits on the table.

"Don't forget the blackberry jelly and Bulger's honey," Beth added as she reached into the top of the cupboard and got the crockery jars filled with last summer's bounty.

"I guess that's it," Bulger said as he surveyed the table. "Let's bow our heads and give thanks for this good hot food and warm surroundings in here---even though it's cold and wet outside." Everyone bowed their heads and closed their eyes as Bulger gave thanks. "We thank ya Lord, for your blessings; our family, good food, sturdy shelter, and steady health. Be with us in all we do and say, and forgive us our sins. Let us take this food and use it to your glory. In Your name we pray, Amen."

A unisoned, "Amen" came from around the table and everyone's heads popped up at the same time. "Pass the biscuits!" exclaimed Beth.

As Eli reached for the platter of hot bread, his eyes fell on Bulger who had just picked up his cup of hot coffee and carefully poured it into a matching saucer. He raised the steaming liquid to his lips and gently blew on it to cool it. As he sat there with his elbows propped on the table holding the saucer of coffee, it seemed not to be Bulger that Eli was seeing, but Grandpa back in his chair sitting at the worn table in his kitchen before Eli and his family left on their journey. Eli felt a deep cold jell in his stomach and quickly squeezed his eyes shut tight to hold in hot, wet tears that threated to seep out and track down his cheeks. His breath quickened and his heart hammered with the vivid memory of that past morning. He filled with hot pain remembering the hurt and disappointment of leaving Grandpa in Kentucky while he traveled to Georgia. He kept his head lowered and gulped down a sob as he willed this awful feeling to pass. With a blink of his eyes and deep breath, he slowly raised his head and glanced to see if anyone had detected his sorrow. All he saw was passing of bowls and all he heard was the scraping of forks. He grasped his fork and dug into his breakfast. His breathing eased. Thankfully, no one had noticed.

THREE

Eli leaned back in his chair and tapped his tummy. "Boy, I'm full as a tick!" he exclaimed. "I think I need to get up and walk off some of this gravy."

He pushed back his chair and stretched. "You know, I had to leave my place before five o'clock this mornin' and walk all the way here in the snow. But, Miss Claudie, I must say it was worth every step. I sure don't get this kind of eatin' at my place."

"Don't thank me, Eli," Miss Claudie said with a grin, "Thank ya sisters here. They did most of the work. They're growing into two fine young ladies; smart, too." Lizzie blushed with the compliment.

"Speaking of smart young ladies," Eli said, "I just remembered I picked this up at the post office when I was in Franklin yesterday." He reached to his back jeans pocket and pulled out a wrinkled envelope: a letter! It was addressed to Lizzie. He handed it over the table to her.

"For me?" she asked. When she read the return address, she quickly ripped the envelope open. "It's from Ginger!" she squealed. Skimming the words, she stammered, "Oh, Miss Claudie, she says she can come if it's okay with you. Could she? Could she? Beth could sleep on a pallet on the floor and Ginger and I could share the bed. What do you think, Miss Claudie?"

Shaking her head as she rose from the end of the table opposite Bulger, Miss Claudie grinned, "Well, Lizzie, looks like we have to work on those quilts so Beth will have a soft pallet to sleep on. When can she come?"

"She'll come as soon as she hears from me. Can I write her right now?" Lizzie jumped up from the table and started for the pine desk near the door to the breezeway, or dogtrot, of the house.

"Whoa, girl," Bulger admonished. "Don't ya think the table needs clearing and dishes taken care of first? We can't get that letter to the post office any sooner anyway—things got to be done around here 'fore we can get to town."

Lizzie blushed again, knowing she had jumped the gun with her excitement and quickly put the letter in her apron pocket. She began scraping what little was left on the dishes into a dishpan. Bulger had a sow out beside the barn in a pen and a couple of barn cats that took quick care of all their leftovers. "Sure thing, Bulger. I just got in a hurry. But I just can't wait until Ginger gets here!" Holding onto that thought, she couldn't help but tap her toes as she skipped to the sink.

Bulger looked at Miss Claudie and smiled and shook his head. He'd never let on, but he was really happy the children were having a visitor from back home. He knew their grief still spilled over from the loss of their parents. Ginger's visit would add another good time to the enjoyment he and Miss Claudie already felt with their new family. Each day came with joy and thanksgiving that God had placed him and Miss Claudie in the right place at the right time to rescue the three lost children that day on the bank of the flooded Chattahoochee River. He realized God's blessings were not meant only for the care and protection of Eli, Lizzie, and Beth, but He had blessed Miss Claudie and him, too, with unthought of love and devotion from three wonderful children. He rose from the table and moved to sit with Eli beside the hearth. "Tell me how ya comin' along with ya house, now, son," he asked as he pulled his pipe and tobacco pouch out of his overalls pocket. He pinched tobacco out of the pouch and tapped into the pipe bowl, lit a match, and sucked the pipe stem until a bright red glow showed in the bowl. He blew smoke from his mouth, tossed the burnt match in the flames, and leaned back in the rocker and crossed his long legs, waiting for Eli to catch him up on the progress on his newly acquired farm.

"Well," Eli began, "you know I was tickled plumb pink that

that parcel of land so close to your homestead was still open and couldn't believe it when I really got it. I still can't believe it," he said as he leaned forward and put his elbows on his knees and clasped his hands together. He continued, "I can never thank you enough for helping get everything squared away. You and me got a lot done since then: a spot cleared off for the house and whew," he said as he remembered the hard work, "felling and cleaning up all those trees." He shook his head. "Boy, will I be glad to get in a house with a wood floor and sleep on a bed with a real shuck mattress. That canvas tent is getting old! It keeps the rain out, but the cold keeps me company. Thought most of the cold weather was over. March is kind of late for snow, isn't it?" he asked, raising up and looking at Bulger.

"Usually done by now. We have had some ice this late in the past, and believe me, snow is better'n ice any day. Ice hangs on and pops tree limbs and makes a mess. At least snow melts fast and the slush is gone in a couple of days." He changed the subject. "I was wondering how ya come along since we got them logs cut and your couple of acres cleared off. I wish I could'a done more, but with Bossie calving and having to keep close eye on Bessie, I been tied up here making sure both of them would make it. Looks like Bossie and her calf are gone be fine and if Bessie does as well, I'll be on back to help you 'fore long," Bulger explained as he slowly rocked back and forth in his rocker.

"And guess what?" Beth broke in. "Bossie's baby is a beautiful red little girl with a bright white star right in the middle of her forehead and I named her Star."

"Why, that's a great name." Eli replied to Beth. He turned back to Bulger and continued. "Since we got the logs cut and ready to notch and stack for the house, I met a guy in town who's staying with the Jones's and helping out at their store. You remember, Mr. Jones who runs the general store? He has those four cute girls." With that, Eli grinned a shy grin, sat up straight, and continued. "Anyway, he said he'd be glad to come over in his spare time and help raise the walls for the house. His name is Cullie and he seems strong and willing. He sure is friendly and has the best joking way about him. I think the three of us could get the logs notched and up, and I know he'd take a lot of work off you." With that, he sat back and put his hands behind his head and teasingly added, "Guess you can be the supervisor. Lord knows, I need one!" he laughed.

Bulger chuckled, too, "I can sure be the boss, and I'm really glad ya will have some help besides slow old me. Ya need t'be gettin' the house finished 'fore plantin' time. That reminds me, we gone need t'get a shed built for Little Man. Ya could take him and get the stumps pulled up in ya clearing and ready to plant 'fore the spring rains come and the ground is too soft. I still have Moses to work here, and he's all I'll need with the vegetable garden. We can swap out our time and work our new ground with both mules so we can get done faster."

"Yeah, we can work that in. I'm sure Cullie can help. He can finish stocking shelves and sweeping up early and have plenty of time to come over to my place."

Just then Miss Claudie was standing beside Eli wiping her hands on her apron. "All finished!" she said. Beth jumped out from behind Miss Claudie's skirts and right on Eli's lap.

"Come on, Eli, let's go outside and look at Bossie's new calf while Lizzie writes to Ginger. She wants you to mail it on your way home this afternoon." She pointed to Lizzie sitting at the desk, bent over paper with her pencil flying. She had a slight frown across her forehead and the tip of her tongue peeped out between her teeth. She was indeed intently focused on her task.

Eli stood and tossed Beth into the air and caught her. "Hey, Little Bit, you're heavier that you were the last time I tossed you up! What has Miss Claudie been feeding you, lead peas and iron cornpone?" he teased as he placed her feet on the floor. "Well, come on. I can't wait to see Star, either. Run on and get your coat. Got to ask Bulger a quick question and I'll meet you in the barn." He popped her behind as she dashed to the door and grabbed her heavy brown coat off the wall peg. Beth shrieked with delight as she flew out the door.

"Hurry!" she shouted behind her as her feet hit the porch and the door banged shut.

Eli turned to Bulger as he slipped on his coat. "Wanted to ask you before I mentioned it to Beth, but Mr. Parmer over the ridge has a redbone hound with pups. I thought I'd get a couple for Beth to keep her company. I know sometimes she slips off to the Indian village to play with the children there, but thought she might like to play around with the pups and be more contented playing here where you can keep an eye on her. They might be good company when she's going on the trail to the village, too, just in case of snakes or bears. Or those Muscogees. Heard they're moving around up here, further north than usual, making mischief and messing around with a few raids stealing cows, hogs, and mules when they can. I don't trust them one little bit!" He playfully tapped Bulger on the shoulder and grinned. "And you could train the pups to be fine huntin' dogs, too. They come from a good bloodline according to Mr. Parmer. What do you say?"

It took Bulger only half a second to think about it. "Sure, love to have'm. Been thinking 'bout getting' a pair of good hounds, anyway. I loved huntin' when I was younger and been missin' it. Mebbe I'll train Beth to shoot and go along with me."

Miss Claudie flipped him on his thigh with the tip of her dishtowel. "Hey, Claudie, what's that for?" He faked an ugly frown and threw his hands in the air.

"For trying to make my little girl into a gun totin' sharpshooter!" she grinned, but suddenly quieting and looking concerned, she added, "but if what Eli says about the Muscogees proves to be true, I'd feel better with her havin' a little protection as she tramps around in the woods and goes on her Indian trail to visit Warm DayRah." she replied with a deep, worried expression.

Bulger shrugged. "Nothin' wrong with that," he replied. Slapping Eli on the back, he declared, "Ya tell Mr. Parmer to pick out the two best pups and send'em on over. We'd love to have'm."

"Thanks," Eli said as he reached for the door. "I'll bring them next week. Can't wait to see Beth when I tell her!" He said as he closed the door.

FOUR

Eli pulled his collar tighter around his neck as he crossed the yard to the barn. It was still cold, but the snow had stopped falling and the morning sun was melting spots of standing snow in the yard making it look like a huge jigsaw puzzle that needed putting together. He looked up and saw that Beth had detoured to the side of the barn and was perched on the fence watching the sow in the pigpen. She had jokingly named the old sow Ole Crip. One day last summer, the sow had plopped down in the cool barn hallway, snoozing peacefully; probably dreaming of an extra helping of slop, when one of Miss Claudie's baby goats came running around the corner into the barn and unable to stop, hopped right up on the sleeping hog, bounced off her, and slid to a stop in the hay. Being so rudely and suddenly awakened, the sow struggled and rushed to stand. Ole Crip pulled a hamstring. She seriously hobbled around for a couple of weeks, but finally grew well enough to limp from place to place. After the unfortunate accident, Miss Claudie developed an aversion to goats and Bulger had to make the farm goat-free. Mr. Levens, their neighbor down the road, became the proud owner of five rambunctious kids and their watchful mamas.

"What'cha lookin' at, Beth" he asked, crossing the yard.

"Hurry, come here!" she shouted, excitedly gesturing with her outstretched arm. "Ole' Crip's got her babies. Look how little and pink they are," she giggled.

Eli reached the fence and peeked under the shed in the pen. Sure enough, Ole' Crip had given birth the night before.

"How many are there?" he asked.

"Not sure," Beth answered. "They keep wiggling around trying to scoot in and get a teat." She laughed again. "And Ole' Crip is just laying there being poked around. Look at her fat sides jiggling like jelly and she's paying no mind at all. Just listen to them babies grunting. Let's see, one, two, three, four….twelve, I think! An even dozen. Ole' Crip done good, didn't she Eli? She gave us twelve perfect little gifts!"

"Sure did. Do you think Bulger knows about this? He didn't feed Ole' Crip her slop yet this morning and I'll just bet he hasn't been to the pen. Guess he was hurrying to get back in the warm kitchen and was planning to check on Ole' Crip when he slopped her after breakfast. Why don't you run back inside and get him out here?" Eli suggested.

Beth jumped off the fence and raced to the porch. As she dashed through the door, Eli moved to the warm barn and checked inside. There was Bossy and her new calf in one stall and Bessie in the other. Bossy was contentedly chewing her cud and her baby nursing, sucking so hard she had white foam dripping from the corners of her mouth. But Bessie was walking from side to side, making a huffing sound, and when she turned, Eli gasped. She was pushing hard and a big bubble was protruding out!

"Uh, oh," Eli thought aloud. "This may mean trouble. She must have been okay when Bulger milked this morning, but she seems to be going slow with her calving and looks like she wants to go down. She might not get up of she does." He quickly moved back out the side barn door and met Bulger and Beth as they arrived at the pig pen.

"See," Beth babbled as she held Bulger's hand tight and dragged him to the fence. "Babies, I told you, didn't I? Isn't this a great surprise? Aren't they soooo cute?" She let go of his hand and pulled herself up on the planks surrounding the pig pen and looked over at Ole' Crip and her piglets.

Bulger looked in and scratched his head. "Well, I'll be." He remarked. "I thought she'd be another few days. Guess I miscalculated. They all seem fine." He said with wonder in his tone. When Ole' Crip heard Bulger's voice, she picked up her head and rose to shake off her babies, ready for something to eat. "Think she's ready to eat her breakfast, too," he chuckled. "Need to get the slop and add in some extra grain and fodder. We better go get the slop bucket from under the kitchen sink." He pushed away from the fence and turned to go back inside. Beth trailed after him.

Eli was in a pickle. He needed Bulger inside the barn to check on Bessie, but didn't want Beth along. She'd never seen a birthing, and so young that she didn't need to just yet, and there might be more involved than Bessie's natural birthing. She might need help since this was her first time calving. "Beth, how 'bout you running in and telling Miss Claudie to add what extra scraps of food she has to the slop today. Bulger will be in in a minute." Bulger stopped and glanced back with his eyebrows furrowed questioningly. Eli sent a silent s.o.s. with a slight nod of his head toward the barn. Thankfully, Bulger got it.

"Yea, Beth, run in and help Miss Claudie find some extra vittles for Ole' Crip. I'll be in to get the bucket in a little while. Ya may want to ask Lizzie to add a special message to Ginger from you, too. Ya can check on how Lizzie is finishing her letter and get her to add your p.s. and get it ready for Eli to mail."

"That's a wonderful idea, Bulger!" Beth agreed. She hopped along and skipped around the sloshy melting mush to the house. She turned when she reached the porch and added, "I'll be sure Miss Claudie adds a bunch of extra biscuits to the slop for the babies, too!" and disappeared through the kitchen door with a bang.

For ye were sometimes darkness, but now are ye light in
the Lord; walk as children of light:
For ye fruit of the Spirit is in all goodness and
righteousness and truth:
Proving what is acceptable unto the Lord.
Ephesians 5: 8-10

FIVE

Bulger moved to Eli and he explained. "While Beth was fetching you, I checked on the cows. Bessie is really agitated and looks like she's tiring fast. I think you need to take a look."

They hustled inside and to Bessie's stall. Bulger gave a low whistle. "What I was afraid of," he said. "I'll watch and if that calf ain't here in a couple of hours, it may need pullin'. Do ya mind hanging around just in case I need ya to help?" he asked.

"Sure thing. I don't mind staying a little longer, anyway. There's not much I can do at my place until I get the walls of the house up and the top on."

And they left the barn and trudged back to the house.

Time crept by like a snail crawling up the side of front porch steps. Lizzie and Beth finished their letter to Ginger and Eli placed in his coat pocket. He promised to stop by the Franklin Post Office and put it in the next mail. Miss Claudie set out biscuits and leftover bacon for dinner, but only Beth decided to eat. Everyone else was still full from the huge breakfast.

After dinner, Miss Claudie, Lizzie, and Beth pulled out the quilt they'd been working on since February and began whipping the hem close along its edge. Bulger could wait no longer and gathered his coat from the peg on the wall. He grabbed the slop bucket for Ole' Crip and moved to the door, but Beth didn't miss his movement.

"Where ya' going, Bulger?" she asked as she anchored her

needle in the fabric and started rising out of her chair, "Can I go, too?"

He stopped and playfully shuffled his big feet. "First I'm gone feed Ole' Crip, then I'm gone go to Rags, then on to Wrinkles," he said with a grin and twinkle in his eye. "Be back 'fore dark."

"Oh, Bulger," Beth said, plunking herself back down with a thunk. "I know that just means you don't want me along."

"Sorry, not this time, Little Bit," he replied. He glanced toward Eli and barely nodded his head. Eli understood. He'd give Bulger a few minutes and make his exit, too.

"Come here, Beth," Eli said, "Get that frown off your face. You'd be in a mess of trouble if it froze up that way! I got something to tell you before I leave for my place that should make you feel better."

Beth dragged up, still scowling, and shuffled her way over to Eli and leaned against him. He put his arm around her waist and lifted her chin with his other hand. "How would you like a couple of puppies to play with?"

Beth came to life like a wilted weed after a rain shower. "Whooop!" she shouted and clapped her hands and jumped all over the room. "Tell me, Eli, tell me. What are they like?" Finally calming enough to stand, still squirming, beside Eli.

"Well, they're about eight weeks old full-blooded redbone hounds. Mr. Parmer said we could have a pair and I'm gone bring'em when I come next week." He explained.

"What are their names?" Beth questioned.

"Don't know yet. I'll let you come up with those. I think I'll pick a boy and a girl. Now you come up with something good and I'll see you soon. Time for me to be going. Be dark before long and I've got a way to go."

Eli stood and gave Miss Claudie a hug and kissed Beth. He crossed to Lizzie and leaned down and kissed her forehead as she finished the last stitches on the hem of the new quilt.

"Be careful," she whispered, "don't forget to post my letter."

"I will," he replied, "and don't you worry one bit about the letter. I promise it will be in the first mail out."

"Since yo're leaving and haven't had anything since

breakfast, here's a sack of biscuits and bacon and a few tea cakes to take with ya," Miss Claudie said, and handed Eli a flour sack filled with goodies. She gave him a quick hug before letting go of the sack. "Ya be careful, now. Watch out for those Muscogees and hurry on home—don't dally around." She stepped back.

Holding the flour sack tightly, he walked to the door, put on his heavy coat, and gave the women a warm good-bye as he quietly left. Then he hurried as fast as he could to the barn where Bulger was waiting. As he approached the barn door and reached to pull it open, he glanced back at the house. There, standing in the cool late of day stood Miss Claudie at the top of the steps; one hand wrapped across her waist and the other resting on the porch rail.

When she realized Eli saw her standing there, she tentatively raised her hand from the rail and lifted it palm up in a silent good-bye. He saw her chin tremble and a quick shake of her shoulders as she tried to control a sob rising from her chest. Then, with tears glistening in her eyes, a shiny single tear slid slowly down her cheek. He smiled and nodded slightly to acknowledge her silent message. Miss Claudie sent a soft good-bye wave. Then, still filled with lonesome loss, she slowly pressed her clinched fist tightly against her quivering lips, turned her gaze away and quickly entered the kitchen. Eli watched, humbled, as she closed the door. His felt a tender fluttering in his heart and thought it would burst with love. He was comforted remembering how she repeated this same tender gesture every time he left ---no matter how short the visit---and he knew she'd do the same the next time. He knew her act wasn't an omen of impending danger; she simply loved him so much it was hard for her to watch him leave. It was a gift that she gave them all, and he'd always feel that she was sending protection and asking God to place His protective hand over him in his journeys. His heart swelled to burst with the realization that God had sent him such love.

Eli, brought back to his and Bulger's problem at hand cleared his throat and moved inside, shutting the barn door.

"What do ya think?" he asked as he hurried to the side of Bessie's stall.

Bulger stood with his hands on his hips looking at Bessie. "Nothing's changed and she's huffing and puffing hard. I guess we'd better get to the water pump in the yard and get washed up. We got a job to do, and one I dread doin'." They took off their coats and rolled up their shirtsleeves as they left the barn. They took turns pumping the handle of the water pump and washing their arms.

"Get that bucket and fill it, too. We gotta wash Bessie's backside off good. Sure don't want any infection to set in and she's gone be real weak after this." Bulger indicated to a wooden bucket sitting on a barrel next to the barn door. Eli hurried to fetch it and fill it with water. "Wish we could warm it, but Beth would be flyin' around like a bee on a bonnet if she knew what we was up to."

Together they entered the barn. "Get that rope off the nail there," Bulger told Eli, pointing to the side of the stall. "And pull the doors shut. Then tie the rope around her horns and pull her head up to the support beam. Make sure it's tight, now, so's she can't move around. We'll have to pull hard and don't want her backing up on us."

Eli wrapped the rope around Bessie's horns and down around her neck, too, but not so that she'd choke, and pulled her up tight, looping the rope several times around the beam and tying it off. While he worked on securing Bessie, Bulger had her backside washed off and his arms lathered with soap. He looked to see that Eli had secured Bessie. He took a deep breath and reached inside her to turn the calf to the right position for birthing, and tried to pull it. The baby wouldn't budge. "Whoo lordy, it's a big'un."

He shook his head and said, "I guess we'll have to do it the hard way. I got to get chains around the calf's front legs, just behind the fetlocks and check to be sure its head is down right." He grunted as he pushed his arms in again and fumbled to get the chains around the calf's legs, and then down around the feet, too. "Gotta make sure these feet are secure," he said as he worked. "Those little hooves are sharp; don't want them cutting Bessie none as we work the baby out." He stepped back. "Okay, Eli, hold the chains and get that side and I'll get this one. Pull hard. Ya may have to brace your foot on something there and pull. Then I'll pull on this side. We'll work back and forth until one of us gets one side of the calf's shoulder through, and then just hang on tight so it won't slip back in until the other of us gets our side pulled out, too, 'til we have the shoulders free. Then we can relax a bit and let the baby breathe a few times."

The men pulled and grunted. Sweat popped out on Eli's forehead and Bulger's arms bulged as they pulled. Their feet slipped in the straw and manure in the stall and Bessie tried to flay her head. It was hard keeping steady pressure on the chains, but they kept the lines taunt. Both of them were breathing hard when the little head emerged. Eli got his side of the calf's shoulder out first and Bulger put his foot against Bessie's rump and gave a massive pull and then both shoulders were clear.

"Whew," Bulger groaned as he let his chain relax and wiped sweat from his forehead on his shirtsleeve. He told Eli to take a breather and examined the baby and confirmed that it was breathing. "Okay, one more pull and it's over. Hand me ya chain." Eli and Bulger exchanged chains. "When I say 'go', pull hard. One . . . two . . . three . . . go!" Bulger counted. They gave a great last pull and the beautiful red baby slid to the ground with a heavy thud. It was tired, but was breathing and within a minute, trying to move its legs.

Eli looked at Bulger grinning like a possum. "Never done that before," he said as he dropped to his knees to free the chains from the calf.

"And probably won't be ya last, either," Bulger replied as he moved to Bessie's head to free her. She was exhausted, as the men were, but motherly instinct made her turn around and begin cleaning her baby.

"Another heifer," Bulger noticed. "Glad of that. Ya can take one to your place when she's old enough. She'll make ya a fine milk cow."

"Look here," Eli pointed as he moved away from the calf to let Bessie do her job. "On her head between her ears, a perfect little white crescent moon. Tell Beth I beat her to the naming this time. I'm naming this baby Moon." He stood and stretched. "Well, you think Bessie will clean off alright?" he asked Bulger as they both washed in what water was left in the bucket and grabbed hands full of clean hay to rub their hands and arms dry. Eli tossed his down with a grimace.

Bulger sighed and turned to Eli. "I'll check her later, but she'll still have a few more contractions and the afterbirth will come. I HOPE it comes, that's really a mess to deal with compared to the pullin' if it don't. She needs its nourishment so she will be able to keep her strength up." Bulger tossed his dirty hay down and lowered himself so that his knees rested in the hay on the barn's floor. He looked over the baby and a soft smile crossed his face. "Look there, Eli," he said as he nodded his head toward the new life. "It's plain hard to imagine how good God is. Then this little thing comes along as God's miracle. He's promised us all we need, and most of the time, if we just stop long enough to think about it, He gives us a whole lot of what we want, too. All we have to do is trust in him and follow his Word." Standing, he added, "We always gotta do our part, too. But every time I witness a birth, see new leaves, smell fresh snow, and drink in all God's goodness, it just fills my heart." Eli and Bulger stood quietly and let the sweetness of the moment sink in.

In no time, the baby was trying to stand, but with each effort, she promptly crumpled back down. Finally she got all four legs moving and bumped and wobbled her way down to Bessie's bag and latched on. Moon's little red tail began swishing back and forth as she pulled on Bessie's "dinners" and got her first delicious taste of warm mother's milk.

Eli and Bulger watched and laughed at the baby's efforts. "Looks like everything's just fine. I'll make sure they're both okay when I look in on them 'fore bedtime." Bulger picked up the water bucket. They walked together through the hallway, left the barn and shut the door behind them.

Thrusting out his hand to Eli, he said, "Well, son, I'da never done it without ya."

Shaking Bulger's hand, Eli felt awkward, but proud. "Aw, nothin' to it," he grinned. As their hands dropped to their sides, he added, "Got to get on toward home. It'll be plumb dark before I get there. I'll be glad to pile up in my down comforter in the tent tonight and I know I'll sleep like a log. Don't mention to Lizzie that I'm gone miss stopping in Franklin on the way home, but I'll get her letter out daylight tomorrow for sure. G'night, now." And he buttoned his coat, picked up the flour sack of food, and started off into the twilight.

Bulger watched after him for a long moment and with a look of pure satisfaction, mumbled, "That's a fine boy, there." Looking up over the trees and letting the beauty of pinks, yellows, and blues of the clouds and the setting sun fall over him, he whispered softly up to Papa and Mamma. "Yep, there's a fine boy there. Ya can be really proud of him."

And Bulger, as the last of the day's light flashed over the horizon, crossed the soggy yard, feet splashing through mud to the porch where he stopped to stomp it off before entering the warm, kerosene lamp lit kitchen.

SIX

Eli stuck the flour sack with his food into the front of his coat and hunched his shoulders deeper under his collar. He pushed his hands to the bottoms of his pockets. He stopped and glanced back as Bulger shut the kitchen door and all he saw was the soft glow from kerosene lamps glowing in the windows. He turned and entered a worn path through scrubby underbrush and tall hardwoods. The trail was open and with the light from a full moon, traveling was easy.

He slowly trudged along until he met a wider, rutted dirt road that led into town. The temperature had dropped a few degrees, and almost all the snow had melted and there was no threat of more. Thankfully, it was windless, cloudless, and the surroundings were bathed in almost daylight from the brightness of the full moon.

He'd follow the much-used muddy dirt road until he came to a little used trail, a deer trail most likely, and cut off there and continue along that tiny path until he reached a small stream that ran along beside his home site. As he walked, his mind swirled with snatches of good things that had filled his day: a welcoming homecoming, Godly fellowship with his loving family, delicious food, and miraculous births, and especially what he had learned about the importance of caring for farm stock and the unusual calf delivery. He absently smiled at that thought, even though he was bone tired after the effort. As he hiked along, he thought, too, of a worrisome threat coming from the Muscogees; Indians who lived just to their south. He hoped with all his heart that they didn't find their way to Heard County. Recent treaties should protect the settlers and friendly Creeks here, but he had an uneasiness quivering in his belly that made him expect trouble. Most of the time, his feelings pointed accurately and these made him feel even more wary.

His thoughts traveled on. Treaties, but what did treaties mean to a people who loved this land and had been here hundreds of years? Just this year, in the Treaty of Cusseta, all Creek nations living in lands east of the Mississippi River 'gave' all but a small strip of their land along the Alabama and Georgia border to the government.

What about their livelihood: farming, hunting, fishing, living in their villages without threats of more land being taken? he wondered. Or worse, what about being forced to leave their homes as so many Cherokees had been made to do. Eli shook his head.

What would he have done in the same situation? he wondered.

They were left with so little. And, too, was their struggle to feed their families as they faced competition with settlers for game. Settlers cleared hunting land for farming and that destroyed hunting territories. He thought of Roanoke, Georgia, that had been attacked and burned by angry Indians in retaliation for their homeland being taken by the U.S. government. As a result of the Indian attack on Roanoke, federal officials met with Creek leaders in the village of Cusseta on the Georgia side of the Chattahoochee River—about seventy-five miles south of where he walked now---and the group of Creeks from the larger Muscogee tribe were compelled to agree to the terms—lose more land. True, some of the Indians, like Skipping Rock's Creek tribe, had been granted land claims in former Creek territory and lived near here. Many others who had been granted their own land lost it when it fell to greedy and dishonest whites who beat them out of it: a disgrace and travesty that made Eli feel ashamed, even though he hadn't taken any part in the trickery. He shook the bad feelings away, breathed crisp, cool night air in deeply, and continued along the winding, rough path.

His mind turned endlessly as he walked and he was

surprised when he came up on the frequently traveled dirt road leading to town. Time had surely flown! Quickly he ducked his head and plowed on into the night. As he slogged along in the moonlight through mud left from melting snow, it coated his shoes and made each step harder. Finally, he moved to the edge of the road and stomped around in the dry weeds to knock off clumps of aggravating mud. Then he continued marching in semi-dark down the road.

He practically missed his turn-off. The monotony of his walk and the quietness of nighttime had almost lulled him into sleepwalking. He stepped off the winding muddy road, raked his boots across high grass growing along the side to rid them of more mud, and continued on along the winding, twisting animal trail through the woods. It was really overgrown, darker shadows danced across the path, and he found it extremely hard to follow. When he had almost reached the halfway mark, snap! Crunch, crack.

The sound of breaking twigs and rustling limbs. Nighttime animals? Eli wondered. Listening closely, peering cautiously around, and not hearing any sounds again, he kept on alert as he continued along.

Swish! Again. This time he was sure he'd heard something and bent, with one hand across his forehead to shelter it from the soft moonlight, and peered deeper into the brush. With shadows cast by the moon and thick forest limbs and undergrowth, he couldn't see a thing. But paired with the upsetting noises, he *felt* as if he was being watched. He tried slipping along more quietly, cautiously, but the feeling of not being alone grew sharply. He felt fear lumping in his belly and his head began to throb with each heartbeat. He began to walk faster.

Again, an ever-so-slight noise, like the sound of a small limb returning to its place after being pushed aside. Instinct told him he truly was NOT alone. Every hair on his body stood on end and he strained to see the path out front. Time from each passing minute became maddening; his imagination ran wild and created more fire in his belly and caused him to hyperventilate. His breath came in short gasps and he started trotting along the narrow route to reach the stream. He looked behind and tripped over a root protruding from the path. He caught himself and continued, feeling as if he was being chased by the devil himself.

Suddenly he *knew* he wasn't alone and he couldn't count on his vigilance for safety. In faithful desperation, he dropped to his knees, right there in the middle of the woods, and bowed his head. "Lord," he prayed. "I call on you to place a hedge around me, all about me and all around me on every side, bless me, oh Lord, and keep me safe." Immediately he felt the arms of Jesus envelop him and bring sweet calmness throughout his body. He rose and began a fast, sure step along the shadowed trail again, now with comfort and knowledge that he was safe. "Thank you again, Lord." He whispered. He trotted along with quick breaths, eyes hurting from searching through the dimness for the end of the trail.

Just as he thought he'd collapse, he sighted a dim light! He'd made it to the rambling creek at last! Running out of the timber and thick underbrush, he stumbled to the bank of the stream, bent and put his hands on his knees to breathe deeply. He kept watch along the tree line, but saw no sign of life. Finally, his heart slowed and he turned to follow along the creek bank to his campsite.

He arrived in a trot and quickly dived into his canvas tent. Reaching for the ties, he secured the flaps and snuggled into his down covers. Remembering the sack of food, he quickly pulled it from inside his coat, but didn't take his coat off, just tossed the sack to the side and pulled the cover over his head. Sleep didn't come quickly. He continued to listen until his head roared with silence. "I know I'm safe, the Lord is with me," he prayed again in a soft voice. In the early morning hours, he finally drifted off.

He woke in a warm cocoon as sunshine beamed down on the canvas, warming his bed. He sat up and stretched, untied the tent latches and peeked out. All seemed quiet and safe. Eli emerged from the tent and, working his arms and legs, ambled down to the creek to wash his face and get a cool drink. He bent over the water to scoop a handful of the cool, clear water when he noticed footprints; moccasin prints in the moist dirt at the edge of the water. Hair raised on his neck. He rose and turned to survey the area. Then angled his head for a second look. Satisfied that whoever had been there during the night was long gone, he bent and was about to dip water into his cupped hand when he felt, rather than heard, someone behind him. He dropped the water and stood, trying to turn at the same time, and found himself tangled in his own legs. All he could see was the silhouette of a tall body against the brightness of the rising sun.

"Hey!" he heard a voice holler.

Finding his balance, he breathed a sigh of relief. It was only Cullie coming to help with the notching of logs for the house.

Laughing to himself, he shook his head and grinned. "Whew, you scared the daylights out of me. Why are you sneaking around like that?" he asked.

"I'm not sneaking!" Culled said with a hint of irritation in his voice. He spread his arms and gestured to the stream. "That water's splashing over the rocks and that's why you didn't hear me coming up. If you don't want me here, I'll just go on back to town." he snapped and mocked a turn as if to leave.

Eli attempted to smooth Cullie's aggravation. "Sorry, but I sure got spooked last night." And he told Cullie all about his walk home in the dark.

"Man!" Cullie said in disbelief. "I don't know what I'da done. Do ya really think something or someone was out there with ya?"

"I'm certain of it," Eli replied. "And I have a good suspicion that it was at least one, if not more, Muscogee. You've heard about them roaming up in these parts, haven't you?"

"Yeah," Cullie replied with a worried frown. "Just yesterday I overheard Mr. Parmer saying that his hounds pitched a fit the other night. He went out and tried to get'em quiet, and finally had to lock'em in his barn, and when daylight came, he discovered two of his steers missing. He believes the Indians took'em. From what I've heard, most think it's a part of the Panther Tribe. They may be taking what they need or what they think is due them, but when a rogue bunch like that breaks from their village and starts stealin', trouble is sure to follow."

"You're right about that," Eli agreed. "Well, there wasn't anything around here for them to take. Maybe they've moved on." He brightened. "Hey, you want a bite to eat before we get started?"

"Sure," Cullie said, hunching up his shoulders and spreading his arms. "But where do ya think you'll get anything? Ya ain't even started a fire yet."

"Just follow me," Eli instructed. "I got Miss Claudie's ham and biscuits and tea cakes for toppins."

"Lead the way," Cullie grinned. "I always work better when I got something in my stomach."

And the boys jogged to Eli's tent and retrieved the flour sack of food. When they finished, they drank their fill from the tumbling clean water of the stream. Just as they finished brushing the final teacake crumbs from their overalls, Bulger came swinging his arms and his long legs ate up the yard. "Ya'll ready to go?" he asked, passing a second care package filled with food from Miss Claudie to Eli.

"Sure are, Bulger," Eli said, peeking inside the brown wrapping paper to see what goodies Miss Claudie had packed. "This is Cullie I told you about yesterday. Cullie this is Bulger, my second Pa," Eli said, making the introductions and quickly jumping through the tent's doorway and putting his meal inside.

Bulger's breath caught. This was the first time any of the three children had ever referred to him as a parent. He felt warmth fill his chest as he reached his hand to Cullie. "Glad to meet ya," he stammered.

"You, too," Cullie replied. He grasped Bulger's hand and was pleased to feel a good, firm hold. He dropped his hand and added. "Where do I notch?" He asked as he picked up his ax and walked to the stack of logs.

"Just follow the boss's directions," Eli said with a laugh as he walked back to the two. He grabbed his ax and moved to the far end of the log Cullie was standing beside.

"Measure along here," Bulger directed as he moved to the stack of wood and pointed to the end of a log. Then we'll move the log and put it on the rock foundations we've already set in place." He pointed to the house, indicating the foundation. "Eli and I already got floor joists nailed in. We took pine logs to Rogers's Sawmill just outside town," he said as he turned toward Cullie. "I was mighty glad that Mr. Denney brought the train close enough to Franklin and the Rogers found the place they wanted to settle. Eli will get more logs down later, soon as he can, and have them sawed and planed for the floors." He looked at the sky. "I hope we get along with the walls before quittin' time."

Eli agreed. "How about working straight through until 'bout three this afternoon and make a quick fishing trip so we can have trout for supper? I'm cookin'," he grinned.

"Can't beat a good fried fish supper," Cullie said as he swung the ax hard, arching his arms and flexing his back muscles, and chopped out a proper chip. "We'll have this cabin up in no time," he guaranteed through a broad smile.

"Ya boys can carry on. I'm gone have to get on back to the house as soon as I get ya'll started and ya'll know what to do from here on out," Bulger replied. "I got things need doin' myself. Where you puttin' the shed for Little Man?" he added.

Eli stopped chopping long enough to indicate a level spot near the back of the yard. "Over there, I think. It's close to water and the tree line will help keep the wind away in winter and give some shade in the summer."

"Good choice," Bulger approved. "Ya'll see if you can get something started there, too. Little Man needs a home where I can bring him when we finish up my plowing." He looked around. "Well, what're ya waitin' on? Get going." He teased.

Eli looked at Cullie and grinned. As Bulger's lanky body disappeared along the stream's bank, Eli said, "Told you he'd be the boss. Can't believe he really thinks we'll get to the shed today." He shook his head and raised his ax.

Throughout the day the only sound was the echo of axes hitting logs and occasional grunts that erupted when a log was heaved higher along the wall into place. The boys worked up a good sweat and by lunchtime they were working without shirts and their bodies glistened in the sun. By two o'clock, one wall was up and braced, windows and a door framed out, and a second half wall up.

"Let's call it a day," Eli offered. "Hard to think we've got this far. It sure looks good. Maybe when you can get back up here we can finish and get the rafters in for the roof. I'll check on them when I get to town. By the way, would you mind

Sunrise

putting a letter in the mail for me? I promised Lizzie I'd get this posted as soon as I could, but didn't have time to get to Franklin yesterday." He said as he reached in his tent and pulled out his jacket. He retrieved Lizzie's letter to Ginger and handed it to Cullie.

"Sure thing," he agreed. "I'll run it by the post office soon as I get to town. I'll put it in the mail before I go back to the store."

"Come on," Eli urged as Cullie folded the letter and pushed it in his back pocket. "Grab that pole standing next to that tree yonder," he pointed. "We can find some grubs under some rotted logs for bait. And let's get some fish."

They gathered their poles and together started along the creek to Eli's fishing hole, looking forward to lip-smacking fried trout for supper.

All the while they had worked and joked, and even now as they made their way to the fishing hole, Eli felt a niggling worry in the back of his mind: Panther Clan; Muscogee.

And he saith unto them; Follow me, and I will make you fishers of men.
Matthew 4: 19

SEVEN

That night, back in the farmhouse, Bulger spent a near sleepless night. He worried about Eli's safety alone there in his tent, about Bessie and her new calf, and about rumors of threatening Muscogees in the area. He was up before daylight.

First thing was checking the cows and calves. Bossie and her baby had fed and were napping. Bessie, munching on loose hay, looked fine and so did her new baby. Moon danced from side to side; bumping her nose against her mom's udder, busy getting her morning breakfast. Next he looked in on the piglets that were eagerly tugging on their mama and getting sweet breakfast. He grinned and mumbled to no one in particular, "Well, think I'll get on in and get breakfast, too. Seems like everybody else around here is," and he ambled back to the porch and pushed the kitchen door open.

Miss Claudie stood at the stove singing and the radiating warmth was chasing the chills away from every corner of the room. "Mornin'," she said as she looked up as Bulger lumbered in. "How about country ham and redeye gravy to go with biscuits this mornin'?" she asked.

"Sure sounds good to me," he answered as he moved to the fireplace and held his hands to the flames. "Hard to believe there was snow on the ground day before yesterday," he mused. He stood and turned toward Miss Claudie. "Want me to set the table? Seems like our girls gone sleep in today."

"Go on ahead," she remarked, dishing up the steaming hot, thin red pork. "They'll wake up when they hear the plates hittin' the table, I'll bet," she added with a chuckle. Sure enough, one clunk of a plate and both girls' heads popped up from the covers.

"What time is it?" Lizzie asked in alarm as she looked around the kitchen. "Get up, Beth! We been sleeping and Miss Claudie's almost finished up. Lordy," she continued as she threw back the cover, burying Beth underneath, and threw her legs over the side of the bed and hit the floor with a plop. She pushed back her hair and noticed Bulger beside the table.

He pretended not to notice her standing there in her nightgown and walked and picked up the egg basket. "Gone get the eggs since Little Bit over there can't find her way out of a mess of quilts," and he was out the door quick as a bird after a worm.

Lizzie slid out of her gown and tossed her dress over her head and shoved her stocking feet in her shoes. "Beth, get up, lazy bones!" she scolded as she dashed to the cupboard and gabbed the remaining dishes, cups and glasses, and forks to finish Bulger's table-setting job. "I can't believe I didn't get up," she muttered as she flew around the table. "Beth, I said get up!" she called out sharply.

"Don't get your undies in a wad!" Beth shouted back. "You're the one who got me all tangled up in this cover. Dolly and Patty are lost in here and I can't find the edge of the quilt and---and I'm just stuck in the dark!" she complained as she fought covers like a cat trying to get out of a bag.

Lizzie slowed long enough to have a closer look. Beth was indeed thrashing her arms and the cover was refusing to leave her head. It slipped this way and that, but kept her under cover. Lizzie and Miss Claudie burst out laughing and Lizzie moved to the bed.

"Hush, ya'll!" Beth cried. "Don't just stand there, get me out!"

Lizzie pulled the colorful quilt off the bed and gave it a shake. "Okay, Little Bit, now you're free. Hop out and get dressed. You're already so late that Bulger had to gather your eggs. At least you can get the bed made and fill the woodbox before breakfast."

"Okay, okay," Beth replied as she flung the sheet back to

find her dolls. She grabbed Dolly, her old rag doll, and sat her on the foot of the bed and searched for Patty, the wooden doll made by Eli and Lizzie for her last year's Christmas present. Finally she found her on the floor next to the wall. She bent and grabbed her up. "Patty, what were you doing down there?" she said as she plopped her down beside Dolly. She straightened the cover over the bed and stripped her nightgown off and pulled her dress over her head. "Will you braid my hair before I get started, please, Lizzie?"

Lizzie looked over her shoulder at Miss Claudie who passed a smile and nod of approval. "Sure, Beth, come on over here and sit in this chair by the table." Lizzie moved to pull out a cane-bottomed chair and get a brush while Beth finished straightening the pillows. She scooted to the chair and sat down and Lizzie deftly twisted her hair into a lovely long braid. "All finished!" she said as Beth bounced out of the chair and pulled her sweater over her dress. She was out the door to fetch wood in a jiffy.

≈

The woodbox was filled; Bulger and Beth sat at the table.

Miss Claudie, deep in thought at the stove, shook herself and snatched the oven door open and grabbed the biscuit pan. "Lordy, me, I 'bout let the biscuits burn!" She dumped them on a platter and told Lizzie to go to the springhouse by the well and get the butter crock. As long as it was deep in the cool water, it stayed firm and sweet.

"Okay, let's finish up breakfast and get on the road!" Miss Claudie said as she set sizzling salt ham and hot biscuits on the table. Lizzie put out crocks of butter, jelly and honey. Bulger said the blessing.

With their bellies full and the stove simmering heat, Bulger pushed his chair back as Miss Claudie and Lizzie rushed to clear the table. "Think I'll check the mules' gear and throw my plows on the wagon to be sharpened at the blacksmith's. I just can't get them heavy ones up to sharpen in my shop. It's dry enough to see to first plowing. I need to get my fields plowed a little earlier than usual so I can help Eli get his ready." As an extra thought, he turned to Miss Claudie and asked, "Ya want me to plow up the garden spot, get it cleaned up, 'fore I get to the fields, Miss Claudie?" he asked as he stood.

"That would be nice," she answered. "What do you girls want to plant?" she asked. She knew this spring was their first with Bulger and her, and she knew the importance of including the girls in their plans. "Ya think a trip to town to look over what seeds Mr. Pollard has in the feed store would help you decide?" she added.

"That's a great idea!" Lizzie answered. "I'd love a trip to town. How about you, Beth?"

Beth thought a short instant. "Yep, I'd like that. Maybe we could find some flower seeds and plant them for Mamma and Papa," she said.

Lizzie remembered when they'd stood beside the graves at the first of the year and she'd promised Beth she'd help plant flowers at Papa and Mamma's graves when spring arrived. Spring was here and it was time. "Flower seeds first thing," she told Beth and reached over and gave her younger sister a hug.

"And guess what, Little Bit? We got a new calf in out in the barn." Bulger had managed to keep the second baby a secret until he knew Moon was up and healthy. Somehow Miss Claudie kept Beth busy checking on the piglets and she'd stayed out of the barn. Beth was content to watch while Ole' Crip lay in her sty or stand by her trough and eat her fill. As usual with each litter, the babies were allowed to run around and slip through the fence to explore the yard. Beth laughed and ran all over the place, trying to shoo them back together and into the pen with Ole' Crip.

Beth jumped from her chair to run out and look at the new calf, but Bulger stopped her short. "In a minute, Little Bit, let me get my coat. Ya can go out with me while I get the mules ready to hitch up. The baby's name is Moon—your brother Eli already named her. She's just like Star but has a white crescent moon shape on her head where Star has her star shape."

"That's so sweet!" she cooed as she clasped her hands together.

"Let's go, Little Bit," Bulger said as he headed for the barn. "Time to see the new heifer and get the mules hitched while Miss Claudie and Lizzie get breakfast cleared away." She grabbed her coat and followed him out.

In no time, Bulger popped his head into the kitchen and announced the wagon was hitched. Outside, Moses and Little Man had their tails twitching and hooves stomping to be on their way. The air was cool enough for the mules to be frisky and the road dried out enough for a double-bumpy ride. Bulger fairly leapt back across the yard and onto the wagon seat and grabbed up the reins and was ready to head out---yesterday!

"Let me get my bonnet!" Miss Claudie said as she folded the dish towel over the sink and grabbed her hat off the peg beside the door. "Better get yours, too, Lizzie. And bring Beth's. Bulger won't wait long. He has plowing on his mind and nothing else will matter 'til that ground is tilled up. Come on, now, hop to the wagon."

Miss Claudie raced out the door and Lizzie shut it hard. Miss Claudie reached up and Bulger took her hand and helped her to the seat while Lizzie joined Beth in the back--well away from the heavy plows.

"Giddy-up!" Bulger hollered as he popped the reins on Moses's and Little Man's backs. The mules were ready to go and lifted their heads high as they cantered out of the yard and to the road to town. Miss Claudie planned to get new material for aprons and dress material for Beth; Bulger's thoughts were of seeds for the fields and garden; and Beth could picture colorful blooms around Papa and Mamma's graves. Lizzie was the only one not thinking of gardens, sewing notions, or flowers. She was excited to be going to town and walk along wooden sidewalks and look in all the windows. Oh, just to be part of a busy place, no matter how hectic it may be, compared to her daily routine on the farm. Part of her excitement, too, was to check the post office. Who knew? There might be a letter from Ginger!

EIGHT

Eli stepped back and looked at his house. He and Cullie worked overtime the last week to get the walls up. Cullie borrowed Mr. Jones's wagon and together they carried logs to the sawmill and had them dressed smooth. It was much easier to lay the flooring and attach the roof rafters than stack those heavy logs. Eli modeled his house after his family home. It looked a lot like Grandpa's and for that he was glad. The doors and windows were still bare holes and today was the day that Eli decided to hang the doors. He picked over wooden planks left from his floor and found just the right ones. He measured and cut, braced and nailed. He brought out a paper-wrapped parcel he'd bought during his last trip to town and unwrapped beautiful hand-crafted iron hinges, and even a matching door latch for each door.

Eli measured his four doorways: one from outside into the kitchen, one from the kitchen to the dogtrot, one from the dogtrot to the bedroom, and the last from his bedroom outside, and set the hinges. It was painstaking work to lift the heavy doors and line them so that the hinges made the doors hang just right; in perfect balance. He had just enough daylight left to trim windows: two in the kitchen and two in the bedroom, before dark. He'd make wooden shutters later that would close tightly during the rain, cold, or wind, and he'd leave them open for fresh, open air in fair weather.

Even without a roof, this house was home. Eli decided to move his down sleeping covers inside and sleep on the floor. After a light supper from Miss Claudie's package of leftover buttered bread, potato patties, and some water from the creek, he gathered the bedding from the tent and moved it into the house.

It was a perfect spring night. A soft warming breeze slipped through the open windows and blew across his face. Clouds continued to float by, changing shapes and colors as the sun dipped out of sight.

Just as the stars began peeping through the few wispy clouds, Eli lay on his 'bed'---in his bedroom---locked his hands behind his head, and looked skyward. The last of sunlight slipped away and he heard the first night bird of spring. It sounded again: "Whip you I will!" The Whippoorwill called again. Eli chuckled. He remembered Mamma telling them that if they didn't wash their feet good and clean, the Whippoorwill would fly through the windows and whip their legs with its wings.

Hope the bird skips over me tonight, he thought. He didn't take time to wash at all, much less clean his feet. He lay there, listening to the bird's call in his long johns and socks, covered with his soft down cover. He remembered that when he was little, in his imagination, the bird was huge: wings spread as wide as he could stretch out both arms, had glowing red eyes and a wicked, sharp yellow beak. Big and fearless and always searching through the night for children who hadn't washed their feet before bed—then it would attack. He smiled as he remembered when he'd first seen the actual bird. A small, drab thing that shuffled its nest out on the ground for a place to lay its eggs. About the size of a dove, and about as harmless, he imagined. He shifted on his pallet and turned his thoughts heavenward.

His prayers came easy. He asked blessings on his family and gave thanks for God's blessings; for allowing him to make such good progress, fellowship and giving from the people in the area--both the Indians and his neighboring white settlers, and feeling God's loving protection. Long before the night birds ceased their chatter, Eli succumbed to his tired body and slept.

He woke and it took a moment for him to realize where he was. As he shook the cobwebs in his head free, he heard a familiar voice calling. "*Osiyo!*" Eli scrambled out of his cover and pulled his new door open to see Skipping Rock standing outside.

"Well, hello to you, too! Look what the possums brought in!" Eli joked. He jumped down from the threshold onto the ground and rushed out to meet his friend. They shook hands and stepped back and studied each other. "*Dtohitsu*? Did I get the 'how are you' right?" Eli tried to use common terms the Creek did as often as he could. He felt humbled that Skipping Rock had mastered the English language so well and he was stumbling so with simple Indian words. "I've got to ask what you have there before we get down to talkin'," he pointed to the pile of gourds. "Put them down and come on in while I get my clothes on."

Skipping Rock laughed. "Good to see you, too! And yes, my brother. I am well, or *osiquu*", he joked. He placed his bundle on the ground and followed Eli. "These are gourds we have left from last summer's crop. We plant them well away from our pumpkins and squash so they won't mix for reseeding, then dry them and clean them to use in the spring. It's time now to hang them."

Eli, still not comprehending Skipping Rock's apparent gift, pulled on his shoes and nodded. "Hang them?" he asked as they went outside.

"Yes, hang them," Skipping Rock said. He picked one up one of the gourds and ran his finger around the neat hole he'd cut in the side. "Insert a length of wire through these two holes in the narrow part here at the top and hang them along the branches of a bare sapling, one that you've stripped bare of leaves and cut off most of the limbs. Or you may want to tie a strong rope between two trees and hang them from it. Either way, toward the end of this month, birds, Martins, I think they're called, will come and build their homes in them."

"So," Eli prompted.

"Oh, you'll see," Skipping Rock replied, "these beautiful birds eat flying insects by the thousands. You will be thankful when you're able to stay outside in the evenings without being attacked by mosquitoes. The males' feathers glisten from black to purple and sometimes blue and green when the sun hits them, and they sing a chatty song as long as they're here. They'll leave in July after raising their young, but sure are a pleasure to have around---in more ways than one---as you'll find out. We can hang them later today if you'd like."

"Sure would!" Eli practically hollered. "That's a great idea. It sure will be nice to have a bug-free yard to relax in this summer." Stepping back, Eli noted, "You've changed a little," Eli remarked, eyeing his friend. "Your hair is different; shaved along the sides and long along the top and back, and your shoulders got broader. What are those, tattoos on your arms?"

Skipping Rock, puffing up his chest just a bit, explained. "I've completed my quest and have become a man in our village and so I've changed. It is good to see you." Skipping Rock explained. "Now I am responsible for gathering meat and providing for mother and Warm DayRah. I have come to ask, if it is all right with you," he paused and began again, losing his proud stance and shifting his feet with uncertainty, "I hope you will allow me to hunt on the land you have claimed. It is harder and harder to find game to keep those in the village fed since our hunting grounds have been lessened by the government's treaties. We will plant corn, beans, and have squash in the coming summer, and gather wild berries as we can, but we men need to go further out to find meat. Will you permit me to shoot on your land?" he asked, lifting his warm brown eyes to meet Eli's.

"You know you can come here anytime you want, take what you need," Eli returned. "I'll never forget that leg of venison that 'appeared' by our lean-to beside the river after our accident last winter. You proved your generosity then. Only fair to offer you mine now." Then as a second thought he added. "By the way, were you through here a couple of weeks ago? I found tracks along the creek here. Thought it might be a bunch of Muscogees, but really would feel better knowing it was you."

Skipping Rock furrowed his brow and crossed his arms across his chest. "I wish I could tell you it was me, but it wasn't. I have heard about the Panther Clan, my southern brothers roaming this area. Perhaps they, too, need to find more hunting grounds. Or perhaps they are resentful and thieving," he said in a low voice.

He squatted, indicated for Eli to sit, and continued. "It is known that once all Creek from here, along with the Muscogee who lived south, were proud to be brothers in The Cherokee Nation; one of the mighty Five Civilized Tribes." He dropped his head, picked up a stick, and made marks in the dirt. He continued. "Those of us who were able to stay after the army of the United States relocated many Indians found our lives changed, but we hoped to continue to live here in our homeland in peace." He looked up and thrust out his chin. "We have helped our white neighbors; ask Bulger. He has learned much about planting from us; watching the moon to know when to plant, using fish to help the plants grow strong, and harvesting every part of the corn plant for use. But now I, too, am afraid. Some of my brothers from the Panther Clan have broken the treaty and are disrespecting their forefathers and bringing shame to all of us." He stood slapped his hands together to shake the dust away. Eli stood as well, amazed at Skipping Rock's words. "It saddens my heart that my brothers have chosen to ravage and steal; lie to my white brothers and walk away from the true path of honor. If I could, I would speak to them and try to turn them back to the rightful way of walking in peace, but they have separated themselves from us and the truth is no longer in them." He paused. "On one hand I can understand their feelings. We have lost so much." With a heavy sigh, he continued. "Times have changed. My people must realize that we must live in today-time; we cannot go back to the old ways. I can only hope that you, my friend, do not consider me a part of that dishonorable group that I no longer call my brothers."

Eli could read the sorrow and disappointment in Skipping Rock's voice and hurried to reassure him. "Skipping Rock," he declared, "you are my friend. Your actions led me to find comfort and helped me through the darkest time of my life, and I am forever grateful. I'll never forget that venison you and Warm DayRah left at our pitiful campsite that morning after we lost the wagon at the river. Be at ease, I will never think of you or anyone of your village in a hateful or vengeful way. On my word."

"Thank you,--*wado*--," Skipping Rock relaxed hearing Eli's

promise. "My heart no longer is in pain from worry. I will always know you are my brother." Pulling a pouch from his vest, he opened it with delight. "With that cleared up, would you like a bit of something to eat this morning before we get the birdhouses hung?" holding out the bulging deerskin bag.

"Just you come on in to my kitchen," Eli was relieved the strain of gloomy conversation had passed and even more so at the sight of Skipping Rock's full food pouch. "And we will sit down and I'll catch you up on what everyone's been up to." He hopped up through the doorway and turned and reached out a hand to help Skipping Rock up into his new house. As Skipping Rock stretched his leg up to climb inside, he looked behind at the ground in confusion. Realizing the awkwardness of their entrance, Eli chuckled. "My porch has to wait awhile, but I think it's 'bout time I built steps, don't you?" he asked. Skipping Rock, stepping onto the rich-smelling new wood floor, nodded in agreement.

They sat cross-legged on the bare floor to eat. Skipping Rock squirmed and fidgeted. Eli noticed his apparent discomfort as Skipping Rock readjusted his seating. "Trouble getting comfortable?" Eli asked. "I'm working on a table and stools over in Bulger's shop, just don't have them finished yet," he added, hoping to hide his embarrassment. Skipping Rock moved yet again. "Got a stove ordered from Mr. Jones's store, too. Miss Claudie found Pa's money. Mamma sewed a pouch out of heavy material and put their money in it. She kept it pinned to her slip for safekeeping. Miss Claudie saved it and gave me enough to get started. It was a godsend. I'll have this place made homey in no time."

Skipping Rock suggested. "I know you will; just takes a little time and hard work." He looked around the room. "You know, Mother can weave a mighty good floor mat. Don't know if you'd be interested, but I think you'd really like one."

Eli was astonished. "I do remember seeing a woven rug on your floor when I visited, but never thought much about it." He nodded in approval of the idea. "I'll visit your village and for sure get your mother to make me one. It will help keep out that cold winter air later on. That's a great idea." He realized then just how hard his bare floor was on his backside, too, and laughed as Skipping Rock watched Eli readjust his seating to find a more padded spot.

Skipping Rock looked up and saw sky and Eli laughed. "Just haven't made it that far, yet. Cullie, from town, is coming over. I just don't know about the roof. I'm not sure where to get shingles around here. I don't think the sawmill is cutting them yet, and I don't have time enough before planting to cut them myself—not that I really know anything about how to go about it," he chuckled.

Skipping Rock gazed around. "You might do as we do in the village. I know where there are thick rushes. Our women cut them and bind them together and together we overlay them along our house rafters. You'll have to nail down other rows of small planks crossways on your rafters to help anchor the thatching, but that should be no problem. The thick dry grass and reeds holds up against almost anything and keep our houses warm and dry." He looked up again, surveying the hole on the top of Eli's house. "I can get Warm DayRah and mother to help get the grass ready, and if Cullie is willing, or if I can persuade a few of my fellow clansmen from the village, we can put you a thatched roof on in no time. I can help with your chimneys, too," he said as he noticed the opening for the fireplace. "We can get river rocks from your creek and I'll show you where there's a place where we can get whitemud. It will look nice rubbed on the inside of the fireplace and around the mantle when it's finished. We can use hardier mud to chink between the logs and the chimney rocks. That's the waddle and daub like we use, except we cover all our walls with it." He nodded to himself with satisfaction.

Eli didn't have to think twice about the offer. "Sounds great." He felt a huge relief knowing plans for his farmhouse were coming together. He smiled as he settled down and watched his Indian friend untie his pouch.

Skipping Rock unselfishly shared his meager meal with Eli. He bubbled out news about Warm DayRah's planning to attend school on the outskirts of town the coming year and learn to read, and about his mother's mare's spring foal. Eli listened intently and in turn, shared information about his family with Skipping Rock. It was good to catch up, and it was like time had turned back and they were sitting in Skipping Rock's house in his village talking and laughing. Finally, as Eli finished telling Skipping Rock about how Beth had grown, and Lizzie had learned to quilt, and Bulger was getting ready to plant their summer crops, a spirit of urgency filled him.

Bowing his head and asking for guidance, for the words he needed, he quietly asked, "Skipping Rock, do you know about our God?"

"Yes, some," Skipping Rock replied. "On some mornings we can hear music from the building near the canes at the head of the creek close to our village. It is very beautiful, but some of the words we don't understand. We pray to our Great Spirit and he comes and enlightens us and gives us comfort when we need it."

Eli knew the place. It was the church where they attended. He loved going there and worshipping God. The plain board church sat at the head of a creek that eventually wound its way into the Chattahoochee and joined its waters. He plunged on. "God is our Great Spirit. I'd like for you to get to know his son, Jesus, too. God came to Earth in the form of a man named Jesus so that all peoples could know him and when they pass on, they live forever in a place called Heaven."

"I have heard of that," Skipping Rock affirmed. "We, too, believe that our spirits go to dwell with the Great Spirit when they leave our bodies. I wish to know more. Perhaps you can tell me more as we visit in other days."

Eli was thrilled. He was filled with hope that Skipping Rock would learn and understand and accept Jesus as his Savior.

Sitting in his kitchen, sharing morning food with his friend, Eli was grateful that Skipping Rock had come and they could share their first meal together in his new home surrounded by the God's sweet Holy Spirit.

NINE

Bulger pulled the wagon to a stop in front of Mr. Marshall's blacksmith shop at the edge of town. "Ya'll stay here and I'll drop these plows off for Mr. Glenn to sharpen," he directed. "I imagine he'll have them ready by the time we leave." He climbed down from the wagon, handed the reins to Miss Claudie, and moved to the back of the wagon to unload the heavy plows.

Mr. Marshall came from inside the hot shop to help. "Mornin' Bulger," he said as he hefted a plow and carried it inside. "What can I do for ya this mornin'?"

"Just need these plows sharpened up," he replied. "Reckon they'll be ready after dinner?"

Mr. Marshall looked over the heavy plows now resting on the dirt floor of his blacksmith shop. "Yep, think so. I need to finish up these horseshoes for Mr. Huddleston and then I'll get right on them for ya." Bulger stuck out his hand and Mr. Marshall shook it with a firm hold.

"See you in a few hours, then," Bulger said as he climbed back on the wagon seat. He gathered the reins and clicked to the mules and they slowly pulled the wagon on into town. He pulled up right in front of the Post Office.

Lizzie, dazzled by all the hustle and bustle found in a busy town, found her eyes resting on the lettering above the door of the building where they'd stopped. Post Office. Post Office! She jerked herself erect, grabbed up her skirts, and fairly cleared the side of the wagon as she hopped out. "Miss Claudie, the Post Office! May I check and see if I have a letter from

Ginger?" she stammered.

Miss Claudie, laughing at Lizzie jumping around like she was standing on hot coals, shooed her along. "Go, go on. Check it out. Beth and I will be over at Jones's General Store. Meet us there." Bulger chucked, too, as he helped Miss Claudie and Beth from the wagon.

"I'll meet ya there," he said as he followed the wooden sidewalk up the main street. "I'm gone check on some seeds at the feed store." And he lumbered on. He reached Pollard's Feed and Seed in no time, his long legs making giant strides along the wooden walk. The path turned to dirt before he reached the Feed and Seed, and he looked around admiringly at the goods Mr. Pollard had brought in from surrounding towns and settlements to help people here in town with various supplies. He walked to the counter. "How're ya doin' Isaac?" he asked.

"Just fine, for now, Bulger. How ya'll been? Askin' 'cause I've had a wagon of nails and gun powder get lifted on the way in. My driver's got a gash in his head but the wagon's intact. He was unconscious for the ride in, but them horses brought in that wagon like a pigeon homing in. Sure gave me a fright," he said as he moved behind the tall wood counter. "I think those Muscogees lifted my goods." He said with a shake of his head. "I'm might uneasy about them Indians. Just hope they don't get the Creeks out your way flamed up, too."

"Ain't heard of anything around home, but ya never know. I sure hate to hear about ya man and supplies." He shifted his weight to one leg and crossed his arms. "I'm not too worried about the Indians around home. I knowed most of them for years. They're having a hard time, but I think they'll come to us for help 'fore they start stealing and hurting folks." He felt sure he was right about that.

Mr. Pollard straightened. "Sure hope so," he added solemnly, then looked up. "What'd ya' need today?" he asked, slapping his hand on the bare countertop, back in the farmer supply mode.

Bulger pulled his list out of his pocket. "Need to get my plowing done and get ready to plant so's I can help my boy, Eli, get his in. This is his first crop and I want him to do good."

Looking at the paper in his hand, he read, "Bushel and half corn seed, squash and bean seed, tomato if you have'm, pea seed, and a half bushel of wheat seed." He finished. With an afterthought he added, "Better throw in couple'a bags of fertilizer, too, sure don't need to forget that!"

Mr. Pollard snapped his fingers and pointed one skyward, "Got ya' covered!" he crowed, and turned and got busy filling Bulger's order.

When Mr. Pollard returned with the seeds, all weighed and placed in small brown paper bags and baskets, he added, "Say, Bulger, would ya like some sweet potato slips to plant this year?"

"Sure would," Bulger frowned, "but where ya gone get them? Didn't know any could be found around here."

Mr. Pollard grinned. "Some folks who traveled in on Mr. Denney's wagon train managed to salvage most of the sweet potatoes they brought along with them. They kept them buried in barrels of sawdust while they traveled. It was the Huckebas, I think. They settled down by the lower creek and kept the 'taters safe and protected from the late frost, covered'em, and let the eyes grow out. They have a few slips ready. 'Spect they'll have plenty ready for planting later, but thought of ya with these here," and he placed a dozen or so slips on the counter.

"Wrap'em up," Bulger said. "Miss Claudie will be happier than a frog with a fly to have these. Now what do I owe ya?"

Mr. Pollard counted up his due and Bulger counted out his change. He gathered up his items and balanced them in his arms, ready to leave the store. About the time he reached for the doorknob, the door swung open and Mr. Denney, the former wagon master, came in. He looked at Bulger, cocked his head sideways, and stuck out his hand.

"You're the man who took in those three children who lost their parents from my train when they tried to ford the Chattahoochee last January, aren't ya?" he asked. "Mighty fine family," Mr. Denney remarked. "How are the children holding up?"

Bulger balanced his packages and shook hands. "They're doin' just fine, I think. Boy's had to grow up fast and the girls are a mighty help to my wife and me. We're fortunate to have found'em and proud they've chosen to stay with us. Those three are mighty fine; been brought up right." He changed the subject. "Thought you'd be out of here. You decided to settle close by?" he asked.

Mr. Denney slapped his hand softly on the side of his leg. "Yep. After that last trip, with the fever and all, I decided it's time to quit and let some younger men take on the responsibility." He shifted on his feet and moved closer to Mr. Pollard's counter where he propped his arm. Bulger stepped back and turned to follow. Mr. Denney continued. "After most of the folks on the train decided to stay close by here, in Heard County, I found I liked this part of Georgia, too. Went back home, got the missus, and coming through Carroll County, a little north of here, saw my dreamland, and believe me, I've seen a lot of beautiful country." He chuckled, "I said 'my dreamland', more'n likely I need to say 'the missus dreamland'. She fell in love with a little spot near Roopville on a ridge between here and Old Carrollton, the Carroll county seat. And here we are."

Mr. Pollard spoke up. "Heard came from a part of Carroll County, ya know. That part of land is the last ceded by the Creeks in 1825 with the Treaty of Indian Spring. Chief McIntosh, chief of the Lower Creeks; 'White Sticks,' I think they called them. Northern Alabama Creeks were the Upper Creeks, or 'Red Sticks'. Anyway, this land was the last of what the Creeks owned in Georgia at that time. Story goes Chief McIntosh got murdered near here 'cause of it." He looked thoughtfully toward Mr. Denney. "Just a ways from where you're settled, probably. Carroll was a real big hunk of land before it started gettin' carved up." He grinned. "Named for Charlie Carroll out of Baltimore. One of the good men who signed the Declaration of Independence." Leaning back, he added with a chuckle, "Glad we got a chunk of it here in Heard."

Bulger, thinking about the history lesson, added. "You know, we still got some fine Indians here about, but in case ya ain't heard, there's a bunch of no-good Muscogee broke off from their group. Muscogees generally have been friendly, too, and good people. Can't figure out why this bunch's decided to go off on their own." He shook his head. "Just keep an eye out."

Mr. Denney nodded.

"Well," he said, shifting his bulky purchases, "I need to get over to the store where my missus is and see how much damage she's done."

"Give my best to her," Mr. Denney said. "Tell those chillun' hello for me, too. I don't usually get this far down; find most of what I need at Craven's store up the road. Been there?" he asked.

"Not in a while," Bulger said. "You talkin' 'bout that little shotgun store off the side of the road above Parmer's Ridge?"

"That's it," Mr. Denney agreed. "Just needed some salt fish and they were plumb out. If I don't get my mess now, I'll have to wait 'til next season. Hoping Mr. Pollard here has a few left," he said, turning to the storekeeper.

"Sure do," he said, "but you'll be getting the bottom of the barrel. Will be mighty briny—be sure to tell your wife to give them an extra soakin'."

The men laughed and Bulger turned for the door as Mr. Pollard and Mr. Denney checked out the barrel at the end of the counter.

"See you later," Mr. Pollard called as Bulger used his foot to pull the store door shut behind him.

Miss Claudie and Beth crossed the street and walked along the walk in the opposite walk from Bulger to Jones's store. They pushed the door open and walked inside and were met with the most wonderful smells: dried apples, coffee beans, cinnamon, and cotton fabric. Beth was instantly drawn to the large candy jar nestled in the front display cabinet. When she looked up from the candy and peered through the glass in the counter, two blue eyes were staring back at her. She jumped with a start. She heard a wind-chime like laugh and watched mutely as a blonde-haired little girl stepped from behind.

"Hi," she said with an assured smile. "I'm Melody. Who're you?"

Beth stood there tongue-tied.

Melody laughed and swished the hem of her dress. She

prodded Beth and good-naturedly asked, "What's the matter? Cat got your tongue?"

Beth snapped out of her shyness and stared at Melody. "Hi," she managed to whisper. "I didn't know there were any more girls like me around here."

"Sure," Melody replied. "Why ain't you in school with us now? We won't get out until sometime in June when the corn and gardens need planting. Folks need their children to help out and then we'll start our studies back in hot summer and not out again until fall harvest. I'll start my second year then. Bet you will, too."

"My sister is teaching me at home. We didn't get to Miss Claudie's until January, and with the weather and all, decided to wait until the new school terms starts," Beth explained. "I guess Miss Myline will figure out which year I'll be in," she added.

"You're comin' to school though, aren't you? Daddy says we'll be out soon, and when all the crops are planted Miss Myline will be calling all of us back for lessons. I love Miss Myline. She's soooo sweet, and pretty, too. You gotta meet her."

"I don't know about starting school right now, since ya'll will be finishing up your year soon," Beth replied thoughtfully. "Lizzie, my sister, is teaching me and our friend Warm DayRah our letters and numbers and we can read a little. My Mamma taught her and my brother to read and write before we left home to come here." She thought a moment and added, "I'll ask Miss Claudie about it, though. I'd really like to go to school and play with other children."

"Yes, it's so much fun!" Melody said. "You have a brother and sister?" she asked. "I don't have a brother, just three sisters and I'm the youngest." She began counting on her fingers. "There's Susan, she's the oldest and helps out here at the store." Then with a sly twinkle in her eye and whispering as she glanced around secretively, she added, "I think she's sweet on Cullie. He helps Pa in the store, too. He's big and strong and can pick up big boxes and reach real high to put up stock." Then she straightened and continued counting on her fingers. "Next are Melinda, then Luanne, then me. Lu and I go to school. Melinda and Susan's already gradjatated." She said with an affirmative nod.

"My brother, Eli, is working on his house and getting ready to plant, and Lizzie, my sister, helps Miss Claudie and Bulger. We live with them since our parents got killed." Beth said with a sad voice.

"Oh, I'm so sorry," Melody replied and reached out her hand to take Beth's in hers. "Would you like a piece of peppermint candy?" she asked kindly.

Beth's face brightened. "Sure would. You think Miss Claudie would mind?"

"Not a bit," Melody said as she led Beth behind the counter and slid the glass door open. "Here, take some for Lizzie, too."

And after Beth took two candies, she popped one right in her mouth and slipped the other in her apron pocket. Hand in hand they wandered to the back of the store, chatting and giggling all the way and sat on the steps. The beginning of a beautiful friendship.

While the girls sat, Beth felt a sting on her arm. She looked down and covered the red spot, rubbing it with her hand. She turned back to Melody to continue their conversation. Just then, another sting and she noticed something bouncing away, across the alley and heard a soft snigger. She looked around, but didn't see a thing. Sitting straighter, and drawing her arms close into her lap, she returned her attention to Melody. Again, Ping!

"What IS that?" Melody asked. "I don't see any bugs out here, but something has you really jumping." Again, the sound of a giggle, just a little louder. Melody jumped up and rushed to look behind rain barrel sitting near the corner of the store. She squinted her eyes in mock anger and propped her hands on her hips. "Get out of there right now, you bother!"

Beth's eyes popped wide open when the mischief-maker revealed himself. It was Sonny from the train! She jumped up and stopped short of grabbing him and giving him a hug. "Sonny! What are you doing here?" she asked.

He grinned his well-known wide grin, showing gaps where his front teeth still hadn't grown in, and drawled. "We're living here now. Mr. Denney brought the wagon train close by and Mamma and Pa decided to stay. We have a house on the edge of town and rent rooms. Pa helps Mr. Pollard down at the feed store. I sure was surprised to see ya here, glad, too," he added.

Beth was overjoyed to meet someone she knew. She had found Sonny to be a lot of fun and they had bonded with a strong friendship on the train. She had really missed him. "We're out of town on a farm there. We have chickens and cows! Pigs and babies, the mules, and I'm getting some new puppies." She looked at Melody and Sonny. "Maybe ya'll can come out one day and play a while."

In unison, the boy and girl answered, "Yeah, we'd love that!"

Miss Claudie watched from a short distance with Mrs. Jones. "You must come to town more often," Mrs. Jones said. "Melody really needs another girl her age to play with. Most of the other girls are just a tad too old to play little girl games with her, and I'm a little afraid Sonny will turn her into a right-out tomboy," she laughed.

"I think you're right, Mrs. Jones," Miss Claudie agreed. "I remember that Sonny. Beth needs more company than we can give her at the farm. We'll see that we come in more often. Then too, school will be starting soon, won't it?" she asked.

"Soon as the crops are in the ground," Mrs. Jones replied. "Our former school teacher, Miss Bonnell, had to leave and go back east with her new husband, Mr. Dowdy. The school trustees placed an ad in the Atlanta newspaper and Miss Myline Walls replied. She came out and interviewed and was accepted right off. Mr. and Mrs. Caswell, who live near the schoolhouse, give her room and board and the trustees pay her a small allotment each month. She really seems to love the children and relishes teaching. I sure hope she'll be around a while." Mrs. Jones explained.

"She sounds real nice," Miss Claudie agreed. She began moving to the cloth table. "Now let me see what I can find before Bulger gets here. I know he'll be in a hurry to get back home so he and Eli can get their bottoms plowed early." She reached for a bolt of cloth. "I'd like something bright. I plan a surprise for Beth and would like a lively little print to make her a new Easter dress for church."

TEN

Lizzie rushed along the wooden sidewalk and stopped right in front of the Post Office. She was so nervous she was afraid to go in: a letter or not a letter? She so hoped there was one. Taking a deep breath and throwing back her shoulders, she boldly pulled the door open and heard a light jingle from a little bell. The postmaster, Mr. Wright, looked up and greeted her with a welcoming smile. "Now who might you be, young lady? I don't remember seeing you around here," he remarked.

"I'm Lizzie and I live with Miss Claudie and Bulger a ways down the road outside town since our Papa and Mamma drowned when the water in the Chattahoochee got high and we tried to cross in our wagon and my…"

"Whoa, slow down a little, I got plenty of time to hear you out," Mr. Wright coaxed.

Lizzie blushed and sucked in her breath. "I'm so sorry, but I can hardly wait to find out if I have any mail. My brother, Eli, was supposed to post a letter to Kentucky to my best friend for me a couple of weeks ago and I thought maybe she'd written back."

"Eli?" Mr. Wright asked with his forehead furrowed in thought. "I remember a new boy picking up a letter to someone named Lizzie a while back, but he hasn't been by since."

Lizzie's heart dropped. Eli hadn't posted her letter! She was both devastated and mad at the same time. Mr. Wright knew by the look on her face she was about to pop, and added, "But let me look, he could have come in while I was out." And he hurriedly turned to go through a box of unclaimed mail. Suddenly he brightened and held up an envelope. "Whatta'ya know?" he said, waving the envelope. "You do have one." He quickly leaned over the counter and held out the letter. Lizzie stood mutely for a moment, hardly believing the paper was real. Then she reached and fairly grabbed it from Mr. Wright's fingers. He chuckled and added, "I hope you find all the good news you expect," and leaned and crossed his arms on top of the counter, grinning as Lizzie turned to go out.

She realized she hadn't been polite and quickly turned and waved the envelope in the air, "Oh, thank, you. I'm sure all's well. I can hardly wait to read this!" she said as she grasped the letter in both hands and shot out the door. As soon as she was on the sidewalk, she found a quiet spot and leaned against a store wall and ripped the envelope open. Her eyes flew down the neatly written lines and she let out a whoop that made a frightened stray cat scoot down the alley. "She's coming! Ginger's coming!" she laughed. She shook herself loose from the wall and rushed down the street to Jones's store.

Just as she reached the middle of the street, she noticed a somewhat familiar figure rounding the corner to the Livery. She stopped up short right in the middle of the busy street and stared as the image vanished inside. The excitement of Ginger's coming visit disappeared momentarily while she wracked her brain trying to remember why the tall young man had caught her eye. Who on earth could it be? Surely she should know, but who?

No! No way, she thought. For a minute there, she was certain it must be Jimmy from the train. But he was going to Alabama. He couldn't be in Franklin. She shook her head and started to Jones's, moving slowly. Her face was wrinkled in deep thought when her eyes fell on the white paper clutched tightly in her hand. Ginger! All thoughts of Jimmy vanished as she giggled to herself and was caught up and filled with excitement of Ginger's visit all over again. She couldn't wait to share her news!

≈

Mrs. Jones and Miss Claudie had their heads bowed over the colorful material and murmured approvals of each print. Finally Miss Claudie chose her favorite: a soft pink with mint green and pale yellow flowers. Flowers! Miss Claudie almost forgot. "One more thing, Mrs. Jones," she added. "Do you happen to have any wild flower seeds? I promised the girls we'd plant some this spring."

"As a matter of fact, I do. I usually don't get any in, but for some reason, we got several free packets when we ordered our new spring cloth." She walked to the counter, bent down and pulled out a drawer. "Here you are. Anything else?" she asked, placing two packets of flower seeds with the material.

Miss Claudie answered absently, "No, not today." She knew exactly why the 'surprise' packets of seeds had been sent. God had been looking after the children, even before they knew they'd need flower seeds, and provided for their needs. She rejoiced at the Goodness of God!

Mrs. Jones had both packages tied neatly in a brown paper bundle propped on the counter and asked, "Are ya'll planning to be at church next week? Preacher Arp will be coming through and have services at Caney Head."

Miss Claudie responded, "Oh, for sure. It seems like it's been forever since the preacher has been here. I know it's hard for him, making his circuit and all. We'll have dinner after services, won't we?" she asked.

Mrs. Jones laughed lightly. "I don't think Preacher Arp thinks the service is fully over until the last of the food is packed in the baskets after we finish dinner on the grounds. That, along with getting reacquainted with everyone, is the highlight of his coming. I sure do hope we have some souls saved. I'm ready for a good spring baptizing."

Miss Claudie nodded her head and reached for her parcels just as Bulger appeared.

"Got my field corn seeds," he said, raising a huge basket. "Enough for Eli, too. And I didn't forget your garden plants; cabbage and onions either. Even a dozen or so sweet 'tater slips! Ya got your other garden seeds saved over from last year, all dried and separated. Ready to go, Miss Claudie?" he asked, attempting to rush them out.

She smiled a 'told-you-so' grin at Mrs. Jones and chirped, "Ready, Bulger. Just give me time to pay Mrs. Jones and get Beth. She's got a couple of new friends—some that speak instead of mews, moos, or grunts," she joked as she nodded her head toward the back steps where the trio sat, still engrossed in deep conversation.

Their heads bobbed up as Lizzie whizzed in the door and shouted, "Ginger's coming. She'll be here in a less than a month!" She danced in place and waved the letter over her head and Mrs. Jones dropped the coins that Miss Claudie was handing her. They tinkled and twirled along the countertop and finally came to a rest. Mrs. Jones grabbed them and placed them in the till.

Miss Claudie looked from Lizzie to Mrs. Jones and explained with a happy face, "That's our other girl, Lizzie, and I suppose you can guess she's excited that her friend from Kentucky is coming for a visit." Mrs. Jones simply nodded and smiled as she pushed the drawer shut in the cash register.

Beth jumped up from the doorway and ran to Lizzie. "Did you say Ginger's coming?" She asked.

"Sure's shootin'!" Lizzie laughed and lifted Beth up and twirled her around.

"Hey, girls," Bulger admonished, gesturing for Lizzie to put her sister's feet back on the floor. "Ya'll settle down." He turned to Mrs. Jones. "Sorry for the interruption, but we really do need to be on our way." And he nodded to Miss Claudie indicating he wanted her to shoo the girls quickly to the wagon.

Melody ambled to Beth. "This is your sister?" She asked. "She's pretty," glancing toward Lizzie.

"Thank you, Melody." Beth looked at Miss Claudie for approval and replied. "I hope you can come to the farm and visit with us. We'll be looking for you one day soon."

A man that hath friends must shew himself friendly;
and there is a friend that sticketh closer than a brother.
Proverbs 18: 24

Just then Lizzie noticed a little boy standing shyly beside the door. "Sonny!" She threw up her arms and rushed across the floor and grabbed him. She gave him a quick peck on his cheek and his face turned bright pink before she let go and stood back. "What are you doing here?"

He stammered, "We settled here, too." He nodded to Beth with further explanation. "Beth can tell you about it."

Beth piped in, "Can Sonny come out when Melody does, too, do you think?"

Miss Claudie was so proud that Beth remembered her manners. She, Lizzie, Beth, and Melody's heads all turned in unison toward Mrs. Jones.

"How can I say 'no' to all of you?" she twittered. "I'm sure we can get Melody out to visit one day real soon and I'll speak to Sonny's Ma about him." Melody clapped her hands and danced over to her mom while Sonny grinned from ear to ear.

Bulger gathered his ladies together and shushed them out the door. "What do I have to do to get ya'll in the wagon?" he prodded good-naturedly. "We got to get to Mr. Glenn's and get the plows, and them mules better high-step it gettin' home." He put his arm around Lizzie, "And you can fill me in on the details of Ginger's visit on the way," he added.

They reached the wagon and piled in and settled themselves in for the bumpy ride home. As they pulled into the yard, they thought separate thoughts about how it had been a full, satisfying day. They were tired and happy to get home and as soon as the mules were settled and all the things done: mules and cows fed and watered, chickens checked, pigs slopped, seeds put safely away, lamps lit, supper warmed and eaten, and table cleared, they fell into bed and slept soundly.

ELEVEN

The next several days flew by in a busy whirl. The house was cleaned from top to bottom, quilts and shuck mattresses "aired" in the soft sunlight, and Bulger found time to build a trundle bed that fit underneath the girls' bed in the kitchen. Beth could still sleep with Lizzie, and Ginger would sleep close by on the trundle bed; nestled underneath Lizzie's bed during the day and pulled out for sleeping at night. Lizzie warned Beth again and again that when Ginger came to keep her mouth closed, go to sleep early, and let her and Ginger catch up their news. Beth, though, knew she wouldn't sleep early, but just might stay quiet so she could listen in on the big girls' conversations.

At the end of the week, Eli made a special trip to the farm and brought two little red-bone hounds to Beth, just as he'd promised. She knew the minute he walked in the yard that he had the pups, and she ran to meet him with wide eyes and flying feet.

"Oh, Eli," she shouted, "Put them down. Let them run to me." And he did.

He stooped and opened the guano sack and held it wide; watched as the nosey pups pushed their heads out and began sniffing. They lifted their heads and their noses twitched. Suddenly they spied Beth. There was no holding them then. They opened their mouths in wide grins and struggled to free themselves. Eli helped a little and shook them out. They were long and lanky with gangly legs and huge feet. They moved like their limbs were tied together with loose string. They bounded toward Beth with oversized ears flapping. Beth held out her arms and squatted to meet them. They reached her and their momentum carried them right into Beth and knocked her flat on her back. Her arms went wide and her feet reached for the sky. Eli dropped the sack and concern replaced his delight as soon as he saw Beth hit the dirt. She was screaming, and Eli raced to reach her.

"Beth! Are you all right?" he asked, trying to shove the playful pups aside. As soon as he got one pup away, it leapt right back. Beth kept screaming, almost lost her breath. Eli tried his best to reach into the frazzle and lift Beth, but she was kicking her legs and wrapping her arms around the dogs. "Beth, come on, help me get you up." He pleaded.

"Noooo," she yelled in breathless glee. "They're giving me kisses. Look, Eli, they are so happy to be here with me."

And with that, Eli sat back on his heels and studied the picture. Sure enough, Beth wasn't in harm's way; she was overjoyed and was in dog heaven with the two hounds slobbering all over her face. He laughed and grabbed a handful of loose skin on both dogs' necks and picked them up. "Okay, Little Bit, get up and dust yourself off. You've got to get to the sink and wash your face."

Beth hopped up and brushed off her skirts and followed Eli into the house, trotting closely along and petting the pups as they went. "Miss Claudie, look, Eli brought me some puppies!" she declared as Eli set the dogs on the kitchen floor. They shook and dirt and dust flew everywhere.

Miss Claudie set her hands on her hips and frowned. "Them dogs are not to be in this house." She declared.

"We could'a guessed that, but I had to get Beth in here somehow to get her face washed. Them hounds slobbered all over her but good!" Eli explained.

Beth, still petting and cooing over the puppies, could hardly pull herself away and wet her face. "I'm goin' to see Warm DayRah and show her my new babies." She said. And started out the door with the dogs clambering behind.

"Whoa, Little Bit. You gone leave before I get a hug?" Eli asked.

Beth quickly turned and threw herself in Eli's arms. "Thank

you, thank you, Eli. I love them so much," she said and mashed her lips hard into Eli's cheek. MMMMuah! she pulled away and started in a great hurry for the door. The dogs were waiting, impatiently, on the porch; tongues wagging and drooling, and whole bodies wobbling back and forth and feet dancing in anticipation.

"Hey," Eli said, stopping her. "You gone leave before you tell me their names?"

Beth turned with a grin spread across her face; one hand on each dog's head. "The boy is Jack and the girl is Bell," she said, and turned and ran outside to the edge of the yard where her much-used trail to the Indian village began.

"She's in hog heaven," Miss Claudie remarked. "I doubt that I'll be able to keep them dogs out'a the house. Never had a dog inside, but do reckon Beth will find a way to sneak them in." She shook her head and reached for the broom.

"I think you mean 'dog heaven'," Eli laughed, "And I think you got that right and you'll have a couple of house dogs," Eli stated. "But I feel a whole lot better knowing she's not alone on that trail through the woods. I haven't mentioned it, but Muscogees have been close by my place. I got my house finished up good enough so that I'm locked inside at night good now. I still need a roof and I'm praying for rain to hold off, but I did see Indian signs before I got the house done—and it wasn't Skipping Rock."

"Eli!" Miss Claudie exclaimed, raising her hands and pressing them to her lips. "How could ya not tell us?"

He shrugged his shoulders. "Just didn't want no worry." He said quietly.

Miss Claudie gave him a sharp look, grabbed the broom and fairly beat the dirt left from the dog's romp off the floor. "What are we to do with ya, child?" she mumbled as she swept the dirt out the door.

Lizzie came in from gathering quilts off the line. "Smell these, Miss Claudie," she said, not noticing Eli. "They smell so fresh and clean. Just in time for Ginger!" She looked up and saw Eli propped next to the table. "And I guess it was you I heard making all that ruckus a little while ago?" she asked.

"Yep," he replied. "Me and Jack and Bell met up with

Beth.

"Where is she?" Lizzie asked, looking around. "And who are Jack and Bell? Do we need to put on extra supper?"

Miss Claudie and Eli laughed. "No, just the two pups I promised Beth. Mr. Parmer was ready for them to go. She's taken them to the village to show Warm DayRah and the other children. She'll be back before supper."

"Glad of that," Lizzie said. "Oh, yes, before I forget," and she placed the quilts on the bed and reached for Ginger's letter.

"As if you could," Eli mumbled.

"What?" Lizzie said sharply, snapping her head toward Eli.

"Nothing," he voiced, raising both hands in surrender.

Lizzie crossed the room and showed Eli Ginger's letter and asked if he would be able to meet the stage and bring her home on his way. He gladly agreed, knowing he could easily walk into town and borrow one of Mr. Jones's wagons. "Let me keep this so I'll be sure to be on time." He knew Bulger would be too busy to stop his work and run to town. Bulger knew the springtime weather was mighty unpredictable and wanted to finish getting the ground broke up and be ready for planting around Easter after the ground warmed. He watched the moon and insisted getting his seeds in the ground according to "the signs".

Or saith he is it altogether for our sakes? For our
sakes, no doubt, this is written;
that he that ploweth should plow in hope; and that he
that threasheth in hope should be partaker of his hope.
1Corinthians 9: 9- 10

TWELVE

Beth skipped along the worn path from Bulger's to the Indian village. She usually visited at least twice a week and enjoyed playing with the children. Most of the time she carried either Dolly or Patty, or both, since Warm DayRah and her friends had dolls, too. They loved playing school and talking. Beth had learned several Creek words: "*Osiyo*, hello; *dtohitsu*, how are you?, and *wado*, thank you." She looked forward to playing with Warm DayRah and learning more of their language and hoped she would eventually carry on conversations with her in native Creek. And Warm DayRah, she was a sponge soaking up the English language. She was good at numbers, too, and made Lizzie proud. Beth thought about their days with Lizzie sitting inside Minshue's warm home, or at the kitchen table at Miss Claudie's as she bustled over the stove and Bulger worked in the barn.

On the days when Warm DayRah's mother could spare her, she visited Lizzie and Beth at Miss Claudie's. Lizzie laid out slate tablets and markers and they practiced spelling and arithmetic. Bulger brought various flyers and ads from town and they used them for reading practice. Both young girls were apt learners and Beth knew Lizzie truly enjoyed her role as a teacher. Lizzie completed her schooling in Kentucky and all she needed to do to be a "real" teacher in Georgia was pass a requirement test. She'd not told anyone but Beth that she had secretly mailed an inquiry to Atlanta and requested information. She hoped to hear back soon. She planned to have time to take it between planting and laying-by time of the crops. She really hoped she'd be a teacher one day soon. She knew she would have lots 'waiting time' on a farm—plant seeds in the ground; wait for them to grow; lay them by---plow one more time and add fertilizer to help them grow strong and wait for a great harvest. Of course there was the constant weeding, mulching, and fertilizing the garden and taking care of Papa and Mamma's graves--tending flowers there.

Beth could feel Lizzie's pride of her and Warm DayRah and knew Lizzie dreamed to add more little Indian children to her school roster soon, especially those who wouldn't be able to attend "real" school near town. She slowed to a walk and Jack and Bell obediently fell in beside her. Beth watched as both dogs constantly inspected, smelled, and listened to the trees and objects around them. Once in a while, Jack would pause, lift his head and perk his long ears forward. Beth laughed when he did this; his ears crept further up on his head, but were so long and floppy they'd never stand at full attention. Bell walked a few steps behind Jack, letting him take the lead, but constantly on alert for back-up. She was a beautiful puppy. Her body long and sleek, hair glistening copper red when Beth led them through a patch of sunlight breaking through new leaves high in the trees. Jack was just as beautiful, but he had an added rippling of muscle strength already showing in his young body.

Beth could hardly wait to get to the village. There were dogs there, but none like hers! She knew Jack and Bell were extra special and Eli had given her a wonderful gift, and as any gift, she must cherish it and share it as she could. Suddenly, her young mind understood the 'gift' that Preacher Arp had talked about a few Sundays ago. They were in the little church at the caney head of the creek and Preacher Arp explained about God's gift of Jesus and how anyone who accepted that gift became a new person. She felt love wash over her and fill her with tingling happiness. She wanted that right then: to accept Jesus as her Savior and share his love. She looked down at her puppies and thanked God for Eli's gift that had helped her understand: She prayed for Jesus to come in and live in her heart; she wanted to share the Good News. Beth stopped and stooped to hug her dogs, tears streaming down her face. When she stood, she felt protected not only by the presence of Jack and Bell, but by the presence of the Holy Spirit, too. She stepped lightly and hurried to the Indian village. She had a lot to tell when she arrived.

Jack and Bell loped ahead and met several village dogs at the edge of the settlement. Beth felt the same awe every time she stepped into the busy village. She stopped and watched as her pups made friends with the village animals: sniffing, ears back, circling each other, and then suddenly jumping back, behind up and front legs low on the ground. With a sudden sprint, they started chasing each other, running and playing in a wild, puppy way. Laughing, Beth stepped into the square village and found Warm DayRah's house. She entered the inviting home, watched as Warm DayRah's mother, Minshue, weaved a large mat. She stood a minute and looked at the beautiful Indian. She was tall for an Indian woman and her jet black hair fell down her back in a long braid. Her black eyes darted around the room looking to Beth, her circle of fire, and back to the mat. Minshue's high cheekbones sat in perfect balance above her smiling lips.

"Come in, Daisy Face," Minshue said with a welcoming smile. Beth loved her Indian name, Daisy Face, which Minshue had given her. Since there was no "B" in the Cherokee alphabet, Minshue gave Beth a perfect name. Beth thought it was perfect, too. She drew closer to Minshue and sat on the woven floor mat.

"*Osiyu*, what are you doing, Miss Minshue?" she asked. And as she looked around, she asked a second question before Minshue could respond, "Where is Warm DayRah?"

Minshue, fingers flying through the dry grass producing a beautifully crafted mat answered, "This, little Daisy Face, is a floor mat to cover your brother's, floor. Skipping Rock has been by and told me about how hard Eli's floor is and how a mat would really dress up his room and make it more comfortable." Then she added, "And Warm DayRah is helping her grandmother plant squash and beans today. She'll be here for our midday meal soon."

Beth thought about that for a minute. "That's good." She sighed and continued, "I haven't been to Eli's yet. Maybe we can go soon. He's almost finished a table and stool. They're in

Bulger's shop. I think Eli's goin' to get Mr. Bussey and Mr. Folds to witch him a well. Mr. Bussey can hold a forked willow stick and when he walks over water in the ground, the stick will bend right down. That's the spot they'll dig Eli's well. Bulger, Mr. Bussey, and Mr. Folds will all help him dig it, and Mr. Todd will build a well-house over it with a windlass and bucket." She bopped her shoulders up and added as she let them fall, "Mr. Bussey really has a gift for helping people find water." Then she became more thoughtful. "Miss Minshue, do you know about God's gift of Jesus that He gave for all of us?"

"Yes," Minshue replied, "I have heard of your God, and He is wonderful. Many of our villagers have asked His Son, Jesus, to come into their hearts. We have our traditional celebrations, but God is our center here in our village. Skipping Rock is almost ready to accept your Christ. I do know Eli has talked to him about salvation, too." Minshue adjusted the mat and continued. "You know, God has many names and is always present with us. As long as we cling to Him and pray for Him to keep us safe, it doesn't matter what we call Him. He is our Father God, our Great Spirit, who lives with us. If we face dangers or hardships, we can find assurance and peace knowing He is with us and will help us." She smiled at Beth, and Beth realized how important and loved she was: not only by one family, but by many.

"I felt him on the trail here," Beth acknowledged. "I know He has saved me and will protect me whatever comes."

Just then, Warm DayRah rushed in. "Hi, Daisy Face," she beamed. "I knew someone special was here when I saw those beautiful dogs. Are you goin' to teach them to hunt?" she asked as she plopped down and crossed her legs beside Beth.

Beth raised both hands and shook her head, "No, not me, but they are hunting dogs and I expect Bulger and Eli will train them one'a these days." She looked thoughtful. "It will be nice to have more fried rabbit and gravy, squirrel stew, and roast possum."

Minshue moved her matting aside, "Speaking of that, are you girls ready for our midday meal?" she asked as she rose from her stool. "We have bread and what is called poke salad today. The cornbread is ready and the poke is bubbling in the pot outside. Come along and we'll eat."

The girls followed Minshue to the cooking area which was always outside in the summer; in winter the family moved to their winter house--one safer for indoor fires and made especially so that smoke rose and drifted through a hole in the roof.

Minshue crumbled cornbread in three bowls and ladled the green poke salad and pot 'likker' over it. It smelled so good! Beth took it with a little trepidation.

"Miss Minshue, Miss Claudie says poke is poison if it's not cooked right."

Minshue laughed. "Sure is, Daisy Face, but it's safe. I've boiled this three times in fresh water and seasoned it well. We say that three good meals of poke salad in the spring will cleanse your blood and make you healthy. Eat up!"

Beth lifted the bowl and drank in the warm broth and sucked in a mouthful of tender greens. Boy, Minshue was right! It was delicious and her bowl was emptied in a jiffy.

When they finished, she and Warm DayRay carried the bowls and rinsed them in the nearby creek, rubbing white sand inside to scrub them clean. With the final rinse, they returned to the house where Minshue was finishing Eli's mat.

"All done," she exclaimed, holding the edge of the mat and tucking in the last of the dried grass. "I'll roll it and tie it so Skipping Rock can drop it off the next time he visits Eli."

Beth felt suddenly tired and a little sleepy. She looked at Warm DayRah and realized she was nodding off, too. "I guess I'd better round up my pups and start home," she said and she looked into Minshue's face and added, "And I know I'll be protected and safe all the way."

Minshue extended her hand and smoothed back Beth's hair. She bent and kissed Beth on her cheek and said, "Yes, little Daisy Face, you are loved and protected in more ways that you know."

Beth walked to the door and looked back. Warm DayRah was sound asleep on their woven floor. She laughed. "Tell Warm DayRah my dogs' names are Jack and Bell. I didn't think to tell her, and now I don't think she'll hear me!"

"I will, sweet Daisy Face," Minshue replied with a loving

smile. "Be safe and please tell Lizzie I'll send Warm DayRah in two moons for her schoolwork. She's really coming along. I'm so glad Lizzie takes the time to help. Maybe she can come here and work with all the children before long. Now be on your way. Keep your dogs close and hurry along the trail." She watched as Beth clapped her hands and her pups came running. She continued watching as Beth and her dogs disappeared into the woods. "Oh, God, our Great Spirit, please keep that little one safe from harm."

And as she turned to move across the room and picked up a light blanket to cover Warm DayRah, she couldn't help but feel a surge of unease reaching inside her with a disquieting chill. Skipping Rock had told her of the marauding Panther Clan. Desperation could cause good people to do bad things, and Minshue only hoped and prayed none of her loved ones got in their way. But the feeling she had; a forewarning of danger, refused to leave.

THIRTEEN

Early the next week, Skipping Rock delivered the grass mat. Skipping Rock bounced into the kitchen and untied it. "Here you go," he smiled. Together they held Minshue's beautiful floor mat and spread it over the bare wooden boards. Eli walked over it, around it, and sat on it, and put his hand down and rubbed it like it was a new kitten. Skipping Rock laughed at Eli's pleasure. Waiting outside were three of his friends and two horses who had come along to work at Eli's. There were huge bundles of dry grass tied to the sides of the horses to use for Eli's roof. Working all through the day, with help from Skipping Rock and his friends, the thatch was quickly on the house.

"Look, Skipping Rock," Eli said, sitting on a rafter and tying the last of thatch. He thrust his chin up toward the sapling full of hanging gourds. "Just like you said. The birds came in the day after we hung the gourds and have been swooping and diving ever since. I wake to their 'talking' and love listening to them during the day. Thanks again!" he added and Skipping Rock smiled with pleasure.

Roof finished, they used the horses to pull in large rocks from the creek and heaped them in piles next to each end of the house. It was backbreaking, and Eli was amazed at the fortitude and resolve of the Indians. Even through their tireless efforts, they joked and bantered. Sometimes Eli was the brunt of their jokes, but he loved it. It was like working with brothers he never had.

They had fine-working chimneys standing sentry on both ends of Eli's house in less than three days. Skipping Rock suggested Eli bring in white mud and daub it over the face of the fireplace and hearth to make it look clean and fresh. Naturally, after next year's winter fires the fireplace's face would be blackened and covered with soot, and the mud daubing would become part of his spring cleaning. Skipping Rock came again early the next morning.

"While we have my friends and their horses working," Skipping Rock suggested after days of rock-hauling, "Let's haul more rocks and stack them for steps." Skipping Rock looked earnest, so solemn; then broke out in hooting laughter as he placed his hands on his hips and stood tall—throwing out a challenge to Eli.

Eli's arms ached and his back was stiff, but he dared not turn down such an offer. Eli blew a great gust of breath and his body shrank. He was bone tired, but he'd never stop while his new friends were willing to help. Besides, he'd never back off a dare.

Noontime passed and the sun got higher. Horses broke a sweat and were pleased to work in the cool, wet, shallow branch pulling large, flat rocks. The horses slipped on the damp banks, but make good time getting rocks attached by chains across the yard to the doorways where steps were needed. Then the backbreaking work began. The Indians grunted and heaved to stack rocks and get the rise just right. Eli found smaller rocks to chink in between the large creek rocks to level them. Finally they were finished. Eli was proud and bowed low as he gestured for Skipping Rock to be the first to try them out. He climbed up and hopped into the kitchen, then lithely stepped back down. He surveyed their work appreciatively.

Eli looked approvingly. "Now I can skedaddle out of the bedroom fast and not break my neck getting to the outhouse," he said flippantly.

"Outhouse?" Skipping Rock laughed in response. "Do you think we can...."

"Oh, no," Eli interrupted, waving his hands in defeat. "I can't do anything else today, thank you. I'll get my outhouse done just fine. Give me a day or two and I'll have the hole dug and my toilet finished. That's one thing I think I <u>can</u> do myself." He snickered.

"Well, then," Skipping Rock said, "Looks like you're about to become a settled settler," he said as he reached and held the horse's halter. He patted its head and let his hand slide down the reins. "I'm glad to have a good neighbor like you," he added.

Eli beamed with the compliment and shrugged his shoulders and said, "Me, too." The work had been hard, but the time spent sharing the work with the Indians was priceless.

Eli's knowledge about house building and maintenance swelled as he worked and learned from the industrious Indians. His admiration and gratitude spilled over as the Indians finished and prepared to leave. "I can never thank you enough. Please," he asked, "if there's ever anything I can do for you, please call on me."

The Indians, grinning knowingly at each other, agreed and pounced on Eli's words, "Eli, our friend," they bantered. "Just one little thing. One small deed would repay us in full." They looked from one to the other and Skipping Rock urged them on. "We're looking for a good meal with all the trimmings, some music, and a little dancing to celebrate your new home!"

A little surprised, but pleased, he agreed. "You bet!" He answered, slapping his hand on his leg, "That's a wonderful idea! I'll send the invitation by Skipping Rock."

The group of hard-working, and tired, young men laughed and joked as they left Eli's yard. Having no word for 'good-bye' they called as they wandered into the woods toward their village, "*donadogohv*?" or "Let's meet again." Eli waved and returned the message. He was bone tired, but so thankful for the finishing of his home. He chuckled at the thought of the Indians loving a good time just as much as he did.

Later that evening, Eli thought that as soon as his well was finished, he'd invite everyone for a house-warming. The Indians, Cullie and the Jones's—especially the girls--Miss Claudie and Bulger, Mr. and Mrs. Parmer, the Rogers, and his other neighbors. He imagined Miss Claudie and Lizzie would cook themselves silly and love every minute of it. He chuckled as he hopped up his new steps; pulled open his new door by the hand-crafted latch, stepped inside, and softly closed it.

Since his house was basically completed: just moving in his furniture, setting up the stove when it arrived, and digging the well, he decided to go to Bulger's and hitch Little Man and help him finish up his last ten acres, and then they'd move to Eli's clearing. He only had about five acres, but with the help of Bulger, they'd have it plowed in no time.

≈

The next week, waking the morning after getting his field broken up, he thought he'd walk to town and check on his stove. He figured Cullie would bring it out as soon as it arrived, but it was a couple of days past what Eli had supposed it was due. He grabbed some cold cornbread, swiped a glob of butter across it and gulped it down—a little dry, but a cool drink of stream water fixed that. As he left, he made sure the door was tightly closed. The day started out cool, then warmed quickly as he reached town. He looked westward and noticed a few dark clouds hanging low and rolling over each other, the wind pushing them his way. Looks like it's coming up a cloud, he thought, and hurried on.

As he reached Jones's store, he saw Cullie struggling with a large crate and three more sat on the delivery wagon. "Whoo!" he shouted and waved to Cullie.

He looked up and returned the wave, almost dropping his box in the process. "Come on over," he shouted. "This is your delivery and I can use some help. Mr. Jones said he's put it on your bill. He don't have much room to keep big orders for long."

Eli trotted over. "Mr. Jones is a good man. I'm proud Miss Claudie found Mamma's money pouch. Without that, I'd a never been able to get this stove, and not much of anything else. Why don't you leave this on the wagon and I'll ride with you back to my place and we can unload there? I'll get it put together when Bulger comes by," he said.

"Now why didn't I think of that?" Cullie grinned and propped his elbow on one of the larger boxes resting on the wagon's tailgate. "What a coincidence you showed up when you did. You really saved me some time." He went on, "I need the wagon to make a delivery later out to Mr. Denney. You know, I think he's your old wagon master. I heard Mr. Jones talking to Mr. Barker yesterday about Mr. Denney's deciding to quit the wagon train business. He and his wife have settled just up north from here in Carroll County. There's only a small general store between here and there; the Cravens run it. They carry trading stuff for the Indians and basics for settlers, not big goods like your stove here." He added.

"Well, what'd ya know about that?" Eli asked. "Bulger did mention something. I'm glad to hear Mr. Denney and his family will be living close by. Did you hear about any more folks that traveled with us?" he asked. He really hoped several families had settled close by and they could rebuild their relationships. The people on the wagon had become like family and he found himself anxious to hear about them.

"Yep, I did," Cullie said, standing, "You'd be surprised what you can learn working in a big store like Mr. Jones's. How about I tell you what I heard on the way back to your place?" he asked as he hopped on the wagon seat. Eli was quick to follow. "Them clouds are coming in fast," Cullie remarked, glancing in the distance.

Eli glanced up, too. "Do you think it will blow over?" he asked. "Preacher Arp will be coming in on Saturday for our Sunday Meeting at Caney Head. He'll be staying with the Huckabas and everyone around will take dinner for after the meeting. You planning to come?" He asked Cullie, still eyeballing the strange-looking sky.

"You bet I'll be at church!" Cullie replied. He glanced skyward, "Probably get some rain tonight or tomorrow. Just hope I make it back from your place and get your stove inside before it hits." He cracked the reins and they rumbled out of town and on the road to Eli's.

"Have you heard about Miss Minnie?" Cullie asked. "She traveled with you on the train, didn't she?"

Eli thought a minute. "Yes, she did," he remembered. "She traveled with the Worleys, and she had her three daughters along with her." He saddened as he recalled Miss Minnie's situation. "She was a widow." Eli drooped as he explained further, "Her husband drowned like Papa and Mamma. Mr. Worley died along with a Mr. Brown, I think it was. They'd been to town and had to cross the Chattahoochee to get home. For some reason, they didn't make it." He paused and looked thoughtful. "She said they'd been paid some wages or won a little money at a friendly poker game and mighta' had some money on'em. There was some question about the drownin' not bein' an accident, ya' know," he said with a dip of his head.

Cullie nodded.

Eli went on, "Anyway, the men were in the water several days and their bodies went down to the bottom and hadn't drifted to the surface, so the men in town floated a cannon out onto the river just below the jailhouse. When they set it off, the vibrations caused the men's bodies to come to the top." He shuddered with flashing memories of his own: river; parents; water; death. Then continued, "I heard Mamma say they laid Miss Minnie's husband on a big ole' flat rock sticking out from the Chattahoochee's bank and the only way Miss Minnie could identify her husband, him bein' in the water so long and all, was by checking for a patch she'd sewn on his shirt. When she saw that, she knew it was him." He continued. "The other man came up further down the river. I know she's had a hard time with her three little girls. Lizzie met them; their names are Sara, Dara, and Vara." He brightened. "Hard to forget, huh?" He went on. "She joined the train to travel further south and find a better place. What do ya know about her and the girls?" he asked.

Cullie had been listening intently. "Oh, boy, what a thing to happen!" He commented. "Well, I heard when the Worleys found a place to build, Miss Minnie and her girls stayed with them. Then she heard about Mr. Sheets's family. His wife was really bad, bed-ridden, and they have about eight children, I think, and one of'em a near baby. Mr. Oscar was having an awful time keeping them fed and the work kept caught-up; housekeeping, cooking, getting ready for planting, and tending the animals. His children helped as they could, but they were young and things were getting behind, besides caring for their mother. Well, anyway, Miss Minnie went to work for them and was a real worker, I heard. She cooked, washed, cleaned, and tended the children and took care of Mrs. Sheets. When Mrs. Sheets passed away, the only natural thing was for Mr. Sheets to ask Miss Minnie to stay on—as his wife. And she accepted. They live out on Red Oak Road just west of town near Alabama. I heard this about a month ago, so I guess she and the girls are here to stay. Mrs. Jones said the community is blessed to have them all here and remarked how God works in mysterious ways. And, man, how everything worked out just has to be a part of God's plan." He finished and was quiet a minute.

"I can't wait to tell Lizzie. She really liked those girls." He and Cullie kept plodding home. "Anymore news to fill me in on before we get to my place?" he asked.

Cullie frowned and squished up his lips in deep reflection. "Do ya know a boy named Jimmy?" he asked.

Eli jumped to attention. "Jimmy, a tall boy with blue eyes and blonde hair?" he asked excitedly.

"I think that would be him," Cullie countered. "Didn't hear anything about him, though."

Eli sat back, deflated. Then lifted his head. "Why did you ask me about him, then?" he demanded.

Cullie chuckled. "Cause I didn't hear anything about him. I talked to'em yesterday in the store." He could hardly wait for Eli's reaction and it came fast.

"You what!" he shouted. "Why didn't ya tell me about this first? What did he say? Where's his homestead? When will he be back?" he shot out.

"Slow down!" Cullie grinned. "First things first. He came in yesterday to pick up some horseshoes from Mr. Marshall at the blacksmith. He'd left an order for them a couple weeks ago." He glanced over at Eli and smiled more. "He's building a house just across the Alabama line and is coming along pretty good, from what he says. He's been livin' in his wagon while he gets a one-room dwelling finished, and is working on his barn. He seems to be a go-getter; really smart. I ordered a couple pair overalls and boots for'em. They should be in next week." Cullie finished.

Eli thought and rubbed his chin with his hand. "Next week. I can't believe he's settled close enough to come to Franklin to get his goods." He turned and faced Cullie. "Do ya mind if I write him a note when we get to my place? Would'ja mind giving it to him when he comes in to pick up his order?"

Cullie laughed as he pulled into Eli's yard and stopped the wagon with the end next to Eli's new steps. "I'll be glad to deliver ya note. Thought you'd be glad to hear he was close by."

The boys hopped from the wagon and dragged the biggest box to the back of the wagon and hoisted it up. They struggled to get it inside and placed it down. Eli was huffing and Cullie was puffing. Between breaths, Eli added, "I'm mighty glad to hear about Jimmy. He's a fine fellow and a good friend. Let's finish up getting the rest of my stove in and I'll write that note." He headed out the door to the wagon with Cullie on his heels. ---and I know a little lady back at Bulger's who will be a whole lot happier to hear about him that I was---Eli thought with a chuckle.

Dark clouds began gathering over the tops of nearby trees and the wind picked up. "Better get these last boxes unloaded and get your wagon back to town pretty quick," Eli instructed Cullie as both boys rushed to the back of the wagon. Cullie pushed the boxes to the back and as they balanced on the open tailgate, he and Eli struggled to lift each and get them inside.

Eli, sensing a storm brewing, hurried and scribbled a short note to Jimmy.

With Cullie's help, the stove, pipe, and stove legs were safe in Eli's kitchen. "Whew," Cullie said as he grabbed the paper and stepped off the bottom step and trotted to the side of the wagon. "I'm a little worried. Looks like the weather is gone storm. Hear that thunder rumbling out there?" he asked. Cullie vaulted onto the wagon seat and gathered up the reins when they heard a loud, "Halooo." They looked to the edge of the yard and saw Skipping Rock. He waved to Cullie and Eli.

"*Osiyo*! Just in time, Skipping Rock," Cullie said, raising an arm in greeting. "You and Eli can get the stove put together. It sure will be easier to arrange it so the stove will be out of harm's way. Don't want any loose embers hitting that dry grass mat and burning the house down." Looking back at Eli, he added, "Got to get back before dark. I don't want to be out when this weather hits. And I've heard more stories about those Muscogees," he looked at Skipping Rock apologetically. "No disrespect meant."

"Sure thing, Cullie, none taken," Skipping Rock answered. "I'm the same way. It's a sad thing that a few ruthless Indians cast a bad view on all of us, and I try to avoid them, too." He and Eli waved as Cullie slapped the reins and pulled the wagon out of the yard and onto the road to town.

"Come on in," Eli gestured to Skipping Rock. "I'd sure appreciate some help getting my new stove together before nightfall." He looked around. "Second thought, maybe you'd better get home. Cullie may be right. It looks mighty stormy and that thunder is getting closer. I'll work on the stove tonight; it will be dry inside and give me something to do. I can go to Miss Claudie's in the morning and get enough staples to start cooking and have a hot meal from a stove instead of the fire outside."

"Sure wish I could stay and help, but look around. There's a greenish-yellow cast to the air. From times past, that's definitely not a good sign. I expect the storm to blow in hard and hit heavy. I need to be home when it gets here, but I'll check on you later," Skipping Rock remarked with a worried face.

Eli noticed the change in the air, too. It was a strange color and the air pressure dropped heavily. "Go, Skipping Rock. And be safe," he urged.

Quickly Skipping Rock leapt out the door and landed directly on the ground in front of the steps. He didn't look back as he dashed into the woods toward home.

Closing the door securely behind Skipping Rock, Eli surveyed his kitchen. He pried open the crates and found that he was apt at assembly. He moved the "body" of the large black stove into place, off the mat, and fitted the pipes into place. He had a difficult time steadying the tall pipes and guiding them into the hole in the roof he'd cut out, but he balanced on his stout ladder and got the job done. Stove ready, table and stools ready to bring in from Bulger's shop, floor covered. All I need are cooking utensils, a bucket of lard, some flour and eggs, and I'll be ready to go, he thought.

He smiled and lay on his back on the floor and pulled up his knees. He reached behind his head and rested his head in his hands. I'm almost done, he thought. Tomorrow I'll visit Miss

Claudie and Bulger, next day; work more on the mule shed and then the outhouse. That celebration won't be long in coming.

Bulger will arrange a proper barn-raising, or at least a sturdy corn crib, before I gather my corn. He closed his eyes and thanked God. Life is good, he realized. Our community is growing and Jimmy is close by. Oh, boy! Just wait until I tell Lizzie! He thought.

Night wrapped itself around Eli's home and the windows filled with darkness. He sat up and walked over and pulled the kitchen window shutters closed and moved across the floor mat so lovingly made by Minshue. 'Gotta thank her for this,' he reckoned, as he touched his toe gently to the edge. He left the kitchen and crossed the dogtrot into his bedroom. He barely got his overalls off and hung on its peg, flopped on his rustling shuck mattress, and pulled the covers up to his neck before his eyes shut in dreaming anticipation of the days to come. In his dreamsleep he heard the pattering of rain tickling the thatch and the wind chatting through the trees, relaxing and lulling him to sleep.

FOURTEEN

Softly, sunrise came, chasing away darkness and sending shadows running. As the sun made its morning appearance, Eli's bedroom suddenly filled with bright white light and the house vibrated with thunder. It was no longer a pattering rain he heard; the sound was more like a thousand shooting bullets pelting the house. Eli sat straight up, wide awake and trembling. He threw his cover off and practically fell out of bed. He started groping for his overalls, and suddenly he saw them plainly as they were illuminated against the wall by another bright streak of lightning—then BOOM-M-M-m--m--m-mmm. He rushed to open the door and was surprised when he had to hold on tightly to prevent the force of the wind from ripping it from his hands and forcing it to the wall. He managed to hold it open a crack and peer out to see green pea-soup air, hailstones, some the size of cat-eye marbles and others as large as owl pellets, flying down and dancing across the yard. Some came to rest in small, round, icy piles. Rain continued pelting the side of his house and he could hear it hitting the ground as it ran off the roof. Instantly, another bright lightning---and he heard a loud crack from the woods nearby.

A strike! he thought. Thunder rumbled and tumbled through the house and rocked on through the woods. Eli pulled the door shut and latched it tightly. He groped his way back to the wall and grabbed his clothing and jerked on his shirt and overalls. He slid his feet into his boots and then wondered what in the world he was doing. Where did he think he was going?

He was safest where he was; all he should do was get back on the bed and wait out the storm. As he lowered his body onto the mattress, the sound of the storm suddenly changed. Instead of the crackling of lightning, the continual booming, crashing sound of thunder, and hail pelting the house, he heard a mighty roar; a roar that was growing louder by the second and sounded as if it was headed straight to devour his home.

Fright didn't begin to define the fear he felt. He was frozen in place and sat and grasped the edge of the mattress until his knuckles turned white. When the crescendo of howling demons reached its peak outside, screeching and wailing above his rooftop, he rocked to life and dove to the floor and covered his body with the mattress. He curled into a ball and put his hands over his head. His body trembled and jerked underneath the shuck-pad with such force that the covering mattress almost toppled off. The walls shook, but stood; the roof swayed, but stayed. Doors and windows popped, groaned, and clattered, but remained shut. They refused to let the beast outside claw its way in.

Then there was silence; deathly silence. Eli peeped from underneath the mattress, teeth chattering and eyes wild, and started to stand when a second ferocious wind slammed into the house. He dove back to his prostrate position and prayed…and prayed. The second assault lasted only a few minutes, but seemed like a week. Just as suddenly as it hit, it left. Eli remained, cowering on the floor, shivering and listening. When he was sure it was safe, he rose up, pushing the mattress away. He moved to the door to the dogtrot and slowly opened it. The wooden hallway was soaked and covered in fresh, new spring leaves that had been whipped off nearby trees.

Eli walked from one end of the dogtrot to the other. He couldn't believe it, but the house was intact! It had weathered the storm and was soaked, but standing. He inspected the kitchen and found rain had dripped down the chimney—as it probably had in the bedroom-- but he had hardly noticed---and leaked in around the outside door and windows. Okay, he thought, this can be cleaned up easy enough.

He opened the kitchen door and looked outside. Limbs were littered across his yard and scattered in the stream. Debris was everywhere. This would take a little longer to clean, he realized. He noticed the poor Martins. Miracle of miracles, the gourds still swayed on their ropes. Birds flew all around, checking out their homes and making sure the flock was safe. Then another consideration hit him: Bulger's farm. He hit the steps with both feet, door slamming, and ran as hard as he could toward Bulger and Miss Claudie's. He didn't breathe; he sobbed choking breaths as he made his way, jumping and ducking through the downed trees and broken limbs. He ran as he had run last fall when he was rushing to Grandpa's to tell him his good news about their move; but this time he had no idea what he would find when he reached his destination.

    He jumped over fallen trees and sidestepped broken limbs. He noticed trees with barren limbs; stripped of their new, tender, green leaves. Just yesterday they had stood like proud soldiers, guarding the trail, and today they were bent and shattered, their beautiful green suits shredded and strewn across the ground. Suddenly he stopped in his tracks, stunned by the sight in front of him. He stepped into a cleared path as wide as two wagons and running straight down to the road. Eli gingerly stepped around dark tree trunks sticking from the ground like grotesque fingers pointing upward. When he reached the road, his legs began pumping and rushing him on his way to the farm where his sisters were. He couldn't bear the notion: were they alive or would he find them dead?

FIFTEEN

Miss Claudie swiped the last pebbles from the yard with her "broom" made from dogwood limbs and bent to pull a straggling bunch of grass from the yard. She had spent the last couple of hours sweeping, getting it ready for Ginger's visit. With a sigh, she propped one hand on her hip and turned to survey her work. The yard looked wonderful; clean and inviting. She knew her handiwork would have to be re-swept before Ginger arrived, but she was proud of making the yard welcoming by adding a back and forth pattern in the soft dirt with the ends of the twiggy broom. She lifted her chin and looked toward Eli's--- over the top of the barn and over treetops beyond---and noticed dark clouds. Low and menacing, forming on the horizon. The air felt different, too; heavy and still, and had turned almost yellow. She felt prickles dancing along her arms, and hurried to prop her yard broom against the house. She quickly made her way up the steps and onto the porch. She stopped and lifted the dipper hanging from a nail on a porch post and dipped it in the water bucket sitting on the narrow porch shelf. As she drained the water, she continued to scan the sky. She dropped her gaze long enough to scoop another dipper full of water and pour it into the small wash pan sitting on the shelf beside the bucket. She returned the dipper to its nail and as she reached in the washpan to rinse red dust from her hands, she looked across the yard and to the pasture behind the barn.

This funny color to the air can't mean nothin' good, she thought, drying her hands on a porch towel and slowly walking to the kitchen door. Last time I saw somethin' like this, bad winds came in and we lost some trees down by the field.

"Did'ja notice anything unusual outside as ya came in, Bulger?" she asked as she tossed a chunk of wood into the cook stove.

"Nope," he answered. "I 'spect it will rain tonight, but that's a blessing. Time for it to come. I'm proud Eli and me got the corn fields broke in. Soon as weather warms up, the plantin' can be done and the seeds ought'a come right on up." He keyed in on exactly what Miss Claudie had asked and turned to her, "What are ya talking about, see something unusual out there?"

Miss Claudie shrugged her shoulders. "Oh, nothing. Just a feeling. But I'm thinkin' several years ago we had a bad spell when the weather looked like this and it got bad," She set the pot with dinner's leftover pintos on the stove to warm. "Just let me mix up a fresh pone of cornbread and fry some potatoes and onions and supper will be ready."

"Sounds good to me," Bulger replied, watching Miss Claudie closely. He noticed a small furrow between her brows. She's worried about somethin', he realized and began rocking beside the fireplace. He gazed into the flames, puzzled over her behavior.

Lizzie and Beth came bustling in the door, chatting and laughing, shaking off cool raindrops. "Whew! We got home just in time! Rain's startin' to come down out there." Jack and Bell scooted quickly between the girls and trotted over to warm on the fireplace hearth.

Bulger chuckled at the hounds. "Look at them dogs; they don't have a care in the world."

"You should have seen them rocking and shaking out there on the porch!" Lizzie grinned. "Water was spraying all over the place. Better be glad they got rid of all that before they came inside. I know Miss Claudie would have had a fit if they'd shook themselves off in here."

Beth laughed as she removed her wet shoes and stood in her stocking feet. "Jack and Bell are so good, aren't they Miss Claudie?" she asked.

"Well, I guess so," Miss Claudie answered absently.

Beth continued, nonstop, "I sure do love goin' to see

Warm DayRah at the village, don't you, Lizzie?" Beth asked, hanging her bonnet behind the door.

"I do," Lizzie replied, shaking her shawl and hanging it, too. "There are so many children, especially girls who come to our reading classes now, and more boys are showing up. I hope they will be able to go study with Miss Myline when school begins next week."

"What will you do, then?" Beth asked.

"Oh, I'm sure there will be families who need their children to stay in the village. They don't have enough time for full-time studies in town. I'll go and teach them when there's time," she replied.

Bulger spoke up, "Have ya heard anything from Atlanta about ya teaching test?"

Lizzie frowned and cast a sideways glance at Beth, "Not yet, but I know I will soon. Maybe next time we go to town there will be a letter." She noticed Miss Claudie peeling potatoes. "Potatoes and onions, Miss Claudie?" she asked. "Want me to get the onions ready?"

"Sure would be a help," Miss Claudie nodded. "I think we ought'a finish supper up quick and get to bed earlier tonight."

Lizzie washed her hands and gathered a couple of onions from the bin setting in the far corner of the kitchen. As she moved to the table to join Miss Claudie with the peeling, she asked, "What's the matter? You seem a little distant tonight. Aren't you feeling well?"

"Just a feelin'," Miss Claudie replied, scooping up diced potatoes and onions and dumping them into the hot lard in the black iron skillet. As she stirred, she added, "Just a feelin'. Tomorrow's sunrise may be a long time comin'. Let's say a special prayer tonight 'fore sleep for the Lord to keep us safe through the night."

Lizzie wondered at Miss Claudie's words. She had learned to trust Miss Claudie's instincts and she, too, felt a little uneasiness creep into the room.

After supper was cleared and the few leftover pintos scraped into the pig's slop bucket and leftover cornbread mixed with some sweet milk fed to the dogs, Miss Claudie admonished the girls to get to bed. She and Bulger kissed them good-night and crossed the dogtrot to their bedroom and climbed into their bed. Bulger was soon snoring soundly, but Miss Claudie lay awake, listening to the rain dancing lightly on their shingled roof. "Lord, keep us safe through the night. Protect us from harm and give us strength to do the things we should. In Jesus's name, Amen." It was only after her prayer that she felt the Holy Spirit's hands holding her; safe and sheltered and she could slip into sleep.

Early the next morning, just before daylight, Bulger went to milk the cows. Jack and Bell, usually standing at the door, waiting and wriggling all over to get out and do 'their things', seemed sully and nervous and walked warily outside. They were back scratching at the kitchen door to be let in before Bulger shut the barn gate. When Miss Claudie pushed the door open, both dogs tore through the first crack, and with their ears pushed back and eyes apprehensive, scooted across the room and got as far under the girl's bed and next to the wall as possible. This didn't improve Miss Claudie's forewarning, uneasy mood at all. Still standing at the door wondering what in the world had gotten into the dogs, she was pushed backward as Bulger tromped through the door.

"Can't get them blame cows to give nothing," he huffed, plunking the empty milk bucket down in the sink with a thud.

"Oh, if you'll get the wood in the stove and meat frying, I'll do the milking this morning," Miss Claudie offered.

Bulger reached for the woodbox. "Be glad for you to try," he said as he tossed wood into the stove.

Miss Claudie crossed the kitchen and checked to make sure there was enough water in the bucket to use to clean the cows' udders. She called over her shoulder as she reached the door, "Lizzie, Beth, better get up. Lizzie, mix up the biscuits, will you please? I'll be back in a jiffy. We got a good bit of cookin' to do today after breakfast. Dinner on the ground tomorrow after church."

As soon as she closed the door and stepped on the porch, she noticed the rain had begun falling harder and the air seemed cooler. The air still appeared a peculiar yellow-green, too. No birds sang or called a distant twitter. The Martins were snug in their gourd homes, fluffed up and trying to stay warm. As she passed the hog pen, she noticed Ole' Crip had her babies nestled close and they were hunkered down near the barn's foundation; on the lee side where no wind could reach them. Unusual, she thought, most of the time Ole' Crip stayed close to the feed trough and her babies wandered around the yard. Now they were scrunched as close to her as they could get. Only their pink backsides with their tails twisted up showed. Hitching up her shoulders, she ducked her head, stepped into the rain and hurried to the barn.

Miss Claudie entered the cow stall and spoke soothingly to Bessie and Bossie, picked up the milking stool and stepped through loose straw to stand beside Bossie. She was fidgeting, wide-open eyes, and swishing her tail; hind feet stepping lightly back and forth and paying no attention whatsoever to her feed. Miss Claudie cooed, "It's alright, girl, settle down," and began rubbing Bossie's side. She turned and eyed Miss Claudie with her big, brown eyes. She thrust out her tongue and licked her nose, blinked, and turned back to her feed, more relaxed. Miss Claudie, feeling more comfortable with Bossie getting calmer, sat on the stool and gently washed Bossie's udder. She tossed the remaining water from the milk bucket to the side of the stall and sat the bucket underneath the cow. Murmuring softly, Miss Claudie began milking. Milk came slowly at first, but Bossie's bag was stretched full, and with each pull, milk sang as it rhythmically hit the bottom of the bucket. Suddenly, two barn cats appeared and sat expectantly in the door of the stall. Miss Claudie smiled and bent one teat, aimed and squirted a stream of warm milk right into one waiting cat's mouth. The other rose and arched her tail high, rubbed against her sister, sat and mewed. "Okay, you're next," Miss Claudie promised. With a second clean shot, she jetted a stream of milk to the waiting calico. "Good shot," she mused, giving each cat a second drink. "Hang around a little longer and ya'll can have a drink from Bessie, too." As she returned to her milking, both cats licked their faces and chests. Before they had almost finished, they lifted their heads and looked toward the rafters, perked their ears, and suddenly darted away, hiding in the hay. Miss Claudie heard the new sound, too; a constant barrage of loud explosions coming from the barn's tin roof. She jumped with fright when she heard a high, screeching sound as nails were pulled from a piece of tin and the popping and banging as the tin peeled away. As she looked upward toward the source of the sound, she saw tin disappearing from the next stall and felt rain and hail blowing in and splattering through the gaping hole. She grabbed the milk bucket, full of frothy, warm milk, and made for the door. Bessie would have to wait.

Inside the kitchen, Lizzie had the biscuits in the pan and Beth had their bed made and the table set. Bulger was lifting the last slice of bacon when they heard a riveting of pellets hitting the housetop.

Miss Claudie, milk sloshing, dashed across the yard, covering her head with one hand, trying to protect it from the falling hailstones. "Oomph!" she cried as a large chunk of ice cracked her wrist. Winds pushed her face-on, knocking her backwards, and her whole body was smashed with hard volleys of ice. Her skirts stood straight out behind her and she was pushed and shoved backwards by the howling, angry wind. It was all she could do to maintain her balance. She ducked her head further and leaned into the wind and fought for each step. Finally she reached the house and shot up the steps and set the milk bucket beside the washpan on the sheltered porch shelf. She leaned forward and stretched out, using both hands to reach for the kitchen door's latch.

And the rain descended, and the floods came, and the winds blew, and beat upon that house; and it fell not; for it was founded upon a rock.
Matthew 7: 2

When she lifted the latch, the door flew open and out of her hands. The force of the wind pinned it against the wall. Bulger stood, wide-eyed, with his hand outstretched to open the door. When he heard the hail begin hitting hard and the wind picking up, he rushed to yell for Miss Claudie to hurry, to get back to the house.

"Help me!" Miss Claudie screamed, but the wind caught her words and tossed them over the porch and into the woods. Bulger grasped her wrist and yanked her inside. He scrambled to grab the door latch and pull the door shut. It took all his strength to finally get it closed and firmly latched. Miss Claudie stood wordlessly just inside the door, watching in a daze.

"Get across the 'trot to the bedroom!" Bulger yelled and snatched Miss Claudie by her arm and pulled her along. Lizzie gripped Beth by her arm.

"Patty and Dolly!" Beth yelled. She detoured to their bed and scooped up both dolls. Lizzie held Beth tighter and lifted her onto her hip and quickly followed Bulger and Miss Claudie. Bulger jerked the door open and they ran across the dogtrot to the bedroom door and thrust it open. "Under the bed, all of ya!" Bulger cried as he pulled the door closed and rushed across the room. He bent and helped Miss Claudie stoop low and crawl under after the girls. She managed to get to the floor and struggled to roll under the bed. Lizzie and Beth huddled, clinging together with the dolls, next to the wall and Bulger fairly shoved Miss Claudie under as he pressed himself in last.

Together they nestled, shaking with fear as the storm raged around the house like a shrieking, starving hawk trying to grab a wailing rabbit and fly away. Beth sobbed quietly and Lizzie pulled her closer. Suddenly Beth pulled back and cried, "Jack and Bell..."

"Shhhh, they're safe, remember they hid under our bed," Lizzie assured. Beth calmed and hid her face in her hands. Lizzie held tighter.

Huddled together beneath the bed, Bulger pressed Miss Claudie close to his heart and buried his face in her loose, windblown hair. Through sobs, Bulger heard Miss Claudie's stammering words, "Our father, who art in Heaven, hallowed be Thy name..."

The wind howled and screamed; roared like a lion and scratched like a tiger. They heard wooden shingles pulled from the roof and clatter to the ground. There were other unidentified sounds; thumpings and drumming, hammering and slapping. Suddenly, there was silence. They looked around in the twilight darkness and listened. Nothing. Then the gentle pattering of soft rain.

"Stay here," Bulger ordered. "Let me check and make sure it's safe." He climbed from under the bed and hesitantly stood. Listening, cocking his head, he crossed the room on his tiptoes and opened the door. He could see daylight at each end of the dogtrot and heard a scuffling noise. Then, appearing in the open kitchen door, he saw Jack and Bell coming out to investigate. They stopped when they noticed him, sat down and began grinning that loppy, tongue-hanging hound dog grin and slapping their tails against the wet porch boards. That's when Bulger knew the storm had passed. "Ya'll can come on out, now," he declared, looking back and signaling to Miss Claudie.

Miss Claudie, stiff and sore, managed to scramble from under the bed and sat with her back against the rails. Lizzie and Beth crawled out and stood. Miss Claudie, still propped on the floor, looked up and asked, hopelessly, "Well, are ya two gone leave me here? Help me up so I can inspect things myself. Who knows what damage this storm has brought? Thank the Lord the house still stands and we're all okay."

Lizzie reached to hold Miss Claudie's arms and Beth took her back. Together they lifted and pulled until Miss Claudie found her feet and dusted herself off. "That was some storm. I don't think we've ever had anything like that pass through here before, not this close, anyway. Come along, let's check on the animals." Miss Claudie hobbled to the door and the girls followed close behind.

Bulger passed through the kitchen which had, luckily, been left unscathed. "Come on, ladies," he coaxed as he reached for the kitchen door latch. The women gathered behind him as he pushed the door open to examine what damage they might find outside.

The door swung open and the foursome tentatively stepped onto what was left of the porch. They gazed upward and were amazed to see fluffy white clouds sprinting across blue sky; only a soft mist falling. The top of the porch was completely ripped from the house! They looked across the yard and past the fence. Only scattered, broken rafters and jumbled shingles could be seen across the landscape. Unexpectedly, Bulger and the girls heard Miss Claudie's laughter.

They turned and heard her bubbling over in amusement. What on earth? They wondered. Had she been hit over her head and completely lost it?

She looked at them with tears running down her cheeks and hiccupped. "Look on the shelf," she pointed. There, untouched by the tornado, sat the bucket of milk. A few bubbles still glistened on top, and minute specks of trash floated there.

Bulger stared in disbelief. "Well, don't that beat all." He, too, smiled. "Not too much damage done there, the milk bucket and washpan and dipper are still settin' just where we left them," he said. "Looks like the barn-'sept for that piece of tin---and Ole' Crip made it just fine, too. We can fix this up in no time."

"Halloo! Hey," they heard the voice before they saw Eli. "Are you all right?" he shouted.

Lizzie and Beth squealed and jumped up and down and Miss Claudie clasped her hands over her mouth. Tears sprung up anew and she was filled with joy and thanksgiving. Eli was safe! Even Jack and Bell joined in the hullabaloo with their loud baying as they danced out to meet him.

Eli stopped short when he saw them standing on the roofless porch. "Is everyone all right?" he asked in disbelief.

"Looks that way," Lizzie answered. "How'd your place stand up? Did the tornado hit you?"

Eli took a deep breath and slowed to a walk. "It came through, all right, but must have passed over with most of the force high up. I saw where it came down and hit just past the road to town. It's really a mess there, but not much more at my place that some pickin' up won't cure."

Bulger shook his head and laughed. He motioned with one hand for Eli to come on in and reached for the milk bucket--still sitting on the porch shelf---with his other. He turned to go inside. "Get the bacon and biscuits put up. We can eat them cold for dinner. Get this milk strained up!" A worried look crossed his face. "Need to get out and check on the neighbors and make sure they're all right."

And they stirred themselves to move. Women wrapped arm-in-arm, stepped inside the kitchen to put things in order. Eli and Bulger hitched the mules and got the wagon---pressing was the need to know if their friends were safe.

Sunrise had indeed come, but not as they expected. That morning's sunrise was filled with fear, intimidation, and danger. Sometimes it comes that way, but like Miss Claudie's faith proved, it passed. Daylight triumphed and darkness was chased away one more time. The Lord was with them, kept them, and after the storm, gave them peace.

SIXTEEN

In their urgent need to know how their neighbors fared, Eli and Bulger found travel exasperatingly slow as they made their way along the road. They were forced to stop and clear away trees and broken limbs before making their way on. They traveled southward away from their house and would circle back to enter town from the main road, following the road close to the banks of the Chattahoochee. Bulger wanted to check the flooding while they were out.

Eventually they came to the bend in the road that led to the first farm. The Hulls bordered Bulger's farm. A large family lived there and their house reflected it. There were five or six bedrooms that had been added on as the family grew. Eli remembered Bulger saying that many of the surrounding children, Indians included, visited the Hulls in the summertime and together they easily made two teams and played stickball—the Hulls comprised one team alone!

Bulger could hardly believe his eyes and Eli was speechless. All that was left was a sign still hanging over the single lane that led from the main road to the house that read God Bless this House, and beyond stood nothing other than the main bedroom. The rest of the house; gone. The barn; gone. A few chickens walked around in a daze and the milk cow roamed over pasture terraces bellowing for her lost calf.

"Giddy-up," Bulger shouted to the mules. The wagon lurched forward and they bounced down the lane to the lone structure. "Haloo," he yelled and pulled the mules up sharply.

Eli sprang from the wagon seat and ran to the door. He stopped short as the door slowly opened and a head peered out. "Is anyone hurt?" he asked.

Mr. Hull's head slowly moved back and forth. He seemed to be in shock as he glanced to his rear. "Come on, ya'll," he whispered.

Then, in single file, his family stumbled out the door and stepped to the ground. Mrs. Hull came first, then the older boys carrying the youngest children. It was eerie; not a single one of them spoke a word as they emerged from their hiding place and formed a line beside the wagon. Suddenly, the baby began a heart-wrenching wail and the family snapped from their stupor.

"Can't believe it," Mr. Hull said, shaking his head and running his hand through his thinning hair. Mrs. Hull began to sob quietly as she moved down the line of her children and touched and hugged each one; making sure none were injured. Several of the older boys, usually too grown-up and dignified to cry, found themselves sniffing back tears; simply thankful and relieved that their family had come through the harrowing ordeal safely.

"It's a miracle," Mrs. Hull remarked in a raspy voice as she reached and pulled her youngest child into her arms. Suddenly, in unison, the children made fast work of circling their parents and swapped hugs and praised the Lord for protecting them.

"Hop on the back," Bulger instructed. "We'll get you to town and find you a place to stay."

"Wait a few minutes and we'll get what blankets and quilts that are left," Mrs. Hull said. She motioned for two of the older girls to go inside and they handed out covers, clothing, and diapers to the boys who packed them on the back of Bulger's wagon.

Mr. Hull walked around the yard and surveyed his homestead. He shook his head in disbelief. "I can't believe it," he said again. "All this destruction; barn, shed, and house, and my family spared." He took a deep breath and turned to check on his livestock. "Guess the horses are either gone or hid out in the woods." Just then, the cow appeared at the edge of the barnyard, calf close behind. She jogged to the spot where her feed trough had been and stopped. "Got a rope, Bulger?" Mr.

Hull called. "I'd like to lead the cow along behind. At least she can give us milk."

"Sure thing, Mr. Hull," Bulger called and reached under the wagon seat for a length of rope. He passed it to Eli who carried it over to Mr. Hull. He noticed some of the chickens' feathers were poking out a bit out of place, but otherwise they seemed fine.

Mr. Hull noticed, too. "They'll be fine. There's plenty for them to eat until we get back." He finished slipping his hand-tied halter over the cow's head and tied her to the back of the wagon. As soon as everything useful was loaded and the children safely in the wagon, he pulled himself up to sit beside Eli and Bulger. "I just can't believe it," he said again, more to himself than to anybody.

Bulger turned the wagon and made his way back to the main road. "We'll go directly to town and find ya'll somewhere to stay. Me and Eli gone go around a few more places 'fore night and check on more folks. I know the sheriff, Mr. Bledsoe and his wife, will take care of ya'll."

Mr. Hull nodded. The wagon bounced and rocked toward Franklin. "Looka' there!" One of the boys called and pointed toward the edge of the road. Two horses came trotting along, falling in behind the cow. "It's Jake and Bill! Them horses done found us!" he added with a wide grin. When the horses joined their masters, the mood changed and hearts felt lighter; a sense of hopefulness and reassurance that the future would be full and before too many more sunrises, they would be back on their farm, working and laughing as usual.

Later, unloading Mr. Hull's family at the jail, Mrs. Bledsoe oohed and aahed as she ushered Mrs. Hull and her family into the building. Sheriff Bledsoe talked quietly with Mr. Hull and in the end it was agreed that the Hulls were welcome to stay in the empty cells housed in the second story above the area where Sheriff Bledsoe and his wife lived below. There were plenty of beds and blankets there, and the family would have meals with the Bledsoes. Mr. Hull, not wanting anyone to think he'd take any charity, assured the sheriff that the boys would keep plenty of wood cut and stacked, and the girls would keep the cells clean and neat. In the coming days, Mrs. Hull proved to be Mrs.

Bledsoe's second hand and together they planned and cooked up fine meals. The cow was an added blessing, she was a good milk producer and they would enjoy fresh milk every day.

As Eli stepped onto the seat, he turned and asked about the Sheets. Sheriff Bledsoe, sure enough, had news and it was good. The tornado completely missed Miss Minnie and Mr. Oscar and their children and skipped over that part of the county completely. "Ya think they'll make it to preaching tomorrow?" he asked as Bulger made his way up to the wagon seat.

"I'd bet on it," Sheriff Bledsoe answered. "You know Mr. Oscar is a preacher. Been thinking about asking the church trustees to invite him to preach on Sundays when Preacher Arp is making his circuit."

Bulger spoke up. "That's a fine idea, Sheriff. With all the young folks that've settled in, we would have a houseful. Plus, idle hands do the devil's work, and we need to be training our young'uns up right."

Eli thought the idea was a great one! What better way to meet and talk to the lovely young ladies in the community? Since he held the reins and Bulger hadn't made any gesture to drive, Eli made an exit. "See ya'll tomorrow, Sheriff. Take care." He looked over at Bulger and Bulger tipped his chin, a clear indication for Eli to head out.

"Guess we need to swing by the Tuggle's on our way back," he said. "Take the long way 'round. We can check on other neighbors and make the Tuggles last. Cut down by the blacksmith shop and head out from there. Lead on."

When they'd traveled about a half mile out of town, Eli broke their silence, "Did you notice the sign Mr. Hull had hanging beside the drive down to his house?"

"Sure did," Bulger said. "And you know, God did bless that family. Even though they've lost most everything, they still have each other, a roof over their heads, and food. Tomorrow will be a day of blessings when we get to church. I just hope everybody will be well and able to attend."

Eli agreed and they followed the rising Chattahoochee along its banks to reach the road back to their farm. Eli watched the water swirl and tumble. Sometimes a log or treetop floated along. He turned his head quickly away, remembering the last time the river looked this menacing and angry. "You didn't get to steal anybody this time," he whispered to the 'Hootch. "Just keep on running. Pound your way down river and don't stop until you're calm and happy again." He breathed in deeply and stared ahead.

Bulger, having lived with Eli and the girls for only a few months, still had instinctively picked up on their moods and body gestures. He knew exactly when Eli's mind flashed back to his family's past winter ordeal and Papa and Mamma were drowned in the water. He knew, too, when Eli's mind passed over the horror and he tucked the memory away and returned to the present.

Eli popped the reins on the mules' backs and urged them further along the road.

A few long miles later, they passed several houses still standing, looking unscathed. The Crocketts, Gores, Souths, and Sheppards waved an 'ok' as they passed. They rambled along the road past their house and turned into the drive leading to the Tuggles'. As the wagon lumbered around a hedgerow and the house came into view, both gave a sigh of relief. Mr. and Mrs. Tuggle and their two children, a boy and a girl, were outside cleaning debris from the yard and barnyard. They stopped and walked to meet Bulger.

"See ya must have made it through," Mr. Tuggle remarked.

"Lost our porch roof, and part of the barn tin. It was mighty scary there for a while," Bulger answered. "Gone get things fixed in no time flat soon as we get back. Miss Claudie and Lizzie are cooking up a storm for tomorrow's service at church. Ya'll gone be able to come?"

Eli looked at him and grinned.

"What?" Bulger innocently questioned, eyes wide.

"Did you really have to say 'cooking up a *storm*?" Eli chuckled. "I think we've all had just about our fill of storms around here for a while."

Bulger's face wrinkled up in thought. Then he grinned. "Yeah, I see what ya mean. Well, Miss Claudie and Lizzie are cooking up a dizzy," he added, making his point by twirling his finger high in the air. Then noticing the Tuggles, standing with grins, too, he asked again. "Will ya'll be at church, ya think?"

Mrs. Tuggle quickly answered. "For sure. I'm praying everyone around is safe. As soon as we get most of this trash cleared away, 'Loris and I are starting on our dinner for tomorrow. I know Preacher Arp will have a fine message," she dropped her head, "and I know we will be filled with the Holy Ghost. Lord knows, he's been covering us all through the past hours." Then she added, "You heard from anyone else around?"

Bulger said, "The Hulls were hit pretty bad, but are doing all right now. They're in Franklin and will be there, probably a while. I'm sure there will be plenty of help to get their place back up and in shape. Everyone along the south road is okay. All of us who came out safe will be ready to pitch in and help rebuild. The storm was bad, but its timing was good. We don't have to worry about the fields. As far as I know, everybody is 'bout ready to get their fields planted. Won't put in seeds until after Easter anyway." He shrugged. "Good thing it's comin' 'bout a week later this year. Usually comes around the first of April. Got early garden plants in and the ground will have to be replowed before other seeds can go in; soil needs to be warm anyhow, so time to clean up is no problem."

Mr. Tuggle declared, "That's right a'ready. We can make plans and get our things and Mr. Rogers will make sure to have extra wood set aside for anybody that needs it. Don't know why everything shouldn't be put back in order for the Hulls by layin' by time."

Bulger nodded in agreement. "Well, better get on back and finish up things at home. See ya'll t'morrow if nothing else happens."

Mr. and Mrs. Tuggle raised their hands to wave good-bye. Eli glanced back in time to see Mrs. Tuggle walking toward the house, one arm around her son and the other around her daughter; heads bent in close conversation. Mr. Tuggle stopped and picked up the last of the trash in front of the barn before shutting the doors and following his family inside. Eli turned forward on the wagon seat. He and Bulger continued along the roadway toward home and spied a wide clearing where the tornado had touched down.

"Hold up, Bulger," Eli said. "I see something over in them treetops down over there, near where the damage begins. That must have been where the funnel hit the ground." He stopped the wagon and jumped off and trotted through the twisted tree trunks and broken limbs toward whatever he'd seen. He reached the edge of a tumbled, twisted pile of debris and fished out a torn Indian blanket. He gathered it up and carried it back to the wagon where Bulger was waiting, curious to see what had caught Eli's eye.

Handing the colorful woven blanket up to Bulger, he said, "What'd ya think of this?"

Bulger sighed. "Muscogee," he said. "I hoped they might'a give up and gone on back to their homes. Looks like they were camping here for the night, off the road and down in that thicket, and the storm came in and caught'em." He looked around. "Wonder where they are now. Guess they had to skedaddle out of here in a hurry and the winds whipped their blanket away." He shook his head and shoved the blanket under the wagon seat. "When we get to the house, hide this somewhere good in the barn. I don't want to worry Miss Claudie none." His body slouched and he put his hands together on his lap. "You drive on in, will ya? I think I'm kinda tuckered out right now. If the storm didn't beat us up around here good enough, we still got them danged Muscogees to deal with."

Eli silently whipped the reins and the mules pulled. Eli had never seen Bulger so tired-looking. He wondered what Bulger was thinking, but the heaviness that had fallen about them prevented him asking.

He was so glad he and Bulger would be home shortly. He'd already made up his mind to stay the night, go to church, and work on his yard the coming Monday. He was filled with a longing; a cold missing of his birth parents, and would be glad to be back at Bulger's, sitting in front of a warm fire, full of Miss Claudie's biscuits and gravy.

SEVENTEEN

Skipping Rock came by just after Bulger and Eli's return home. He reported that all was well in the village and no harm was done there; just a few rotten limbs scattered about; but it was a good thing to rid trees of diseased or dead limbs.

"We have plenty of shingles stored in the barn loft," Bulger explained. "Do ya boys have time to help me get'em nailed down over the porch? Think we can get that tin back on the barn, too."

Eli looked at Skipping Rock and grinned. "Sure, Bulger, lead the way."

Bulger instructed Eli to climb the skinny steps that led to the barn loft. There, just as Bulger said, lay two bundles of wooden shingles. Eli strained to slide them across the floor and to the hay-hole in the middle of the loft. He lifted the double-doors that, when closed, made a firm flooring. When hay needed to be thrown down for the livestock, the doors were opened and hay forked down and the animals had good eating without Bulger having to go to a lot of trouble.

When Eli had the doors open, he hitched a hook to the ropes tying the bundles together and gently, using the hay winch, dropped one to the floor. Skipping Rock reached high and guided it down. Soon both bundles were in the barn's hallway and the loft doors closed. Eli and Skipping Rock hoisted the shingles into Bulger's large homemade wheelbarrow. Together they pushed and made it to the porch where Bulger had finished re-securing the porch rafters. "Aw' right, boys, I'm turnin' this over to ya'll. I don't think I can handle hammering and standing high on the ladder at the same time. I'm tuckered."

Eli climbed to the rafters and Skipping Rock passed him shingles. The only sound drifting throughout the rest of the morning was the tap-tap-tapping of Eli's hammer as each shingle was nailed in place. When the last one was secure and the final corner covered, Skipping Rock exclaimed, "Now get that tin on the barn." It was nailed back in no time flat. "Well, I do think we've done a pretty good job," he added.

"That's the truth!" Bulger grinned as he watched Eli finish up. "Don't know what we would do without ya help. Let's see what the women have been up to."

"Sounds good to me!" Eli shouted as he popped over the edge of the barn roof and found footing on the ladder. He scrambled down like a raccoon skinning a tree and landed on both feet. He handed the hammer to Bulger and dusted his hands. "I think I could smell something good while I was up there," he said, nodding toward the kitchen.

"That ya did!" Miss Claudie finished his thoughts as she opened the door. "Have some chicken dumplings and cold sweet milk just waiting for ya'll to fill up on."

The men hurried across the porch and into the kitchen, mouths watering. When everyone was settled, Bulger prayed a prayer of thanks. They were safe, their stock was safe, and hopefully, all their neighbors safe. After the 'Amen', forks were clanking and milk was slurping and the meal was finished.

"Ya'll get on out, now," Miss Claudie said. "So glad to know the others made it through the storm. We'll finish up here." And as she placed the last dish in the dishpan and poured in hot water, the men were out the door and headed to the barn. Lizzie grabbed the broom and started sweeping the kitchen, working her way toward the porch.

"Can I go outside and start clearing the yard?" Beth asked.

"That would surely be nice," Miss Claudie replied. "Just be careful, now, don't wander too far off. As soon as Lizzie finishes up the sweeping, I'm filling the woodbox on the stove and we're getting' some cakes baking and starting a batch of stew to simmer for church tomorrow. I'll get up early in the morning and kill a couple of chickens and fry them up."

"Ugh!" Beth remarked. She hated to lose her chickens, but knew the older ones needed thinning out so others would thrive. Besides, not much could beat Miss Claudie's fried chicken. She rushed to the pigpen to check on Ole' Crip and her babies. Ole' Crip was rooting around near the feed trough, looking for something leftover from yesterday's slop, and her babies wandered through the yard and around the edge of the barnyard searching for anything edible. Beth sighed, "I'm sure glad to see all of your babies, Ole' Crip," she said. Quickly she ducked into the barn to make sure Bossie and Bessie and their babies were out of harm's way, too. She decided it would be safe enough to open the back door and let them graze a while in the pasture. She knew they'd be back for their late afternoon snack of sweetfeed.

As she watched the cows and their calves shuffle along their cowtrail, snatching mouthsful of fresh, green grass as they went, she smiled. Even though the storm was mighty and forceful, it had come through with a cleaning. Everything looked and smelled so fresh, so new! Beth turned and skipped back to the yard to begin her cleaning-up job, stooping to pick up limbs and twigs as she went.

She started stacking limbs, leaves, and other light debris in a pile near the edge of the woods, just out of the yard. There were broken shingles scattered across the yard, too. She'd worked long enough to work up a sweat and was tired and thirsty. She'd cleared the yard and started back to the porch for a drink from the water bucket when she stumbled over a lonely shingle. With a 'tisk' of her tongue, she frowned and picked it up.

"How did I leave you here?" she asked. "I'm just too tired to walk and drop you on the pile; I'll toss you right on over." She turned and aimed the shingle at the large pile of trash. She pulled the shingle near her side, eyed the trash pile, bit the end of her tongue, and with a flick of her wrist, she let the shingle fly. But it didn't fly smooth and straight. It angled off to the side toward the barn. Beth's eyes grew wide and her mouth formed a silent 'o' as she watched in horror as the shingle glided perfectly toward one of Ole Crip's babies.

"NO!" she shouted and ran to try to catch the flying

shingle, but she'd never catch it. It twirled and turned, flying furiously through the air. The baby pig noticed the movement and looked up. Beth screeched to a stop watching as the shingle came to a stop-- smashing right into that little pig's forehead right between its eyes---and before the shingle hit the ground, that pig dropped down dead as a doorknob.

Beth was aghast. What had she done? Her knees got weak and she grabbed her head with both hands. "MISS CLAUDIE!" she screamed.

Miss Claudie heard the high-pitched scream and knew something was *really* wrong. She ran from the sink, not even wiping her hands, and rushed to the door. Lizzie, finishing sweeping, dropped the broom and was close behind Miss Claudie as she flew across the porch.

"What on earth?" Miss Claudie cried, shaking the water off her hands as she ran. They saw Beth standing near the edge of the yard, trembling like she was being jiggled by a dozen puppet strings. Lizzie passed Miss Claudie in the middle of the yard and reached Beth first.

"What's the matter, Beth?" she huffed, all out of breath.

Miss Claudie caught up and grabbed Beth by her shoulders and looked her over. "Don't see any bite marks or blood," she said, feeling and examining Beth closely.

Beth, between sobs, pointed toward the pig. "I, I, I didn't mean to. . ." she bawled.

Miss Claudie and Lizzie followed Beth's finger and spied the pig, sprawled dead where it had been standing.

"I, I, I threw a shingle toward the trash pile and it hit the baaaa-by," she wailed louder.

"Shhhh, shhhh, child," Miss Claudie comforted, pulling Beth close and patting her back. "It's gone be fine. Don't worry none. Come on back to the house and get cleaned up. Lizzie will take care of the pig," and she motioned for Lizzie to move the dead pig.

Lizzie looked at Miss Claudie with round eyes, shrugged her shoulders, spread her arms and made a 'why me?' face. Miss Claudie paid her no attention at all. Lizzie's shoulders slumped and she looked toward the pig; then back and Miss Claudie leading Beth into the house. She remembered the box under her bed where she kept the letters from Ginger. Guess I'll find somewhere else to store those letters, she surmised as she crossed the yard to get the box.

When Miss Claudie got Beth calmed down and Lizzie had wrapped the pig in a soft dishtowel and placed it in the box, all three gathered underneath the largest oak tree at the edge of the yard. Lizzie dug a shallow grave and they stood together and placed the little pig in its 'coffin' down into the fresh ground. Miss Claudie asked the girls to join hands and said a kind prayer. Finally, Lizzie gently covered the box with moist dirt. Beth held a dandelion flower, ready to place it on the soft mound as soon as Lizzie patted the last shovel full in place. Beth squatted and solemnly placed the little yellow flower on the grave. A lone tear escaped and dropped on the fresh grave. Her little chin quivered as she rose. Lizzie had to wipe a tear and swipe her nose, too, and noticed as Miss Claudie turned her head and tried to hide her tears as she wiped her face with the hem of her apron.

Miss Claudie and Lizzie followed behind silently as Beth bravely, shoulders back and head high, walked to the house.

EIGHTEEN

Miss Claudie and Lizzie had the stove popping when the day's chores were finished. The women baked two meal pies and had two egg custards and a caramel cake resting in the pie safe and a pot of stew and fresh wild greens bubbling in a black iron pot. Lizzie made a huge pone of cornbread and mashed potatoes for their supper. Miss Claudie said for them to eat their fill of greens and cornbread, and help themselves to one pie. She'd save the leftover greens for dinner the next day and bake fresh bread to go with them. To speed up the next morning's cooking, Lizzie set aside a bowl of potatoes for potato salad, and Eli made sure they had a chicken or two ready to dress for frying. Miss Claudie would be up early to get her dinner basket filled and packed before heading out to church.

It was satisfying for Eli as he sat beside the fire after his filling evening meal. Bulger sat, smoking his pipe while Beth played with Dolly and Patty. "Better get ready for bed," Bulger instructed the girls. "You can wash off in warm water from the stove's warming tray first thing in the morning. I know Miss Claudie will have that stove hot early."

Beth sighed, but obeyed. She shucked off her dress and put on her gown. As she pulled the covers back to put Dolly and Patty in bed, she asked, "Eli, is it this coming Tuesday that Ginger will be here?"

Eli sat straighter, "I think so. The coach will be coming in town about nine. That will give us plenty of time to get here and for me to be back home by dark."

"Good," Beth yawned. "I can hardly wait to see her." Then she added. "Are you coming to bed soon, Lizzie?" she asked.

Lizzie laughed. "Right soon. Just need to have everything ready to get started cooking early in the morning. We have to be at church by ten-thirty. I'd like to be there early enough to visit a little before the service. I know the Jones girls will be there, and 'Loris, too. Guess the Hulls will come on, Mrs. Hull always has more than enough food for everyone, but, Lord knows how she does it and is still on time." She added, shaking her head. "Beth, did . . . ," she began. As she looked over at the bed, she smiled when she saw Beth and her dolls, all propped up on pillows, sound asleep.

"Well," Eli began as he stood and stretched. "I guess I'm gone go on to bed, too." He opened the door to the dogtrot and pulled out the extra cot that was always ready for him. Miss Claudie, who followed closely and brought out covers and a pillow from Bulger's and her bedroom, handed them to Eli. He took them and bent for Miss Claudie to place an angel kiss on his cheek before turning toward the kitchen.

"G'night," she whispered, and she stilled herself and simply delighted in the perfectness of the moment.

"G'night, love you, Miss Claudie," Eli said.

His prayer that night was a prayer of thanks. He drifted off to sleep with 'thank, you Lord' lingering on his lips.

Miss Claudie nodded and smiled before joining Lizzie and Bulger in the kitchen. "Lizzie, girl, time to put these things to rest. Get to bed. Move it, Bulger. We need to get to bed so these young'uns can get some sleep. I think we done all we can for tomorrow."

Bulger slowly pulled himself up from the rocker and lumbered out. He nodded to Eli lying on his cot as he passed. When Miss Claudie followed, Eli was already snug in bed, covered with warm quilts, ready for the chill that spring nights brought. Miss Claudie studied him for a moment and quietly entered the bedroom, clicking the door behind her.

Lizzie quickly got into her nightclothes and hopped in bed beside Beth. Just think! She imagined. This time next week Ginger will be here. We'll pull out the trundle bed and talk and whisper all we want. She closed her eyes and was asleep in a wink; her thoughts spilling over into dreams of Ginger visiting.

Miss Claudie was up before the rooster was. Lizzie woke, too, the instant Miss Claudie walked in the kitchen. Together, they peeled potatoes, boiled eggs, baked bread, warmed greens, fried chicken, and even found time to make a custard.

Bulger and Eli woke early, and did the 'things'; fed the animals, milked cows, and checked on Ole' Crip and her babies. When they finished the yard and barn chores, they drew fresh water from the well, shaved, and slicked back their hair with cold well-water from the washpan on the porch shelf. They circled back to the dogtrot and to the empty bedroom and put on a fresh white shirt and clean pants. Bulger used a shoe brush and dusted his shoes, just in case Miss Claudie noticed the barn dust on top of them. They entered the kitchen just as Lizzie finished putting dishes on the breakfast table.

"It'll be a short breakfast this morning," Miss Claudie remarked as she flew around the room. "Eat up and help get our baskets packed." She flitted across the kitchen and grabbed a couple of split-oak baskets off the top of the pie safe. Bulger had made them especially for carrying dinners. They were big and had double handles, just right for filling with Miss Claudie's good food.

Breakfast was gobbled up and swept away. Miss Claudie had the baskets on the table and a towel folded in the bottoms before Lizzie could get the dishes rinsed. "Cover that bread with this cloth," she instructed as she shoved a red and white checked cotton cloth to Lizzie. "Bulger!" she scolded, "don't ya'll have that wagon hitched yet?" Then, mumbling, added, "Do I have to do ever'thing around here?"

Bulger jumped up and reached for the doorknob and Eli was close behind.

Lizzie, having covered the bread and placed the pies and cake on the table, got the washpan and poured warm water in it and ran to get Beth. "Come on," she urged. "We got to get washed and dressed. We can put on our clothes in the bedroom," and they grabbed a fresh cloth and 'hit the high spots', scrubbing their faces and necks, arms and hands. Then they snatched their Sunday dresses off the pegs above their bed and ran across the dogtrot to pull on their Sunday best.

Bulger pulled the wagon to the porch steps as Miss Claudie opened the door. "Eli, will ya get these baskets and set them on back of the wagon? All I need to do is take off my apron and comb through my hair. Girls! Are you ready?" she called, rushing back into the kitchen.

"All ready, Miss Claudie," Lizzie answered.

"Get that cake, Lizzie, and you, Beth, will you carry the milk pitcher to the wagon, please?" Miss Claudie asked as she whisked through the door. The girls hurried to put the items in the wagon and Beth trotted back to the house.

"What'cha doing, Beth?" Eli hollered.

"Gotta get Dolly and Patty!" she yelled back.

Miss Claudie, still patting her hair with her hands, exited the house and Beth followed. "Up, now Little Bit," she said as she helped Beth to the wagon step. Eli reached over the wagon's side for her. Miss Claudie hauled herself up and plopped down on the wagon seat.

"Are we ready, now?" Bulger said with a bit of amusement.

Miss Claudie gave him an annoyed, side-ways glare and Bulger chuckled and slapped the reins to get the mules moving. They were finally on their way to Sunday church.

"Whew," Eli whispered to Lizzie, "Good thing we only have services and dinner on the grounds a few times a year. Don't think Bulger would ever make it through many Sundays like this."

The mules danced along the road. The beautiful little church came into view, framed with lovely shades of green. Early yellow-green fresh buds deepening to blue-green pine boughs blended together making a delightful, calming glen to house the church. A small, bubbling stream cascaded over smooth pale rocks and rambled alongside the building. Soft moss grew along its banks. Just at the head of the stream where it sprang from the earth grew tall canes much like the ones Eli and Papa found refuge in during the snowstorm. Long, green fern fronds uncurled among tiny white flowers blooming in bright patches alongside the path to the church. There were already several wagons tied to trees beside the bare wooden building, and horses tethered nearby in fresh, lush grass.

Some of the children ran and played tag or hide-and-seek.

Beth's eyes busily scanned the crowd for Melody and Sonny. When she spied them, she moved to stand up.

"Whoa, Little Bit," Bulger warned. "Let me get the wagon stopped before ya even think about getting off."

"Hurry, Bulger," Beth pleaded. She clutched her dolls tightly.

Bulger led the wagon to an empty spot beside the Tuggle's wagon. Lizzie smiled at 'Loris and she waved in return.

Beth and Lizzie jumped from the wagon while Bulger, Miss Claudie, and Eli moved slower. "Tie the mules over by the canes, Eli," Bulger said. "We'll go on inside and get our seats for the meetin'."

Eli led the mules around the canes to a grassy spot, and was surprised to see a familiar figure following. He looked closer, not believing what he saw. Jimmy! How in the world did he get here?

"Hey!" Jimmy called as he walked abreast of Moses and patted his rump.

"Hey, yourself!" Eli said back. "What are you doing here?" When he got the mules secured, he stuck out his hand. Jimmy grabbed it and pumped it up and down—hard.

"I got your note. I made it to town just before dark yesterday," he began, "and stayed over with Cullie. Then got up early and rode in with the Jones's. I wanted to surprise you."

"Well, you sure did that!" Eli grinned. "Come on, let's get in. I can't wait to see Lizzie's face when she sees you."

Jimmy's face turned a bright red, "To tell you the truth, I can't either." He dropped his head as they walked side-by-side to the church. "But I gotta' tell you, I'm a might nervous about it," he added as he pushed his hands deep into his pockets.

Eli stopped dead in his tracks. Ha! He couldn't believe it! Jimmy was keen on Lizzy! He laughed out loud and slapped Jimmy on the back. "Let's get on in. This is gone be priceless!"

Jimmy shrugged his shoulders and together they headed toward the church.

The little church had a steep roof and no porch. There were two doors reached by steep stone steps that spanned the entire front: one for men on the left and one for women on the right. The couples sat respectively inside in the same manner.

Children usually sat in the back, too afraid to whisper, but often slyly exchanging written notes. Benches were separated by a massive black pot-bellied stove sitting on a dark, square tin sheet right in the middle of the church. The tin covered wooden flooring underneath the tall stove and protected the floor from the stove's massive heat in winter. That stove's belly would burn red-hot and still not keep the far corners of the building warm. Everyone sat as close to the stove as they could to feel its warmth, just as they spread out and sat near open windows and kept their Stutts Funeral Home fans swishing in summer to try to stay cool.

Eli and Jimmy rounded the corner of the church just as Lizzie and a group of girls were coming from the opposite direction. They met, face to face, almost bumping into each other and skidded to a halt. Eli stood back and grinned, looking from Jimmy to Lizzie and back from Lizzie to Jimmy. This was his moment and he wanted to savor it.

Lizzie gaped upward into Jimmy's face and looked like she'd swallowed a goose egg. Jimmy's face was red as a ripe tomato and his Adam's apple was jumping up and down like a bobber with a fish on the hook. Neither Lizzie nor Jimmy moved—not even blinked.

Suddenly, Lizzie's friends started giggling. Lizzie looked quickly away and fussed with her collar. The girls covered their mouths with their hands and giggled louder. Eli stood by and kept grinning. Jimmy stood there, glancing over Lizzie's head at the girls and over to Eli. Finally, Eli could stand it no longer.

"Aw, come on, ya'll," he said, and grabbed both Lizzie's and Jimmy's arms and ushered them away from the keyed up group of girls. They walked, Eli between them, to the edge of the woods beside the wagon. "Okay, Lizzie, meet Jimmy," he said gesturing his hand toward Jimmy. "And Jimmy, this is Lizzie," he added, sweeping his hand toward his sister. "I'll meet you inside," he nodded to Jimmy. And he turned on his heel and marched back to the church. When he reached the steps, he was grateful that Mrs. Gore had come out when she heard the ruckus and shooed the girls inside. He looked back to the couple once more, whispered, "Oh, my," and lightly bounced up the steps and inside.

Mr. Eddie Denney finished his morning scripture reading and the congregation sang 'Happy Birthday' to Miss Doris, one of Preacher Sheet's daughters. Preacher Arp stood behind the pine podium in front of the congregation. He looked over the chatting flock and gave a loud cough. Folks took the hint and quickly quieted down, and Mr. Eddie nimbly sat on the men's bench right across from his wife, Miss Glimmer, on the women's side. Eli skimmed the men's side and saw Bulger motioning for him to hurry on up and sit beside him. He scurried and slipped in his saved seat.

Preacher Arp spoke, "Brother Barker, will you please come and lead us in our first hymn."

Mr. Demmie, the very same known for his possum suppers, rose and moved to the front. "Please stand as we sing 'Rescue the Perishing'", and he began pumping his arm up and down to keep time. He sang with exuberance and enthusiasm and in unison, the congregation's voices joined in beautiful harmony that carried all the way through the trees and into the Indian village. With the last, lingering note, Preacher Arp motioned for everyone to be seated. He began his sermon.

He opened with a lovely and moving prayer. His message was one of perseverance and courage; trust and faith. He told how Abraham took his only son to the sacrificial altar to kill him. And what would become of God's promise of Abraham's family? Of God's promise that it would be numbered as stars of the sky; flecks of sand? To kill his son would end his lineage—but he trusted God. And because of Abraham's total faith, courage, and trust, God's promise was fulfilled. Preacher Arp continued, explaining that Abraham probably thought he was in a dark time in his life—a total absence of light—a dark future without his son.

But God brought sunrise, light, and hope. The sun rose with Abraham just as it had with them there after the frightening storm. They were all secure, like Abraham with his son, and darkness and fear was banished. Preacher Arp spread his arms wide to emphasize how God's light covers everyone and everything. It had been a lengthy sermon, as every Circuit Riding preacher tended to give, and carried a mighty message. Eli was filled to overflowing. He realized he had lived, during his short life, through a time of darkness and was now in God's light. He resolved to live more abundantly and walk closer to Him every day.

Beth, however, listened halfheartedly. She sat beside Miss Claudie, squirmed and wiggled, arranged and rearranged Dolly and Patty, and generally wished it was lunchtime.

The older girls in the back hardly listened at all. They passed quick notes, 'Who was that boy with Eli?" and 'Did you see how cute that boy is?" Feeling a little envious of Lizzie and her mysterious new beau.

Finally Preacher Arp bowed his head. The congregation followed his example. "Dear Lord," he began, "We thank you for your protection during the terrible storm. Today we have come together today for another blessing. You have spilled your Holy Spirit among us and filled us with hope and love. We ask you to speak to our hearts and condemn us of our sins so that we will seek forgiveness. We ask you, Lord, to come into our hearts and fill us with your light. Lead us, help us, and protect us in all that we do. We ask these blessings in Your Holy name, Amen. Mr. Barker, would you come and lead us in our invitational hymn?"

Mr. Barker stood and said, "All rise. Our invitational hymn is 'Oh, Lamb of God, I Come'."

Preacher Arp raised his arms and continued, "As we sing, the doors of the church are open. Ask the Lord to save you and come down today. Do not wait! Tomorrow may be too late…Mr. Barker…" And he gestured for the closing hymn to begin.

And the people of Caney Head sang and the Spirit of the Lord moved. The Huddleston boy, the Parmer's daughter, and Mr. and Mrs. Crockett's daughter, Victoria, came forward to profess that they had been saved by the grace of God.

Preacher Arp, blessing the candidates for church membership, said, "These have accepted our Lord Jesus as their Savior. With no objections, they will be baptized in Mr. Dessaw Wall's bottoms there in the creek next Sunday." He continued, "And what couldn't be a more fitting day, Easter! The very day God's son rose from his grave will be the same day our baptismal candidates will rise from the water, their sins washed away, down in the waters, and rising anew in Christ!"

There rose a hearty chorus of "Amens" from the men's side.

No one objected, and as women wiped their eyes and men shook hands, the young men and women were greeted in God's name.

Preacher Arp boomed. "Now we will gather under the trees for our midday-meal. If the gentlemen will move the sawhorses and boards to make the table and womenfolk get their food ready, I will ask blessings on the food outside." With that, he closed the meeting and everyone began filing out.

Parents of the saved rushed forward to hug their children as most of the men moved outside to the back of the church where the sawhorses were stored under the building. They pulled them out and lined them up under the trees next to the church. Next, they placed wide pine boards across them and the women used short brooms to dust them off and spread clothes over them. With help from their husbands and children, women brought baskets, trays, and arms full of food to the table. When it was spread out, Preacher Arp rapped on one of the boards with his pocket knife to get everyone's attention. "We will say blessings over our food," he continued, and he closed his eyes and reached his arms high. "Father, Lord, we ask you to bless this food to nourish our bodies and use our bodies for Your service. Amen."

Eli grinned at the short blessing. Undoubtedly, the preacher was hungry, too! He wondered about Jimmy and Lizzie. Where were they? The last he'd seen of them, they were standing beside Bulger's wagon in shock. He didn't look behind him at the pews while Preacher Arp delivered his sermon; Mamma had stoutly forbid them to do that. Rude, she always said. So he knew better than to turn around and stare at latecomers. So what had become of the pair?

He walked through the churchyard and down toward the creek. Suddenly he heard Lizzie's laugh. He'd found them, sitting beside the creek, talking away like they'd never left the wagon train. "Here ya'll are," he said as he squatted down beside Jimmy. "What have you two been up to?"

Jimmy looked sheepish and admitted, "Well, we walked

about a dozen times to the well and back, then decided to come down here by the creek." He looked around. "It is nice here, ain't it?" He said, picking up a leaf and ripping it in half along the middle vein.

"Yep, that it is," Eli returned.

"We've been catching up," Lizzie broke in. "Jimmy's started his place just in the edge of Alabama, but with nobody to help, it's going slow. He barely has a one-room house up and barely any crops ready at all." She grinned and glanced at Jimmy. "Guess that means he'll have to stop by our place a lot."

Jimmy simply shook his head and tossed the leaf into the water. "Don't know what I'll do, but I'll be okay." He looked up at Eli. "When I sold our place after Pa died, I kept the horses and traded our work wagon for the wagon I had on the train." He dropped his head. "I hid what money I had from the sale of the place under a board beneath the wagon seat." He looked at Lizzie and grinned a soft smile. "I still have most of it, even after getting things set up for the house. Mr. Jones is a good man, and he's helped me a whole lot. Me and Lizzie heard enough of the preacher's sermon out here and that I know God is good, and He's gone work things out for the best."

"That He'll certainly do," Eli agreed, "but right now, if we don't get to that dinner table, we gone leave here hungry!"

Lizzie and Jimmy laughed and rose, and walked along with Eli to join the happy churchgoers at the homemade dinner table.

Sunrise

Therefore shall a man leave his father and his mother, and
shall cleave unto his wife;
and they shall be one flesh.
Genesis 2: 24

The men went along the table first, dipping and forking food to heaping on their plates, then moved to a smaller table with water and milk buckets. They filled their cups and gathered in small pods to eat and discuss how their farm work was coming along. Questions and reassurances were abundant concerning the effects of the tornado, too.

Next came the women, choosing dishes made by well-known bakers and cooks. They, too, moved into small groups to eat and chat.

Finally, it was the young folks' turn to fill their plates; and that they did! Eli, Jimmy, and Lizzie inspected each bowl and platter, and even though the grown-ups had filled their plates to overflowing, there was plenty of food to choose from. Some moved to the dessert table first, but watchful mothers shooed them away and toward vegetables and meats. Desserts would come after a generous lunch.

Lizzie noticed Beth balancing her plate in one hand with her dolls clamped under her other arm. She giggled aloud. Jimmy and Eli looked at her and asked, "What'cha laughing at?"

She nodded toward the table and they saw Beth, her plate, her dolls, and Sonny. He had his plate loaded with potato salad and fried chicken in one hand and teetered along in front of Beth dipping from the table, spooning food on her plate with his other. They looked like a pair of clowns at the fair; ducking and dodging to hold their plates steady and find a place to sit and eat. Lizzie stood and walked to take Beth's plate. "Come on over here," she offered. "You can eat with us."

"Thanks," Sonny grinned. Lizzie noticed his front teeth had finally grown in. He looked older. He was a generous and helpful boy. She was thankful Beth had chosen him for a friend.

Eli was almost—almost—too full for dessert when he heard the loudest screech he'd ever heard! The others stopped chewing and looked toward the squealing coming from the far end of the table.

"IEEEEEE!" It came again.

Eli swiveled his head to see a rather large lady from town with hands waving high, her plate flying through the air like a wounded duck, and food smattering down everywhere. Then the lady's arms came down and her fingers made a tight ball close to her sides. She began shaking all over, slinging her hair, stomping her feet, and simply having a hissy fit.

"IIIIeeeee," again.

"What in the world?" he said as he watched Preacher Arp hurry to the woman's side.

"What's the matter?" Preacher Arp asked.

The woman, clutching at her chest and gasping, stuttered, "There's a lizard in my plate!"

Preacher Arp looked around, totally puzzled. There were no lizards being served that day. "What do you mean?" he asked.

The woman rushed to the other side of the serving table and pointed upward, fingers shaking. "From there!" she motioned. "I was standing underneath that tree and suddenly a huge, HUGE, green lizard landed right in my plate in the middle of my mashed potatoes!" And she covered her face with her hands and sobbed.

Eli noticed Preacher Arp moving his face a bit to the side to keep the terrified woman from noticing his grin—almost an outright laugh popped out! He composed himself and patted the woman on her shoulder. "Come now, let's get you another plate and you can start over. I'll even have you a chair brought out and you can sit over by the wagon---well away from the trees."

Eli shoved a spoonful of peas in his mouth and bit off a chunk of cornbread. He chuckled softly as he watched Preacher Arp gracefully lead the woman to her seat. Mrs. Huckeba rushed over with a fresh plate and chatted cheerfully beside the woman, trying to reassure her. Nonetheless, Eli noticed the woman's eyes constantly, tentatively glancing upward as she finished her meal.

NINETEEN

The sun rose bright on Monday morning. Sunbeams burst over the top of the barn and scattered shimmering pools of light across the yard. Lizzie was up way before the sunshine chased the last shadows from the house, and Miss Claudie joined her, sleepy, but ready to go.

"Tomorrow's the day, ain't it?" she asked.

It was almost time for Ginger's arrival. Lizzie was as nervous as new daddy waiting for his firstborn to be delivered. She was busy, dusting and tidying everything. "It is, and I can hardly wait!" she said as she pulled the chimney off the kerosene lamp and dumped it into sudsy water. She rubbed it with vigor—more from nerves than anything—Miss Claudie assumed.

"Well, as long as the sun is up, I'm out to sweep the yard," she said. "I need the early morning air and the exercise will do me good. Beth!" she shouted. "Come on and get up and run to the village and see if Minshue will let Warm DayRah take ya to the whitemud hole. Take the old bucket with you and fill it. We need to wash down the hearth and clean it good. Don't think we'll be needin' much more heat outta' the fireplace from now on in." She looked over the yard and spoke to herself. "Maybe I'll have enough to cover the tree trunks, too. As high as I can reach, anyway. That'll sure make this yard look better and keep some of the critters off'em."

Hearing Lizzie's bustling and clattering and heeding Miss Claudie's call, Beth sat up and rubbed her eyes.

"Wha'cha'll doin'," she asked. "I'm trying to sleep here.

And you've woke up Dolly. Good thing Patty is a hard sleeper. If it's left up to you, none of us would get any rest." She rose and stretched. Then her eyes grew wide and her mouth made a little 'o'. "It's tomorrow!" She threw back the covers and jumped out of bed. "Tomorrow's the day Ginger's coming, ain't it? Com'on, Jack; here Bell," she clicked to her pups and they dragged themselves from underneath the trundle bed and stretched. "Get up, you lazy hounds," Beth said. She shed her gown and wiggled her dress over her head and shooed the dogs outside.

"Oh, no," Lizzie thought out loud. "Gotta find somewhere else for those dogs to sleep, and Beth won't like that. Ginger can't have them snoring and scratching under her bed. She'd never sleep a wink!" she uttered absently. Beth danced around Lizzie and gave her a huge hug.

Lizzie laughed and grabbed Beth's hands and danced around in a circle. "Yes, tomorrow it is!" she tittered. "Hold on, I can't get my breath!" Lizzie said at last. "Everything has to be just right when Eli gets here with Ginger. I'm so happy!"

Beth let go and ran to make the bed. "I'm happy, too. Ginger's coming. Oh, yeah!" She quickly pulled the bed covers to tidy it. She ran outside and grabbed the rusty bucket. "Come on Jack, here Bell," she chimed. "Gotta hurry and get that mud to wash over that smutty fireplace. Don't want Miss Claudie upset!"

Miss Claudie, hands on her hips watching the two girls, got in a hurry. She dodged Lizzie, who was rushing across the room to replace the sparkling lamp chimney. "And I'd better be out of this girl's way," she muttered as she left the room and stepped into the first morning light. "Breakfast can wait until Bulger gets the things around here done and Beth gets back, and by then we'll all be hungry." She walked to the side of the barn and retrieved her brush broom and started sweeping the yard. She watched Beth skipping along the path swinging her bucket and the two dogs investigating bushes along the way. She smiled as Beth disappeared into the green thickness. The quietness of the morning, coolness of early spring air, and monotony of her strokes led her body and mind to a relaxing rhythm.

Lizzie, having worked herself down and rid herself of most of her butterflies flitting around in her stomach, looked around the room. "I sure want everything to be pretty," she said. She hurried outside to the edge of the garden and broke a handful of blooms—just weeds, and some newly budding wildflowers, and rushed back inside. She quickly put them in a tall green Indian pottery pot, filled it with water, and sat them on the table. She remade Beth's and her bed; arranged and re-arranged pillows and covers.

"Everything looks as tidy as a mouse's nest," she said. "But Bulger's gone be hungry as a bugger when he gets in here. Miss Claudie's sweeping the yard, and Beth's on her errand, so I guess it's me to make late breakfast. Better get the eggs after I mix up the biscuits," she said, reaching for the dough bowl. She gathered the sifter and looked around the sparkling kitchen as she began sifting the light, powdery flour. Lizzie felt relief. Everything was in perfect shape. Breakfast would be long cleared and cleaned, late breakfast meant early supper, and that meant one night 'til Ginger arrived. She kept her hands and mind busy working on breakfast and refused to let her worries leap forward. She had gotten up early because she couldn't stand the worries: Ginger missing the stage; Ginger sick and cancelling the trip; stage breaking down; and Eli forgetting to go to town and pick up Ginger. Well, too late for all that! Just good thoughts today; and Ginger would be here before tomorrow's nightfall!

TWENTY

Eli woke early and walked to town. He believed he'd stop by the Post Office and check on any mail for Bulger since he'd be going out there anyway.

"Howdy, Eli," said Mr. Wright. "Looking for something special?"

"Not today," Eli replied, propping his arms on the mail shelf between himself and Mr. Wright. "Just thought I'd check and carry anything in since I'm heading out to Bulger's."

Mr. Wright turned and checked the boxes behind him. "Well, you're in luck. Got this in for Miss Lizzie. Looks important," and he handed the long letter through the metal mail slots.

He turned the envelope over and looked at the return address: Georgia Department of Education. Well, he had no idea what it could do with Lizzie, but the envelope was a fat one. He poked it inside his jacket pocket and thanked Mr. Wright before walking out.

"Tell everyone out at the farm hello for me," Mr. Wright called.

"Sure thing," Eli waved over his head as the Post Office door bumped shut.

Eli had made arrangements with Mr. Jones to borrow a buggy and Cullie had it ready and waiting when Eli got to the general store.

"Expecting someone special, huh?" he asked.

"Yeah, a girl from back home. She and Lizzie are best friends and Lizzie's in a tizzy," he and Cullie both laughed at the rhyme.

"Is she cute?" Cullie asked.

"Not particularly," Eli answered. "She's just a girl like Lizzie. Kinda plain, but real sweet. I never paid much attention. She was always comin' around to see Lizzie." He tried to remember how Ginger looked but couldn't bring her to mind. Focusing on the present, he continued, "Guess I'd better get on out and meet the stage. Don't want Lizzie to give me the what for if I'm late. Tell Mr. Bob I'm mighty thankful for the use of his buggy. I'll get it back tonight." And he sauntered out the store door and drove to the stage depot and pulled up next to the walk where passengers exited the stage.

It wasn't long before he heard the tramping of horse's hooves and whistling of the stagecoach driver. Then the stage came into sight. It was beautiful: six bay horses pulling the swaying stage along the road, manes dancing as they raced toward the depot. It was near enough for him to hear the huffing of the horses as they worked to pull the heavy coach, and he could smell their lathered sweat. The driver yelled, "Whoa," and the coach stopped beside the walk. The driver quickly wrapped the reins around the brake handle and climbed down. He opened the stage door and reached in and put down a much-worn stool for passengers to step on as they departed. Eli strained to see Ginger. First in view was a tall man with a colorful bow tie. Next a lady with tall, fluffy feathers in her hat holding a little girl's hand. Girl too young, Eli reasoned, but where was Ginger?

Then came a man dressed all in black with a huge mustache; next a girl in a blue dress holding a blue parasol. She reached for the driver's hand to help her down. She stepped to the ground and smoothed the front of her dress and gracefully turned and walked to the back of the coach to retrieve her bags. She opened her parasol quickly and held it to keep the sun off her face. Eli noticed her dark hair was twisted up on her head and her dress fit her most pleasingly. She walked with good moves, too. He could hardly take his eyes off her and pull them back to the stage door to watch for Ginger to get off. But no one else did. He sat there, confused and worried.

Oh, would Lizzie be disappointed! he thought. But if

Ginger had missed the stage, it wasn't his fault. He pulled the reins to turn the horse around and take the buggy back to Mr. Jones just as the girl turned toward him. She had the parasol in one hand and her bag in the other, just standing there. He looked again, leaned forward and looked closer. He could hardly believe it, but THAT was Ginger! His knees tingled and his hands went cold. Boy, he was surprised, pleasantly surprised. He managed to swallow and stiffly shifted the reins to one hand and shakily raised the other and waved to her. She smiled and his heart melted. As he sat on the seat in a daft trance, Ginger shifted her heavy bag and began trudging toward the wagon.

How thoughtless! Eli realized as he found his feet and hopped out of the buggy, almost losing his hat in the process. "Hello, Ginger," he stammered as he rushed to her and reached for her bag.

"Hello, Eli," she said.

He couldn't take his eyes off her as they walked side-by-side to the wagon. Eli threw her bag on the back and extended his hand to help her up. A hot tingling began where her fingers touched his hand and shot up his arm. His mouth went dry and he didn't want to let her go. She sat and looked at him and slightly raised her eyebrows and looked toward his hand holding hers.

"Um, oh, well," he babbled as he quickly dropped her hand and scrambled up and grabbed the reins. He stared straight ahead and as he popped the reins across the horse's back, he barely managed to shout through his dry mouth, "Giddy up!"

And the horse pulled away from the passenger platform toward waiting Lizzie. Ginger sat straight on the wagon seat beside Eli, not looking right nor left, wearing a slight smile as the miles raced along.

Too soon, Eli thought, they arrived at Bulger's and Miss Claudie's. Eli discovered he was a little disappointed to turn Ginger over to Lizzie. He wished he could keep on driving through the spring morning with her. The sun shone and the horse felt good. He felt so comfortable with Ginger sitting beside him; just like she had always belonged there. As he pulled the horse to a stop, he looked once again at the graceful young lady sitting next to him. Whatever happened to that long-legged tomboy, that annoying friend of Lizzie's they'd left back in Hooverville, he wondered. He couldn't help but stare; she was beautiful!

Lizzie's shriek brought him out of his reverie. He jumped and Ginger shot to her feet. She was down from the buggy before Eli had time to blink. He leaned back and watched as the two girls hugged and danced all over Miss Claudie's freshly manicured yard—whitened tree trunks and all. He heard the screen door slam as Beth, followed by Jack and Bell, ran and jumped from the porch to the yard. She joined her sister and friend, dancing and laughing. The dogs started barking and leaping circles around the trio.

Bulger came trotting from the barn and Miss Claudie stood in the kitchen door, eyes twinkling, as the girls enjoyed their meeting.

Finally Lizzie caught her breath. "Bulger, Miss Claudie, this is Ginger!"

Bulger extended his hand and Miss Claudie hobbled down the porch steps to greet her.

"Glad to meet'cha," Bulger said, and shook her hand.

"And I'm Miss Claudie, so good to finally meet ya. We've heard so much about ya, seems like we've known ya all along," Miss Claudie added with a hug. "Come on inside and get the dust off and have a cool drink. Supper will be ready early since Eli needs to be home before dark." She looked to the wagon, "Eli, bring in Ginger's bags, will ya? We can visit a little as we eat."

Lizzie and Ginger led the way into the house. Beth followed, along with her dogs, and Miss Claudie came behind. Eli handed the bags down to Bulger and he sat them on the porch. Then he followed Eli and the buggy into the barn where they unhitched the horse, put him in a stall, and tossed in extra hay. Bulger, watching Eli closely, sensed something a little different. It didn't take much guessing to decide what it was. He was in love. Bulger beamed.

As the two made their way to the house, Bulger placed his arm over Eli's shoulders. "How ya' feelin', son?" he asked.

Eli looked up, confused, "I feel fine; why do you ask?"

Bulger laughed out loud. "Well, boy, ya look a little

flushed." And he clapped Eli hard on his back a couple of times before letting his arm fall to his side. "I do think ya got the fever, mebbe ya just don't know it yet. Don't know what we're gone do around here. Seems the fever has hit hard." His long leg skipped over the first porch step and his foot landed on the second. "Gone get mighty interestin' before this fever gets cured."

Eli stopped stock-still when Bulger removed his arm. He watched in disbelief as the old man fairly skipped up the steps and across the porch. What on earth is he talking about? he wondered. He shook his head to try to clear his thoughts and slowly followed Bulger into the kitchen. Everyone was laughing and talking and getting settled. Eli absently stuck his hand in his coat pocket. The letter! Well, there's too much goin' on now to hand it over to Lizzie, he sensed. Noticing the newly whitewashed fireplace, he moved to it and propped the letter on the mantle. Someone would be sure to notice it and Lizzie could read it later. No hurry, he was sure.

Miss Claudie smiled from ear to ear. Beth talked nine miles a minute. Jack and Bell danced back and forth across the kitchen, eyes from Ginger to Beth, and Lizzie still held Ginger's hand in a death grip.

"Come on in, Ginger. We could hardly wait for ya to get here," Miss Claudie said. "Get ya things put away over by the bed and we'll wash up for supper. We'll finish up and have time to talk a little before bedtime. Eli has to get Mr. Jones's buggy back to town and walk on home 'fore it gets good dark." She whooshed out a breath. "I'm so thankful the days are finally getting a little longer. I won't worry so much about him walking alone; he won't be in the dark traveling now." She didn't mention that she'd found that Muscogee Indian blanket hidden in the back of the barn. She'd discovered it while looking for the calico's new kittens and she found them all right; the mamma cat had used the blanket for her babies' bed. That blanket could mean only one thing-- the menacing Indians were still skulking around.

Lizzie helped Ginger slide her bags near the end of the bed and explained how Bulger and Miss Claudie had made a special bed for her. Lizzie would pull it out from under theirs when it was bedtime and they could sleep together in the warm room. As long as the nights stayed cool, it was very pleasant; but in summer, they might move the beds to the dogtrot where it usually caught a breeze and was much cooler.

Beth placed plates, forks, and glasses on the table while Miss Claudie dipped up supper. Bulger said grace and they dug in.

Eli couldn't help but sneak glances at Ginger; she was really pretty. Most often than not, Bulger caught him and Eli turned red every time. Bulger grinned and caught Miss Claudie's eye and winked. She smiled a knowing smile, and noticed that Ginger was giving Eli 'the eye', too. Everybody but Lizzie and Beth knew that Eli was truly smitten. And Ginger did nothing to cause Eli any worry otherwise.

When the table was cleared and dishes on the shelf, Bulger retired to his rocker and pipe, and the women folk sat around the table. "Eli, it's about time ya started back. I packed ya a basket of leftovers to take along. They should last until ya can get back by," Miss Claudie said as she handed Eli a large basket of bread, fresh eggs, fried chicken and crocks of milk. "Don't forget to set the milk in the creek down by your house when you get in; it'll be spoiled 'fore mornin'."

"Sure thing," Eli mumbled as he took the basket and started for the door. He was startled to hear a soft voice behind him.

"Bye, Eli. See you soon?"

He turned to see Ginger standing beside Lizzie. He blanched as he recognized the look on Lizzie's face when lightning of realization hit. Her eyes widened and her lips pursed. Ginger and her brother? She couldn't believe it, but it was plain as the whiskers on Ole Crip's nose.

Eli ducked his head and avoided Lizzie's gaze. He looked up at Ginger and, not typically, shyly whispered, "Sure, soon." And quickly turned on his heel and dashed out the door.

Bulger began rocking and grinning. Lizzie plopped down in a kitchen chair in disbelief, and Miss Claudie sighed. Only Beth kept both feet solidly on the floor.

"Tell us about your trip on the stagecoach," she said. "Me and Dolly and Patty sure want to hear all about it."

The spell was broken and the kitchen filled with chatter and laughter until the mantle clock struck ten times. Time had flown and Beth's yawns prompted everyone to turn in. New sunrises were coming bringing summer days, lots of work, and bushels of fun.

Everyone slept soundly that night. Everyone but Eli. He tossed and turned, wishing he hadn't enjoyed Jimmy's discomfort being with Lizzie at church quite as much. Now he knew exactly how Jimmy felt; and he, like Jimmy, felt like a fish out of water. He thought his heart would pound out of his chest and a hundred buzzards flew in his belly. He was hot, then cold. Just before he finally drifted off to sleep, he prayed. He licked his lips and with eyes clinched shut, asked for guidance and understanding. He knew he was entering a new, wonderful part of his life, and he wanted to know he was walking with God and could follow His guidance. The Holy Spirit enveloped him and his fingers relaxed their hold on the hem of his quilt, Eli breathed deeply and finally found his soft, safe place in assured sleep. A new day was coming filled with sunlight and joy.

TWENTY-ONE

The new week broke bright and clear. It seemed that winter wasn't in a hurry to stay around and warmer weather was emerging with leaps of higher degrees. Jack Frost was long gone and April showers were light and welcomed. The earth drank the nourishing liquid and was covering herself with a colorful cloak. Butterflies popped out, birds sang as they built nests, babies of all descriptions appeared, and as Bulger noted, love was indeed in the air.

Eli woke early on Friday morning, eager to get back to Bulger's and Miss Claudie's. He wondered if he had dreamed about Ginger and if he had, it was a beauty! He looked around his new house and breathed in the fresh-wood smell. Earlier when Bulger had brought the mules over to break Eli's fields, he also hauled in the table, benches, and bed he helped Eli craft in his shop. Eli rubbed his hand over the smooth top of the oak table before chunking wood in the stove. As the stove warmed, he walked to the stream and dipped water for coffee. Midway back to his house, he stopped and turned a complete circle, looking at everything he and his neighbors had managed to build. He was filled with gratitude and thankfulness. Taking a deep breath and closing his eyes to savor the moment, he thanked God for His blessings. With a light step, he crossed the yard and his feet barely touched the stone steps as he reached the door and went inside.

≈

Ginger woke with a strange sense of being watched. She turned her head to look up right into Lizzie's eyes.

"I couldn't wake you, and I still can't believe you're really here," Lizzie remarked as she propped her head higher on her pillow.

Ginger smiled. "I know. Me neither." She turned and adjusted her pillow, too, so that she could see Lizzie better. "You have a wonderful place here, and Miss Claudie and Bulger are the perfect couple." She dropped her gaze to the covers and picked at a loose thread. "I can't believe your Papa and Mamma didn't make it. It must have been horrible."

Lizzie's mind flashed back to the past January when Mamma and Papa perished, along with most of their belongings. She shivered and simply nodded in response.

Ginger continued, "I'm so thankful that you and Eli and Beth are here."

Lizzie's somber spell broke. "We have been blessed. Without Miss Claudie and Bulger and our Indian friends, we never would have."

"Indians!" Ginger gasped. "You mean there are Indians around here?" she shot up in bed and held the quilt tight against her chest.

Lizzie laughed and tossed off her cover, checking to make sure Beth still slept soundly. "Come on, let's get up and surprise everyone with breakfast. And yes, there are Indians around here. I can't wait for you to meet them. There's Warm DayRah, Beth's friend, and Skipping Rock who's been wonderful to help Eli and has given him so many good ideas to help with his house, and Minshue their mom." She stood and opened the door to the dogtrot and stood behind it to change clothes. When she was dressed, she motioned for Ginger to do the same.

"After we finish up here, we'll walk to the village and you can meet them. Beth loves to go and has made herself a second daughter to Minshue. She's learned more of their language than I have, but I go two or three times a week and help the little ones learn reading and some math. Warm DayRah is like a sponge. I think she'll grow up to be an important ally for the Indians and probably be a great go-between for her people and our government one day. Hope so, anyway."

By then, Ginger was dressed and Lizzie had the fire going in the stove. "This feels good," Ginger said as she rubbed her arms. "Got a few goosebumps." She looked at Lizzie and grinned. "Don't know if they're from this morning's cool or from the idea of Indians. I gotta get used to that."

"Don't worry," Lizzie laughed. "You're gonna love them."

Beth woke just as Miss Claudie came into the kitchen. "Bulger's on his way in. How did you sleep, Ginger?" she asked.

"Oh, wonderful!" she responded.

Bulger came in, looked around, and grinned. "I think I'll get the things done in the barn fast this morning. Can't wait to get back to my room full of girls today." He picked the milk bucket up and made his way out.

Lizzie looked at Ginger's puzzled gaze at the closed door and burst out laughing. Beth and Miss Claudie joined in. "Don't worry," Lizzie assured. "Bulger has a great sense of humor—but he does love us ladies."

The morning passed with lively chatter and merriment. They talked about families that Ginger would meet at the baptizing on Sunday and how Eli had built his house. Lizzie noticed a slight flush in Ginger's cheeks whenever Eli's name was mentioned. She was afraid to hope Ginger might become her 'sister' one day soon, but thrilled to hope her wish would come true.

Eli arrived late that afternoon and announced he was spending the night. The girls got busy making sure everything was in order; supper cleaned up and cot ready on the dogtrot. The night was warm so they moved chairs outside on the kitchen porch where they sat and quietly talked.

"Look! Lightning bugs!" Beth shouted.

"Look in the pantry and get a bottle. We'll catch some," Eli directed.

Beth shot inside and was right back out with a tall, transparent-greenish old vinegar bottle. Eli jumped up and together they ran to the edge of the yard where most of the flashing was. "Come on!" Eli shouted and waved his hand for Lizzie and Ginger to join them.

Bulger and Miss Claudie sat and watched their brood run

and jump through the early twilight. Bulger slowly rocked as he sucked on his pipe and Miss Claudie sat in her short rocker with her hands clasped in her lap, smiling softly. The spring night was warm and slightly moist; the bugs were twinkling like a Christmas tree. Soon the bottle held enough lightning bugs to be a beacon.

"Watch!" Beth said. She caught a firefly and just as it blinked its greenish glow, swiped it on Lizzie's head. Suddenly, there was a luminous streak shining through her hair! Then Eli caught one and swiped its glow on Beth. They all ended up with green glow somewhere on them, and as darkness crept in like a mouse at midnight, Miss Claudie and Bulger watched a show of peculiar iridescence swishing and swirling around their yard. Finally the quartet of bug catchers ran out of steam and made their way to the porch. Beth lifted the lid on her bottle and watched as the once-imprisoned fireflies danced back to their woodland homes.

Eli held Ginger's hand as they made their way back into the house.

Miss Claudie smiled and warned, "Ya'll better get a washcloth and get that lightning bug goo off 'fore you go to bed. I think it's beginning to disappear and you'd better wash while you can still see it."

Lizzie got the washpan and a cloth for each of them. There was a moment of hesitation and a little embarrassment as they scrubbed and wiped, but eventually all evidence of their evening escapade was washed away.

"I guess I'd better get on out to my cot," Eli said. He glanced at Ginger who reacted with a different glow—there was a special radiance all around her. Lizzie knew she had nothing to worry about. She would definitely be getting another sister. The only question was: when?

Bedtime came a little later that night than usual. Finally everybody was dressed for bed and they tucked their tired bodies under the covers. After prayers were said and the girls drifted off to sleep, Beth said, "Lizzie, will you take Ginger and me to the village tomorrow? I want her to meet Warm DayRah and the other children."

Lizzie reached over and tucked Beth in tighter. "Sure, Little

Bit. First thing." Before she could arrange her corner of their shared quilt and say goodnight to Ginger, Beth had dropped off to sleep.

"What a wonderful day," Ginger murmured, yawning and closing her eyes. "See you in the morning."

"Yes, a wonderful day," Lizzie agreed. She settled her head into her pillow and reflected on the day's events. She fell asleep with a smile touching her lips.

≈

Daybreak on Saturday proved to break as nicely as the previous days had. Sunrise was bright and cheery and all the morning's chores were finished in a flash. Lizzie wanted to carry the Indian children a treat, so she was up extra early and made teacakes to take along. As they cooled, she walked to the fireplace to get a basket from the hearth and as she looked up, she noticed an envelope perched on the mantle and picked it up. It's addressed to me! She noticed. Then she read the return address: Board of Education and with that, she tore into it. With shaking hands, she read the letter enclosed with a thicker bundle of sealed papers. In short, she had her test in her hands! She reread the letter. Instructions were complete: she should carry the unopened test packet to the courthouse or to the probate judge's office. There he, along with the acting headmaster of the school, would open the packet and with the headmaster would witness as she completed the test. She would leave it with the judge and he would be responsible for mailing it back to Atlanta where it would be scored. She couldn't believe it. It had been here---how long? Eli must have brought it when he came with Ginger. Ohhhhh, she questioned. Why didn't he tell me? She shook the papers and turned on her heel. Just as suddenly as she felt indignation at Eli for forgetting about the letter, she felt relief and elation. It didn't matter! The test had arrived and she was already feeling nervous about taking it. As much as she'd looked forward to visiting the village, now she could hardly wait for the day to be over so Eli could take her test to the judge's office. She had to let Miss Myline know since she had to be present during the test. So much to do....

She shouted for everyone to get to the kitchen. Bulger ran from the barn and Miss Claudie rushed through the door followed by Eli. Ginger got her bed only part of the way hidden under Lizzie and Beth's bed and jumped up to gawk at Lizzie standing in front of the fireplace. Beth had scattered half her apron of corn for the chickens, but when she heard Lizzie's loud voice, she shook the rest to the ground in a pile and ran for the house. They all reached Lizzie at the same time and came to a strained halt—what on earth had happened?

"It's here!" Lizzie shouted, waving the letter in the air. "I'm finally going to take the test and be a real teacher!"

Miss Claudie let out the breath she'd been holding and Bulger grabbed his hat off his head and hit his thigh with it. Ginger and Beth grabbed Lizzie and squeezed her so tight they cut off her breath. "Le, le, Let me go!" she gasped.

Eli stood at the edge of the gathering with a sheepish, uh-oh look on his face. He'd completely forgotten about the letter and Lizzie had found it. He was sure she was going to give him the 'what fors' and fuss him out for wasting time. Instead, she reached and grabbed him and gave him a huge hug.

"Oh, thank you, Eli, for bringing my letter out! I'm so excited!"

He broke loose and shuffled his feet uncertainly. "You're welcome," he mumbled.

Lizzie managed to calm down and everyone slowly went back to their chores. Miss Claudie snatched Eli aside before he had a chance to escort the girls to the village. "I really need'ja to help me get these last cabbage and onions in the garden," she said. "I'm putting in more this year since we got more mouths to feed." Then she added with a twinkle in her eye. "You got any ideas on adding to the number?"

"Aw, Miss Claudie," Eli blushed. "I don't know what you could be talkin' 'bout."

Miss Claudie straightened and shoved a hoe his way. "Well, old eyes do see new things," she chuckled. "Get on out there; I want to finish up early so I can get to work on Beth's Easter dress. That material has been laying on my dresser a month. I can't waste any more time gettin' it sewed up. She's gone look sweet as a peach come Sunday."

Eli threw the hoe over his shoulder and lumbered out to the garden, Miss Claudie on his heels.

Lizzie, keeping her letter close, patted it in her hand once more and replaced it on the mantle. She bent and picked up the basket and skipped to the table to fill it with her fresh teacakes.

"Are we going now, Lizzie?" Beth piped up.

"Yep, you bet'cha," Lizzie said, ushering Ginger, Beth, and the two dogs out the door.

They ambled down the well-worn trail toward the Indian village. Lizzie chattered nonstop along the way. Beth ran ahead following and clucking to her dogs like a hen watching over her chicks, and like chicks, the dogs rambled and snooped in every shadow and hole along the path.

Ginger was unusually quiet. She held one side of the basket of cookies and Lizzie held the other. It swung gently between them as they walked along. In no time they reached the edge of the village. They knew it was near before they could see it. There was a nice smoky smell in the air and they could hear various sounds: nickering and tramping of horses, clanging of metal utensils against iron pots, mammas' voices urging their children to be careful, and the happy, tinkling laughter of children playing. When the village came into view, Ginger and Lizzie stood at the edge of the clearing and soaked in the scene. It was like walking into another world. Busy. Colorful. Happy.

Beth was right in the middle of it; Jack and Bell, too. Some of the children were playing Lacrosse while their mammas watched closely as they shook the dust from colorful blankets, stoked fires, braided hair, and worked their own gardens. Every now and then the women looked over the group of children, earnest in their attempt to score a goal, just to be sure all was right. Some of the younger children took turns trying to throw rocks through a rolling hoop that had been sent scooting along by a partner. And others played hide-and-seek or tag.

The men, older ones not on a hunt, sat quietly and watched the children, smoking their pipes or propped back against the side of the houses enjoying the warming sun. Everything was in order, peaceful, and contented.

"See, I told you," Lizzie said to Ginger.

Ginger smiled and they walked together into another

world. Their arrival had already been announced by the baying of Jack and Bell, and many heads turned and friendly hands lifted to wave toward them as the girls walked to Minshue's house. The Lacrosse game ended unexpectedly when several of the children left to run and meet Lizzie. Together they walked through the village to Minshue's.

"Come in," Minshue invited. "*Dtohitsu*, Daisy Face," she smiled and held out her arms.

"*Wado*, Minshue," Beth replied, "and I *am* fine." She ran and fell into Minshue's arms and squeezed her tightly.

Minshue turned Beth loose and moved aside so that Lizzie and Ginger could enter. Lizzie sneaked a peek at Ginger and stifled a giggle. Ginger's eyes were as large as a new moon in August and she looked uncomfortably pale.

Beth passed the basket of teacakes to Minshue. "We made them this morning."

"Oh, thank you. Come, sit," Minshue instructed. The girls moved to a low bench covered with a colorful woven rug and sat. "I am sorry my house is in such a state, but we're getting ready to move to our summer house. The days are warming and we should be making ready to bake outside in our ovens and sleep in our open, light summer homes. I must keep myself busy. Skipping Rock has left with some of our younger men to seek the Muscogee and persuade them to return to their village." She dropped her head and smoothed her long skirt. "Those rambling Muscogees are nothing but troublemakers. I am uneasy thinking about Skipping Rock. I know he intends to help bring peace, but I have a cold shivering through my belly and trembling hands as my thoughts are with him." She moved and picked up a wooden dough bowl and a lone tear slipped down her cheek.

"Oh, Minshue," Lizzie said, rising from her seat and moving to touch Minshue's arm. "I'm sure he will be all right. Skipping Rock is smart and knows how to speak so well. He will persuade the other Indians to leave, I'm sure."

Minshue looked at Lizzie and sighed. "Yes, you are right. He will be fine. And you are Ginger," she said, looking at her. "How do you like being here so far?" she asked.

Ginger didn't know what to say. She felt overwhelmed in

these new, different surroundings. Thankfully, Beth wasn't shy at all.

"She's doing great!" Beth blurted. "She gets to sleep in the room with us. Bulger made her a bed that slips right underneath ours during the day and we pull it out and Ginger sleeps there at night. Eli comes over almost every day, now. He thinks we need him to help with the planting, or he wants to borrow something, or SOMETHING, so he's around a lot," she said, nodding her head innocently to make her point.

Minshue looked from Ginger to Lizzie and back at Ginger again. Suddenly her eyes sparked and she glanced knowingly at Lizzie. Lizzie was grinning like a possum perched high in a loaded persimmon tree.

Well, Minsue thought, looks like Eli might be setting up housekeeping for good and Ginger might be staying for quite a spell. Just then, a holler rang through the village and they heard pounding feet running toward the path leading from the village.

Minshue's face blanched ashen, and she ran through the door out into the village courtyard. The three girls followed.

Lizzie wanted to turn away, but the revulsion of what she saw held her. Ginger grabbed Beth and turned her away, leading her quickly away from the sight.

Two young Indians were carrying a third between them. The wounded Indian could hardly move his legs as his friends struggled to drag him into the village. A crowd gathered around them, shouting questions and offering concern. Minshue reached the returning men and her voice rose to an agonizing wail. It was Skipping Rock they were dragging along, and he was covered in blood. His friends had not come home unharmed, either. One could hardly see through blood that seeped from a gaping wound along his hairline and dried in a crackling, brown rivulet across one eye. The other had one arm tied close to his body, apparently broken, and struggled to hold Skipping Rock around his waist with his other. As soon as men from the village reached the tired, bloody trio, all three fell into waiting arms and were carried to their respective homes. Mothers cried. Dogs barked. Children became unearthly quiet as they followed.

Minshue gathered water from a pot hanging over the outside fire before entering the house. As soon as the Indian men laid Skipping Rock on his cot, they single-filed outside, out of the way, and Minshue rushed inside.

Lizzie and Ginger gathered Beth and told her to call her dogs. They quietly slipped through the Indian crowd and stood respectfully out of the way. When they knew more about what happened, they'd get Bulger and return to check on the hurt men.

Minshue knelt beside her son and soaked a cloth in the hot water. She washed blood from his prostrate body. She hadn't heard him utter a sound since he had been carried into the village; not even a soft moan. She wiped and rinsed until the water in her bowl turned red and she hurried to refill it with clean water to finish washing her son. All the while, she choked with muffled sobs and her shoulders shook as streams of tears ran down her face and dripped onto her breast.

As she rinsed away the blood, she saw that he had taken a beating. There were bruises, some already turning yellowish green around the edges. Thankfully she found no broken bones, but she was afraid there was internal bruising; maybe a worse fate. A shadow passed over her face and she looked up to see the village medicine man standing in the doorway. She moved aside to let him minister her boy.

The doctor moved his hands gently over Skipping Rock. He turned him and examined his back and felt through his hair. Ever so gently, he massaged Skipping Rock's arms and chest, rubbed his neck, and finally dripped water into his mouth. "I will be back shortly," he said to Minshue. "Keep him wrapped and give him sips of water until I return."

He was back before Minshue could refill her water bowl, carrying a pouch of medicinal supplies. "Bring in boiling water and pour over these leaves," he instructed. Minshue scurried to obey. When the water had cooled and turned to a light green color, the medicine man lifted Skipping Rock's head and poured the warm liquid down his throat. Skipping Rock sputtered, but swallowed the bitters. "Give him a cup of this every hour throughout the day and until sunrise," the doctor ordered and handed the bag of medicine to Minshue.

"Bring the clean cloth strips from my basket," the man charged.

Minshue reached for the medicine man's large woven bag and pulled it open. She reached inside and lifted a handful of neatly folded linen and handed it to the doctor.

"Watch," he commanded. "You will need to change these tomorrow. I might not be available to return to do this." He gently placed one end of the linen on Skipping Rock's chest and began winding the cloth tightly around his body. Skipping Rock moaned each time the doctor lifted him to continue wrapping around his back. Finally, "There. That is all I can do. I will return to check on him as soon as I can," the doctor said, sitting back on his heels and viewing Skipping Rock with a long face.

Minshue looked at Skipping Rock and realized he looked much better.

"What of the other boys?" she asked, looking up.

The medicine man gathered his breath and let it out in a rush. "They will be fine. Only a broken arm for one and a scalp wound on the other. Both are doing well." He looked again at Skipping Rock and rose. "From what I gather, Skipping Rock was the speaker. He led his group to the Muscogee, it was indeed the Panther Clan, and noticed two of our village's horses tethered near their fires. When he asked for the horse's return, one of the Muscogees refused. Skipping Rock asked again, and again he was turned down. When Skipping Rock moved to untie the animals, the Muscogee attacked."

The doctor shifted his feet and finished the account. "It was no fair fight. There were about fifteen Muscogee and three of ours. They were lucky to return home alive. When the Muscogee finished with them, they threw them out from their circle of fire and taunted them halfway home. I am afraid there will be more bloodshed to come," he said with a mournful whisper.

Minshue thanked the doctor and followed him outside. She stood, arms across her chest, watching as he slowly moved to another house and entered there. When she turned to go inside, she noticed Warm DayRah huddled in a tiny wad, leaning against the wall next to the door. Her face was lined with tracks of tears and her eyes were red from crying. Her playful mouth was puckered in a tight line and she hic-upped so hard her whole body jerked. Minshue reached and grabbed her little girl and Warm DayRah's small arms wrapped around Minshue's neck so tightly she could hardly breathe. What had she been thinking? She hadn't been thinking! All the while, her baby girl sat outside, listening to her mother's whimpering sobs and to the soft splash of water dripping into a bowl; afraid of what it meant not hearing Skipping Rock make any sound. Minshue's heart broke a second time that afternoon. "Don't cry, my baby," she crooned. "Don't cry. Skipping Rock is resting. His breath is better. He will be all right; together we will care for him." She carried her second child inside and through the door. Together they would tend Skipping Rock. Together they would sit through the night and wait for the morning's sunrise.

≈

While Skipping Rock and his two friends lay helpless in their beds being tended by their mothers, another group of men were ready to seek justice. Creeks were well-known for their quick tempers and willingness to attack—and attack hard.

Several young braves were adamant to form a search party and seek out the enemy band. Koatohee, the Tribal chief, gathered everyone together in the Council House in the center of the village and tried to calm them.

"I have spoken to the grandmothers. We are in agreement. We have too much to lose if we act rashly," he said. "We've lost most of our land already to the U.S. government. If we attack the Panther Clan, we will be asking for retaliation from the Muscogee Family—and rightly so. Listen, my brothers, we are safe and prosperous here. We get along with our neighboring Creek Brothers as well as our white neighbors. Think! Think! If more warring occurs, the government will step in and take what we have here. We must stay alert and be ready at all times to protect our homes. But we must NOT become hunters of man, killers, or seek revenge. Revenge will come, and come mightily, for those who are in the wrong. We cannot go back to our old ways; time has come for us to bend a little. We must follow more peaceful ways." He looked around the group of young men, sorry that their way of life was quickly coming to an end.

The young men slowly, ruefully realized Koatohee spoke

with good judgment; it was true, his words. They were angry and bitter; ready to revenge their friends, but they were also wise enough to know when truth and common sense were spoken. They agreed, reluctantly, to go back to their homes and work for peace in their village. They may have lost a battle, but they saved a war.

TWENTY-TWO

Lizzie, Ginger, and Beth stood mutely near the open window on the side of Warm DayRah's house. The three girls heard only whispered conversations concerning Skipping Rock's condition. Outside, Lizzie reached for Beth's hand and squeezed it tightly while inside Minshue and the doctor ministered to Skipping Rock. Lizzie strained to hear his voice, but none came; only those of Minshue and the doctor. She breathed a deep breath of relief when she heard the doctor's words as he left and Minshue's comforting words to her daughter.

"Come on," Lizzie urged. "We need to get back home and tell Bulger and Miss Claudie about this. Maybe there's something they can do to help."

Slowly they slipped, single file, along the edge of the village to the path in the edge of the woods leading home. All the while they walked the short trail, they were obsessed with private thoughts. Even Jack and Bell were silent, walking one on each side of Beth, their master. Every half-dozen steps, the dogs lifted their heads and gazed soulfully at Beth, sensing that something unusual, something clouded with threat, had happened. When the silent trio finally reached the edge of the garden; home at last; Beth and her dogs started running. Her chest throbbed with sobs and her feet hardly got her to the house quickly enough. As she turned the corner of the barn and rushed into the yard, she saw Eli.

After finishing work in the garden, Eli planned to go to the village, eager to see Skipping Rock. His friend had seemed withdrawn the last time he'd visited, still Eli had missed his company.

He went inside to Bulger and Miss Claudie, "Got the garden clean," he announced, and gobbled down two cold buttered biscuits filled with white sugar and drained a glass of milk. "I'll meet up with the girls and visit in the village a while myself," he'd told Miss Claudie. Then giving her a quick peck on the cheek, he was out the door, headed for the trail.

As he passed the smokehouse and headed for the barn, Beth rounded the corner. Eli sensed at once that the girls had seen something very upsetting: The two grown ones were pale and frightened; Beth scared out of her wits. He opened his arms and Beth fairly flew into them. He held her tightly and lifted her off the ground. She held his neck in a death-grip and he felt her body suddenly wracked in sobs. The dogs sat on the ground in front of them and watched silently.

"Oh, Eli," Lizzie whimpered, "Skipping Rock is hurt, and two of his friends, too."

Eli's grip on Beth tightened. "Hurry, get in the house and tell us about it."

Together they rushed inside. Eli placed Beth in Bulger's rocking chair and Miss Claudie moved to gather her in her lap and gently rock, crooning soft assurances and holding her tightly. Eli joined the girls and Bulger at the kitchen table. Lizzie and Ginger told about their frightening morning.

"That don't beat all," Bulger said, shaking his head after hearing their story. "I knew them Muscogee Panther Clan was no good. They're a shame to their folks, all right. You girls had better stay close by the house from now on." He rose and removed his rifle from over the mantle. "Eli, I want you to carry this with you when you're out. Don't shoot unless you have to, but shoot if you must." He crossed the floor and handed the gun to Eli.

Eli's face was ashen. "I remember Mamma worrying about Indians here. It was one of her 'what ifs'. Remember, Lizzie, she had a list of 'what ifs' and one of them was 'what if the Indians aren't friendly?" He took the rifle and laid it carefully on the table.

Lizzie nodded, remembering the time of planning with Papa and Mamma. Mamma's worry had come true. Not from the local tribes, but from those further south; those who shouldn't be here at all.

"Time will tell," Bulger continued. "Most likely the hoodlums will lay low a while and hope their lickin' Skipping Rock and his buddies will keep folks away." He knitted his brows and rubbed his chin. "They ain't all that strong, though. If you say there was a bunch of them and they jumped Skipping Rock and two more, seems they're more cowards than brave. One thing for sure, they ain't got the brains to know when to back off—even when offered a peace offering. They ain't brave, but a careless, arrogant bunch of Indians and that can mean trouble for all of us around here." He stood and banged his hand on the table, making Miss Claudie jump and Beth peek around to see what was happening. "Well," he said, hooking his thumbs through his overall galluses, "they may have just stepped into the wrong stall in the barn!"

Eli grinned, and Lizzie and Ginger sat back in relief. Bulger had, in his own way, given them assurance that in spite of trouble and threats, they were in a safe place and all was going to be just fine.

"Let's get this show on the road," Bulger said as he reached his long arms out to Beth. She laughed and he lifted her into the air. "Miss Claudie, how about making a batch of fresh bread and we'll take it to Minshue and Skipping Rock. Bet he will feel better after eating your good bread."

"Already got it rising," Miss Claudie replied. Lizzie and Beth helped Miss Claudie bake three loaves while Eli kept Ginger company sitting on the porch steps. Bulger contemplated every situation he could think of concerning his friends in the village and the plundering bunch of bandits. His thoughts were interrupted only when he noticed the glow coming from Eli's cheeks and the soft chuckles from Ginger as they sat, shoulders touching.

Two loaves of bread were wrapped while still warm, and

placed in one of Bulger's hand-woven oak baskets. Together they returned, rifle in hand, to Minshue's village to share it and, for Bulger, to gather information he needed to help keep the Muscogee bandits in check.

As they entered the village, they noticed quietness prevalent throughout the square. A few children's heads peeped outdoors, and dogs gave a howl to warn their owners of visitors' arrival. Beth led Bulger and Miss Claudie to Minshue's home. Miss Claudie called out softly and Minshue immediately ushered them inside. Beth ran to Warm DayRah and handed her the basket of nourishing bread. Warm DayRah's smile seemed to bring a little more light into the room.

"How's the boy?" Bulger asked Minshue.

She gestured to a low cot settled neatly near the far wall. "See for yourself. He is badly beaten, but the doctor has brought medicines to ease his pain. He has never faced such a beating; both of the body and of the spirit." She seemed to shrink standing before them. She wrung her hands and tears seeped into her eyes. "I hope he will be able to overcome this. His heart is so good. His wish was that he could persuade the Muscogee brothers to return home. To find another way to provide for themselves. He wished for them to make their parents proud and contribute to their family—not steal from and hurt others."

Bulger quietly moved and knelt beside Skipping Rock. He noticed Skipping Rock's breathing: shallow but steady. He realized, too, how this trial might affect Skipping Rock. He did have a huge heart. One that was filled with goodness and fairness and a desire for everyone to work, prosper, and reap benefits from being a good neighbor. "Miss Minshue, would'ja object to me praying over ya son?" he turned and asked.

Sunrise

To another faith by the same Spirit; to another the gifts of healing by the same Spirit.
1 Corinthians 12: 9

Minshue simply, quietly moved her head from side to side.

"With your blessing, I will ask God to bless your son and your house." He bowed his head and placed one of his old, calloused hands on Skipping Rock's forehead and the other on his chest. He began. "Our Dear Heavenly Father, Loving God. We gather here to ask your healing blessings on this young man, Skipping Rock. He ventured on a mission of your own: to show others love and understanding, to encourage them to fill their lives with honest work and sharing love. Faith, Dear Father, is what ya ask of us. He has shown faith in his attempt to face an adversary and hoped they would follow. He demonstrated his faith with works. He has done what many of us have failed to do: honor our faith with works. He is suffering, Dear Lord, for deeds he has done for good. Give him strength, Father, and bless him and his family. Allow him to grow strong again and to remain steady in his beliefs that good will overcome evil. He has shown integrity, been a true leader, and has reaped only suffering. Take away his pain, we ask, and bring those who've harmed him to a true understanding of the love he has offered. We ask all this in the name of your blessed son, Jesus Christ. We believe ya will touch this young man, heal him, and restore him. Amen."

Tears were flowing down Minshue's face and the tracks shone in the reflecting light from the fire. Miss Claudie went to her and held her, shedding her own tears. The children sat or stood motionless, letting the Holy Spirit move through the house with its healing power: healing and strength for Skipping Rock, for Warm DayRah's fears, Minshue's worries, and peaceful understanding for Bulger's family. Each one felt the Spirit move in his or her way: a stillness in the heart; a tingling of skin; a breaking out of goosebumps, or feeling a sudden wisp of cool breeze.

Bulger stood and Miss Claudie stepped back from Minshue. Beth instinctively went to Lizzie and grasped her hand. Bulger nodded to Minshue.

"*Donadogohv?*" she whispered. The promise of another meeting; let's meet again.

Bulger's face relayed all Minshue needed in assurance of any help she needed. He softly touched her shoulder as he passed, and his family quietly followed him through the door of their friends' home.

The moon rose before they reached their house. They had a quick supper and Eli moved his cot to the dogtrot. He wished everyone a goodnight, but the special goodnight wish was bidden to Ginger. His first dreams were of her as he slept, wrapped in Miss Claudie's warm quilt.

The new day broke warm and sunny. Sunrise came early and everyone carried on as usual—harboring uneasy concerns of Panther Clan attacks carefully tucked in the back of their minds. Bulger, having fears of danger high on his mental list, hitched the mules and headed for town early to seek out more news, and hopefully join forces with neighbors and townspeople to work out a united protection plan.

"Time to get things done for Sunday," Miss Claudie said after Bulger left. She tried to pull her treadle sewing machine from her bedroom onto the dogtrot. "I think I can get Beth an Easter dress made today if I can get this thing out where the light is better." She struggled with the heavy machine. Eli noticed and scurried over to help.

"Where do you want this?" he asked.

Miss Claudie put her hands on her hips and nodded toward the eastern side of the dogtrot where the sun was beaming in. "Over there," she said, pointing to the sunlit edge of the 'trot.

Eli had the sewing machine and a hardy chair set up quick as Bossie could swish a fly off her side with her tail. Miss Claudie disappeared to her bedroom and emerged holding lovely material wrapped in brown paper that she'd purchased earlier at Jones's store. She crossed the dogtrot and into the kitchen where she laid the package on the table.

Eli followed. "Miss Claudie, I think I'll go back to the village and check on Skipping Rock. Then back to my place before dark. I'll take the rifle and be careful." He leaned to kiss her on her cheek, noticing her familiar tears of concern puddled in her eyes. "Don't worry, now. I'll see ya'll sometime Saturday morning." He lifted her head and looked into her loving eyes. "Don't worry, Miss Claudie. Everything's gone be all right." He turned and lifted Beth. "See you Saturday, Little Bit," he said and gave her a big hug before letting her go. He tipped his hat to Lizzie with a grin and walked to Ginger. Lizzie and Miss Claudie tried to be invisible but kept one eye on the couple. Both felt their hearts fill to bursting when they witnessed Eli's arm gliding around Ginger's waist and she leaned closer to him. And after a quick hug, Eli and Ginger parted and Eli was out the door.

"Come on over here, Beth," Miss Claudie mumbled, quickly turning to untie the package on the table. She reached and wiped her eyes as she pulled away the last string. "I need to get some measurements and get this dress ready for meetin' Sunday. And I gotta get my things ready to start cooking." She straightened. "Need to check on the garden, too, come to think of it." She shook her head. "My, my, my. Time's flyin' by. Come on, girl. Lots to get done and not much time to do it."

Beth jumped up and let her dolls fall with a plop to the floor. "A new dress? For Sunday?" she asked, her face shining.

Miss Claudie instructed her to stand on a stool and proceeded to mark off measurements for the dress pattern. "I saw this real cute thing in the catalog at the store. I think I can make you one like it—close to it anyhow." The next ten minutes were spent silently. Beth holding out her arms, turning this way and that, and Miss Claudie wetting the tip of her pencil on her tongue and making marks on the brown wrapping paper.

Lizzie went to Ginger and held her hand. As Ginger looked away from Eli's fading form and into Lizzie's eyes, both girls burst into wide grins. "I know," Lizzie leaned and whispered in Ginger's ear. And Ginger squeezed Lizzie's hand tightly as they walked onto the porch and into the morning sunshine.

"And I know," Ginger replied. "Jimmy will be coming to Eli's on Saturday and they'll be joining us late and spend the night so they'll be ready for church on Sunday morning!" she beamed.

Lizzie's heart skipped a beat. She grasped Ginger's hand in both of hers and laughed out loud. Together they skipped across the yard and climbed the fence to perch there where they talked and planned wonderful girl secrets.

"Now don't get too far off," Miss Claudie cautioned Beth. "I'll need ya to fit to my pattern when I get it cut. Then ya can plunder with your dogs a while, but don't leave the kitchen," she warned. Beth jumped down from the stool and Miss Claudie gave her a loving swat on her behind and sent her to play. As Miss Claudie pored over the brown paper, snipping and cutting, Beth, Patty, and Dolly had their own conversation discussing new dresses for Sunday meeting and the baptizing that followed.

Miss Claudie cut the paper and Beth hopped back onto the stool a dozen times before Miss Claudie was happy with her pattern. "All right, I think I got it now," she said with a satisfied look, holding half dozen brown paper pattern pieces. "Ya can go on."

Beth carefully put her dolls to bed and called the dogs. "Come on Jack and Bell," she called. The dogs came running through the kitchen door from the dogtrot where they'd been sunning on the warm boards. "Let's go check on the biddies!"

Miss Claudie watched as they bounded out the door and left it to shut with a bang. She spread Beth's dress material carefully on the table and pinned the new pattern down. With careful cutting and making her scissors sing, she had the dress cut in a few minutes. Carrying her bundle to the sewing machine waiting in the sunlight, she began working on Beth's new Easter dress.

Concentrating only on pedaling her machine and keeping her stitches straight, Miss Claudie forgot about dinner and preparing supper. Thankfully, her brood ate leftovers for dinner and Lizzie and Ginger proved competent in the cooking department and a good, hot meal was waiting for Bulger when he returned from town.

Just as the sun dipped low over the tree line west of the house, Miss Claudie clipped the last threads from Beth's dress. "Finished but for the hem," she muttered, holding up her masterpiece. She folded the dress and shut her sewing machine. Bulger had finished putting away the wagon and feeding the animals when he saw Miss Claudie struggling with the heavy sewing machine, trying to drag it back to its place in their bedroom.

"Here, woman," he laughed. "Let me give you a hand. You look like one of our laying hens after that tornado passed through." He moved the machine effortlessly through the doorway and settled it in place before Miss Claudie could smooth back her untidy hair. She held the new dress over her arm and quietly slipped it under the pillow on Lizzie's bed. Then together, she and Bulger joined the girls at the supper table.

Bulger said grace and everyone plowed in.

"Make any progress in town?" Lizzie asked through a mouthful of cornbread.

"Some," Bulger replied. "Men are gone take turns patrolling the area, then report if anything or anybody shows up and we'll take it from there."

Miss Claudie nodded. "Sounds good. Guess that's all we can do until something really does happen. That Panther Clan is smart, though. I just hope ya'll won't have to get together and hunt them down; hope they'll just finish up their thieving and get on out."

The girls looked up, and Bulger reassured them. "It'll all turn out fine." Pointing his fork toward the boiled potatoes, he huffed, "Pass them 'taters, Little Bit. They're sure fine eatin' tonight."

After the table was cleared and Bulger had a trail of fragrant smoke curling from his pipe, Miss Claudie called Beth back to her stool. "Take off your dress, Bulger won't look, will ya?" she asked as she grinned and shot Bulger a warning look. Beth turned and Miss Claudie unbuttoned the line of buttons down the back of Beth's dress and pulled it over her head. "Fetch me that dress under your pillow on the bed, Lizzie," she said.

Lizzie pulled the pillow off the bed and held up the dress. "Oh, Miss Claudie, it's beautiful!" she gasped. Quickly she handed it to Miss Claudie who pulled the dress over Beth's head. Beth was so stricken with the beauty of it, she was speechless.

Lizzie laughed. "Can you believe it? Beth can't say a word!"

Beth smoothed the front of her dress as Miss Claudie fastened the last button and tied a neat bow behind. "Now all I gotta do is mark the hem," she said. As she reached for the pincushion, she glanced as Beth, standing on the stool in her new dress. *The little girl only makes the dress more beautiful,* she thought.

Hem marked, Bulger set off to bed and girls got in bed. An extra lamp lit so she could see, Miss Claudie worked late, hemming Beth's dress in the softness of the evening. Long after the girls' whispers had ceased and Miss Claudie heard the soft breaths of her three girls, her needle and thread wove in and out of the lovely fabric. She smiled and hummed 'Amazing Grace' quietly as the fire in the hearth burned down and the wick in the lamp began to flicker. At last, the dress was finished. Miss Claudie shook it out so heartily that loose treads flew and unwanted wrinkles smoothed. She held it out at arm's length and looked at it in the lamplight. She smiled a faint, satisfied smile and quietly slipped across the room to hang Beth's new Easter dress on the peg Bulger had just set in—precisely for the dress. She tip-toed across the room and picked up the lamp, banked the fire in the fireplace, blew the girls a goodnight kiss, and quietly closed the door on her way out to her own bed.

TWENTY-THREE

Saturday was filled with lively chatter, laughter, the banging of pots and pans, and Lizzie's and Ginger's frequent trips to the door to look for Eli and Jimmy. Miss Claudie and Bulger worked, grinning and humming happy tunes as they watched the girls. Beth was oblivious to everything and stayed in the yard playing with her pair of dogs.

Suddenly, Jack and Bell lifted their noses to the air and their tails arched in a beautiful curve over their backs. They threw back their heads and bawled the loudest 'A-A-w-w-ooooo', the boys were headed in! Sure enough, before the dogs could take a second breath to cry out their ear-splitting welcome, Eli and Jimmy reached the yard and trotted right on in, each carrying a huge bouquet. Both were loaded with arms full of colorful wildflowers they'd picked along the trail. Lizzie and Ginger grabbed each other's hands and lightly jumped up and down before rushing to meet their matches. Beth stood with her little fists propped firmly on her hips, one foot tapping the clean ground, watching Lizzie and Ginger receive their beautiful flowers and demanded, "Well, where's mine?" Quickly the girls pulled out sprigs of blooms and made a third bouquet for Beth, making her frowning lips turn into a smile. "Come on," she said, "let's get our flowers in water and then we can play!"

"Well, we can put the flowers in water, but I don't think we'll be able to play with you today, Beth," Lizzie said, throwing a careful eye to Jimmy. "I think we have to see to other plans this afternoon. Maybe we can come up with a game or two after supper." And the two couples led the way toward the house.

Beth followed, mumbling to Jack and Bell. "Well, I never!" She rearranged her flowers and bounced after her brother and sister. "Don't you worry," she said to her dogs, "we'll have more fun without them anyway."

After the flowers were standing in crocks---one the table and one on the cupboard shelf, Bulger and Miss Claudie found chores to keep themselves busy. Beth forgot all about her planned playtime with the couples and contentedly followed her dogs in their searches and investigations, and the couples wandered out of earshot.

Knowing it was inappropriate for two 'sweethearts' to be alone without chaperons, the four meandered together through the edge of the garden and to the joining wood's edge. Finding themselves in the cool shade of huge trees, Lizzie and Jimmy sat on the mossy ground with their backs against the huge tree's trunk and were almost alone. Ginger and Eli walked slowly along a deer trail, still in sight, but out of hearing range. Ginger glanced back, saw the resting pair, and smiled. She let her hand fall to her side and Eli quickly reached and held it tightly. They, too, found a comfortable spot to rest, and sat huddled together, laughing and talking nonstop.

Lizzie found herself without words. She was nervous and felt ever so shy. Her tongue felt thick and fuzzy and her mind couldn't stop its fleeting thoughts; all of which seemed too silly to utter. Jimmy, too, was shy. They sat for a few minutes, Lizzie busy tucking the hem of her dress under her feet and Jimmy breaking a twig into minuscule bits and letting them fall to the forest floor.

They both spoke at once and immediately flushed with embarrassment. "You first," urged Lizzie.

Jimmy blushed and picked at a ladybug crawling over the moss near his boot. "I guess I just wanted to say how glad I am to be here," he stammered.

"I'm glad you're here, too," Lizzie agreed.

Jimmy laughed. "You know, when I first saw you on the wagon train I could hardly keep myself away." He dropped his head. "You probably guessed that I used the kids as an excuse to be close to you." He looked up. "When I found out about your Pa and Ma, I was so afraid I'd lost you, too. I couldn't believe you'd stayed here and not tried to get back to Hooverville after the accident." He took her hand. "I know I won't be able to visit very often, but I have a book," he removed his hand from hers and reached into his coat pocket. "I have this little daybook and I'll write in it every day. I can get to town and give it to Cullie and he can pass it on to Eli for me. Then Eli can get it to you on Sundays. If you will, you can write back to me and I'll pick it up from Cullie the next week." He seemed embarrassed once more. "I'm not that good a writer, but at least this way, I can still talk to you." He leaned his back on the tree next to Lizzie's. "I don't think I can get away from my place very often, I got so much to do with the house and all…"

"I know," Lizzie responded. "I think the daybook is a great idea. Sometimes people can write more than they can say in person, anyway."

Jimmy's heart swelled to its limit. He might not be able to see and talk to Lizzie as he wanted to, but with the daybook, at least they'd be able to stay in touch.

"Tell me about your teaching," he urged, hoping to keep the words flowing.

Lizzie perked up immediately. "I got my letter from the Board of Education and can take my test as soon as school is out and I can meet with Miss Myline and the judge. Finding time for all of this is the problem. I hope it will be before summer session so I'll get the test results sooner. I'm so nervous, already. I try not to think about it, but really do want to get it over with."

"Too bad Miss Myline is here for a while, I wish she'd get married and you'd have a chance to teach."

"Oh, that's okay," Lizzie said. "I can still teach in the village." She sighed, "But it would be good to get to teach in town with in a real schoolhouse with a board, books, and all."

"Yeah," Jimmy agreed. He grinned, "Married women have to stay home and keep house," he teased. "Just the single girls can teach."

Lizzie balled her fist and whopped him on the shoulder. "Well, I'm a single girl who'll have her teaching license before long and I just might fill some good teaching shoes!"

Jimmy laughed and Lizzie wondered: could he be tossing out a marriage hint? She gazed into his eyes and gave his hand an extra squeeze.

The look Lizzie gave Jimmy at that moment made his head swim and he felt his blood rush to his ears. He held her hand tighter and they sat underneath the tree, quietly in its shadows, simply relishing being together.

≈

Eli and Ginger seemed to have an endless supply of words. Eli laughed as he recalled his disbelief when he realized who that good-looking girl really was that got off the stage. Ginger swatted his arm as he told her about how he described her to Cullie: kind of plain, just a girl.

"We *have* known each other most of our lives," Ginger admitted. "But after you left, time just flew. I couldn't wait to visit and Lizzie's letters were always filled with so much— sounding so good. She made me so impatient to get here, and I did want to make a good impression," she grinned.

"Oh, that you did, M'Lady," Eli returned, bending at his waist and pretending to tip an imaginary cap. He leaned his back against the trunk of the pine tree and breathed in the deep woody scent. "It's so good to be here with you." He looked deeply into her eyes and added, "And I hope you'll never leave."

Ginger's heart stopped beating and she gulped for air. "Oh, Eli, you know, even when I was a little girl, you were my hero. I've always wanted to be close to you; closer that you've ever imagined of being with me," she added, dropping her eyes.

Eli grinned and lifted her chin so that her eyes met his. "I never knew you existed before, that's for sure. You were always that little kid Lizzie ran around with. But you've changed and got all grown up. Would it be too soon to ask if I can write your father and ask if he'll allow us to marry? Will you stay on here and marry me? I'll have my place set up right in a couple of months, and have my crops in, and with Bulger's and Miss Claudie's help, we could set up housekeeping near the time to get the corn gathered and my other things finished."

Ginger's hands had grown cold and her lips numb. She finally got her eyes to focus and found her voice. "Oh yes, Eli, yes!" She reached her arms around his neck as his arms found her. Their first kiss sent fireworks spinning and the ground shook beneath them.

When they parted, Ginger, bursting with happiness, jumped up and pulled Eli's arms, urging him to stand. "We've got to go tell Lizzie and Jimmy!" she giggled.

"Now?" Eli asked dolefully. "Why we gotta go now?" he pulled her hands down gently, urging her to sit again.

"Now!" Ginger insisted, letting his hands go and twirling around, scattering pine needles as she did.

Eli moaned and groaned as he rose and dusted himself off. "We were having such a great time here," he mumbled. Ginger laughed loudly and grabbed his hand and pulled him along the path toward the tree where Lizzie and Jimmy sat.

Jimmy heard the couple before he saw them. He and Lizzie stood and walked around the tree into the deer trail to meet Eli and Ginger.

Lizzie looked at Jimmy questioningly. "What in the world is going on?" she asked.

"Dunno," Jimmy remarked, feeling a little alarm. "They sure seem to be coming in a hurry." Suddenly his fingers tightened on hers. "You don't think the Indians. . ."

Lizzie paled at the threat of a Muscogee attack; here so close to their house. Then she heard Ginger's laughter and peered harder down the lane at the pair. Ginger was in the lead and seemed to be dragging Eli behind. He was clomping along with a goofy grin spread across his face. "I don't think it's Indians," she uttered. "But something's sure going on."

Jimmy held to Lizzie's hand as Ginger and Eli slowed to a stop in front of them. Ginger's face was flushed and Eli still had the goofy look.

"Guess what!" Ginger gushed.

"What!" Lizzie demanded.

"Eli and I are getting married! Just as soon as we get news from home that it's okay and Eli gets his place in order. Maybe August or September," Ginger said, grasping Eli's arm with both her hands and pumping it up and down making his shoulders jump. Then, out of words, they simply stood there like two squirrels waiting for the last acorn to fall from the tree.

Lizzie and Jimmy watched and listened, speechless, staring and not knowing what to say. Finally Jimmy stood and stuck his hand out to Eli, "Congratulations," he offered.

That broke the ice and Lizzie squealed in delight as she jumped up and hugged Ginger. "You're gonna be my sister!" she piped. "Come on! Let's go tell the others!" She linked her arm in Ginger's and they fairly skipped down the path. Jimmy and Eli followed mutely.

When Miss Claudie heard the good news, tears spilled down her cheeks in mighty trails and had to detour around the corners of her upturned, happy mouth. Bulger slapped Eli heartily on the back and they slipped out to the barn where Bulger slyly offered him one of his special drinks: 'the eye of the tiger', kept hidden away in the corner of the barn, well away from Miss Claudie's prying eyes. Beth had Dolly in one hand and Patty in the other, swinging them around while Jack and Bell danced and yelped with the excitement. Finally the mirth died down and everyone found regular breaths. Miss Claudie beamed and Lizzie could see wheels turning in her head, rolling out plans for the wedding.

Bulger prayed an extra special prayer that night at the supper table. One for thanks, and love, and joy that they'd all felt, and for its continuance. Unknown to Lizzie, during the blessing, Jimmy lifted his eyes and gazed lovingly into her face. His heart was happy, yet heavy. He so wished he could offer the same promise of marriage to her, but as he closed his eyes and bowed his head; he knew he had a long way to go before he could ask Bulger for her hand. His heart would burst with sorrow if he proved to be unable to provide for her; or worse, if she found someone else before he could make her his own.

TWENTY-FOUR

Sunday morning broke in splendor. All was quiet in the house. Miss Claudie let her family sleep while she milked the cows, fed the animals, gathered eggs, made early breakfast, and had most of the dinner packed before the sun shot its colorful rays across the top of the barn. She looked out the window above the sink as she rinsed the last pot. She was so blessed! Never had she dreamed that Bulger's and her lives would be filled with such wonder, happiness, and love. Bulger broke the spell as he stomped around on the dogtrot to wake Eli and Jimmy who were sleeping there. Then he came barreling through the kitchen door like a mamma bear yowling after her runaway cub. The girls jumped straight out of bed and ran for their clothes.

"Ah hah!" Bulger shouted and dashed across the kitchen floor and grabbed Miss Claudie around her waist and kissed her neck.

"Bulger! The children!" she admonished somewhat weakly. Seems everyone woke in a good mood.

Breakfast was hurried. Coffee and milk poured. Blessing said. Biscuits and gravy sopped, and plates gathered and in the sink. Miss Claudie washed while the girls finished wiping everything down and the menfolk drew water from the well and tidied themselves up for church. By the time the mules were hitched and dinner baskets packed away under the seat, the womenfolk had gotten themselves all gussied up and trotted out to the wagon.

Bulger tossed on extra hay for the mules and Eli and

Ginger settled in one pile while Lizzie and Jimmy sat in another. Beth and Miss Claudie sat up front on the wagon seat with Bulger. He jiggled the reins and the wagon jerked forward. He didn't stop until they reached the churchyard at Caney Head.

Preacher Arp was already there, along with many from town. Sheriff Bledsoe and his family along with the Hulls, the Tuggles, Huckebas, Wiggins, Jones, Gores, as well as others in the community. A family had recently arrived from South Carolina, the South's, and proved to be wonderful neighbors. Mr. South proved to be apt at veterinary services and had 'the gift' of helping and healing animals. Glovis, his wife, was an animal lover, too, and together they took in any stray or hurt animal and nursed it back to health.

Eli looked for Cullie and led Ginger along. It was obvious when Eli broke his good news to him, Cullie's face broke out in a smile and he grabbed Eli in a bear hug. Thankfully, he only gave Ginger a tip of his hat.

As Miss Claudie made her way inside and Bulger hitched the mules and spread hay for them to munch on, more families came in: the Folds, Pollards, Marshalls, Barkers, Busseys, Cravens, Walls, and Maxwells. Miss Myline arrived with the Caswells, and the Crockett family brought the Sheppards along with them. More new folks arrived, and Bulger learned they were the Todds. The menfolk's reputation as reliable carpenters spread rapidly through the community. There were others coming in, Bulger noted, and he decided he'd better get inside and find a seat or he might not get one. He was surprised to see Mr. Denney and his family attending the little church. The reputation of the little church; good folks and good Sunday dinners had spread, and the congregation was growing week by week.

Preacher Arp opened service with prayer and Mr. Demmie lead the congregation in two rousing songs. Mr. Gore and Mr. Pollard passed the collection plate and Preacher Arp opened up. He started slow and soft. The sermon gained momentum and his voice rang through the rafters and the Bible almost jumped off the podium when he banged his fist beside it—just to make a point. Just as Eli's heart slowed down from the shock of the preacher's noise, he heard the doors of the church creak. In spite of Bulger's warning, in spite of being considered rude, he *had* to look over his shoulder and peek at who was coming in so late. His breath caught in his throat and he punched his elbow in Bulger's side. Bulger looked at Eli and turned too. His face softened; it was one of the few times Eli had ever seen Bulger touched to the point of tears, he saw Bulger's old eyes become watery as he gazed to the church doors. Slowly, one-by-one, others turned.

There, standing in the doorway with morning's light shining so brightly behind them that they seemed like ghostly silhouettes, stood Minshue, Skipping Rock, and Warm DayRah.

Eli slowly rose from his place. He stretched out his arm and motioned for his friend to join him. On the far side, in the women's group, Miss Claudie stood and welcomed Minshue and Warm DayRah to the women's' pew. Slowly the Indians moved down the aisles and sat.

Preacher Arp was obviously moved. He resumed his message with more fervor. He spoke of the cross, reminded the congregation of the suffering Jesus endured on Good Friday. "And why is it Good Friday when such an atrocity occurred? Jesus, our Lord and Savior, falsely accused, falsely condemned, and killed in such a horrible way. *Good* Friday---how can that be?" He paused and let the question hang in the air.

There was a hush throughout the congregation. Often wondered that myself, Eli thought.

Preacher Arp continued. His gaze swept over each and every one.

"Good Friday. Without that day, Jesus would never have risen!" His voice rose as he stretched himself to his tiptoes and lifted his arm and pointed toward heaven. "To rise again! For you!" and he whipped his arm down and pointed to a young man. "And for you!" He turned on his toes and pointed to a woman. "And for me!" He added as he pointed to himself. "Without Good Friday, without his loving goodness; sacrificial goodness, we, the Gentiles, the sinners, could never be with our risen Savior Jesus Christ when we die and our spirits RISE with him! Oh, how good of him to give himself for us." He paused and continued. "This Easter morning, as the sun rises over the horizon, God's S-O-N has risen already, rolled the stone away and is with God his Father in Heaven everlasting! In his goodness he has provided for us to rise with him. Easter is here; He is risen!"

As twelve o'clock closed in and Preacher Arp's voice wound down, the service came to a close. When Mr. Demmie led the closing hymn and Preacher Arp opened the doors to the church for membership or prayer, one of the Jones girls and a young Levens boy came forward. The congregation gasped in unison as Skipping Rock, Minshue, and Warm DayRah moved to the front of the church with the others. Preacher Arp was, for once, without words.

"May I speak?" Minshue asked.

Preacher Arp nodded and gestured for her to continue.

"My son was beaten and thrown away by his tormentors, left half dead. His two friends, also hurt badly, managed to drag themselves back to our village. There, we prayed. Our medicine man came and ministered to my son and did all he knew to do. Late in the afternoon, Mr. Bulger and his family came with food. More importantly, they came sharing their faith of their Lord Jesus Christ. Mr. Bulger prayed over my son. He had been unable to utter or hear a word since he was beaten, but he heard the words of Mr. Bulger speaking of a loving Father, healing and forgiving Savior, a loving Jesus." She paused. "I heard them too, and they spoke to our hearts. As we stood there in the quietness of my home, this Holy Spirit came. We felt Him. I know He is real for He healed my son." She gestured to Skipping Rock who nodded his head in agreement. "We have come today because we long to be a part of your God's family. We have heard your songs and felt His Spirit. We know He is real and wish to become a part of His kingdom."

Mrs. McIntosh, a saint if there ever was one, raised her hands and shouted praise. Mr. Barker, tears streaming down his face and his chin quivering, raised his hands and slowly began clapping. Then Bulger, and others, until each person in the church building was clapping and crying; welcoming their new brothers and sisters into the fold. There would be a good crowd gathering down in Mr. Dessaw's bottoms for the baptizing in the afternoon.

Dinner was spread and lots of good food vanished. After a

short rest, Preacher Arp invited everyone who wished to, to drive down the road to Mr. Dessaw Walls's bottoms where the baptizing would take place. Miss Claudie noticed hay spread in several wagons, and mammas had spread quilts over the soft layer and many small children napped on them. She climbed in beside Bulger and made sure all her brood was accounted for, and Bulger headed for the bottoms. Minshue and her son and daughter were included and rode along as part of the family.

Wagons pulled up side-by-side along the creek bank. People slowly moved to the sandy area where the water glided by. Willows dipped their new leafy branches in the cool water, soft cattails burst out along the banks, and countless ferns, bushes, and white, yellow, and pink wildflowers nodded their heads in the soft breeze. It was a day made for baptizing!

Mr. Demmie gathered everyone together and led two verses of 'Shall We Gather at the River' and then Preacher Arp waded up to his thighs out into the creek. He read from the scriptures.

One by one, candidates for baptism joined him in the water. One by one, they were immersed into the cold creek as sinners and broke forth new brothers and sisters in Christ; their sins washed away. Preacher Arp admonished each new church member, as well as witnesses standing on the creekbank, to remember their salvation; never forget the day they were saved and the day they allowed themselves to be washed clean by the blood of Jesus Christ. And to revel in the fact that their church family had grown, and to love and uphold one another. The Word of God spread and with the adoption of their Indian family, it would spread even further. "Praise and Praise be to God," he shouted in closing.

Mr. Demmie ended the warm, filling service with a rounding full verse singing of 'Amazing Grace', and the baptizing came to an end. Only it hadn't ended—it was carried home in the hearts of each and every person to be shared and shared again. The loving story told, and in many cases, written down so the memory could be cherished for years after.

TWENTY-FIVE

April rushed out, frost gone with May, and days were well into June. Corn shot up; growing fast, as were beans, pumpkins, tomatoes, and squash in the garden.

One warm, early summer day when Eli and Bulger were plowing, or 'layin' by' the corn plants---now knee high---Miss Claudie called Lizzie and Ginger to the well and handed them a bucket filled with fresh, cool well water.

"Let me get this lid on tight," she said as she pushed the wooden top down. "Now, that's good. That'll keep the water cool and it won't slosh out. Take this water to the lower field for Eli and Bulger," she said. "I know they're dying of thirst right 'bout now." Then she added, "Here," reaching for the tin dipper hanging from a nail on the porch. "Don't forget the dipper!"

The girls held the bucket carefully between them and made their way to the cornfield. Waving the dipper carelessly, Lizzy said, "Eli brought Jimmy's daybook with him this morning when he came to hitch up Little Man," and looked up with a sly grin.

"What did he say?" Ginger asked, but then felt intrusive. "Sorry, it's none of my business," she dropped her head.

"No mind," Lizzie answered. "He's still working on his house. With little to no help, he didn't get many trees felled before the sap rose and only finished one room. I'm worried he'll never get things ready." She stepped lighter, trying to hide her disappointment from Ginger. She saw through Lizzie's mask easily.

"Don't worry so much. He's doing everything he can and I know he loves you. He'll ask you to marry him as soon as he can."

Lizzie slowed. "I know." She turned to Ginger. "I do know. It's hard to write back and sound happy and content when I'm really impatient and anxious." She sighed.

"Well, write! He needs to know you're there for him no matter what," Ginger prodded.

Lizzie could only nod a slight knowing nod. It seemed a quick, short time and they heard Bulger's irritated shout, "I said 'gee' Moses. Quit that 'haw' stepping and get these rows straight, dang-burned mule!"

They reached the field where Eli was plowing Little Man, and in a nearby row, Bulger followed along behind Moses. Both mules were hot and tired, but trudged on with their heads dipping low. The men always plowed until nearly dark. They needed to finish up as quickly as possible to get the last fertilizer out and early weeds killed, and besides, it was cooler plowing in late afternoon. Bulger saw the girls coming before Eli did.

The men pulled up and stopped at the end of the nearest row. "Whew!" Bulger said to Lizzie as he took the bucket. He carefully pried off the lid. Lizzie handed him the dipper and he filled it and lifted it to his lips and gulped greedily. Water filled his mouth and leaked down his chin and onto his sweaty shirt. When he'd downed about three dippers full, he passed it to Eli and wiped his lips with the back of his sleeve. "That's mighty good, girls," he grinned.

Following closely, Eli gulped his cool water. Ginger watched as his Adam's apple bobbed up and down with each swig. He, too, used his sleeve to wipe his mouth.

They replaced the lid on the bucket and sat it on the ground, balancing the dipper on top. "Tell Miss Claudie 'thank you', and we're mighty thankful to you too, for bringing that water out. We'll finish it off before coming in for supper and bring the bucket back. Maybe Miss Claudie will fill it up again tomorrow and ya'll can bring us some more," he said with a wink.

Lizzie watched as Ginger and Eli gazed lovingly at each other. She wished it was Jimmy plowing so she could bring him some cool, refreshing water.

For I was thirsty and you gave me drink.
Matthew 25: 35

The girls talked continuously of the up-coming wedding on the way home.

Lizzie, naturally, was to be the maid of honor. Ginger chose light blue for Lizzie's dress, and Beth would wear a matching color as flower girl. Jimmy would be best man, and Cullie stand in as second. There was no way Eli could not include Cullie, as much help has he'd been getting everything ready.

Ginger's family graciously gave permission for her to marry; they had known the family from Hooverville and loved Eli as a son already. Eli's house would be finished in time so that Ginger's parents and little brother could stay there during the week-long preparation and wedding festivities. They were bringing along her dowry: pots and pans, dishes, bedding and other linens, and a little cash. Miss Claudie had been putting aside special items of her choosing, too. Then there would be a 'pounding' given by the women of the church. Each woman would give a pound of this or a pound of that to the newlyweds and their pantry and larder would be filled when they set up house. Sometimes, the younger ladies would give the new bride a shower. It was mostly a time of fun and gossiping about who would be the next to walk down the aisle, or who was keen on whom. The older ladies, moms and aunts, stayed away from this occasion, and the young singles and newly wedded girls loved this fun time together.

Time passed swiftly, rushing to the wedding date, and Ginger was getting more nervous with each passing day.

They reached the yard and found Beth goading the dogs to find a crow's nest. Sonny had told her if she caught a young bird and slit its tongue, she could teach it to talk. She was on fire to prove him right. Unfortunately, Jack and Bell weren't crow dogs, so her progress was extremely slow. They heard Beth, "All right, now, Jack. You're the oldest. You can do this," she shook her finger in front of his nose. "Find that crow nest. It'll have babies in it now. I need one bad!" But all Jack did was stretch out his tongue and lick her finger. "Ugh!" she grunted.

Lizzie and Ginger hurried up to 'save' the dogs. "Come on in, now, Beth. It's too hot and the dogs are tired. You can get Sonny to come over one day when it's cooler and ya'll go find a crow for yourselves."

"I guess you're right," Beth pouted. "But I sure want one of them talking crows!"

Chuckling, the girls led Beth to the porch. Lizzie drew fresh water and poured some in the bucket on the porch shelf and the rest in the shallow washpan. They took turns rinsing their faces before going inside to help Miss Claudie with all the never-ending summer chores. Ginger watched as Lizzie slipped Jimmy's daybook from her apron pocket and grabbed a pencil off the cupboard before stealing quietly out the kitchen door to the dogtrot to write a message for Eli to carry back.

The still summer afternoon's solitude was cut sharply by Jack's and Bell's loud barks. They ran to the end of the trail beside the yard and stretched their necks and stiffened their legs, pointed their noses high, whipped their tails to a point, and bawled. They'd let up long enough to get another good breath, and let go again. Bell danced back and forth, glancing back at Beth the whole time.

Inside, Miss Claudie heard the ruckus. "What in the world?" she asked.

She and Lizzie hurried to the porch and watched Beth run across the yard.

"Ya'll hush!" she demanded.

The dogs paid her no attention at all.

From down the road came a creaking and clanking sound. The dogs howled themselves almost into a frenzy; they'd never heard such noise before.

Miss Claudie put one hand on the porch rail and told Lizzie to get inside and gather all the scissors and knives and check the pots for worn places. Lizzie, puzzled, lifted her eyebrows toward Ginger and turned and went inside to complete her chore. "Bring'em out here when ya get'em all together," she shouted.

Lizzie had barely gotten an old pot with handles on each side filled with knives and scissors when she heard a loud, "Howdy, there, Miss Claudie. How's ya doin' now?"

Miss Claudie stepped off the steps and reached up to greet a grizzled, bearded man with long gray hair pulled back in a ponytail, sitting on the seat of the oddest wagon Lizzie had ever seen. It had tall wheels on the back and smaller ones on front. The wagon was pulled by a sway-backed Appaloosa that looked like the next day would be his last. The wagon was covered with a red-painted, box-like covering with colorful writing on each side:

Tinkering for Everything
New pots, Sharpenings, Tools,
and
Tonic for the Body

There were all sorts of different sized pots and pans hanging from the wagon. That's what the odd, strange sound was they'd heard: pots and pans hitting and clanging together as the wagon jostled along. It had set the dogs off to no end!

She and Ginger didn't move from the porch. They watched in fascination.

Jack and Bell quieted down and circled the wagon; sniffing and poking around the wheels, under the wagon, and even tried to climb aboard through the canvas flap in the back. Beth stayed busy trying to contain her dogs, but soon gave up and joined Miss Claudie.

"We're doin' just fine, Sammy," Miss Claudie grinned. "Come on down and get some cold milk and a piece of pie. Lizzie here's got everything ready for ya to go to work."

Sammy nimbly jumped to the ground and tethered his gangly-looking horse to the porch post. "I won't turn down anything ya got, Miss Claudie," he replied with a twinkle in his bright blue eyes. He stepped up on the porch and moved to the washpan and washed his face and hands. Miss Claudie handed him the porch towel. He slicked back his hair and rubbed the towel across his face, dried his hands, and hung the towel back on its nail. "Presentable, now?" he asked.

Miss Claudie grinned and ushered him to the kitchen.

Lizzie and Ginger stared after the odd-looking couple walking arm-in-arm inside the house, and Beth followed wordlessly.

"Run to the barn and get a bucket of sweet feed for Sammy's horse, then get in here and set out a plate for Sammy. We don't get his company more than twice a year," Miss Claudie called over her shoulder to Lizzie and Beth.

The girls moved their feet and got the horse his feed and rushed inside for a plate and mug. Beth brought in the milk from the spring house, and they got settled around the table. Miss Claudie made introductions and explained why the girls were living with Bulger and her.

"Sorry 'bout ya folks," he said. Quickly changing the subject, he added, "Looks like ya'll had some bad wind a little while ago," Sammy said between mouthfuls.

"Sure did," Miss Claudie said, dusting an invisible crumb from the table. "We were mighty feared, but weren't hit bad. Lost the top off the porch, but the boys got things fixed in an afternoon. Many 'round here weren't so lucky. The Hulls lost their barn and house and are staying in town with Sheriff and Mrs. Bledsoe." She paused, and then went on. "I hear their place is almost back to where they can move back. The Rogers cut lumber brought in by neighbors and the community raised the house and barn in less than a month. All they need now is getting some furniture." She straightened. "We women 'round are planning a shower for them and they should be able to get along fine."

"This sure is a close place 'round here, ever'body heppin' ever'body out an' all," Sammy said as he finished his pie and milk. "Now I'll git on outside and git your things sharpened. Look around the wagon and see if there's anything there ya need. Pick it off and bring it on up to the porch where I'm workin' and we'll balance out what ya owe."

He stood and went outside to his wagon and brought out a heavy whit and lugged it to the shade of the porch. He pumped a wooden pedal and the rock wheel began to turn. He held the edges of knives and scissors close; chiseling each one and checking the sharpness with his thumb. He continued until there was a fine, razor-sharp edge on each tool.

Miss Claudie and Beth circled the wagon, inspecting one pot then another. Finally Miss Claudie found two she liked and brought them to the porch beside Sammy.

He placed the sharp scissors and knives in Miss Claudie's old pot and picked up the two new ones.

"How much do I owe ya, Sammy?" she asked.

He rubbed his chin and hummed a low, "Hummm. Let's see. Eight knives and four pair scissors, and two pots. That'll be fifteen cents."

Miss Claudie went back inside and checked her 'honey jar' on the shelf in the wall cabinet and retrieved the money.

"Here ya go," she said, dropping the coins in Sammy's hand. He'd already loaded his large whit stone and was ready to head out.

From around the corner of the barn, Bulger and Eli trudged along. Bulger perked up at the sight of the tinker's wagon, eager to hear any news that Sammy had heard along his travels.

"Hey, Sammy!" Bulger called.

Sammy peeked around his wagon and hollered a greeting in return.

"Good to see ya. Looks like I almost missed ya comin' 'round this time," Bulger said as he reached for a friendly handshake. "This here's Eli, my boy," he said proudly

"Yep, almost loaded up," Sammy said, gripping Bulger's hand firmly. Then shook Eli's. "Good to meet ya. Ya need anything I got?"

"Let me check," Bulger answered. "Walk with me out to the barn and I'll see what I might take off your hands. Eli, you can check out the wagon."

Sammy and Bulger walked into the cool, hay-scented hall in the barn. "Wanted to hear if ya'd heard any news as you got around, 'specially 'bout them Muscogees. Didn't want to worry the women none if ya'd anything to say 'bout that."

Sammy stuck his hands deep in his back pants pockets, kicked at the loose hay, and looked down. "Hate to say it, but I have." He looked Bulger in the face. "They hit hard south of here. Burned out one family close to Bowdon and even hit a small group of Creeks. Stole most of their horses and some food." He shrugged his shoulders. "Thought they were laying low and might go on back home, but looks like they're getting bolder. Ya might want to lock everything up tight around here and keep a keen eye."

Bulger's body sagged. "I sure hate to hear that," he said in a worried tone. "I'll do all I can to keep our folks safe; all I can do." He pushed his shoulders back. "Well, we'll just handle whatever comes. God be with us, we'll get by." He looked toward his tools hanging along the barn walls. "Now let's see if I need replacing any of this. Maybe I can use something off your wagon." They made their way to the wagon in the yard. As they walked, Sammy suddenly chuckled.

"What 'ya thinkin' now?" Bulger asked.

"Jus' thinkin' 'bout them Muscogees," he said. "You know the Craven's Trading Post up near Carroll County line?" he asked.

Bulger nodded.

"Well, the other day when I was by there, I heard a story on Miss Missouri, Mr. Craven's wife. Seems some old dodger had been in lookin' 'round and seen one of the Craven girls. All of'em are good-lookers, ya know, and that old man said somethin' outta' the way to her. After he left, she told Miss Missouri 'bout it and ya know she didn't take good to that a'tall." He grinned and sniffed, then went on. "Next time the ole' man come in, Miss Missouri reached under the counter there and pulled out her pistol and stuck it in his face. She let him know real quick to get out'a her store and not set foot in it agin'. She didn't 'preciate him makin' snide remarks to her girls." He chuckled again. "Lord knows, that man gone have to walk an extra mile to git his supplies." He paused and added with a nod of his head. "Them Muscogees better circle 'round her store for sure."

Bulger slapped Sammy on the back. "Yep, them Panthers better sidestep around that store. They don't wanna be dealin' none with Miss Missouri!"

Back at the wagon, Sammy handed Bulger a brand new saw and two new hammer-heads. "That'll be 'bout forty cents," he said.

"Here 'ya are," Bulger said as he handed over the coins and shouldered the saw.

"Glad ya told me 'bout the Hulls, Miss Claudie, save me a trip that'a way. Good they're getting back home soon." Sammy tipped his hat as he climbed aboard his wagon. "Hope to see ya'll 'fore long," he called as he cracked his whip across the poor-looking horse's back. He raised his hand good-bye and pointed the horse to the road.

Jack and Bell gave Sammy and his Appaloosa a hearty going-away; shepherding them along with a full, loud, boisterous hullabaloo.

TWENTY-SIX

In the schoolhouse at the edge of town after the planting was done and the crops grew and matured in the ground, summer session was coming to an end. Miss Myline wound down the last few weeks of the year—to be finished at last! Children were needed at home during spring times of hard farming chores, and if school was in session, too bad. Their folks kept them home and the young'uns helped with the work. The trustees adjusted the school year to fit the needs of working farming families so there was no school during crop time: planting, plowing, and harvesting. Summer was a time of school, too!

Back in school in late June and most of July, windows were opened wide and children folded accordion-made paper fans to force a tiny breeze across their sweaty faces. Afternoons were atrocious! Hot, still, and nothing stirring but the July Fly's wings singing their monotonous song. Little dust devils danced in the schoolyard, and even Miss Myline longed for the end of the hot school days.

The only fun during school for this time of year was celebrating the 4th of July. On the fourth, no matter what day it fell on during the week; Friday in case it fell on a Saturday or Sunday, the whole school celebrated. Miss Myline got out the flutes, drums, and tambourines and the children made music. They paraded around the schoolhouse and made red, white, and blue flags. They wrote patriotic poems and learned about the founding fathers in a play-act. Older boys played their parts and one special girl dressed as Betsy Ross and sewed on a pretend flag. It was a day of jubilation that culminated a week of fun studies. The celebrations continued on week-ends with a town picnic followed by fireworks at dusk. The heat and humidity of July was worth the trouble, for a few days, anyway.

When lessons couldn't possibly last any longer, August finally arrived and the school year was over! Miss Myline was finished with the last hot summer months. Those completing their eighth grade lessons would be graduated—their 'book learning' over. Only two students were expected to be 'repeaters' and that fact was known only to their families since all the students studied the same subjects in the same classroom.

With school out; the year ended and another wouldn't start until late fall after the corn was gathered and other crops in. Children were finally free to stay home; but it was no vacation. Crops ripened and needed tending. Many families grew cotton and it needed picking. All the field crops needed a good weeding, either from the hoe or plow. The late vegetables were planted and the gardens needed continuous care. Everyone helped gathering summer and fall crops.

Still, before having to work in the fields, children had a few days to swim in the creek, make mud pies in their playhouses, and find doodlebug holes under the cool porches and 'doodle' the bugs out. During their 'off days' children played in cool shades in the edge of the woods and made huts or rode horses made from tall, thin saplings bent and held so their tops touched the ground. When a child straddled the bend of the tree and made the sapling's top limbs dip low enough, he could tip his toes to the ground and push off hard and 'ride' high--only to dip down and push off the ground and 'gallop away' again. Many were 'bucked' from their sapling stallions and hit the ground with a hard smack.

One lazy, hot July afternoon, Bulger suggested they walk through Mr. Dessaw's bottoms and down to the swimming hole. The only problem was the girls and boys weren't allowed to 'bathe' together in the same hole, and the girls had no one to oversee them while they played a little way downstream. Miss Claudie finally gave in to go along. She'd sit on the bank and 'dip in her toes'. She knew how cold creek water was---even in the summertime. She gathered towels and a bar of soap to carry along, "Might as well get these young'uns a good bath while we're down there," she grumbled to herself.

They didn't bother with the wagon, but walked single-file down the road to the cut-off where they passed through some cotton growing in the bottoms. They heard the singing of water over rocks before they came to the creek banks.

The girls, in their lightest dresses and long undies, ran downstream. The boys kept to the deeper part of the creek where a large flat rock stuck out over the swimming hole. Eli and Cullie brought Sonny along to play in the water. Bulger even joined in getting wet, but soon stretched out in the warm white sand to dry and enjoy the sun. The sand was hot and he soon moved into the cool shade of a large 'hicker' nut tree. He watched the boys taking turns diving off the rock. Both Cullie and Eli wore an old pair of cut-off overalls and no shirt and swam in their unlikely outfit. Sonny came bare-chested, wearing cut-off jeans. Since Sonny hadn't learned to swim, Cullie let him hold to the back straps of his overalls, and as Cullie swam around and dove under the water, Sonny held tight and had the time of his life.

Eli climbed to the rock and dove in. Bulger watched as Cullie followed behind, ready to have a quick race across the creek. Cullie's grin gave his plan away: when Eli surfaced for air, he'd jump off the rock and 'cannon ball', splashing Eli and probably sending a spray of water clear up to Bulger's resting place. Bulger sat straighter. He noticed Sonny climbing right behind Cullie. Before he knew what was happening, Eli surfaced, Cullie jumped, and Sonny reached for Cullie's overall galluses—only Cullie was already in mid-air! Sonny's face changed from a happy grin to one of sheer terror. He began tumbling into the deep swimming hole, and Cullie and Eli were completely unaware!

When Sonny hit the water, the boys never noticed. They were horsing around, splashing each other and racing to the far bank.

Sonny went under and didn't come up.

Bulger rose from his shade and started running toward the water.

Sonny flailed his arms and kicked his legs underwater, but didn't rise. He opened his eyes, but saw only murky, sandy creek water, and it seemed the current was moving in slow motion--at a snail's pace. He saw bits of sandy mica floating around in the water, and sunlight danced and sparkled through the water as it hit the floating, swirling sand. 'Beautiful,' his mind whispered.

Neither Cullie nor Eli was anywhere close to realizing what was happening.

Sonny kicked harder but had no idea which way was up. He was bobbing halfway between the sandy bottom and the airy surface, alone and running out of air. All he could do was thrash his arms and kick his legs. He felt his foot touch something, but it was probably his imagination—just a fluttering touch and gone.

He closed his eyes and held his breath. His lungs burned and his chest felt as if it was bursting. Well, he thought, guess it's not true that if you throw someone in deep water they'll learn to swim. If he wasn't hurting so much he'd almost laugh. Funny what goes through your mind when you're drowning; his mind raced.

Suddenly, he felt arms reaching around his middle and he was lifted up and out of the water. As soon as he head broke free, he threw his head back and began gulping air. His arms and legs were limp, and he sucked in the precious air until his throat burned, hanging motionless in Cullie's arms. Then the dirty water he'd swallowed came up—mouthfuls of it, and he started to cry body-wracking sobs. He was a 'big boy', but he didn't care if he cried. He'd almost drowned and couldn't stop the tears. He looked up and saw Bulger running across the sandy beach toward him. Bulger reached out his arms and Sonny grabbed him. He wrapped his legs around Bulger's middle and his arms around his neck and buried his face in his shoulder and let the sobs surge through his body.

Eli splashed his way across the creek to Bulger, and Cullie stood white-faced and shocked. He looked at Eli and explained, "I was swimmin' over to you and thought I felt something hit me. Then I looked on the rock and didn't see Sonny." He sucked in his breath and went on, "I dove and began sweeping my arms around and found him." He turned back to Bulger who was still holding Sonny tightly.

"Go get the girls," Bulger said, "it's time we got goin'."

Cullie wasted no time trotting down the bank and calling to Miss Claudie. She waved back and knowing something was wrong, quickly gathered the girls, snatched up the soap, and handed out dry towels.

She and the girls couldn't believe the story as Eli told what happened. Beth was especially shaken. "Ya all right, Sonny?" she asked, tilting her head back and reaching to touch Sonny's back. He was still latched on to Bulger.

Sonny pulled his face away from Bulger's comforting shoulder and looked down at Beth. He took a deep breath and mumbled, "Yeah," and untangled his legs from Bulger's waist. When he had his feet on the ground, he felt embarrassment fill him from his head to his toes. He hitched up his jeans and looked at Cullie. "Next time, I'll let you know I'm comin'," he said. Then he grinned, sniffed, and wiped his arm across his nose.

Cullie reached over and swiped his hand across Sonny's head and raked his hair to one side. "Yeah, you do that," he said with a thankful grin of his own.

Miss Claudie, quiet the whole time, naturally teary-eyed, wrapped a towel around Sonny's shoulders. "Let's get back to the house. We'll get some tea cakes and milk. Then Cullie can get you on back home."

The boys took the lead, followed by the girls. Bulger put his arm around Miss Claudie's shoulders and gave her a squeeze. Then they followed the children along the trail home.

TWENTY-SEVEN

Picking corn and cotton, preserving beans and other garden vegetables, making jellies, and drying apples and peaches were jobs that had to be done as the fruits and vegetables matured. Not jobs that could be put off---put it off and it was too late; summer vegetables quickly became too ripe, rot set in, or insects and animals would get them first.

During the last of July when the green beans ripened, blackberries did too. Miss Claudie presented each of the girls small tin buckets, and one larger for holding their combined pickins', for berries for jelly-making. Huckleberries ripened around the same time on low bushes growing where fires had formerly cleaned wooded areas, and Miss Claudie knew first-hand how redbugs loved all the berry bushes. Before the outing, she wrapped the girls' wrists and ankles with strips of cloth torn from flour sacks. Then dipped a final cloth strip in kerosene and tied it over the others. She'd made sure the girls wore long sleeved blouses and kept their stockings snug in their shoes. Then she sent them out with their buckets; armed for repelling redbugs.

They started out early, as soon as the dew dried, and walked to the blackberry patches that grew mainly along the fence line. Blackberries ripened on thorny, winding vines, and their hands and fingers ended up stained and scratched at the end of the day's picking.

All the while they picked, the older girls kept a watchful eye for snakes and bears. They kept a keen ear out, too, for sounds of a more dangerous animal: that Panther Clan, the renegade

Muscogees. Thankfully, the bunch of rioters had been relatively quiet since Skipping Rock's meeting: a few chickens here; some eggs there. The land was plentiful and the Indians hunted wild food easily, Lizzie supposed. Still, she heeded Bulger's warning and was ready to run for home if need be.

They picked until their buckets were filled and emptied them into the larger bucket until it was full. Lizzie noticed that Beth hardly ever filled her small bucket, and her mouth and tongue had a marked dark blue stain.

They laughed as they made their way back through the pasture. Lizzie and Ginger held a handle on each side of the big bucket, swinging it between them, and carried the lighter buckets in their other hand. Beth continued sampling berries from her bucket as she walked; and finally they were home.

Miss Claudie met them and was proud of their day's pickings. "Girl," she said to Beth. "You'd better hope you don't have a case of the runs tonight after eatin' all them fresh berries." She shook her head, "but won't doubt it a bit if ya do."

She had a fire under the washpot going in the back yard, and a second galvanized tub filled with hot water standing behind a couple of quilts hanging on the clothesline. She'd sprinkled a small handful of lye in the hot wash water. As soon as the girls shed their outer clothes and stood in their slips, Miss Claudie gathered the clothing and tossed it in the boiling washpot. She instructed the girls to take turns scrubbing and soaping up in the washtub. Lizzie dunked Beth in first and together she and Ginger scrubbed her until she turned pink. They quickly toweled her off and sent her to the house to get dressed. Ginger shed her underclothes and Miss Claudie added them to the washpot. Ginger took her turn bathing, and last of all Lizzie sat in the now cool water and scrubbed. She made sure she scrubbed a second time in the 'redbug places': under her arms, along the banding line across her chest, and behind her knees. She had first-hand knowledge of redbugs and was familiar with their favorite hiding places.

Soon the girls were scrubbed free of redbugs and any clinging to their clothing were long boiled dead. Miss Claudie removed the quilts, folded them, and hung the girls' clean clothes on the line to dry.

Her day's work wasn't finished. Inside, Lizzie and Ginger washed the berries and had them ready to cook when Miss Claudie came in carrying a very large pot. "We gotta' boil these berries 'til the seeds are free and get'em strained out," she instructed. She poured the berries and barely enough water to come to a boil, and let them simmer. She placed a large piece of clean flour sack across the mouth of another large pot and secured the cloth with wooden clothes pins. Gently she poured the cooked berries onto the cloth and the dark purple juice drained through. Finally Miss Claudie unpegged the cloth and gathered the edges into her hand and squeezed out the last drops of juice. "Get that measuring cup, there, Lizzie," she instructed. She measured sugar and berries, two cups sugar for one cup berries, and set the pot on the stove. The air was already heavy from July's heat, and the room heated even more, but the smell was heavenly!

The girls, except for Beth who played outside in the shade, hardly knew they'd enjoyed a fresh bath as they worked in the hot kitchen, sweat pouring off them.

Miss Claudie kept a close eye on the pot; stirring often to be sure her mixture didn't stick and scorch.

Lizzie and Ginger washed and rinsed squatty crockery, and a few odd-shaped bottles--- so few were to be had---mainly scavenged whiskey and vinegar bottles, and put them in a large pot of water to heat. Each container had to be sterilized and prepared for the jelly when it finally cooked down. Miss Claudie hadn't told the girls, but her batches of jelly would be shared between her household and Eli's and Ginger's. Hopefully, she mused, between Lizzie's and Jimmy's too.

When Miss Claudie dipped her spoon into the mixture and held it over a glass of cool water and watched as a drop fell, it made a ball. It was ready! "Come on, girls, we got to ladle this jelly. The faster we get it done, the faster we can get outside and cool off. I'm hotter in here than a hen in a wool blanket!"

Miss Claudie moved the pot to the table. She ladled, Lizzie wiped the mouth of each bottle and crock clean, and Ginger dripped melted wax carefully over the top of each, then wrapped clean, white circles cut from flour sacks over the tops and tied them tightly. It was a beautiful sight when the containers were filled and the pots washed up. Sitting on the table were two dozen dark bottles filled with sweet jelly. What a winter treat to go with warm buttered biscuits! The only downside: huckleberries were coming soon.

Sure enough, all during that night just as Miss Claudie expected, Beth moaned and groaned with a tummy ache. Nine times Lizzie had to get up and hold the lamp high along the path to the outhouse so Beth wouldn't stub her toe. Then back to bed---only to be kept awake with Beth's tossing and turning. Ginger, too, got little sleep.

The next day was green bean picking day, but Beth was excused. During the cool morning, they pulled their long picksacks over their shoulders and tramped to the garden. Each handful of beans dropped to the bottom of the sack. Soon Miss Claudie's sack was dragging along the ground. After an hour, the half-dozen long rows of beans were cleaned, and the women returned to the house. Lizzie pulled three chairs to the porch while Ginger got a dishpan for each. With their picksacks full of beans on the floor, the women sat and filled their dishpans with fresh beans. They nimbly snapped off the ends and pulled each string away and snapped the beans into short, bite-sized lengths to cook. They tossed the ends to the yard where the chickens ran and chased each other for the green, fresh tidbits. Supper would be good tonight! Green beans cooked down with a hunk of fatback, fresh cornbread, a slice of onion, cool buttermilk, and blackberry jelly. Good enough to 'swaller your tongue,' Bulger would say.

He savored his unusual combination. Miss Claudie saved the light, tasty foam she'd scooped from the top of the jelly and Bulger loved it spread over his fresh beans. The only time he could have his treat was during jelly-making. There was always jelly, but the foam was available only on jelly-making day.

To each his own . . .

Snapping beans for supper was the easy part; the relaxing, cool---as it was--part. Lizzie and Ginger were grateful for the sitting. After they snapped enough to put in the pot to cook for supper, they'd prepare the rest to dry. 'Leather britches' were good eating on those cold winter nights. They'd save 'shelly beans' in flour sacks, too, to boil as wintertime staple.

Lizzie and Ginger missed last night's allotment of sleep thanks to Beth's berry eating. Miss Claudie noticed the girls slowing down, and got the ball rolling by asking Ginger how her wedding plans were coming along. That made the girls' heads snap up!

Ginger was glad to elaborate. She worked faster and faster as she talked more excitedly about the wedding. Her parents would arrive the first week in September, and she and Eli would get married at Caney Head the following Sunday. Eli had sent a letter to his Grandpa in Hooverville, and Grandpa'd responded. He was planning to ride on the stage and come in for the wedding! Ginger laughed as she told how excited Eli had been when he read the news. Her pan of beans almost tumbled off her lap.

Only Lizzie knew how hard it had been for Eli to leave Grandpa; the old man was unable to bear the trip with his family on a long wagon train. The established route along the road in the stage, however rough it was, was one that Grandpa believed he could make. Eli was so happy. He could hardly contain himself. Lizzie understood.

Ginger continued. Eli had been working on a new smokehouse and hoped to fill the salt box with hams and shoulders and hang sausage from the rafters after hog-killing. Not to tell Beth, though, that the meat was from Ole' Crip's pigs.

Cullie had helped with digging the 'containing hole' for the outhouse and building the small shed over it. Mr. Bussey had witched the spot for the well and Skipping Rock, now almost fully recovered from his run-in with the Panther Clan, brought his friends to help as well.

Ginger was on a roll...

She reached for the beans faster as she talked. On she went, slipping beans on a string to hang as fast as she talked. She continued her account.

The men digging the well had hit water and it was a good well. Mr. Rogers had the remaining logs that Eli and Bulger had felled cut into boards and there was more than enough for a small dogtrot and extra bedroom where her parents would stay when they came for the wedding. Cullie, Jimmy, Skipping Rock, a couple of the Huckeba boys, and a couple others whom she didn't know, had come, and with instructions from Bulger and Mr. Todd, raised the dogtrot and extra room in a day. Skipping Rock and his friends had the thatch on by the next nightfall. She caught her breath.

She remembered to include that Eli promised Grandpa a bed in the kitchen where the stove was for his visit. His old bones needed the extra warmth.

Miss Claudie listened with a smile. Every once in a short while, she glanced over to Lizzie and grinned. Lizzie grinned back. Miss Claudie caught the slight sadness in Lizzie's smile. She wished with all her heart that Lizzie and Jimmy could make plans and could tell about her wedding, too.

As Ginger wound down and finished her account of everything that had been planned for the wedding, and not wanting to leave Lizzie out of their conversation, Miss Claudie asked, "Lizzie, now that school is ended, have you heard from the judge about getting together for your teaching test?"

"Just a word from Miss Myline. She says she'll talk with the judge when he gets to town, since she'll probably see him before I will. I've passed the test packet on to her, and she'll send for me. I wish I could do something to be more prepared, but I guess I'm as ready as I'll ever be. Miss Myline said not to worry; she did fine and knows I will."

Miss Claudie smiled and agreed. "I know you'll do just fine. Maybe it won't be long now before you can get together and have this test over with. I do hope we get this wedding over first, though. That will let you breathe a little easier when the time comes for your testing. I know you want a clear head to think about your answers."

"Yes, we're all so busy getting ready for Eli's wedding. I'm almost as excited as Ginger, so maybe taking the test a little later is a good thing."

Miss Claudie and the girls sat quietly, listening to summer bird songs, to Beth and her dogs playing, and to Ole' Crip's babies grunting and rooting at the edge of the yard. The pile of green beans shrank and Miss Claudie rose and got the snapped beans ready for supper.

It was hard, hot work, but such a beautiful sight when

lines of beans were strung and hung along the wall of the dogtrot where it was dry and cool. They'd dry in no time and then be hung along long shelves in the pantry and smokehouse.

Miss Claudie would string peppers, put pinto beans and Whippoorwill peas out to dry, and along with the green beans, hang them in sacks high beside the open ends of the dogtrot. Then when they dried, they'd be moved inside the smokehouse to keep safe. Dried beans were a constant food in the winter, boiled slow over a low heat, long hours simmering with strips of pork belly or streak'o lean until the boiling water thickened to a delicious mush surrounding the tasty beans. Summer work meant filling, satisfying winter meals. Lizzie sighed as she hung the last of the beans. Tomorrow, she grimaced, huckleberries.

TWENTY-EIGHT

Eli visited twice during the last of July. Mainly because he missed Ginger so much, and Jimmy had been by and left his daybook for Lizzie to read. He felt guilty not getting it to her any sooner; he wished he could have left his place and taken off to Bulger's the second Cully came by and left the book with him. It lifted his heart to see the eagerness in Lizzie's face almost as much as it did to see Ginger's when he hopped up the porch steps at Bulger's. He'd had to wait a couple of days for Mr. Bussey to get by to witch the well; then mark the spot so Skipping Rock and his experienced friends could come and dig.

With this visit, as soon as Eli shut the door and Miss Claudie gave him his usual welcome peck on his cheek, he slipped to Lizzie and passed her the book. Lizzie gratefully took the daybook and greedily devoured every word. She smiled at some of Jimmy's spellings and cherished every word-- no matter how it was put together. She read that he was well and hoped she was too. The house was coming along, but he was waiting to sell his crops so he could buy more lumber. He was thankful he had the wagon and his horses. . .

She finished reading, but decided to wait a little while before writing her response; she wanted it to be just right, to say what she wanted to. After finally jotting in two whole pages, she slyly slipped the book back to Eli before he started his trip home. The daybook was wonderful; but how much more so to be able to speak to Jimmy; to look into his eyes; to hear him laugh; and to touch him, she dreamed. Her heart ached, but she forced her lips to smile.

July slipped into August. Miss Claudie remarked to Bulger that it would be nice to have a break from the daily work. All the family worked hard during the busy time of summer, and more work was to come. She decided Lizzie, Eli, and even Beth, could invite some of the young people and go down to the Maxwell's where the creek ran wide and shallow and a grove of young sweet gum trees grew close by and have a picnic. There were flat rocks abounding and the water was just deep enough for skipping rocks and wading barefoot. No deep swimming holes for Sonny to tumble in there! Only one spot further upstream where folks were sometimes baptized, but they'd be well down creek from that place.

"Come'on, Bulger, I'm hotter than a firecracker. Today's gone be a scorcher," she said, wiping her face with the hem of her apron. "I'll pack a basket and we can take the young'uns and some of their friends down to the Maxwell bottoms and they can cool off," Miss Claudie suggested.

Bulger liked the idea, and he sent Lizzie and Ginger to Eli's where they hitched Eli's mule, Little Man, and rode to town to invite their friends.

"Be sure to get Melody and Melinda to come. Maybe Lu and Susan can, too, if it's not too busy at the store," Beth chirped. Then she ran over to Miss Claudie and begged, "Can I invite Warm DayRah?"

Miss Claudie chuckled, "Sure, Little Bit, hurry down the trail and keep Jack and Bell close. Be on the watch for them Indians and ya'll hurry on back so we can get out there to the Maxwell's pasture 'fore dinner."

Beth called her dogs and shot through the yard toward the village. Jack and Bell ran alongside, tongues and ears lolling up and down as they ran.

Bulger helped Miss Claudie pack a generous basket of food and as they stepped on the porch, Eli and the girls, along with a small wagonload of friends, rounded the barn and into the yard. Beth and Warm DayRah followed breathlessly.

"Just in time," Bulger called. "Pull up and we'll get this dinner basket loaded."

With everyone on board, Eli clicked the reins and Little

Man picked up his head and they were away.

The day was bright and sunny, less humid than usual, not as hot as Miss Claudie had predicted, and perfect for a picnic. Bulger lowered himself off the wagon and unlatched the pasture gate, securing it again after Eli pulled the wagon through. The wagon jostled along and they bumped their way through the meadow to the picnic spot.

Miss Claudie spread a quilt near the grove of trees, and Bulger brought the basket. Beth, Warm DayRah, Melody, and Sonny ran ahead and picked up flat rocks as they went. Eli tethered Little Man so he could graze, and he and the older ones broke into couples, removed their shoes and stockings, and waded into the creek. Girls screeched and yelped and pretended to lose their balance so their beaus could catch them. Some of the boys ran and splashed in the water, giving the girls a gentle wet, having a good ole' time. Sonny, wary of water still, waded across but stood safely on the bank and demonstrated the technique of skipping rocks to the younger girls.

Nobody noticed the herd or when the cows' heads rose and their ears perked forward.

Just as Bulger got the quilt straightened and the basket lid open, he heard it: pounding hooves and loud, huffing breaths.

Miss Claudie heard it too, and looked up to see the whole herd of Maxwell cows loping toward them with no intent of stopping.

"Run!" she yelled. "Run to the trees! The cows are comin'!"

Bulger's mouth popped open and he reached for Miss Claudie's arm to pull her up and they hobbled as fast as they could toward the thick growth of young trees.

Sonny, too, heard the cows and struck out for the trees, "Come on!" he yelled to the girls as he ran, splashing and stepping high through the water. "Get to the trees!"

Beth and Warm DayRah dropped their stones and ran, feet barely hitting the ground. Melody, a little stunned at the sight, forced her feet to fly and caught up in a flash. They all headed for the trees as fast as their legs would go.

The older group of folks were shocked when they heard Bulger's yelling and stood flabbergasted as they watched Bulger and Miss Claudie shuffling along to the safety of the grove, and

Sonny and the girls racing through the creek right behind. Hearing the strange sound coming across the pasture, they turned their eyes back to the stampede. Nothing more needed saying. The boys grabbed the girls' hands and the girls grabbed and lifted their skirts and they skedaddled across the smooth, rocky creek for the trees.

"Come on!" Miss Claudie urged as she and Bulger reached the thick grove. "Get in; go as far back and as deep in as ya can. The cows can't get back in here! Come on!"

Sonny got across the clearing first and didn't stop at the tree line. He passed Bulger and found a thicker sapling and stood behind it, motioning for Beth and Warm DayRah. They rushed in and got behind him, squatting and shivering, watching with wide eyes between the sweet gum saplings to see what the wild cows would do.

Eli and his group reached the grove last. They scattered through the trees, limbs slapping their faces and scraping their arms, but they didn't stop until they were safely hidden deep in the trees.

"Shhhh," Miss Claudie admonished, bending her shoulders a peeping around a small tree.

The young folks, breathing heavily, clung to thin, tall saplings and watched the stampeding cows with anticipation: would they stop or not? There were cows, calves, heifers, and the bull. Tails high, tongues flopping, eyes wide. Would they crash through the trees and thrash their heads to drive their sharp horns through them? The sound of the herd was like summertime thunder. Lizzie closed her eyes as the animals reached the creek. They didn't stop. Water flew and rocks tumbled. They kept coming, following an old black cow that seemed to have red fire shooting from her eyes and puffs of smoke curling from her nostrils. There was a loud "humph, humph" pushed from the bovine's throats each time their front feet hit the ground. They were big cows . . .

Miss Claudie held her breath. Each tree in the sweet gum grove sensed danger and curled its leaves tighter; not one stirred in the stillness. The air was heavy and grew to a deathly quiet.

Suddenly, the lead cow turned and slowed. She threw her head from side to side, bucked and grunted, and trotted over to the picnic basket. She turned her big head and eyed the colorful quilt, snorted at the basket, but she wouldn't step on the blanket. All the others stopped and gathered around the quilt, dipping their heads and sniffing it. Some threw back their heads and bellowed a low, deep, chest-vibrating rumble. The big bull backed off and thrust his hoof in the ground and with a mighty push sent dirt flying high over his back and splashing in the creek.

Everyone in the grove watched. No one said a word. It was a wondrous time, there with the cows; almost magical there in the woods. None of them, even Bulger and Miss Claudie, had ever experienced such!

The cows circled, sniffed, and pawed dirt around the quilt, but not one of them would touch it. Finally, after a good ten minutes of examining and poking around, their curiosity filled, the old matriarch-leader moved on. One by one, the others followed. Slowly they crossed the creek and wandered out in the pasture, snipping grass and checking for their calves.

Bulger tentatively moved toward the rocky beach.

"Be careful," Miss Claudie warned.

"I think they're satisfied and won't bother us no more," he quietly said.

"Well, enough's enough," Miss Claudie said as she left the 'security' of her spindly tree and followed Bulger. "We're goin' home," she huffed.

Watching Bulger move into the clearing, Eli motioned for the others to leave the safety of the trees and return to the sloping creek bank. Wordlessly and carefully, they kept an eye on the cows as they quietly, cautiously made their way. Miss Claudie grabbed the basket and quickly folded the quilt. Everybody sensed the need to stay quiet. Bulger looked at Eli, rolled his eyes, and jerked his head toward the wagon. Thankfully, Little Man wasn't concerned about the cows at all. He remained contentedly munching tasty grass growing near the water's edge. Eli hitched him to the wagon. Still eyeing the cows, the young folks tentatively gathered their shoes and stockings and climbed on.

Bulger lifted the basket on the back and Miss Claudie plopped the quilt on the seat, and Eli helped her up where she sat straight-backed and stared forward.

It was a quiet ride most of the way home. Until Sonny started chuckling; then burst out in full-blown chortles. It was catching. Eli looked behind at Lizzie and she covered her mouth with her hand to keep from laughing, but it didn't work. She, too, giggled, then Ginger, and one-by-one, they all caught the giggles. Finally Bulger joined in and Miss Claudie turned to toss him daggers from her eyes, but when her gaze hit Bulger's face, she succumbed and sat there on the wagon seat, laughing and slapping her leg as they bumped along the road.

When they reached the house and Eli pulled Little Man to a stop, everyone piled out. Their sides ached from the good laughs they'd had along the ride.

"Can't let all this food go to waste," Miss Claudie said. "Get that basket, Bulger, and ya'll come on." She held the quilt in the crook of her arm and led the way across the yard to the shade of the huge oak. She shook the quilt out flat and Bulger set the basket down. "Gather 'round, ya'll," she said as she opened the lid of the basket. She placed a huge bowl of fried chicken, bread slices spread with fresh jelly and some with ham, and a caramel cake. "Dig in."

And they did.

As the last of the chicken disappeared and only crumbs were left on the cake plate, Sonny sat back and remarked. "Remind me to NEVER let ya'll take me close to any more water. At. All." And he leaned back against the tree trunk, closed his eyes and tapped his full tummy.

Bulger looked at him and grinned, and Eli shook his head and smiled. Beth balled her fist and knocked Sonny on his shoulder.

"You don't go with us to the creek, and you don't get picnic baskets anymore, either!" she scolded.

Sonny opened his eyes and grinned. "Well, I might go to the creek with you, but you can bet I won't get wet and I'll watch for attacking animals!"

Miss Claudie dipped her chin and shook her head. "These young'uns," she chuckled.

≈

Sunrise

Summer wore on. Bad thunderstorms came and passed, followed by dry, hard hot August air that made puffs of dust rise with each footstep. Katydids cried and grasshoppers sang, and dust devils danced in the dusty yard.

Corn stalks dried and the ears had to be gathered and tossed in corncribs. Bulger and Eli plucked them off cornstalks and tossed them into a pile along the center rows in the field. Lizzie drove the wagon along the rows and guided the mules. As she coaxed them along, Bulger and Eli walked beside, stopping at each pile of corn and tossing the plump ears into the wagon as it passed. When the wagon filled, Bulger took the reins and guided the mules back to the crib where the corn was stored.

Say not ye, there are yet four months, and then cometh harvest? Behold, I say unto you, lift up your eyes, and look on the fields; for they are white already to harvest.
John: 4: 35

In winter, Bulger shucked the corn and fed the shucks and corn to the cows and horses, and tossed some to Ole' Crip. He'd shell some in a bucket for Beth to scatter to the chickens. None of the corn was wasted. The leaves, or fodder, were stripped off and used for animal feed.

Some shelled corn was taken to the gristmill and ground into cornmeal. The ears were fed into a tube where the cob and kernels were rubbed between turning wheels and separated. The cob would drop from one chute and the corn kernels fed down to the grinding stones. As the stones rubbed together, the kernels were ground into meal and skittered out between the rocks through small chiseled grooves. The meal was caught in five or ten pound bags and tied up.

Mr. Gore, from the wagon train, settled nearby and built a gristmill. His brother, Lewis, joined him a short while later and together they ground corn, bagged it, and sold it. Of course, they ground corn for farmers who brought in their own from the fields, too.

The same for cotton. After it was picked, it was taken to the cotton gin where the cotton fibers and cotton seeds were separated. Some of seeds were saved for planting, but most were mixed with grain and roughage for cow and horse feed. The fibers were either pressed into bales and sold or kept and spun into homemade cloth.

Then there were pumpkins and squash, apples, and sometimes peaches. Many of these were peeled and dried for use in pies and puddings.

Miss Claudie and the girls gathered bushels of apples in July and August, peeled them, and sliced them thin. Miss Claudie showed Lizzie how to carefully place them on a square of tin and carry it outside in the sunshine. There the water evaporated and all that was left were strips of dried fruit. Miss Claudie packed it in pottery crocks and large churns, lidded them tightly, and stored them in their back bedroom behind the door. During winter months, Miss Claudie dropped some of the dried strips of fruit in water and soaked them overnight. The next morning she'd add a little sugar and boil everything until it thickened. Wonderful to use for fried pie filling.

Fried apple, peach, sweet potato, and even cocoa—a

rarity—fried pies were a treat! Under Miss Claudie's instruction, Lizzie learned to roll out pie dough into thin rounds about the size of Bulger's favorite saucer. She dipped out a tablespoon of the sweet fruit mush and plopped it in the middle of the dough. Ever so carefully, she picked up one side of the dough and folded it over, making a half-moon shape. To seal the edges, she pressed the tines of a fork along the outside. This made a lovely pattern to finish off the pie. When the lard in the black iron skillet barely sizzled as a drop of water hit it, it was ready for the pies. Gently Miss Claudie slid one pie at a time into the skillet, curved side of the pie matching the curve of the skillet. Slowly, she'd slide in the second filling the skillet, and when one side of a pie reached a golden brown, she'd flip it over and brown the other. Two by two, the pies fried up. She'd scoop the flaky pies onto a plate and keep them in the warming oven while she fried two more. As they browned and she transferred them from the skillet to the plate, she'd stack them two by two, straight sides meeting in the middle. Finally, she'd have a tall stack of warm, flaky pies. She and Lizzie worked long and hard for the treat—for they surely didn't last long once they hit the table!

TWENTY-NINE

Eli's house was finished. Lizzie and Ginger visited twice, with Miss Claudie as chaperone, and together they measured windows and oohed and aahed at the fine stove and Minshue's wonderful woven rug. During a trip to town, Ginger picked out fabric for curtains, tablecloth, and bedspread, and Miss Claudie whipped them up on her sewing machine in no time. Eli helped with the hanging of the window trimmings and then was shooed out of the way while the women finished.

They had the house cleaned and new linens on the bed for Ginger's parents and younger brother, Greyson. They were expected on the coming week's stage. Ginger was beyond excited.

The following Sunday at church, Eli and Ginger were surprised with the pounding that Miss Claudie expected. Mr. Eddie Denney, morning service director, called the service to order, read and explained a short scripture, asked for anyone with a recent birthday or couple with an anniversary to stand and led the congregation singing 'Happy Birthday" or 'Happy Anniversary'.

Preacher Sheets conducted the worship service while Preacher Arp was completing his rounds as the regular Circuit Rider. The church people were glad to have Preacher Sheets, Miss Minnie, and their children close by so weekly worship services could be held. Most of the time the church was filled. Miss Minnie played the piano and her girls, Sara, Dara, and Vara sang lovely special tunes that had most toes tapping and many humming the words along. The Sheets girls added harmony and kept the congregation feeling good.

One particular time, Miss Claudie remembered, Vara played the piano and she and Mavis, Preacher Sheets's daughter, sang a duet. Vara got her words mixed up, but kept on singing and Mavis noticed her flummox. She got tickled. She looked at Vara and giggled, trying to keep up and stay in tune. Vara knew she'd bobbled, but was determined to stay composed and not let Mavis get *her* tickled. Somehow they sang on… Mavis managed to finish, but she did have somewhat a giddy time of it. Vara sat and played and confidently rose and returned to her pew when they concluded. Miss Claudie smiled thinking of the times in church when giggling and laughing was a good thing.

It was right after Sunday's service when the men made themselves scarce for about a half hour, while inside women laughed and gave 'words of advice' to the new bride. Ginger was flooded with food staples, canned goods, and enough lard to carry Eli and her through Christmas. It was so exciting!

The day was saddened only because Lizzie should have been sharing the day as a new bride, too. Lizzie and Jimmy were in love, but love doesn't always provide everything a couple needs for security and happiness.

Lizzie received Jimmy's daybook from Eli that morning when he arrived to join them for church, and she carefully read his entry. She was shaken up, excited, and bursting with happiness when she finished reading. Ginger didn't dream her joy was from reading Jimmy's book: she reckoned Lizzie's happiness came from the delight they shared at the church pounding. She was wrong!

Lizzie could hardly contain herself. What Lizzie didn't know was that Jimmy's house was almost finished and his corn crop was better than he'd expected. He'd be able to keep enough for food and animal feed, seeds, and still sell some to the Gores at the gristmill. He'd asked her to marry him! Right there in the daybook!

She could hardly wait to get home and write one big, simple word: YES. She wished he could have asked her in person, but what a story they could tell their children and grandchildren! Papa proposed to Mamma in a book—and she accepted in a book!

As soon as they arrived home, Lizzie rushed to the cupboard and grabbed a pencil. She opened Jimmy's daybook and covered one page with her three special letters: bold and big and black: Yes!

Beth came wandering up as Lizzie closed the little book. "What'cha got, Lizzie, more words from Jimmy?" she asked.

Lizzie laughed and hugged Beth. "You bet. And if you can keep a secret until tonight, I'll tell you one."

Beth hopped up and down and patted Lizzie's cheeks with both her hands. "Yes, yes, I can keep a secret." She leaned close, her nose almost touching Lizzie's and her little hands reaching and smashing Lizzie's cheeks together. "What is it?" she whispered like a conspirator

"MMMuuummm…mmm." Lizzie mumbled.

"Oh, gotta let you go so you can talk," Beth giggled, and let Lizzie's cheeks fall free.

"Jimmy asked me to marry him and I said 'yes'!" Lizzie whispered back.

Beth clapped her hands together and pressed them against her mouth. "Ohhhhh!" she peeped, feet jiggling.

"Shhhhh, quiet. Let's let Eli and Ginger enjoy their special afternoon before we share our news." And she and Beth walked together, grinning like dogs that treed a 'coon, and handed Jimmy's daybook to Eli. He deftly slid it into his coat pocket and grinned slyly at Lizzy. She trusted him completely not to peek and read their entries. She smiled as she and Beth raced back to the kitchen.

Soon Eli helped Ginger and Miss Claudie onto the wagon. Miss Claudie traveled to Eli's to help put their 'pounds of goods' away. After everything was in the pantry or on a shelf, she slipped outside and pulled herself onto the wagon seat and left the two alone in their new home for a few minutes. She didn't have to wait long. They hurried out, hand in hand, laughing and chatting away.

Eli helped Ginger up and then climbed on himself. Simply being with the happy couple made Miss Claudie's heart sing all the way back to the house.

Eli stayed for supper. When everyone was almost finished,

Lizzie asked Beth if she'd like to share some good news she'd heard that afternoon. Bulger and Miss Claudie suspected something was at hand; Lizzie and Beth had kept stealing secret looks and sniggering all during the meal. Bulger laid down his fork and demanded to know what they knew that he didn't. Beth jumped up and bounced around in her chair, unable to contain her joy.

"Go on, Little Bit, tell us what's got ya so happyfied," he said.

Beth could hardly get the words out as she stuttered, "Lizzie and Jimmy's getting' married!"

A group, "what" echoed through the rafters and bounced off the window panes. Lizzie could hold her joy no longer. "Yes, he doesn't know my answer yet; Eli still has it in his pocket."

Beth, Ginger, and Miss Claudie all rushed up and sped around the table to give Lizzie best wishes.

Eli saw and his heart spilled over, love seeping from Miss Claudie's eyes. She stood and quickly wiped the happy tears away before anyone---so she thought---saw them.

"Well, lord'a mercy," Bulger exclaimed. "Will there be no end to this marryin' around here?" he looked at Beth and asked, "Ya ain't plannin' on getting hitched up with that Sonny boy anytime soon are ya, Little Bit?"

Beth laughed and answered, "Aw, Bulger, you know I'm not. I'm not ever leaving you and Miss Claudie." And with that, she left her sister and moved to the head of the table and grabbed Bulger in a huge hug of his own.

≈

Eli and Grandpa exchanged letters to set the time of Grandpa's arrival, and Eli walked to town to borrow Cullie's wagon and pick up Grandpa at the stage station.

"Your granddaddy gone stay a while after the weddin'?" Cullie asked.

"Probably not," Eli replied. "This is an extra special trip for him; a hard one. I don't think he'd make it at all if it wasn't for me." He gazed upward, thoughts spinning. "I think he'd do most anything for me."

Cullie recognized the look and knew there was an unbreakable bond between Eli and his granddad.

The horse in front of the wagon stomped his foot, making a 'thump' on the hard town's Main Street, breaking Eli's thoughts. "Stage will be here soon. Thanks for the wagon, Cullie. I'll get it back quick as a wink."

Cullie laughed. "Sure thing, Eli. Go on, don't need to be late."

Eli jumped on the wagon and trotted the horse to the stage station at the end of the street and waited for the stage to pull to a stop. He tossed the reins across the front seat and jumped to the sidewalk. Timing just right, he reached the stage door just as the driver jumped down. Eli pulled the door open and there, face to face, he looked into Grandpa's great brown eyes. Grandpa's face broke into a thousand pieces as his wrinkled cheeks crinkled and he grinned from ear-to-ear. Eli reached for Grandpa's hand and helped him clamber down. They embraced in a bear hug, and Eli was surprised when he realized he'd lifted Grandpa's feet plumb off the sidewalk! He quickly put him down.

"Com'on, Grandpa," he said, "I got a wagon and your bed is ready at my place. I can't wait for you to get settled. We'll go right on over to Bulger and Miss Claudie's for supper. I know you'll like'em."

"Just a minute, boy," he said, "Gotta git my package outta' the coach." He ambled back and reached inside the stagecoach and pulled out a small bucket. It was covered with a burlap bag. Something, twigs, probably, propped the bag high.

"What'cha got there, Grandpa?" Eli asked.

"Something for Lizzie," He responded with a sly grin. "Your Uncle Alvin sent this. Aunt Lola worked hard all spring and summer to get these ready. She didn't know then how in the world she'd git'em here to Lizzie, but the Lord made a way."

Eli was filled with curiosity, but didn't try to peek under the burlap. He hurried to the back of the stage and grabbed Grandpa's bag and led the old man to the wagon and put his bag in the back. He helped Grandpa up. Eli raced to the other side and climbed in beside Grandpa and gathered the reins. They were on their way home.

"Sure is pretty country here," Grandpa remarked.

"Yep," Eli agreed.

"Never been this far from home before," Grandpa added.

Eli laughed. "Don't worry, I know you'll have a great time. Man, I am so glad you got to come. Got some more news, too. Lizzie's getting married come Christmas, to a boy we met on the train coming down. He's a worker, all right, and a good man. They'll be living over the Alabama line west of town."

"Well, I'll be," Grandpa said, shaking his head and rubbing his whiskered chin. "Hard for me to think of ya'll chillun old enough to be gettin' married." He turned his head and looked at Eli, worry in his eyes. "She understands that I can't stay for her weddin', don't she Eli?" He turned and faced the road ahead. "I'm more tuckered with this trip than I'd a'thought; don't think I can stay that long and then travel back home during the cold." He drooped low on the seat. "Sure don't want to disappoint that little girl, but I gotta git back soon as I can," he pointed to the bucket in the back. "Mebbe this'll help her not be too disappointed."

"Don't worry, Grandpa," Eli assured. "She knows. We've already decided that this trip will be so full that it will carry over for her, too. We're both really glad you're here now, and appreciate your coming. Look here, we're almost home. My house is just over that hill."

And they continued along the road to Eli's where they unloaded Grandpa's old, worn bag. "Leave the bucket in the wagon," he said. "I'm gone go down and sample some of your well water. He made his way to the well and barely lifted the dipper to his lips when he gazed up to see a tall, bronzed young Creek emerging from the trees.

Grandpa dropped the dipper and stumbled toward Eli's house. Eli was stepping off the bottom step when he noticed Grandpa staggering toward him with a terrified look. Eli had a sudden fright. Was Grandpa having a heart attack? He rushed toward the old man and as he reached him, he heard a hearty call, "*Osiyo!*" coming from the far edge of the yard.

Eli followed the call and saw Skipping Rock coming toward

them. Grandpa was making funny little grunting noises, pointing to Skipping Rock, and his eyes were wide, stuck on the Indian.

Eli returned the greeting, "*Osiyo* to you, too!"

Skipping raised his hand in greeting, "*Dtohitsu?*"

Grandpa almost collapsed.

"Grandpa, don't worry, this is Skipping Rock from across the woods. He and his mother and sister have helped us tremendously since we got here."

Grandpa tried to stand, and mumbled, "Wha'd he say?"

Eli laughed, "He said 'hello' and 'how are you?' You want to answer?"

Embarrassed, Grandpa stood, as best he could after such a scare, and extended his hand. With slow, loud words, he leaned forward and said, "I . am . fine. How . are . you?"

Skipping Rock grasped Grandpa's hand and lightly said, "Nice to meet you, Grandpa, I am Skipping Rock."

Eli laughed. "Grandpa, Skipping rock is fluent in English and has been trying to teach me a few Creek words. He's the best friend a guy could have. He and his sister brought us food when we were stranded on the Chattahoochee. Without him, we might not have made it."

Grandpa took this information in with amazement. He straightened and added, more composed, "A mighty thank ya, son. I appreciate all ya done for my grandchildren."

"I wanted to surprise you, and guess I really did, didn't I? I knew Eli was picking you up today, and came by to say hello, or '*osiyo*'. If I can help in any way, let me know." He turned to leave. "I'll bet Miss Claudie is standing on her head waiting for you to get there. I'll go so you can hurry on." He added, "Come by the village when you can, Mother has some dried venison and wants to share with you."

Eli raised his hand. "I'll do that," he said. "Tell Minshue thank you for me."

Before he left, Skipping Rock added, "Best of luck to you and your woman. My prayers will be with you tomorrow, and I'll see you the end of the week to check on how you're making out." With a grin as wide as a new moon, he turned and jogged into the shadows of the forest while Eli and Grandpa hoisted themselves onto the wagon seat once again.

It was late afternoon when Eli pulled the wagon into Bulger's yard.

Miss Claudie and Bulger stood on the porch and Lizzie and Beth sprinted out to meet Grandpa. His feet hardly hit the ground before he was sandwiched between the girls' arms in a hard hug.

"You filled out, girl," he grinned to Lizzie, then looked down at Beth, "and you really growed, Little Bit."

Beth squealed and jumped up and down. "How did you know I'm called 'Little Bit' Grandpa?" she asked.

Grandpa laughed and bowed and gave her another hug. "Great minds think alike," he replied with a grin. "Guess we all think you're a perfect Little Bit!"

He turned back to Lizzie and stuck his thumb toward the back of the wagon. "Got you somethin' from Uncle Alvin and Aunt Lola," he said.

Lizzie rushed and stood on tiptoe to look inside the back of the wagon. Sure enough, there was a strange-looking, burlap bag wrapped bucket. She stretched and hooked her fingers on the lip of the bucket and slid it close enough to lift it out. "My, this is heavy," she huffed as she set it on the ground.

"Go on, take that sack off and see what'cha got," Grandpa grinned, crossing his arms across his chest and looking pleased as a hog laying in sunshine.

Lizzie grasped the burlap by its bottom and gently pulled off the rough cloth. There were half-dozen rose bushes, rooted in dirt in the bucket. A tiny squeak came from her mouth and she raised both hands to her cheeks. Tears puddled in her eyes. "Mamma's rose bushes!" she cried. "Aunt Lola always did have a green thumb and she's rooted these---for me?" she asked.

"Yep, and ya can share with Eli and your little sister."

"Oh, Grandpa, thank you so much, I'll never forget how Mamma loved her roses. That was one of the hardest things she had to do; leave her roses when we came here." She ran and gave him a rib-crushing hug.

Miss Claudie reached and touched Bulger on the arm. "Welcome, and come on in," he called from the porch. Lizzie and Beth released Grandpa and each grabbed one of his arms

Sunrise

and walked him along. Eli followed carrying the bucket of Mamma's rose bushes and set them on the porch. Bulger extended his hand and Grandpa shook it heartily.

Got a strong grip for a man his age, Bulger thought.

"Come on and set a spell 'fore we eat. Tell us all about your trip," Miss Claudie said.

≈

Eli and Grandpa loaded on the wagon once more, after a great meal and lots of laughter and warm talk. As they slowly sauntered back to Eli's, Grandpa remarked, "You chillun were mighty blessed when them folks took you in," he said. "I worried at first, but now I know ya'll are right where the Good Lord wants ya to be. I'll finish up my days knowing ya'll are safe and loved."

Eli swallowed hard and he choked up. He couldn't bear to think of Grandpa's 'last days', but knew this time together would probably be their final ones. Wordlessly, he popped the reins and urged the horse home, trotting in the last of the sun's rays and watching the evening sky flame with its vibrant colors behind the tall trees and low fields.

THIRTY

The following Wednesday Miss Claudie busied herself cleaning and baking a pound cake. Lizzie grinned like a smug cat with one mouse in her mouth and another under her paw. Ginger knew what was coming, but didn't let on. Lizzie had ridden into town with Bulger and given word to the Jones girls to spread the news to the neighboring girls to come by Miss Claudie's the coming Wednesday afternoon for a shower for Ginger. They were tickled pink to issue the invites, and every girl who came to the store heard about the party and shared it with her neighbor. The Jones's experienced an extra benefit from the party. Many girls chose a special little gift for Ginger and Eli from the store. Others made handmade items with sentimental or embroidered monogrammed linens to give.

"Well," Miss Claudie finally said innocently, "Looks like we got company." She sashayed to the door and opened it to a wagonload of chatting girls. "Ya'll come on in," Miss Claudie smiled.

Ginger was surprised, even though she suspected the 'surprise' shower. So many gifts and so much chatter! She made a special announcement after opening her gifts and cutting the cake. "I have news I'll bet none of you've heard about," she taunted the girls. "I know who will be having the next wedding!" Lizzie turned a bright red. Ginger turned to Lizzie and gestured toward her with a fork held high. "Lizzie," she began, "is getting married!"

All the girls screamed and squealed and talked at once.

Sunrise

"Who to?" asked 'Loris.

"Is it that cute tall guy you were with that Sunday at church?" asked Carolyn.

"Tell us, tell us," cried Susan and Melissa.

Lizzie took a deep breath and answered softly, "Yes, it's Jimmy. I met him on the wagon train. He has a place just over the Alabama line west of Franklin. We haven't set the day yet, but hopefully a little before Christmas."

Beth, who had remained quiet during the party, whispered to Dolly and Patty as they sat on the bed, watching and listening to the big girls. "And you know, girls, I was the very first to know!" And she hugged the dolls tightly.

"Oh, Christmas weddings are so lovely," crooned Miss Myline. She leaned and whispered to Lizzie, "Don't let me leave before I tell you about the judge. He's coming in the first of the month and we need to make plans."

"Oh, my," Lizzie whispered back. "I don't know if I can stand all this pressure! So much is happening so fast!"

Miss Myline nodded and turned back to the cake on her plate.

The party wound down, refreshments finished and the cake crumbs swept out the door, gifts piled on the bed, and dishes stacked in the sink.

Miss Myline cornered Lizzie as the remaining girls hugged Ginger goodbye. "Plan on the first Wednesday after the wedding. Be at the schoolhouse by nine o'clock." She said as she squeezed Lizzie's hands.

Lizzie held Miss Myline's hand tightly. "For sure I'll be there. Thank you so much for everything you've done. And thank you for getting this set up."

"Don't worry," the young teacher assured. "You'll do fine." She reached for her wrap. "See you soon." She joined the others and they were soon loaded in the wagon and headed home.

"Well," Miss Claudie said. "I think I'll let ya'll girls finish cleaning up. I'm going straight to bed. Make sure Beth and the men have supper. I've had it for one day." They heard her continue mumbling as she went through the door. "I thought gathering my garden and preserving was hard work, but today beats all."

Beth yawned. "Me, too," she said, and sleepily dressed for bed. She never knew when she no longer heard soft voices and was sound asleep.

Lizzie noticed Miss Claudie's recent tiredness, but passed it off as due to all the extra excitement. Lizzie and Ginger made a light supper and cleaned everything with a happy heart. Lizzie's eyes moved to the foot of her bed where the only thing she, Eli, and Beth had left of Mamma and Pa sat. She folded her dishtowel and laid it across the back of a chair and slowly moved to the trunk. Inside were items they'd saved when the family had attempted the ill-fated fording of the Chattahoochee. The trunk washed into a log jam and Eli found it. Inside were two quilts Mamma had made, the family Bible, and part of Mamma's dishes. Lizzie took a deep breath and rested her hand on top of the worn camel-backed box.

Ginger turned to say something, but caught Lizzie's somber face and subdued manner. She stood still and watched.

Finally Lizzie seemed to snap out of her contemplations and turned to Ginger, a broad smile across her face. "Come here," she said. "I want to give you and Eli something."

Ginger silently moved to Lizzie and knelt on the floor beside her. Lizzie opened the chest. Ginger saw two beautiful folded quilts.

"I want you to pick which you like best," Lizzie said with a sorrowful expression. She slowly lifted both quilts and spread them across the trundle.

"I can't do this," Ginger said. "These are yours. Miss Claudie has already given Eli and me a quilt, and these belonged to your mother."

"And that's why you must choose one," Lizzie said. "I know she'd want Eli to have one, and later, Beth will have the other. I have the memories of her making them. I won't have it any other way."

Ginger stood and caressed both quilts. Which would Beth like? she wondered. And she chose the other. "This one with the flowers is the perfect one for us," she said, "Beth will love the colorful one with all the fans. Oh, Lizzie, I don't know what to say," she cried.

Lizzie folded the fan quilt and returned it to the trunk and shut the lid. "Don't say anything," she replied with a soft smile, "just think of Mamma when you and Eli use it." She folded Ginger's choice; the flower garden pattern, and placed it beside Ginger's other gifts.

"This has been a wonderful day," she said, teary-eyed. "I would never have dreamed everything would ever be this full and good for me." She reached for Lizzie. "God had truly been so good," she said. She stepped back and took a deep breath. She smoothed her dress and untied her apron. "Time for bed, I think," she said.

She and Lizzie quickly snuggled under their covers and all was quiet.

Ginger could hardly wait to get back to 'her' house and put all her new gifts away. Just think, her wedding was less than a week! And then there was Lizzie's to plan. . .

≈

Miss Claudie's feelings were lifted when she ambled into the kitchen the following morning. "Well, this is a surprise!" she said, looking at the spotless kitchen. "I think I'll gather in the last of the 'maters before the sun gets too hot." She tied her apron, slipped out the door and got her basket for the tomatoes before the girls woke.

When she lumbered up the porch steps with her heavy basket of red-ripe tomatoes, she heard voices. She set the basket down and went in where she found Lizzie and Ginger finishing breakfast and Bulger at the table having a hot cup of coffee.

"Where ya been?" he asked.

Her mouth dropping open, she muttered, "Just getting' the 'maters."

Lizzie and Ginger laughed. Beth pulled out a chair and ordered. "Sit down, got your coffee ready and we're gone take care of everything today."

Miss Claudie sat. She looked around in wonder. Then she grinned. "Okay," she said with a grin as she reached for her cup. "I'll do just that. If ya'll can handle it, we'll make a batch of 'mater sauce today." She sat back and sipped her coffee. "I'll give the directions and see how good ya can follow them."

All three girls chuckled as they bustled about finishing up the early morning chores. Finally they were ready to begin Miss Claudie's sauce-making.

"Bulger's got the washpot boiling and the wire basket ready. Let's get outside and I'll see how good'a 'mater peelers ya'll are."

The girls followed Miss Claudie outside. Beth brought out a low rocker for her to sit in as she dictated directions concerning the tomatoes.

"Pick off the stems and put the 'maters in the wire basket--'bout half full," she watched as the girls gently placed them in the basket.

Miss Claudie leaned closer. "Now carefully lower the basket in the boiling water and watch until the 'mater skins start to split." She turned to Beth. "Little Bit," she ordered, "Fill up that dishpan there with cool water from the well while these 'maters are scalding."

Beth ran to finish her job before it was time to lift the tomatoes from the boiling water. She had the water in the pan as Lizzie cried out and pointed. "Look!" she exclaimed, "the peelings are starting to pop!"

Miss Claudie chuckled. "Now lift up the basket and be careful! Ya can get burned! Pour the 'maters slow in the cold water in the dishpan. Ginger, as soon as they get cool enough, start pulling the peelings off and cut out the top core. Cut'em up in this large pot. Lizzie, get another basket ready to scald."

Lizzie repeated filling the wire basket and immersing it in the boiling water; Ginger tested the tomatoes to be sure they'd cooled off and began peeling them.

"Why, these peelings just slip off when I get the knife under the skins!"

"Yep, that's the way to do it!" Miss Claudie said. "Beth, you got that big pot ready for Ginger's peeled 'maters?"

"Right here," Beth said as she plopped it next to the dishpan.

In no time at all, the tomatoes were scalded, peeled, cut up, and ready to carry inside.

"Now," Miss Claudie continued. "Beth, put that pot on the

stove. Ginger, pour in about half gallon of water. Lizzie, find those spices and salt and vinegar we bought at the store last week and sprinkle about four tablespoons spice and a cup of vinegar and one of sugar over the 'maters. You girls can take turns stirring so they don't stick. Watch'em. When they get cooked down, we'll put them in the last of our bottles with the little necks and cork'em tight. They'll have to be given a water bath so's they'll keep. Gotta' be sure to keep the corks clear of the water, but you can count on this sauce bein' mighty good later on."

It was hot in that kitchen with the cooking, but at the end of the day there were eighteen bottles filled with dark red sauce sitting on the cupboard shelf cooling.

"Ya'll girls did a fine job," Miss Claudie bragged. "I'm not tired at all and just look at what ya'll done today."

All three girls, hair drooping around their faces and sagging down their backs, beamed. They were proud of their day's work, and just as proud that they had helped make Miss Claudie's day a little lighter. They were pleased with their summer's work on the farm. The skills they were learning were to be used over and over.

After a 'dull' day of cooking tomatoes, Miss Claudie outdid herself sewing on Friday. She was responsible for getting Ginger's bridal dresses made. The material for the bridal gown was pearl white water-stained organza. Miss Claudie cut and sewed most of the gown together in one day. But for several nights afterward, late, after a full day of peeling and preparing fruits, peas, or beans for drying, Miss Claudie stitched tiny tucks across the bodice and gathered even pleats around the waist. With scraps of ribbon, she added bows with trailing wisps and added tiny crocheted flowerets and embossed the hem, neckline, and wrists with finely tatted lace. When she finished it, it was a beauty, hanging on its store bought hanger behind her bedroom door. Eli would never see it before he viewed it on Ginger as she walked to him down the aisle. Miss Claudie could hardly wait!

Mrs. Jones got in the special order of blue organza at the store for Lizzie and Beth's dresses. After Bulger brought in the huge wrapped package of material, Miss Claudie stitched them in record time; they were plain indeed---compared to Ginger's masterpiece.

She prodded Bulger to make sure the boy bought an appropriate suit, shirt, tie, and new Sunday shoes at Jones's. Bulger assured her that Eli was ready, and chuckled as he explained that Eli was all set--except for the buzzards he said were flying around in his stomach and the nervous jitters that kept him awake at night.

THIRTY-ONE

Beth, usually blessed with most of the attention from her siblings and Bulger and Miss Claudie, felt a little neglected during summer when everyone was busy preserving foods and finishing wedding plans. It seemed that Lizzie and Ginger spent most of their time together and poor Beth was left to trail behind or sit on the sidelines and listen to their chatter. She became apt at tuning out the two girls' voices and letting her imagination go wild. She devised colorful conversations with Patty and Dolly, and sometimes her little friends played and romped with Jack and Bell. When Beth wasn't along with Lizzie and Ginger, she trailed along behind Miss Claudie.

Miss Claudie was glad for her company, but when she was busy cooking, washing, or finishing up her chores, she focused her mind on the task at hand and once again, Beth was left to her own devices.

And Bulger. She tried to help him out on the farm, but with his long legs she was soon left behind. So Beth spent most of the last weeks before Eli and Ginger's wedding in the village with Warm DayRah and the Indians.

Every morning after she gathered eggs and cleared the table, Beth divided the scraps between her dogs and the barn cats. Then, unless there was something to gather from the garden, she was free for the day. She learned that if she let Miss Claudie get started on one of her chores and let the girls get engrossed in their plans for the wedding or house decorating, all she had to do was say a quick, "Be back 'fore dark; goin' to the village," and all three heads would nod and she'd hear a mumbled, "Stay on the trail and keep the dogs with you." Soon she'd be jogging along, keeping a watchful eye out for lazy snakes warming themselves in the open trail or for signs of the rebel Indians. The dogs usually trotted along in front, ready to protect and guard her.

She reached the village and ran into Minshue's house.

"*Osiyo*, Daisy Face, *dtohitsu?*" Minshue said as she gave Beth a hug.

"*Osiquu*, I am well," she answered with a great smile. "Where is Warm DayRah?"

Minshue released her and pointed to the creek. "She's down by the creek rinsing the wash. Go on and help her hang it to dry. I know she'd like the help."

Beth ran out and across the courtyard to the creek bank where Warm DayRah was gathering the last of the day's laundry in a woven cane basket. "Hello! Beth," she called, drying her hands on a soft towel.

Skidding to a stop beside the wash basket, Beth watched as Jack and Bell continued on and splashed into the water. "Eeiiii!" Both girls squealed. "Let's get this basket to the drying line," Warm DayRah suggested.

Beth grabbed the handle on one side and Warm DayRah lifted the other. Together they half carried, half dragged the basket to the line Skipping Rock had strung between two stout trees well away from the Martin gourds. The birds were tidy. They'd grasp the 'poo bags' of their babies in their beaks and carry them away from the gourds and drop them. Clotheslines too close always got 'bombed'.

The girls chatted as they grabbed pieces of clothing and kitchen cloths. They shook them hard enough to hear a good 'pop', and anchored them across the line to dry. When they finished, they made their way back to the house.

"We're tired," Warm DayRah complained to her mother.

Minshue laughed. "It's only mid-morning. I'll get you a snack and you can go play before dinner." She handed the girls a chunk of sweetbread and they wandered outside and joined a group of girls to play. Beth fit right in. She understood the rules of the Indian games and they ran and raced, tagged and stood still, or tossed deerskin bags filled with grain through hoops. Soon they tired of running and sat under an oak tree in the shade. Beth noticed leaves fluttering in soft breezes and her mind flashed back to the past fall on the wagon train traveling, coming here to their new home. She noticed some of the leaves were turning red and yellow. Here and there were oranges and a few purples. She remembered the special game Lizzie played with the girls on the train.

"Look here," she said, rising and plucking bright leaves. "We can make crowns to wear," she added, looking closely for tiny twigs to bind the leaves together.

"Crowns?" the girls echoed, puzzled.

Beth realized crowns were not things readily recognized by her friends and wracked her brain to explain. "Beautiful headbands," she suggested.

"Ohhh," the girls acknowledged, nodding happily.

Soon all the young girls were wearing colorful red, yellow, and orange headbands. They danced around and laughed just as lively as Beth had with her friends on the train. By lunchtime, they were really tired and famished. It was a happy morning.

Minshue was prepared when the girls came in. They sat around the smoldering center fire and ate delicious fish stew with hard bread. Soon their bowls were scraped clean and the bread crumbs tossed outside for Jack and Bell.

The girls yawned and stretched. "Tell us a story, please," they begged.

Minshue smiled and sat. Her chores could wait. She loved sharing tales that had been handed down through generations and knew if her stories were captivating enough, they would continue to be shared through future generations. "All right," she said. "Just one." And she began.

"Do you know, Daisy Face, why the bear has a short tail?" She glanced at Warm DayRah and grinned. Warm DayRah grinned back and looked expectantly at Beth.

Beth frowned. "No, I don't think I do. I didn't even know he'd had any other kind of tail!" she said.

Warm DayRah and Minshue laughed

Minshue began: "A long, long time ago, Bear had a long, beautiful, bushy tail. He was very proud of his tail, and Fox, too, had a beautiful tail, and was jealous of Bear's bigger, lovely tail. One freezing, snowy day, Bear saw Fox coming along the road carrying a long string of fish. 'Where did you get those fine fish, Fox?' he asked.

'I caught them in the pond,' he replied.

Bear smacked is lips. He could almost taste the fish. 'Oh, Fox. Those are beautiful fish. I would love to catch a string for myself. Will you show me where you caught them?'

'Come this way,' Fox said. He led Bear across the meadow to a pond, frozen in the winter cold. 'First you must go out on the ice and chop a hole in it,' he said. 'Then sit and let your tail dangle in the water. Fish will swim along and latch on to your fur. It will sting and hurt, but the longer you sit with your tail in the water, the more fish you will catch.'

'Thank you, Fox,' said Bear. Then Fox smiled a sly grin and went away.

Bear sat on the ice with his tail in the hole a long time. It was very cold but he would not get up. His tail felt tingly and began to hurt, so he knew lots of fish were biting and hanging on. He wanted lots of fish, so he tried to sit a while longer. Soon the sun began to go down.

I must have many fish by now, thought Bear, and he tried to get up. But he couldn't budge. Something was holding his beautiful tail! Poor Mr. Bear! He could not get his tail out of the hole; it had frozen over and his tail was caught in the ice! He tried and tried; pulled and pulled. At last he jumped up fast to get his tail out of the water. It was stuck! He took a deep breath and jumped again--harder. Off came his tail!

And that is why Bear has gone about with a little stubby tail to this very day."

Beth and Warm DayRah leaned back and laughed and laughed.

"That was a really good story, Minshue," Beth said. "I want to remember it and tell it to Eli one night soon."

"I hope you will," said Minshue. She wanted stories, especially from her heritage, to be told and cherished, enjoyed and shared for a long, long time.

Beth stretched again. "I must be going on home now," she said, "before I fall asleep." She rose and called to Jack and Bell who were snoozing beside the door. "I'll see you later if it's okay," she called back inside to Minshue.

"Come anytime, Daisy Face," Minshue said. "*Donadogohv*—let's meet again." She watched as Beth reached the edge of the village and vanished onto the trail leading back to her home.

The next few weeks were filled with many days much like that day for Beth. She never forgot the stories she heard from her friends around the fires at Minshue's home.

Little did she, or any of the family, realize that in a few short years, most of her Indian friends would be gathered together and forced to march a long and deadly trek to Oklahoma where they would be relocated. It would come to be known as *The Trail of Tears*. Beth's time with her friends and the stories she heard were kept in Beth's heart to be pondered and shared with her children and her children's children.

THIRTY-TWO

The last two weeks before the wedding were filled with men's work, too. Bulger, Eli, and even Skipping Rock worked overtime to get the corn gathered and in the corncribs. Fodder from both Bulger's and Eli's fields was pulled and hay piled onto wagons and tossed high up in the barn loft. Eli's, as well as Bulger's barn, was filled. They shared with Skipping Rock and he had an ample supply for his village's horses, too.

The men finished in time to help Mr. Cook pick the last of his cotton and Eli drove the wagon to the cotton gin. Mr. Cook had four bales, several bags of seeds for animal feed, and planting seeds for the coming spring.

Farmers throughout the community made good on their crops that year, and in turn, Mr. Jones's and Mr. Pollard's credit slips got paid off and they were blessed, too. Mr. Marshall's blacksmith shop got a new bellows and Rogers and Son ordered an extra supply of nails and bolts with their added income. It seemed that everybody was bettered when the farmers were blessed with good harvests.

The day for the stage to bring in Ginger's family arrived. Eli borrowed Bulger's wagon and hooked up the mules. He arrived early to meet the stage bringing his future in-laws and his new young brother-in-law. It roared into town in a dusty cloud and pulled to a rattling stop. Eli's bones knocked and his teeth totally clattered from nervousness. He watched as Ginger's Pa got off and turned to lift his hand to help Ginger's Ma step down. They had their backs to him as they chatted and swished the dust from their clothing. Ginger's mom turned to a tall boy who hopped from the stage directly to the sidewalk, skipping the coach's steps entirely. Eli's jaw dropped. This couldn't be Greyson, the little fellow he'd seen on the sidewalk in Main Street, Hooverville as they pulled out last fall. How he had grown!

Ginger's parents turned and looked right through him. Why! They didn't recognize him, either! He rushed to greet them. He enjoyed the surprised look on their faces as he came close and stuck out his hand for a shake. Naturally, if Greyson had grown and changed so much in only a year, he must have, too. It was hard for him to imagine, but he suddenly realized he was no longer a sapling eighteen year old looking for fun and adventure; he was a responsible man, almost a husband who had a home and was getting a wife. It took his breath away and he barely was able to croak, "How do, so glad to see you. Come this way to the wagon and I'll get your things and load them."

"Why, Eli," Elizabeth, Ginger's mom sang as she grabbed him, "I hardly recognized you." She held him at arms' length and stared. "You're so grown-up, so handsome." Behind her, Ennis, Ginger's Pa, was grinning from ear to ear.

Thankfully, Ennis took Elizabeth by her elbow and steered her toward the wagon. Greyson grabbed two of their bags and Eli hoisted the others filled with dowry goods. They struggled with the bags and tossed them aboard the wagon. "Hop in, Greyson," Eli said. "I'll have you home in no time."

Greyson was silent during the ride home, but Ennis carried on a lively conversation the entire trip. He asked about Eli's parents and offered condolences, wanted to know more about Bulger and Miss Claudie, and hinted to insure Eli's devotion to Ginger was a lasting one. Eli felt the wagon seat get hotter and hotter, sitting there with his future in-laws. He sweated as they rode along the road and was grateful when they arrived at his house. Both Elizabeth and Ennis became tongue-tied as he pulled up to the door and they took in Eli's stout, stunning house. He didn't feel on the hot seat anymore and almost puffed his chest with pride. He didn't, though. Bulger taught him that pridefulness is a sin, and he reminded himself to be humble and grateful for all he had.

"You can freshen up here, and I'll get the wagon unloaded. Your room is across the dogtrot and Greyson and I will sleep on pallets. Grandpa is already here and he has a cot in the kitchen." He hopped down and Greyson followed. Ginger's parents slowly got off the wagon and gazed wonderingly as they stepped up the stone steps and into the kitchen.

Grandpa met them just inside the door.

"Remember my grandpa?" Eli made introductions and the men shook hands. Elizabeth did, too.

"Sure do," Ennis replied.

"This is lovely, Eli," Elizabeth admired, turning and looking around. "Ginger will be very happy here. She can come by later and go through her dowry and put things away."

Eli beamed.

Soon after, they were all aboard the wagon again and on their way to supper with Bulger and Miss Claudie.

As soon as the wagon pulled to a stop in the yard, Bulger stood alongside and extended his hand and introduced himself. Miss Claudie stood on the porch, ready to give Elizabeth help. Lizzie and Beth stood just behind her, but Ginger rushed down the steps and into her mother's waiting arms.

"I can't believe my baby girl is getting married," Elizabeth said.

"Nor can I," her father agreed.

"It's a nice surprise for us, too," Miss Claudie added. "We're so blessed to have Ginger join our family."

Eli jumped off the wagon and as soon as he helped Grandpa down, gave Ginger a peck on the cheek. Her smile beamed clear across her face.

"Ya gone get them mules settled, son?" Bulger asked.

"Sure thing," Eli replied, leading the animals to the barn. "Wanna help, Greyson? I could use someone to toss a little hay down for the mules."

Greyson grinned and followed Eli.

"Well, ya'll come right on in," Bulger invited. "Miss Claudie has a meal fit for royalty waitin'." As they climbed the steps and started inside, Bulger continued. "I'm sure you remember Lizzie and Beth."

"Land alive," Elizabeth exclaimed. "You know we didn't

even recognize Eli in town at the stage office. And how these two have grown, too. Lizzie, you're so beautiful, and Beth, you're a lovely young lady."

Lizzie blushed and Beth blurted out. "Lizzie's getting married come Christmas, and taking the state teacher's test the coming Wednesday after Eli's and Ginger's wedding."

"That be a fact? I know you'll do fine on your test. I'm so proud for you." Elizabeth said. Then added, "Well, that young fellow who got you has done a fine thing for himself. Do we know him?"

"I'm not sure," Lizzie replied as they entered the kitchen and found a place at the table. "His name is Jimmy and we met on the train coming here. His parents passed away a few years back and he's been on his own since. I'm the lucky one to have met him." She added.

Eli and Greyson came in and Miss Claudie dished up the food. The table was laden with fresh vegetables, breads, and even sweet tea, especially for the occasion. Bulger asked Ginger's father to bless the food and he did: strong but short. The meal with their extended family lasted until almost bedtime. They sat and ate awhile, let the dishes go and sat and talked a while.

It came time for Eli to take his future in-laws and grandpa back to his house. "I'll get the wagon," he said. He was back quick as a chicken pecks up corn, and everyone said their 'good-byes', and 'see you tomorrows'. Quick hugs were exchanged and the visitors were gone, and Bulger and Miss Claudie and the girls were left alone once again.

Miss Claudie looked across the leftover food and dirty dishes on the table. "Girls, I'm gone do this one more time, but if you tell anybody 'bout it, I'll deny it to the end. Get those leftovers put away and scraps to Jack and Bell and the barn cats, and stack the dishes in the dishpan and cover them with water. They'll wait washing 'til mornin'," and she turned and walked straight through the kitchen door, across the dogtrot, and into her bedroom. "Comin', Bulger?" she hollered after her.

He looked bewildered, pulled himself out of his chair, looked at the girls and shrugged his shoulders. "Comin', Claudie," he answered, and followed her fading steps to the bedroom.

"I'll be," Beth said gazing in wonder after the couple.

Lizzie and Ginger looked around the kitchen in disbelief. Miss Claudie, leaving dishes again? They couldn't believe it.

Lizzie broke the spell by grabbing plates and raking out scraps. She went outside and dropped the scraps in the dogs' pan on the porch and tossed the rest to the barn for the cats. Ginger put what leftovers could be kept for later in crockery and carried them to the springhouse near the well and settled them in the cool water. They'd be good to have the following day. Miss Claudie must be plumb tuckered out to go to bed and leave the cleaning up to them again.

"Be a nice surprise for her to get these dishes washed and put away and the kitchen cleaned before she gets up in the morning," Beth advised. "We got that housewarming Monday evening at Eli's. He invited lots of folks and the Indians who helped him on the house. Miss Claudie will be tired out after cooking for that. We need to help out all we can.

Lizzie and Ginger agreed and they worked double-time and with Beth's help, got the room spanking clean. They were proud of themselves for such a good job.

The girls blew out the lamp, hit their beds, and pulled their sheets lightly up over their tired bodies. They still were in awe at Miss Claudie's actions. "Maybe we should take over a few more of her chores," Lizzie said to Beth. "Ginger will be gone in a few days and it'll only be me, you, and Bulger. We really gotta help out with the housewarming."

"Yeah, let's do that," Beth said, her eyes already closing as the Sand Man sprinkled down sleepy dust over them.

It was only her second, soft sigh and Lizzie was out like the lamp flame, too. The girls slept soundly and dreamlessly. So did Bulger and Miss Claudie.

THIRTY-THREE

Days following up to the wedding weekend sped by. Miss Claudie, true to Lizzie's words, cooked relentlessly and the night of Eli's housewarming was a great success. It was the biggest and best party those parts had had in quite a while.

Saturday, the day before the wedding, passed in a blur. Eli was nervous as a long-tailed cat in a room full of rocking chairs; Miss Claudie and Elizabeth fussed over last minute touch-ups; Lizzie and Ginger worried about the next day's weather, Beth followed Miss Claudie and jabbered continuously; and Bulger, Grandpa, Greyson, and Ennis simply stayed out of the way. After sending Greyson along with Beth to check on the chickens and look for eggs, the men slipped to the barn and sampled a bit of 'the eye of the tiger'---just to calm their nerves. Eli, not used to the joy juice from the small-mouthed jug, sputtered and coughed as he took his swig. Bulger and Grandpa laughed.

"Don't think my future son-in-law takes to this stuff so good," Ennis said.

"Nope," Bulger agreed. "He won't be keeping my friend over by Deer Creek in business for sure," he chuckled.

The day passed, and time for everyone to find their place of night's rest came. "Now, tomorrow night after the weddin' the newlyweds will need their own time." Miss Claudie looked at Ginger's folks and Grandpa. "Lizzie and Beth will make a pallet in mine and Bulger's room, and ya'll can have Lizzie and Ginger's beds," she indicated to Ginger's parents. "Grandpa, ya can bundle up on Eli's cot and Greyson can have a thick pallet. We'll snuggle ya both in on the dogtrot. Bulger made a little nook just for ya and ya won't feel this September chill at all." She looked around and continued. "Bulger will get ya'll to the stage in plenty of time Monday mornin'. Eli and Ginger will have to say their 'byes after the weddin'."

They all nodded in agreement.

"That sounds wonderful, Miss Claudie," Elizabeth said. "We'll have our bags packed and bring them over on our way to the church in the morning. It was good of Preacher Sheets to let our wedding be the service."

Miss Claudie smiled, relieved, and asked everyone to join hands and circle around on the porch for a goodnight prayer before traveling to their household.

"Bulger, would'ja say a thankfulness over us before we break up for the night?" she asked.

Everyone bowed their heads and Bulger began: "Father, we thank you for each of these here tonight. We have found love and caring through the meeting of each one. These children have brought us together; we who would have never met otherwise. Lives have been touched, enriched, and blessed. Lord, continue to bless each one and protect them through the coming days as they travel to their homes. Be with this young couple as they begin their lives together. Keep them in your loving care. May tomorrow be beautiful and untroubled. In your Son's Holy name, Amen."

And, Lord, please include Jimmy in our circle even though he isn't able to be here tonight, thought Lizzie as a round of 'Amens' sounded and nightfall ushered in.

Eli was the last to leave the porch where Ginger lingered. "Just think, Eli," she said, "tomorrow night this time we'll be man and wife."

Eli's eyes bulged out. He was thrilled about the marriage, but it hadn't hit home until Ginger said those words. Him, a married man! He gulped. All he could do was nod, give her a quick, light kiss on her lips, and scuttle to the wagon. He almost tripped as he left the last step, and Beth burst out laughing. Face burning, he pulled himself on the wagon with Elizabeth and Greyson, and Ennis cracked the reins and headed to Eli's.

THIRTY-FOUR

Sunday morning's early quiet sunrise was interrupted by horse's whinnies and thudding boots on the porch. Three tousled heads popped up and Beth's eyes were big as wagon wheels. Lizzie looked at Ginger and scooped the covers off and yelled, "Hide!" She was sure it was Eli on the porch ready to barge right on into the kitchen. All three girls hopped out of bed and Ginger ran and stood behind the door.

"Eli can't see you today before the wedding," she cried, "It's bad luck!"

Ginger stood shivering in her bare feet behind the door as it swung open.

"Anybody up?" Ennis called.

Lizzie grabbed her robe and pulled it tightly around her. "Where's Eli?" she asked.

"Staying on the wagon with Greyson and his second best man, Cullie," he answered. "Elizabeth fairly dared him to come in. He's all dressed to go, nervous as an alligator at the dentist's. Had to stop by and unload our stuff for our stay tonight." He looked around. "Where's that daughter of mine?"

Ginger peeped out from behind the door. "Right here, Pa," she said through chattering teeth.

He reached and pulled her close. "Your Mamma's coming in now. I got orders to hurry back out and watch your fella while she comes in. Eli, Greyson, and me are riding on to the church so you womenfolk can get ready." He gave her a kiss. "See you in a while, baby girl." He looked long at her and gave another father's kiss. Then he turned and left. The girls heard him holler as he crossed the porch. "Okay, Mamma, your turn. I'm gone get that boy to his wedding."

Ginger heard her mother's voice carry to her pa's in passing, "Don't forget to keep that wagon behind the church until we get there. We'll keep Ginger out of sight while Eli goes in the church. Don't want him seeing her before she starts down the aisle so they'll have nothing but good luck!" Shivering, Ginger scurried from behind the door and across the room to grab her robe as Lizzie threw more wood in the stove.

Elizabeth came in with a rush and quickly shut the door. "You girls better get on the ball!" she admonished. "We got a wedding to go to!"

Miss Claudie came in beaming. "Land sakes, Elizabeth. We have to shake a leg to keep up with you." She tied her apron around her waist and set the iron skillet on the stove with a 'clank'. "Did your men-folk already have breakfast?" she asked Elizabeth.

"For sure, flapjacks and bacon, but that'll do'em until after the ceremony," she replied.

"Same's coming up here," Miss Claudie countered. And she got the table set before the girls got dressed. "Don't put on your wedding duds before we eat, girls, save them until after. Don't want any messes on them."

Bulger came in, and after a quick blessing of the food, gobbled his breakfast and scooted to the bedroom to get his Sunday clothes on and out of the women's way. Sure enough, they were busy as hens on laying day and Bulger sighed a big relief when he stepped off the dogtrot and headed to the barn to hitch Moses.

Inside, the women had the kitchen squared away in record time. Beth made the beds and Ginger fidgeted and shook her hands as she darted around the room.

"Settle down, Ginger," Miss Claudie said as she took Ginger's face in both her hands and then smoothed her hair back. "Set here and let your Mamma get your hair up. Beth gathered some late blossoms to go in with the veil." Ginger sat.

"Come on, Beth," Lizzie said, reaching for Beth's hand. "Let's get you dressed and then you can help me with my hair."

Beth flashed a shining smile and ran to Miss Claudie's

room to get their dresses.

Elizabeth hummed as she combed Ginger's hair, wound it beautifully around, and secured it with combs. She pinning white flowers with the veil and softly said. "I remember when I was getting ready for my day with your pa," she mused.

Ginger quieted and let her mamma continue.

"I was so nervous. Your pa had our house fixed up, and I had a good dowry; plenty of linens, pots and pans, and new pillows, but down in my heart, I was doubtful. I knew he was a good man, and would make a good husband and someday, I hoped, a good father. My mamma fixed my hair that day. Daddy walked back and forth on the porch," she chuckled, "back and forth. He had more jitters than I did, I think."

Miss Claudie dressed slowly, listening in wonder, and silently recalled her wedding day. Her day getting ready for Bulger.

Elizabeth continued, "I finally got to the church. I remember your pa's face when he saw me coming down the aisle; he had that same look later when he first looked at you after you were born, and again when Greyson was born." She pinned the last pin and moved to face her daughter. "My only wish is that Eli will be the man you father is, and love and respect you just as much as your pa has me." And she kissed her daughter.

Miss Claudie turned away in reverence for this special mother-daughter moment.

As usual, Beth popped up, "Can somebody PLEASE button me up?" she blurted. "I can't reach back there!"

Lizzie laughed and finished helping her little sister get dressed. Then she handed Beth the brush, sat on a stool, and asked her to 'style' her hair. Puffing up like a turkey strutting, Beth took the brush and brought it through Lizzie's long, shiny brown hair.

Miss Claudie let the sight set in her mind. She wanted to savor this time again and again and was bound not to forget. She had to will out of her daydream. "Don't forget to grab a couple of them left-over biscuits and go sit on the steps and rub your shoes," she chuckled to Beth. "They'll shine like morning dew with the sun hitting it when ya finish."

In short time, the women were dressed and Miss Claudie brought out quilts to spread in the wagon for them to sit on. She spread them as Bulger held the mules steady. Elizabeth led her daughter to the wagon and helped her in. Lizzie and Beth followed. Miss Claudie sat beside Bulger, and Elizabeth settled on the seat next to Miss Claudie. Bulger gave a soft click with his tongue and they were on their way.

Elizabeth sat, quiet and thoughtful; Miss Claudie already had wet tracks from tears making their way to her chin; Bulger sat straight and stared straight ahead, not saying a word. In the back, Lizzie and Ginger held hands so tightly their knuckles turned white. Beth sat like a big girl, smoothing her skirt and patting her curls.

Elizabeth leaned forward as the church came into view, her eyebrows wrinkling together. "Don't see Eli's wagon," she mumbled and sat back, relaxed and satisfied.

Bulger pulled his wagon to the far end, away from most of the wagons and buggies. He got down and said, "I'll let Eli and Preacher Sheets know we're here." He stopped and turned back. "We start 'bout eleven o'clock?" he asked.

Elizabeth nodded. "On the dot, I hope."

Bulger's stooped form ambled across the church yard and to the back of the church.

"Now, ladies," Miss Claudie said, "Ya'll get down here and stand behind me and Elizabeth." The older women stood behind the wagon and Lizzie and Ginger hid behind them. Beth peeped around and watched as Eli, Greyson, Cullie, and Bulger entered the church. She guessed Bulger had threatened to bop Eli on his head if he glanced toward the wagon because he kept his eyes on his boots. Ginger's pa waited on the church steps.

Elizabeth let out a long sigh. "So far, so good," she said. "Well, daughter, time to go meet your father." She looked long at Ginger's face and gave her a tight hug before starting to the door. Lizzie and Beth gave Ginger a quick hug and followed Elizabeth, leaving Miss Claudie with Ginger.

Ginger reached and held Miss Claudie's hand and that opened the door for tears again. Miss Claudie's chin quivered and she reached with her other hand and cupped Ginger's chin. "Ya know I love that boy like he's my own," she said. "When we found him, he was a broken little boy, lost and angry at God and everybody else. We loved him, Bulger and me, and he came to love us, too. He'll be good to ya, and love ya come what may. I ask ya to love him back, and be good to him." She dropped her hand.

Ginger's eyes puddled and she reached to hold Miss Claudie tight. "I will. I'll love him come what may. You've been his ma since he lost his, and you'll always be his ma in his heart." She loosened her arms and Miss Claudie wiped Ginger's tears.

"Well, I guess it's time to go get you and my boy joined up," Miss Claudie said. "Let me get inside before ya start to your pa. Then when I see you ya'll standing in the door, I'll nod to Miss Minnie and she'll start playing. Won't be no turning back then," she chuckled.

Ginger watched as Miss Claudie slowly made her way to the steps. She nodded to Ennis as she passed, and he gave her a quick hug. She turned and smiled and Ginger watched as Miss Claudie's small, frail form disappeared into the inside shadow of the church.

Ginger took a deep breath and held her dress high as she stepped lightly across the yard to meet her pa. As she came to the church, he reached for her hand and guided her up the steps. She linked her arm through his, and together they stood side-by-side in the open doorway, and the Bridal March began to softly fill the church. Her father took the first step to present her to her future husband.

Eli stood opposite Lizzie, and Jimmy stood nervously beside Eli. Cullie stood a little back, enjoying the event.

Beth waited at the door holding one of Bulger's handmade oak baskets filled with petals picked from flowers found around Miss Claudie's yard. She saw Eli's face turn toward the door and it seemed to melt into a glowing orb. She realized he'd seen Ginger. A shadow crossed her from behind, and she knew it was time to walk the aisle; Ginger and her pa had stepped into the doorway behind her, blocking the morning sun. Her steps were slow and measured. She reached into the basket and lifted a handful of petals and let them drift to the floor. Ginger and Ennis walked behind, her lovely dress swishing through the colorful petals. Everyone rose to greet the bride.

Eli watched without blinking an eye as Ginger's pa ushered her into the church and slowly escorted her down the aisle—to him. His chest tightened and his breathing became shallow. He clasped his hands tightly behind his back, just to let them go and then hang limply at his side. He leaned forward and tipped up on his toes and gently rested back on his heels. He couldn't believe Ginger's beauty; and she was his!

Ginger floated along between the pews and came to rest beside him. She passed her bouquet to Lizzie and turned and smiled at Eli and his heart almost burst. Miss Minnie ended her piano notes softly, and Preacher Sheets motioned for everyone to be seated.

Eli heard, through an excited buzz, Preacher Sheets ask, "Who gives this woman to be married to this man?"

Ennis removed Ginger's arm from his and placed her hand in Eli's, and answered, "I do."

And then there were only Eli and Ginger standing in front of the preacher, taking their vows. His eyes never left hers. Before either could realize it, Preacher Sheets said, "You may now kiss the bride." And he did.

They turned and faced the congregation and received a rounding applause. They were now officially man and wife!

Lizzie handed Ginger the bridal bouquet and Ginger and Eli tore hand-in-hand down the aisle.

Cullie joined Lizzie and Beth followed. Then Ginger's parents and Greyson; Bulger and Miss Claudie.

When everyone met outside, it was smiles, happy chatter, and lots of hugs and handshakes. Eli's gaze fell directly on an unexpected guest. Minshue and her family had attended! He was happy that they had chosen to come and celebrate the occasion. When he saw Skipping Rock, he grinned like Beth's hounds with a new bone. To his surprise, Skipping Rock grinned a sloppy grin back, raised his eyebrows, and slanted his eyes to his right. There, just behind his shoulder, stood the prettiest, petite young girl he'd ever seen. Whoa, Skipping Rock had a girl of his own!!! Looking back to Skipping Rock, he nodded and raised a hand as if to say, 'Nice going!'

"Line up, girls, over here," Ginger instructed, pointing to

the bottom church step, intruding on Eli's thoughts. She climbed to the top, turned and looked down quickly and tossed her bouquet over her shoulder. It came down right in Lizzie's arms. Beth jumped up and down clapping her hands and the other girls clapped along with her. Finally, slowly, the girls broke away, moving to their parents' wagons or to whisper a quick 'bye' to their boyfriends, when suddenly Jimmy quietly slid beside Lizzie and reached around her waist, pulling her close.

She gave a start and almost pushed away before she realized who he was. "Oh!" was all she could say. She threw her arms around his neck and they hugged tightly right there in the middle of the churchyard. When Jimmy let go, Lizzie looked to Miss Claudie. She was grinning like a fox in a henhouse.

"All right, ya'll get loaded up and back to the house for dinner. Plenty for everybody," Miss Claudie instructed.

Eli and Ginger climbed into his wagon pulled by his 'new' mule Little Man who would make his home at Eli's. The rest of the wedding party joined Bulger in his wagon. He'd insisted Eli take Little Man home to his house to stay since he had a brand new barn and fresh hay waiting there.

Bulger and his wagonful of folks followed the newlyweds back to the house where Miss Claudie set out a banquet fit for the Queen of England herself. The afternoon was spent building rich memories that would live in everyone's minds long after. Getting ready to leave, Ginger clung to her mother an extra minute before letting go.

"Don't worry, my sweet daughter," Elizabeth said, "Everything's going to be fine. You'll see." She pushed back a straggling strand of hair from Ginger's forehead and leaned and kissed the spot.

Ginger broke from her mother, and Eli bid Ennis and Greyson good-bye, and Eli once again had to bid Grandpa farewell.

Grandpa walked and stood in front of Eli, and his gaze warmed Eli's whole being. "This is it, boy," Grandpa said softly. "I've given Lizzie my best for her and her Jimmy's wedding; don't think I can make the trip back no more. Just too tiring." He placed his hand on Eli's shoulder. "But I wouldn't a'missed this for the world." He pulled Eli close and held him tight. Eli reached around Grandpa and clutched his shirt to pull him closer. "Now don't fret. This is your new beginning. I'll be leaving tomorrow after sunrise to meet the stage, but today will last me a long time. I love you, son, no matter what comes along later."

Eli choked back the tears, stepped back and offered Grandpa his hand. Eli wanted to hold on and never let go. His heart felt like a cold stone: he knew, felt it deep, that this was the last time he and Grandpa would be together. It was the last time he would look into Grandpa's eyes and tell him he loved him.

"I love you, Grandpa," he whispered.

Grandpa grabbed Eli's hand and shook it hard. He clapped Eli on the shoulder and said, through halting words, "I love you, too, son." Then he stood back and smiled. "You'd better get on up there in the wagon with that pretty little thing. Keep her warm tonight," and winked. Eli grinned and climbed in his wagon beside his bride. Claudie had packed them a wedding basket of goodies---which they wouldn't touch until the following day---and after this wonderful, full day, their wedding day was coming to an end and they were on their way home. Eli couldn't bear to look back as they rode from the yard.

Grandpa and Greyson sat for a while in front of the fire with Bulger. Greyson listened as the two wizened men talked about crops, weather, Indians, and hunting. Bulger noticed Greyson's head nodding and his eyes closing.

"Time to hit the hay," Bulger said, rising and hitting his hands on his legs. The women, who had been sitting around the table, rose and gathered quilts and more quilts for Grandpa's and Greyson's beds. Grandpa made it to his cot and Elizabeth had to lead Greyson, so tired and sleepy, to his pallet on the dogtrot. He was asleep before she got his shoes off. Elizabeth and Ennis made their beds in the kitchen, and Lizzie and Beth slept comfortably on the floor in Bulger and Miss Claudie's room.

The night was quiet. Miss Claudie snuggled close to Bulger and he hooked his arm around her and smiled down at her as he pulled her closer. She knew what he was thinking: that first night they were man and wife and how special it was. Miss Claudie closed her eyes and whispered a prayer that Eli's and Ginger's would be as sweet and loving as hers and Bulger's was----all those years ago.

≈

Eli and Ginger pulled into the yard of their new home. Eli helped Ginger down and held her in his arms as he climbed the steps and pushed open the door. "Gotta carry my bride over the threshold," he said. When he passed through the door, let her go and her feet were on the floor, he held her tight and kissed her deeply. She almost melted away right there in the middle of the kitchen.

He stepped away and said hoarsely, "I'll be right back, gotta get Little Man cared for."

Ginger could only smile and nod through glazed eyes.

Eli stumbled out the door and pulled Little Man to the barn. He threw off his harness and tossed hay toward the trough. The barn door banged behind him as he ran toward the house.

When he entered the kitchen, Ginger wasn't there. His stomach fluttered as he realized she'd already gone to the bedroom. His legs went limp and his mind went blank. Somehow his feet took him across the dogtrot.

Ginger was already in bed. The light from the lamp on the bedside table cast a glow that created a soft iridescent halo surrounding her. Somehow he stumbled across the room and stood by the bed. He was filled, simply standing and looking at his beautiful wife. He moved to the lamp and gently blew out the flame.

Ginger heard a soft rustling as Eli got ready to join her. She felt the bed sag and heard the springs sing as he lifted the cover and lay beside her.

Eli wondered if Bulger and Miss Claudie had been this loving and happy on their wedding night---all those years ago.

≈

Sunrise came that morning, beaming brightly across the top of the barn and into the kitchen window. Elizabeth woke with the warm sunbeams dancing on her face and Miss Claudie knocked on the door.

"Ya'll dressed yet?" she called. "Need to get ya fed and in town early for the stage. Won't be another until next week."

Elizabeth jumped out of bed. "Give us a minute," she said. "We slept like logs last night."

Miss Claudie chuckled. "I'll get Grandpa and the boy up while ya'll get ready." And she moved to the dogtrot where the old man and young boy were rousing from their night's sleep.

Greyson stretched and climbed out of his bundle of quilts.

"Did ya sleep good, boy?" Miss Claudie asked, tousling his hair with one hand while reaching for a quilt with the other.

Greyson smiled and nodded.

Miss Claudie folded quilts and stacked them. "Get your shoes on and go see if your folks are up," she told him. She moved to Grandpa's cot and peeked around the protective screen that Bulger had put up to help keep Grandpa warm. "Ya awake, Grandpa?" she asked.

"Yep," he answered, "and ready to get goin'." He lumbered out, pulling his suspenders over his shoulders. "Bulger made a pretty good little room for me there," he said. "Slept like a newborn baby."

Miss Claudie looked at the cot and was pleasantly surprised to see Grandpa's quilts neatly folded. Elizabeth stuck her head out the kitchen door and shouted, "Ya'll come on in, we're finally up and ready to go."

"Come on, Grandpa, let's get the water hot for coffee," Miss Claudie said, holding Grandpa's arm.

Lizzie and Beth rushed in and in no time at all, everyone was sitting around the table, sipping hot coffee and eating buttered biscuits with ham and gravy. Bulger, pulling himself out of his chair, moved to the door and put on his jacket.

"Well, guess it's time to hitch the wagon. I'll go get ole' Moses. Hate to see ya'll folks go, but know ya'll got to get on home and back to your things," and he started to the barn.

Elizabeth sighed. "It has been a wonderful visit. I'm so glad to have got to know all of you. Ginger's in such a good place, with a good family. We won't worry any, will we, Papa?" she asked to her husband.

"Nope," he answered. He rose to gather their bags and set them on the front porch where Elizabeth and Greyson joined him.

Miss Claudie kept herself busy at the sink, quietly washing dishes that had already been washed once. She knew the folks needed private good-byes.

Lizzie and Beth were alone with Grandpa. Beth climbed into his lap and Lizzie pulled a chair close and put her hand on his arm.

"We're gone miss you, Grandpa," Lizzie said in an almost whisper.

Beth nodded and laid her head on Grandpa's chest. Grandpa reached and smoothed her hair. His voice caught.

"I'll miss ya, too. Won't be a day goes by that I won't think of ya'll. Ya know," he said, pulling Beth back and looking into her face. "We built some mighty purty memories while I was here and we'll have 'em for now on out."

Beth reached and put her arms around Grandpa's neck. "I love you, Grandpa," she whispered.

Lizzie's chin quivered and she clamped her eyes shut to keep her tears from spilling."

Grandpa hugged Beth close and coughed. "Now girls," he said in a rough, coarse voice, "Ya'll get up and help me get my things to the porch. Give me a quick hug and I'll get going." He stood and Lizzie and Beth hugged him and held on an extra minute—one to last them a long time.

Grandpa got his bag and the girls followed. Bulger had the wagon beside the steps and Greyson helped his pa pitch the bags aboard. Grandpa turned to Lizzie and tipped her chin so she gazed into his eyes. "Remember the roses, now. Put them in a good place so they'll grow and be a reminder of me and our place back home."

She nodded. "I'll share half with Eli, so he can have a piece of home at his place," she added.

Grandpa dropped his hand and crossed the porch and climbed on the wagon.

The folks were loaded; bags piled high, and Bulger ready to

pull out.

Unexpectedly and loudly, Greyson raising his hand and waving boisterously quipped, "Bye ya'll!"

Bulger, somewhat astonished, mumbled, "Well, I'll be. The boy CAN talk!"

Grandpa didn't look back as they rode out of the yard toward town and to the stagecoach to carry him back home.

THIRTY-FIVE

The first two days after Eli and Ginger's wedding, Lizzie's stomach fluttered and bubbled with anxiousness. Her test would be administered on Wednesday. Bulger agreed to take her to town and drop her off at the schoolhouse. Miss Myline would be there and sign as a witness, and Judge Knight would administer it. It was a two hour test, timed by the judge. Regular curricula subjects; reading, history, spelling, grammar, arithmetic, and geography would be covered, and Lizzie was expected to be fluent in each area. She'd have to write a five-hundred word essay on 'Why I Choose to be a Teacher'.

Miss Claudie made flapjacks and sausage for Lizzie. Bulger's breakfast blessing was mostly concerned with Lizzie that morning. He asked for her to feel peace and have understanding of the questions. His prayer softened her queasy stomach and gave her unexpected confidence.

As soon as the plates were in the sink, Bulger had the wagon waiting at the door. The weather was good; light breeze, soft sunlight, and just enough crispness in the air to keep her mind clear.

She climbed aboard and they rode out. Lizzie looked back toward the house and, as Lizzie knew she would be, was Miss Claudie, standing on the porch. She stood watching after the wagon, one arm around her middle and the other wiping her cheeks. Lizzie knew she'd be covered in prayer all morning while she worked at the schoolhouse.

Trees along the winding road to town were still dressed for

fall. Some wore bright yellow jumpers, some orange and red dresses, and still others in somber purples and greens. Lizzie breathed deeply. She heard geese and looked up to see a large 'V' flying overhead. Their honking filled the air with happy sounds of a comfortable, warm place ahead. *Maybe a good sign for me*, she imagined.

Bulger kept his eyes ahead. "Nervous?" he asked.

"A little," she answered.

He chuckled. "I know ya gone do fine."

She relaxed and tried to clear her mind. Moses clomped on along the road, and before she knew it, Bulger had pulled to a stop in front of the schoolhouse. Judge Knight and Miss Myline were already there. There was a second woman who accompanied the judge. A stately, kind-faced lady who seemed to ooze confidence and sureness.

"Come on in," the judge called. He turned to the woman as Lizzie dropped down from the wagon. "This is my wife, Arphelia," he explained. "I told her about you and how you were to take the teacher's test, and she came along to offer her support."

Lizzie shook hands with Miss Arphelia. "Thank you so much for coming," she said as she dropped her hand to her side. "I sure need all the help I can get."

Bulger moved to Lizzie and reached to give her a hug—something he seldom did. "Best of luck to ya," he said. His face gave away the pride he felt in his heart. Lizzie hugged him back.

"Thank you, Bulger," she said, a little choked up. Bulger wasn't one to let his feelings show.

"I'll be back by dinnertime," he said, clearing his throat. "Gone go by Mr. Rogers's and get more nails and by Pollard's just to chew the fat awhile." He moved his hand to the reins and released her to Judge Knight standing beside the wagon. Miss Arphelia took Lizzie gently by her arm and they joined the Judge and together they walked up the steps and into the schoolroom.

Miss Myline sat near the window in one of the student's desks. Judge Knight's seat was Miss Myline's in front of the chalkboard. She motioned for Lizzie to sit in the desk in front of the judge.

She sat and Miss Myline rose and moved a chair for Miss Arphelia before she gathered two pencils and handed them to Lizzie. She smiled comfortingly, touched Lizzie on the arm, and returned to her seat by the window.

Judge Knight coughed softly. Lizzie's eyes turned to him.

"I have here the test from Atlanta. I am to administer it to you and preside over the testing time and procedures. Miss Myline will witness that everything is conducted according to state rules. Are you ready to begin?" he asked.

She slowly nodded her head.

"Then we begin," he said as he tore the seal on the testing document. "I will place the test sheets before you. When I say 'begin', you will begin reading and answering the questions. At the end of two hours, I will say 'stop' and you will put down your pencil. Do you understand?"

She nodded again.

Judge Knight laid the papers on her desk. She picked up a pencil, poised to begin. The judge held his pocket watch and finally said, "Begin." As she began reading, he quietly walked to the chair behind Miss Myline's desk and sat.

There, for the next two hours, sat the judge, Miss Myline, Miss Arphelia, and Lizzie. Lizzie's nervousness vanished as soon as she began reading. She knew this answer! Quickly she read and marked, lost and immersed in the test. It seemed that she was the only one in the room and time had stopped. She finished the question sections on the test, all areas, and quickly scanned it to be sure she'd not skipped any or gotten any answers out of order. She found two questions she believed she'd marked wrong and changed them and began her essay.

That part was easy. Words flew across the page as she listed reasons why she wanted to be a teacher and described her heart-felt calling. Just as she finished re-reading her essay and making a sentence clearer here and clarifying an expression there, Judge Knight called, "Stop."

She laid her pencil down and Miss Myline breathed an audible sigh of relief. She didn't know if she would be able to stand after sitting still so long, but she was thrilled that Lizzie had finished and seemed to have answered questions easily and confidently.

Judge Knight gathered the test and answers and replaced them in the packet from Atlanta. "There's a return envelope. I'll get your test in the mail first thing when I get back to town." He reached to shake her hand. "Congratulations, young lady. I'm hoping the next time we meet I'll be looking at a Georgia teacher."

Lizzie smiled and stood. Miss Arphelia did, too. "Oh my, I didn't realize how stiff I'd be after all that sitting," she said.

Lizzie looked at Miss Myline who was rising from her chair rubbing her lower back. She grinned, "Know just how you feel," she replied.

They heard the wagon stop at the door. Bulger was back, exactly as he'd promised. Judge Knight nodded his head as a farewell, and Miss Myline walked Lizzie to the door. She almost fainted when she looked out. There beside Bulger on the seat sat Jimmy! He was grinning like a bear eating honey, and held a bunch of fall flowers. He jumped off the seat and ran up the steps to meet her.

"Wanted to surprise you," he said, handing her the flowers.

Lizzie couldn't believe it. "You did!" She admitted.

Bulger called to them, "Com'on you two. We need to be gettin' back. I got things to do, ya know."

Jimmy held Lizzie's hand as they walked to the wagon. He helped her up and hopped up beside her. She waved to Miss Myline and the judge and his wife as Moses led them down the road.

Lizzie was quiet the first few miles. She was tired and when Jimmy's surprise got mixed in her emotions, she was overwhelmed. The test finished; Jimmy sitting beside her; and they were headed home.

Bulger finally broke the silence. "Jimmy's gone take the wagon back with him tonight after supper," he said. "He needs to load some stuff from town and get it back to his place, and I told him he could use Moses and the wagon."

Who cares? Lizzie thought. She reached to hold Jimmy's hand and smiled. *Who cares? Right now I've finished my test and sitting with my future husband. Now I can concentrate on planning my wedding. I'm the happiest girl in the world.*

THIRTY-SIX

With late fall days, time came for potatoes, both Irish and orange-colored sweet ones to be dug and hilled. Bulger hitched Moses to a huge, heavy tiller that cut deep into the ground and threw mounds of dirt to the side. Hidden in the dirt were the potatoes. Lizzie, Beth, and Miss Claudie followed Bulger, picking through the dirt, plucking out potatoes and tossing them in buckets. Buckets got heavy, and many trips were made to the edge of the 'tater patch to empty them. Piles of 'taters mounded up. It was tedious, backbreaking, hateful work. But it had to be done. 'Taters were as much an important winter staple as beans and pork. The 'taters were spread and allowed to dry a while before storing. Then they had to be hilled for the winter months.

To hill them, first a convenient spot, one out of the way yet close to the house, was chosen and cleared. Then a thick layer of pine straw was laid and a layer of potatoes placed on top of that-- and more pine straw-- and more potatoes-- until all the potatoes were 'nested'. Bulger placed a large galvanized tub over the top and lastly, the whole thing was covered with a good layer of dirt. All this made a good-sized 'hill'. Sheltered and snug inside, the potatoes were protected from frost and most freezes. Whenever any were needed, they were merely dug out, tossed in a bucket, and carried inside.

All during the long fall days of harvest, children of all ages toiled on their farms, doing what was needed to help their family survive another winter. Even toddlers followed behind their mothers; picking apples off the ground and tossing them into buckets—not always hitting them---but trying, anyway. Children toiled alongside their parents, bending to pull weeds—and often a few squash or peanut vines were uprooted before the diligent mother noticed; and many a sibling sat under a shade tree tending the baby while their parents picked cotton or gathered crops. It was an angry mother who returned to find a yowling baby whelped with ant bites while the sitter slept soundly.

One cool afternoon after most of the crops had been picked and stored, Eli decided to ask Bulger if he and a few of his friends could have a bird thrashing. They had cleared several acres on his place the past spring and piled the cuttings from bushes, small trees, and limbs from treetops in huge piles. They settled and dried during late spring and summer, and birds found refuge there in the cool fall weather. He was delighted when Bulger gave a 'go 'head', and when he and Ginger rode to town to pick up a few supplies, he asked Cullie to spread the word.

Later, he visited Minshue and asked Skipping Rock to come along. Eli entered the village and found Skipping Rock trimming the hooves of his paint. Skipping Rock let the horse's foot drop as Eli drew close.

"How you doin', Skipping Rock?" he asked. "Don't think I didn't see you with that great-looking girl at my wedding," he teased. He watched Skipping Rock actually blush!

He answered, "That was Bright Star," he said. "Don't be surprised to be invited to a marriage celebration not too long from now," he grinned.

Eli's eyes widened in surprise. "You don' mean it! You?"

"Well, why not?" Skipping Rock retorted. "I think if it's good enough for you it's good enough for me." He added, shaking his finger at Eli, "And you look like it's been a mighty good thing for you, if you ask me."

It was Eli's turn to blush. He quickly shook the red off his cheeks and told Skipping Rock about the bird thrashing; his real reason for the visit, and Skipping Rock readily agreed to come along. He walked Eli to the edge of the village, out of Minshue and Warm DayRah's earshot.

"Have you heard any more rumors of the Panther Clan?"

he whispered.

Eli looked up. He hated to give Skipping Rock the news. "Good or bad first?" he asked.

"Gimme the good first," Skipping Rock answered.

"Well, the Clan seems to have left our area after your meeting with them," he winced, remembering how Skipping Rock and his two friends almost lost their lives at the Panthers' hands. He continued, "And now the bad. Looks like they've moved a little further south, but not back to their homes. They've been really raising havoc; stealing more, getting bolder, even burning out some farmers." He shook his head. "I hope they come to their senses. If they go home, they can be punished there. If not, then they'll face courts here and it won't be nice."

Skipping Rock looked deeply into the forest, silent. At last he broke a twig that he held in his hands and tossed it to the ground. He sighed deeply. "It's too late for punishment from the courts; yours or ours. Their time will come. I only pray that they won't bring any deaths or do anything reckless around here. But, for some reason, I have a really bad feeling." He looked up. "Maybe my feelings will be wrong, though."

Eli agreed, and left Skipping Rock's eyes following him as he walked the trail home.

Late one afternoon the following week, Cullie, one of the Crockett boys, a Huckeba or two, and a couple of the Walls's and Gore's, ambled to Eli's house.

"Ready to get some birds?" Cullie called.

"Be there in a minute," Eli called. He turned and gave Ginger a quick peck on her cheek and dashed out the door. He stopped short when he saw Sonny bringing up the rear.

Cullie noticed his puzzlement and shrugged. "He was in the store after school and heard me telling Ross here. Nothin' to do but let him come along."

"He'll get broke in good," Eli answered. "Seems he's growed a foot since spring, anyway." He turned and said, "We gotta get some limbs ready," and started trotting to the edge of the field. He pulled his pocketknife and cut a couple of long, thorny limbs from a bare plum bush. Cullie cut his 'thrasher' from a wild lemon and the others gathered their own; long, bushy, sturdy, and thorny.

They walked to the edge of the field to the mounds of dried bushes and limbs. "You wanna' go first, Cullie?" Eli asked.

Cullie grinned and walked to the brushpile and slammed the long limb he'd cut down across it. Nothing. He stepped back and grabbed his limb with both hands and whapped it down—hard--again. Out flew two or three birds. Eli and the Hull boys ran, thrashing their limbs in the air and whipping at the birds. One of the Gores got a bird, knocking it dead to the ground. "Whoo-ee!" he hollered. "Knock it agin', Cullie!"

Cullie did and more birds flew. The boys ran, thrashing their limbs and hollering, laughing, trying to knock down birds. More got away than got hit.

"Give me a chance!" Sonny hollered.

"Sure," replied Ross, and he began hitting the brushpile.

When no more birds flew from that huge pile of dried wood, they moved to another and started again.

The 'game' was new to Skipping Rock, but he caught on quickly. He ran around, swatting his limb as well as the others, and fared almost as well as they did. Many of the birds were fit to eat and would make a fine bird supper.

Finally, about dark, they were 'thrashed out', tired, a little sweaty, and happy. They walked back to Eli's. Bulger was there and invited them back to his place for supper.

They rode to Miss Claudie's in separate wagons. She looked at the men and commanded. "Ya'll get right on out on the porch and rub them beggar lice off your pants. Get some of that cotton sticking in the crack by the window."

They went to the porch and laughed as they rubbed beggar lice—little flat seeds that clung to their clothing, and picked off prickly cockle burrs, with wads of cotton.

Once clean and sitting around the table, they ate and talked about the afternoon's thrashing. Skipping Rock gleefully slapped his leg as he explained to Ginger how Sonny ran wildly, whacking around and finally got two birds. Sonny countered with a short account of Skipping Rock running at a bird so hard he tripped over a root. Everyone hooted and guffawed. Hollis, one of the Walls's, broke the mood when said how he dreaded going home. His ma would give him the 'what for' when she saw the long tear in his overalls and had to patch it.

Each of the men shook hands and commented on their good time and complimented Miss Claudie on her supper. "Need to do it again," said Sonny, ready to romp anytime. After a full, merry afternoon filled with lots of fun, and good fellowship over a tasty meal, they all left in time to get home before bedtime.

THIRTY-SEVEN

The days grew shorter and cooler. Skipping Rock stopped by Eli's and asked him to go rabbit hunting. Skipping Rock needed a few pelts for Warm DayRah to make a toasty covering for her head and cozy hand mittens for protection from the coming cold, so he readily agreed.

They decided to walk over to Bulger's and ask him to come along.

When they arrived, Bulger and Beth were stacking wood on the porch where it would be dry and handy for the stove. Eli watched Jack and Bell follow Beth. His eyes widened when he saw what the dogs were doing: each had a small piece of firewood clamped in their mouths! When they climbed the steps and stopped beside Beth, she turned and removed the wood and placed it on the pile.

"I'll be," Eli exclaimed. "You got some smart dogs, there, Little Bit! Reckon they'd like to go rabbit huntin'?" he asked.

Beth puffed up. "Really, Eli. You know these are 'coon dogs. They wouldn't waste their time runnin' no rabbits!" And she tipped up her nose and turned on her heel and shushed her dogs into the kitchen.

Skipping Rock, through his laughter, asked, "How about you, Bulger? Are you up for getting us a mess of rabbits for supper?"

"Time's a'wastin', let me get my gun."

Before any rabbit could give three shakes of his cottony tail, the three hunters set out for the boggy swamps near

Maxwell's place. Bulger and Eli had shotguns and Skipping Rock had his bow. It wasn't long until they reached the swamps where the rabbits grew bigger and had better pelts than those that lived in the woods.

Skipping Rock slipped to the right and Bulger to the left. Eli trudged straight on in. Eli heard a 'wwhiiisssssh' and knew Skipping Rock had let go an arrow. He didn't see Bulger, but heard him. Wish he could get around a little quieter, he said to himself. Bet he's gone scare away any rabbits we might see on this side. Then he grinned as the thoughts kept tumbling; but at Bulger's age, he chuckled, guess gettin' around at all was good.

Suddenly he saw a black shiny dot in the middle of a bunch of swamp fern. A rabbit. He looked closer and raised his gun and shot. The rabbit never knew what hit him. He heard a 'boom' and jerked his head to his left where Bulger was hunting.

"Hot dang," he heard through the brush, "Missed em'!"

Then the brush exploded. There came the biggest, fastest swamp rabbit Eli had ever seen. And it was aiming straight for him! Then a zig; and a zag; again straight on. The bushes where the rabbit made his hasty exit began shaking and whipping wildly once more, and Bulger's big head popped out, his hat covering one eye and a long bleeding scratch along the side of the other.

"Git'em!" he hollered, raising a fist and beating it in the air.

Eli raised his shotgun, but the rabbit was coming too fast to get off a shot. He lost his concentration when he saw, from the corner of his eye, Skipping Rock burst from the bushes with a baffled expression. Eli's mind reeled as he tried to comprehend and make sense of what was happening.

Realizing Skipping Rock wasn't in danger and was only running back to see what all the commotion was about, Eli's snapped his eyes back toward the rabbit. His heart beat faster and the shotgun felt slippery along the barrel where he gripped it. His hands felt sweaty, hot. He tried desperately to level the gun and get a good bead on the incoming grey-haired bullet. All he could see was the flash of fur.

That rabbit was traveling: hind legs pumping his rear high into the air; ears straight and twitching from side to side; black button eyes wide and white tail flashing. Without a doubt, it was headed straight at him.

"Git'em!" Bulger hollered again, stumbling out of the swamp tangles.

Spontaneously, totally on impulse, Eli threw down his gun, clamped his feet together, squatted, and hammered his hands together just as that rabbit hit his knees. The impact to his chest knocked him a step backward and made his hat fly off. When he found his footing and managed to stand up, he was amazed to find he was holding a long, limp rabbit in a vise grip between his fingers.

Bulger came limping up and Skipping Rock was close behind.

"I'll be dang-darned!" Bulger exclaimed, removing his hat and pounding it on the side of his leg. His eyes sparkled and hair stood out wildly at all ends. "You done got yourself a rabbit!"

Eli stood, holding the rabbit in disbelief. "Well, don't know if he broke his neck when he hit me or ya'll scared him hollering and knocking bushes so bad he had a heart attack." He looked at Bulger, "We'll have fried rabbit and gravy for supper tonight, anyway! Got another over in the ferns," he said with a grin.

Skipping Rock added, "And Warm DayRah will have plenty of pelts to work with after we have our rabbit stew, too," he said as he held his bunch of three rabbits high. He shook his head. "I don't know if I believe what I just saw," he said. "And I was standing here watching the whole thing!"

Bulger, feeling bushed, urged the boys to head home. "Com'on, boys. Eli, go get your rabbit over there. We better head out 'fore dark. Got to get these rabbits cleaned and ready for the pot. You can have our skins, Skipping Rock. Warm DayRah will stay warm this winter."

They made their way back along the trail in the boggy swamp; happy but tired. The day was one of those special days when memories were made. The story of the rabbit being caught in Eli's hands there in the boggy swamp would be told and retold....but who'd believe the truth of it? Eli wondered.

THIRTY-EIGHT

Miss Myline worked two weeks full in mid-September to get the schoolhouse ready for the first day of the new school year. Sonny came often to help; rearranging heavy desks so Miss Myline could sweep and mop under them.

Bulger dropped Beth off early one morning as he passed the schoolhouse on his way into town. She wanted to visit Miss Myline, and he wanted to check on the Hulls' progress in moving into their new house and barn.

Beth jumped off the wagon and ran inside the school house.

"Why, Beth, what are you doing here today?" Miss Myline asked.

Beth walked around the room, touching desktops, lifting their tops and peeking inside. "Just wanted to come by and see what's going on," she said. She turned to Miss Myline and beamed, "I can't wait to come!" she said. "I waited all summer to get to come to school and now it's almost time to start."

Miss Myline laughed. "As long as you're here, you may as well make yourself useful," she said. "Grab that rag and wipe the slate board clean."

Beth hurried to help. She rubbed the board and stood in a chair to reach the top. "What do you make marks with?" she asked.

"I have white chalk sticks," the teacher replied. She lifted a desk top and removed a small version of the board on the wall. "Children have these slate boards," she explained. "They make marks with slate pencils, we can't afford chalk for everyone, and I check their figures and they can erase them and try again." She replaced the slate. "We write letters and numbers and spell. Each morning we stand and face the flag as one of the students—a good reader—reads a few verses from the Bible." She smiled. "Then we start our day. I know you're going to love school, Beth. I can't wait for it to start, either! I know it won't be long before you're one of my best readers."

Together they cleaned and chatted and filled the morning, waiting for Bulger to return from town.

≈

Bulger made his way through town and pulled Moses to a stop in front of the Sheriff's office at the jail. Mrs. Bledsoe came out to greet him.

"Hello, Bulger, what brings ya out today?" she asked.

He dropped the reins and looked down at her. "Come to offer my wagon if the Hulls need any help movin' back home," he said.

Mrs. Bledsoe propped her hands on her hips. "I think they're all set now," she said. "Been finishing up their roof and getting the barn ready last week. Moving things in yesterday." She moved and crossed them across her chest. "It's been a blessing," she said, "people coming in with all sorts of things; beds, quilts, food, and building supplies. The town turned out and I think they're pretty well set. Even Sammy the Tinker gave pots and pans and tableware off his wagon." She shook her head. "God works and our good people follow through."

Bulger nodded. "Well, I got extra seeds here for'em," he said, handing down sacks of seeds—enough for next year's spring planting a few acres and some are to grow few garden staples.

Mrs. Bledsoe reached and took the sacks. "Thank you Bulger. The sheriff will get these out to them tomorrow."

"Mighty welcome," Bulger said. "Knew there was a reason we got blessed with extra crops this year. Still have some to share with a couple of neighbors who were hit, too. God has been good!"

Mrs. Bledsoe agreed. "Yes, He certainly has."

Bulger tipped his hat and pulled the wagon around. He headed back out of town and stopped in front of the schoolhouse. Beth heard the wagon and ran to the door.

"See you soon, Miss Myline," she called over her shoulder as she skipped down the steps and hopped up beside Bulger on the wagon seat.

"What'd ya think?" he asked.

Beth clapped her hands together in delight. "I think I'll love it!" she crowed. "I can't wait to get started."

Bulger threw back his head and laughed. "Just what I thought," he chuckled. He clicked his tongue to the mule and together they rambled down the road and back home.

THIRTY-NINE

School started the Monday after Lizzie completed her test. September flew by and October came in with a cold wind that stayed cool all month. There were days sprinkled with warm sunshine, Indian summer, Bulger had said, but the days passed quickly and tumbled into each other. Beth loved school, especially since Warm DayRah was attending.

Bulger dropped Lizzie off to stay with Ginger as he carried Beth to the schoolhouse. They intended to work on plans for Lizzie and Jimmy's wedding in December. Ginger busied herself with her new house and Eli, but not too busy to make sure Lizzie had her 'pounding' at church and a special shower. Ginger's surprise for Lizzie's shower would include local couples as well as single girls and guys.

The last week in October was one of bustle. After Bulger returned from dropping Beth off at school, Miss Claudie pulled out Bulger's old quilted jacket and pulled a toboggan down low on her head and they headed out to gather pumpkins. She planned to save the biggest and best for Beth to carve out a face and put a candle inside and put on the porch. She would love watching it at night. It would be a special treat when the young folks came serenading on the night after the harvest celebration.

When they reached the small pumpkin patch, Miss Claudie sat on the wagon seat and slowly urged the mule along. Bulger walked alongside and placed the pumpkins in the wagon bed. There wasn't a huge crop; but it was ample.

Back at the house, Bulger unloaded the pumpkins near the edge of the porch where any early frost wouldn't hurt them and spread them on the ground. Miss Claudie eyed each one and finally picked one especially for Beth. She sat it on the dogtrot.

"I'll get to work on some of these pumpkins for drying tomorrow," she told Bulger. "Pumpkin pies go mighty good on Sunday dinners." She turned. "Right now I'll get supper started and have the knives ready for Beth to work on her pumpkin when ya'll get back from school."

"Don't forget I have to drop off 'Loris on the way," he said as he mounted the wagon. "We'll be back 'fore dark, though." He headed the wagon toward the edge of town and to the schoolhouse. Miss Claudie picked up an armful of wood from the stack beside the door and went inside. She looked after Bulger and saw Jack and Bell rising and stretching from their resting place under the old oak tree at the edge of the yard.

She chuckled. Them dogs know Bulger's gone after Beth, she thought as she went inside. Funny how they follow that wagon every mornin' to the edge of the yard and lay there all day, waitin' 'till Bulger and Beth pull up every evenin'. Beth's 'bout as happy to see them hounds as they are to see her, she mused.

She tossed the wood onto the waiting embers in the stove and blew on the hot coals to get a flame going. Supper would be short tonight. She couldn't wait to see Beth carving her first harvest pumpkin.

FORTY

Eli and Ginger's first few weeks together were filled with honeymoon bliss. Ginger bustled about all day, cooking and cleaning while Eli never wandered far from the house. He found thousands of reasons to get back inside and be with his bride. He spent time outside finishing up the board and batting on the corn crib, trying to plug any holes where mice and rats could get in to the corn. He knew they'd get in somehow, but was determined to make their job as difficult as he could. He nailed the last nail and heard the familiar 'hallo' coming from the woods. It was Skipping Rock. He raised his hand in friendly salute and bounced into a jog and crossed the yard to Eli.

Eli grinned. "What'cha doin' out today?" he asked his friend.

Skipping Rock shrugged his shoulders and huffed to a stop by the corncrib. "I just wanted to come by and invite you and Ginger to mine and Bright Star's marriage celebration."

"Whoa!" Eli responded in surprise. "I knew you expected you'd marry her, but I never thought it'd be so soon."

Skipping Rock almost blushed. "My grandmother agreed that ours is a good match. Winter's coming on and there is plenty of room in Bright Star's winter house. I will leave Minshue and go with my wife's family."

Eli propped his hands on his hips and nodded toward the house. "Come on in and tell us about your celebration. When and where should we be so not to miss this shindig?"

They crossed the yard and found Ginger making coffee. "I

thought I heard company," she said. "Have a seat. I'll put out cups for coffee and have some of Miss Claudie's tea cakes to go along with it."

"Sounds good to me," Eli responded. He and Skipping Rock sat at the table. "Skipping Rock has some good news to share with us," he said. "We've been invited to his wedding."

Ginger almost spilled the coffee. "Wedding!" she said. "Oh, Skipping Rock. Is it Bright Star? I'm so happy for you!"

Skipping Rock's face turned from red to maroon.

Eli laughed. "I think you got him that time, Ginger," he said. Then to Skipping Rock, "She does tend to get excited about such things. Now, fill us in with the details."

Ginger sat and passed the tea cakes. Skipping Rock cleared his throat and glanced at Ginger, then picked up a cookie. He turned it over in his hands and started talking. "Like I told Eli, I'm eighteen and a man, and Bright Star is fifteen, and my grandmother decided it was time for me to have a wife and, um, start a family," the cookie broke in his hands and he quickly brushed the crumbs into his saucer. He looked somewhat embarrassed, but continued. "We must marry outside our clan. Don't know if I've ever told you, but I'm part of the Red Tailed Hawk clan. We're the keepers of birds and hold all birds sacred. Remember the gourds I brought for this spring's Purple Martin's houses when they return? Anyway, birds are messengers. They may bring messages of joy or warnings of bad weather or possibly let us know a predator is near: animal or human. Our clan color is purple and our clan tree is the Maple."

"Bright Star's clan is the Blue Holly clan. They are known for their knowledge of herbs and making medicine. They are also known as the Blue clan since that's their color, and their wood is the Ash. Grandmother and Minshue believe that the joining of our two clans will be a strong one, so Grandmother went to the Blue Holly clan that's found in Carroll County, just above Roopville. She met with Bright Star's Grandmother and together they decided to see if the union between Bright Star and me might work out. Well, I'd seen her around the Craven's Trading Post and thought she was beautiful. Turns out, everyone I've asked about her says she's as beautiful inside as she is out." He paused and added, "And I think so, too."

"I decided she is the one, so I killed a deer and went and placed it at her doorway. Boy, did I sweat out the next couple of days." He shifted in his seat and sipped some coffee. "Our way says that if she ignores my gesture of bringing meat to her door and sends it back to me--it's no deal—I'm out. I could hardly sleep waiting to know what she'd done with the meat. Two mornings after I'd left the venison, Grandmother came, smiling from ear to ear. She told me that Bright Star had taken the meat and asked that I come for supper. Her cooking my offering and serving it to me meant that she'd accepted me, and boy, was I ever relieved!" He took a breath and noticed that Eli and Ginger were listening closely and went on.

"After the family supper with Bright Star, we became officially engaged. Your wedding was the first outing we've had together. Grandmother was so impressed with your ceremony that she decided ours should be soon, and here I am. Can you come by in ten days' time? That's the first night of the new moon and we'll be beginning our new life together under the new moon's blessing." He looked at them both expectantly.

Ginger looked at Eli and smiled. Then back to Skipping Rock. "We wouldn't miss it for the world," she said.

"Good!" Skipping Rock replied. "I must be going now to Bulger's to pass the invitation to them. New times have come concerning our clan's including white brothers in our celebrations, and your family is a special one to our family. My wedding would never be the one I'd want without you there."

He rose to leave. Ginger and Eli followed and quietly shut the door. When Skipping Rock stepped off the bottom step, he started trotting along the worn trail beside the creek that led to Bulger's. His heart was swelled to almost bursting. He was the happiest young man in Heard County.

FORTY-ONE

Fall officially arrived. The air was definitely cooler and there was a thin covering of ice on Ole' Crip's water trough when Bulger went out to feed the animals. Trees wore their leaves with a last minute splendor that seemed to shout, 'Look at us, this is our glory. Enjoy our brilliance now for we will be reaching to the heavens with bare arms in a few weeks.'

Jack and Bell felt the cooler weather, too. They ran and sprinted around and across the yard and chased squirrels that were brave enough to try to bury acorns there. Puffs of white breath came from their mouths in the early morning play and disappeared as the sun warmed the day.

Most of the summer's crops were harvested and put safely away. Any extra was sold or bartered for goods they'd need during the cold winter months. Miss Claudie traded extra eggs and milk for the end pieces of material left on bolts of cloth at Jones's store. She planned to hold a quilting and have a new quilt ready for Lizzie and Jimmy, come her bridal shower.

Bulger pulled the quilting frames from the rafters in the smokehouse where they were stored. Miss Claudie pushed the kitchen table and chairs to the side of the kitchen and Bulger brought the frames inside. Miss Claudie wiped them clean. She pulled one of the chairs and positioned it just under one of the hooks set in the ceiling. There were four hooks anchored in the ceiling and each formed a corner that would hold the square quilting frame. Bulger stood in the chair and Miss Claudie handed him one thin rope to attach to a hook. One by one, each of the four hooks held a rope attached and hung loosely down. Bulger and Miss Claudie joined the ends of the quilting frames and attached them to the hanging ropes. Miss Claudie stood back and inspected their work.

"Looks mighty good, Bulger," she said. "We quilting ladies can pin the quilt top on the batting and backing and go to town!" She stood back. "We can lift the whole thing high out of the way when we're not using it and push the table back along the wall when we do need it. I'll let the frame back down when the women come to do the stitching. I'm right proud of this," she beamed.

"Look'a here what I done got finished," she said to Bulger as she opened the bottom drawer on the wall cupboard. "I've been working on this and kept if from the girls so it will be a surprise." She pulled out her quilt top and spread it for Bulger to see.

"Why, Claudie, that's beautiful," he said with wide eyes. "Ya outdone yo'self on this one!"

Miss Claudie began refolding the top. "It's a double wedding ring pattern," she explained. "I thought it was the perfect one for Lizzie and Jimmy." She placed the colorful patterned top back onto the shelf and closed the door. "Lizzie gave Eli one of those two quilts left from when their folks drowned, but we never could get all that red mud stain all the way out. I wanted her and Jimmy to have something special to start their new lives together; something with new, good memories."

Bulger felt Miss Claudie's sadness and spoke to break it. "When ya planning' to get the quilting women together to finish this thing up?" he asked.

She snapped to attention and stood, brushing off her apron and frowning in concern. "I thought about next Saturday evenin'," she said. "Most ever body's got their things done and it will be hog killin' time in a couple of weeks, 'bout Thanksgiving time. Folks will be busy then, for sure, getting' the hogs killed and meat ready to cure out."

"Sounds good to me. I gotta go to town and pick up that salt I ordered from Mr. Pollard for the saltbox in the smokehouse. I'm gone salt down our meat this year, 'stead of sugar cure it; think it keeps better that way. Then we can dry out some sausage and eat our fresh as long as it lasts." He paused. "Want me to stop by and pass out invites to the quiltin'? Ya sure ya got ever'thing ya need for it?"

Miss Claudie thought a minute. "That'd be nice. I got my backing and cotton filling and plenty of needles and thread. Gone bake a pound cake. That should do it." She got a pencil and paper. "I'll write down the names to invite so you won't skip anybody. Help me get this frame up and move the table back in place."

Together they got the frame raised high, almost touching the ceiling, and pushed the table back under. Miss Claudie pulled up a chair and began listing her quilting friends. They usually got together two or three times a winter at one or the other's house during the cold weather and enjoyed their days of quilting. They stitched, laughed, gossiped, and enjoyed tasty snacks. By the end of the day, one of the ladies had a new quilt perfect for a gift or topping for her bed. Sometimes if the pattern was a difficult one, a second get-together was needed.

After the quilting, all Miss Claudie had to do was the final hemming, and that was finished up after supper. It was calming and relaxing, sitting beside the warm fire with a new quilt draped over her lap, rocking and stitching the hem; dreaming of enjoyment to come to the proud owners with the use of their new cover.

Miss Claudie made her list: Miss Bea with her tiny hoop earrings dangling from her pierced ears, neat and petite Miss Pearl, Aunt Glimmer, whose tea cake recipe was used by almost everybody, Miss Jessie with her baked sweet potatoes, Miss Eva and her meal pie, Miss Dara with her pound cake, Aunt Della, and the Baptist church ladies: Miss Vivian, Miss Pauline, Miss Nora, Miss Myric, and Miss Capitola. When these ladies got together, laughter flowed and stitches flew. Needles flashed and before they knew it, a new quilt got born.

Bulger put the list in his overalls pocket, set his hat on his head and grabbed his coat. He had a lot of stops to make before he'd get the salt for the saltbox and back home. He chuckled as he opened the barn doors to hitch Moses and finish his outing before dark.

FORTY-TWO

The following Saturday, Miss Claudie made sure Bulger left early with Lizzie sitting high on the wagon. She'd conspired with Ginger to have Lizzie over to help arrange her pantry, and Lizzie was eager to go. She'd missed their time together and wanted to hear all about Ginger's insight concerning marriage.

Bulger and Lizzie were long out of sight when wagons came in the yard like a train pulling up to a station. Wagons lined up and dropped off women carrying their specialized covered dishes and small sewing baskets containing their favorite quilting needles and thimbles. Uncle Eddie brought his wife, Aunt Glimmer, and her sister-in-law Miss Pearl, and Miss Bea. Others doubled up, too, and by nine o'clock the ladies had pulled kitchen chairs up to the quilt fit snug in the frames and with needles threaded, started stitching. A couple of the ladies reached in their apron pockets and pulled out their sweet gum toothbrushes with their spraggled-chewed ends and dipped them in the small snuff boxes they always carried. They popped them in their mouths and chewed contentedly.

Soft chatter filled the cozy kitchen. The kettle whispered on the stove and lovely scents wafted from the oven. Platters of cookies and plates of pies and cakes covered with clean, brightly printed feed sacks stood ready on the shelf of the pie safe.

Beth sat on her bed on the side of the room, watching and listening to everything going on. "Shhhh, Dolly," she whispered. "Let's sneak under the quilt and sit on the floor and play and listen awhile. We won't bother nobody." And she stuck Dolly under one arm and Patty under the other and crawled between Miss Claudie's and Aunt Glimmer's chairs to settle under the quilt.

"Did you know Miss Myline will be leaving us Christmas?" asked Miss Capitola. Miss Myric nodded agreement and kept on stitching.

"Why on earth?" wondered Miss Pearl aloud. She'd been a teacher before she'd married Mr. Demmie. Then, like all female teachers who married, she became a housewife and stay at home mother.

Miss Vivian chirped, "I hear she had a marriage invitation from her beau back home. She's inclined to accept, from what I heard. With the money she's saved from her allowance here, she has a right good chunk to start out on."

"What ever will we do? We can't get another teacher here before Christmas. All the available teachers have jobs and our children will be lacking for sure," said Miss Bea, shaking her head so that her little gold earrings jiggled a little as she talked.

The subject was dropped and Beth heard Miss Jessie ask about gardens. "How did ya'll come out with your gardens this year?" she asked.

There was a jumbled murmuring of 'just fine', and 'all right,' or 'better than last year'.

Miss Nora spoke up to Miss Claudie. "How did ya'll like that Indian marriage ceremony you went to?"

Miss Claudie's hands paused, needle still in the air. Her eyes expressed her delight before words were spoken. "It was beautiful," she said. She looked around to the group of women. "It wasn't like Eli's and Ginger's wedding, but it was a very moving ceremony." She looked down and her fingers began working on the quilt again. "There was such a quiet dedication; a fullness of union." She sighed. "It was really a sweet, sweet, moving time, us being there. I feel blessed and honored to have been a witness to Skipping Rock's wedding." She hesitated and her voice caught a bit. "Sad only that that fine young man won't be as close by anymore. He's gone to live with his bride in her village and can't get by as often. We'll all miss him."

The women, all quiet while Miss Claudie spoke, nodded in agreement. Their fingers slowed as they listened to the account of the Indian's ceremony.

"Well," Miss Nora spoke up, "I'll be glad when that other wild bunch decides to go home or they get put somewhere one. I'm a little afraid with them skulking around. My husband, Alma, heard last week that they'd been seen close by here again." She shook her head and started jabbing the needle through the cloth. "I feel for their folks, but them boys need to be stopped."

With that, the women's conversation picked up and their needles stitched inches and inches of beautiful, intricate details along the colorful entwined wedding rings.

Beth, hiding under the quilt, felt like she was in a tent, listened quietly and heard the door open.

"Come on in, Susan," Miss Claudie said as she rose to round up another chair.

Beth peeked out and was surprised to see Susan, from Jones's store in town, and Melody with her. Beth scrambled out from under the quilt frame and ran up to Melody.

"Hey," she said, "I didn't know you'd be coming. Wanna' get your coat and go out to the barn and see my dogs? Their names are Jack and Bell and they can smell anything. The barn cats are out there, too. We can play in the hayloft while your sister helps Miss Claudie get Lizzie's quilt finished. Wanna' go?" she asked again.

Melody looked at Susan and Susan smiled with a 'go ahead'. Beth rushed across the room, dodging chairs and tossed her dolls on her bed. She grabbed her coat off the peg and together she and Melody scampered off to the barn.

"Sorry I'm late," Susan said. "Mr. Wright at the Post Office stopped me and asked if I was joining the party out here." She laughed. "You know the post master knows all the news. I told him I was in a hurry to leave, but he insisted I stop by so I could bring this by for Lizzie." She pulled a letter from her coat pocket and handed it to Miss Claudie. Her eyes widened when she saw the return address: Department of Education, Atlanta, Georgia. Lizzie's scores had arrived. Miss Claudie's hand shook as she opened the pie safe and laid the letter on the top shelf for safe keeping. As much as she loved quilting and having the ladies over, she was almost ready for the day to end and Lizzie would be back and open her letter. She was as nervous as a worm on a hook the rest of the day.

The morning passed swiftly. The quilt took shape with all the tiny, neat stitches being artfully woven through the material.

Beth and Melody eventually tired of playing with the cats and teasing Moses with bits of hay. Jack and Bell tired and curled up in a corner of the barn and slept. The girls walked slowly back to the house and washed their faces and hands in the washpan on the porch shelf. "Burrrr," said Beth. "That water's cold." She hurried to dry her face and hands and handed the towel over to Melody.

They came in the warm kitchen just as the ladies were taking a break. Chatter livened up as the women circulated and stretched their legs, relaxed their fingers and wiggled their toes. Miss Claudie set out cups and plates and a quick snack put the women back in the sewing mood. Soon they were settled back in their chairs, fingers darting, needles dancing.

Beth and Melody picked over cookies and pies and settled in front of the fire to eat. Before they knew it, Miss Claudie and Susan were shaking them awake and it was time for Melody to go home. Beth looked groggily around. Most of the women were gone already and the quilt was wrapped all the way around the frames to the middle. It was almost finished! The ladies had embroidered their names around the outer edge and all that was left was for Miss Claudie to take it out of the frame and hem it. Would Lizzie be surprised!

Melody asked, "Can you come stay the night with me one night? You can come home with me from school and Mr. Bulger can pick you up the next day from the schoolhouse." She looked at Miss Claudie.

Beth looked expectantly, too.

"I think we can arrange that," she said, her eyes twinkling. "Right now, though, it's time to get going. Beth will see you tomorrow at church. We'll ask Bulger about it then." She helped Melody with her coat and added, "Beth's gotta' help me get this quilt off the frame and folded away 'fore Bulger and Lizzie get back—and that won't be but just a little while now."

The girls pulled themselves to their feet and Susan walked Melody out the door to the wagon where Cullie had come to pick them up. If Miss Claudie didn't miss her guess, that boy had a fool goofy look on his face as he helped Susan in the wagon. She grinned. If there's much more sweet-heartin' going' on now than in spring, heaven help us. She chuckled aloud.

She and Beth waved 'bye to Cullie and turned to get the quilt put away before Lizzie returned home. Hopefully, she would be so eager to tell them about her day with Eli and Ginger that she would never notice there'd been company around.

Miss Claudie's feet were light as she bustled around the room, folding the quilt and returning the quilting frame high to the ceiling. Moving the table and arranging chairs; building the stove fire and humming to herself as dusk slipped in. She lit extra lamps and warmed supper for her family with a full, sweet happiness she hadn't felt in a good while. Beth caught the mood and together they filled the kitchen with love and joy. When Bulger and Lizzie came in, they only added to the rich, warm, affection that packed the room like soft, sweet, cotton candy.

Suddenly Miss Claudie gave a stifled cry. "Oh! I almost forgot!" And she raced over to the pie safe and pulled the door open. "This letter came for you today." She hurried to Lizzie and thrust it forward to her.

"Letter? Came here? How did it get here?" she asked as she took the letter and quickly read the return address. A slight wisp of air escaped from her lips. She asked again, "How in the world did this get here?"

Thinking fast, Miss Claudie crossed her fingers behind her back and told a little white lie. "Susan brought Melody over to play with Beth a while today and she brung the letter with her." She shot a piercing look at Beth.

Beth turned white with the understanding that she should back up the story if Lizzie pressed for more. Well, it's not exactly an UN-truth, she rationalized. Susan did come and Melody came too, and, they *did* play.

Lizzie stood staring at the envelope until Bulger finally said, "Well, don't just stand there—open it!"

Lizzie wasted no time, ripped through the envelope and unfolded the letter. She scanned through until her eyes found what she was looking for. There it was: 'we are pleased to inform you that you have passed the Georgia Department of Education's qualifications to become an accredited teacher'. She couldn't believe it! She screamed and everybody laughed and danced all over the kitchen like happy rabbits in a hayfield.

When the excitement wore to a point where Lizzie had to sit to get her breath, she continued reading the letter. There was even more good news. She'd scored the highest of that quarter's testing group in the whole state!

She dropped the letter to her lap. "Oh, my," she said. "This is so wonderful." Then she sniffed and tears wet her eyes. "To be so happy, yet to know this certificate," and she held up the printed certificate with its gold seal, "will never be used. I'd thought I'd teach in a real school, but I'm going to be Jimmy's wife in six short weeks." She looked up and a lone tear rolled down her cheek. "Now I have my first wish, but I won't be able to fulfill it." She stood and took a deep breath. "I'm glad I did my best and I'm glad I know I can do whatever I set my head to do, but being a married woman, this certificate is as good as a blank piece of paper." She folded the letter and certificate and replaced it in the envelope. She smiled, "I wouldn't change my life for anything. Jimmy's my life and I can hardly wait to share it with him."

Miss Claudie gave her a reassuring hug. Beth took the envelope from her hand and placed it back on the top shelf of the pie safe. Bulger sat in his rocking chair by the fire and lit his pipe. God's grace came and surrounded them all and washed them in contentment and peace. This day became a special day of memories that Beth cherished and brought to mind many, many times as she grew in body and soul.

FORTY-THREE

The next morning, sunlight poured over the top of the barn and spilled into the yard making mottled smudges throughout the yard. Jack and Bell bounded out the kitchen door and Beth laughed as she watched them jump from shadow to shadow. They soon tired of their game and trotted to the edge of the yard, noses down, scenting around dead leaves and under fallen trees. They ducked in the woods and did their 'things'; scratching the ground and making dirt fly from their hind legs to indicate a job well done.

Miss Claudie stood at the kitchen sink, washing up the last of morning's dishes and gazed out the window. So blessed, so blessed, she assured herself. Ah, so blessed to count my and Bulger's blessings. God is so good, she thought.

Lizzie and Beth covered the lunch basket with sparkling white flour cloths and Bulger hitched Moses. Today was a special day at church. It was Preacher Arp's day to deliver the message, and Lizzie's pounding would follow dinner.

Bulger pulled Moses next to Eli's wagon in the churchyard. Ginger hurried to give everyone a hug, but Eli held back. He picked up Beth and swung her around, making her squeal with delight. He hugged Miss Claudie, and shook hands with Bulger and turned to Lizzie. He grinned and raised his eyebrows as he reached into his coat pocket and brought out Jimmy's daybook. Lizzie was de-lighted.

Her hands shook as she slipped the thin, worn book into her purse. She could hardly wait until she could get home and read it. Holding the clasp on her purse tightly, she followed her family into the church.

Uncle Eddie finished his scripture reading early and Bulger prayed the mid-morning prayer. Preacher Arp came to the stand and everyone's attention turned to him.

The sermon was to the point: get saved or go to Hell. Preacher Arp waved his arms and pounded the podium. As intense as it was, the service ended in thankfulness and gratitude. He echoed Miss Claudie's morning thoughts: God is good.

Mr. Demmie came forward and concluded service with 'Amazing Grace'. It was time to eat.

Instead of serving food on tables outside in the cold, the men slid two church benches together and the ladies put the food on the seats. They'd have to reach over the backs of the benches to get the food, but it was warm and dry inside. After a filling meal, the men folks moseyed outside and sat in buggies or lounged in the back of a wagon out of the wind while Lizzie and the women enjoyed a good time inside unwrapping all sorts of good things. It was never too cold for children to romp outside. Beth, Melody, Sonny, Warm DayRah, and several others played hide-and-seek and Red Rover. They managed to work up a sweat and had their mothers in a dither to clean them up enough to go home.

Night came soon during the early weeks of November. Once they arrived home, Bulger hurried to unhitch Moses and rushed to get inside the warm kitchen.

Bulger had made a large chest and presented it to Lizzie as a wedding present. She stored her goods in it until Jimmy could come by and pick it up. She hoped Eli might offer to hitch Little Man and carry the gifts to Jimmy's and her new home. Either way, she wouldn't worry about lacking for basic food stuffs during most of the winter months. Lizzie and Beth giggled as they packed Lizzie's goodies in the fragrant pine chest that Bulger had made. He'd carved a heart and Jimmy's and Lizzie's initials inside the heart right on the front. Lizzie loved it!

It had been a wonderful week-end. The next four weeks would fill to overflowing. Hog killing coming up at Thanksgiving, followed by Lizzie's shower, then the wedding, and Christmas! Time flew and everyone worked hard to keep up.

Hog killing was both thrilling and exhausting. Thrilling for the children and exhausting for the grown-ups. One of the best things about it for Lizzie was that Jimmy would be there. He'd stay with Eli and Ginger at night and help work up the meat during the day. But he'd be close and Lizzie was happy.

Most hog killings in the community took place down near a spring in Mr. Lewis's woods just below his chicken pen. Likely as not, at least two families brought in two or three hogs each and every one worked together to get the meat 'worked up'.

Miss Claudie and the girls started on Monday getting everything ready. They scoured washtubs and dishpans, checked knives, washed lard buckets, and gathered spices for making sausage and pressmeat.

Beth wasn't sure about what was going on, but was happy about having fresh meat. She never connected fresh meat and Ole' Crip's pigs—which had grown enormously during the summer. Miss Claudie made arrangements for her to stay with Melody during the killin'. Next year she'd be old enough to help, but the butchering might be too much for her this time. Bulger would drop her off for school, return and load the pigs, and they'd head to the spring.

Bulger spent all of one day working on a sturdy cage-like contraption that fit on the back of the wagon. He made a long raised gangway with high sides from inside the pig pen to the top of the fence. He'd back the wagon to the gangway's high opening, a perfect meet to the cage, and run the hogs up the gangway and into the crate on the wagon so he could transport them to Mr. Lewis's.

Mr. Lewis had made the area near his spring accommodating for hog killing. He'd built a couple of tables for cutting meat and placed a low slatted wooden pallet near the spring, directly under a large pine. There was a stout limb just above the pallet, and a cleared area to the right of the pallet where a large fire would roar. He had buckets ready for anyone to use hanging on nails driven in trees nearby.

Bulger dropped Beth off at school and had the hogs loaded in no time. He'd chosen three: one for each family in his household to have. They'd work up the meat at the spring and bring it back to the house for grinding and mixing the sausage; salting down hams, a couple of shoulders and the belly, or streak'o lean. They would cook up the cracklins in the washpot in the yard and as soon as the cracklins were strained out and the remaining grease cooled, pour it in the waiting twenty-five pound lard buckets.

As soon as everything was loaded on the wagon and the dogs shut in the barn, they headed for Mr. Lewis's.

When Bulger arrived, Eli and Ginger, Jimmy, and Cullie were already there, along with Sonny and the Sheppards who'd brought two hogs to be slaughtered. The Gores arrived with only one hog. Bulger noticed Sonny peeking from behind a tree, grinning like a kid at Christmas.

Bulger shot a look at Cullie and asked, "What's that boy doin' here?"

Cullie looked sheepish and answered. "You know Sonny. His ears are everywhere and if he can help with a day's work, he's ready."

Bulger shook his head and pointed his finger at Sonny. "I'm gone get the good out'a ya t'day." He promised. Sonny grinned and started gathering wood for the fire.

Eli already had three washpots filled with water sitting on a lively fire in the clearing. He and Ginger, and Jimmy and Cullie stood with their backs to the fire warming while their breaths puffed out in white wisps. It was cold! Killing hogs in freezing weather was a must; the meat had to stay really cold or risk spoilage. The weather had to stay bobbing around freezing a few days following the slaughter, too. Killing lasted more than one day.

Lizzie jumped from the wagon and rushed to Jimmy and wrapped her arms around his neck. He gave her a quick peck on the cheek and looked around, embarrassed. Lizzie laughed. Together they watched as the hog killing began.

Mr. Gore had a rope around his hog's neck and got him off the wagon. He had his .22 under his arm and led the squealing hog to the edge of the clearing. The woods vibrated with the high-pitched hog's screams. Mr. Gore tied the rope around a tree and pulled it tight so the hog had to stay still. He held the rifle and placed the end of the barrel between the hog's eyes and pulled the trigger. The squealing stopped. There was a 'whump' as the hog dropped to the ground. All Lizzie could hear was the echo of the shot through the cold trees. She put her hand to her mouth to keep from gagging as her stomach turned. She didn't know if she could bear hearing the shots from the slaughter of the rest of the hogs.

Mr. Gore stuck his long knife in the hog's main artery in its neck and let the blood run. When the bleeding stopped, the men went to work. They pulled the hog to the wooden pallet and lay him on his side. Mr. Sheppard kept the fire hot around the pot and Cullie and Jimmy started dipping scalding water from the iron pots. They gently poured it over the hog and Bulger and Mr. Gore began scraping the hog's coarse hair away with sharp butcher knives. They had to be careful not to nick the skin. Cullie and Jimmy had to be careful with the scalding water, too. If they let too much run over one spot on the hog, it would soften, or slightly cook the skin and it would come off with the hair. Messy.

When the hair was gone on one side, they flipped him over and finished the other. As soon as the hog was scraped clean as a newborn babe, Bulger took his knife and stuck it through the hog's back ankles and ran a stick through its tendons and tied it tightly at each end with a rope. They threw the other end over the stout pine limb and began pulling. The tendons held the stick in place and kept the hog's back legs apart while the men hoisted it in the air. When the hog was lifted completely off the pallet, they tied off the rope and the hog hung there. Eli grabbed a large galvanized tub and placed it on the ground underneath the hog's head. Cullie grabbed one of the hog's hind legs and Jimmy held the other, pulling them apart and making the hog's belly tight. Bulger stepped up and began cutting. He reached high and cut around the hog's butt opening and slit the skin enough to pull the intestine forward. Mr. Gore was ready with a piece of twine and tied the end of the gut off tight and stepped back.

Bulger then, ever so carefully, started slitting the skin down the belly. One slip and he might cut an intestine and that would be more than awful—nasty, smelly, dirty contents would contaminate the meat and cause extra time and work to clean. As Bulger cut, Eli stood as close and reached to hold back as much of the insides as he could. Finally, the whole mess dropped into the tub. Mr. Gore tied off the throat-end of innards and Eli and Jimmy moved the steaming tub filled with entrails, stomach, liver, and everything else to the side. Bulger cut off the hog's head and dropped it into a smaller tub. It would be boiled and used for pressmeat, or maybe a spicy stew. They'd have a mess of brains and eggs for breakfast and hog tongue sandwich the next day for sure.

And I heard a voice saying unto me, Arise, Peter; slay and eat. But I said, Not so, Lord; for nothing common or unclean hath at any time entered into my mouth.
But the voice answered me again from heaven, What God hath cleansed, that call not thou common.
Acts 11: 7-9

In the cold, the warm meat and especially the exposed insides, gave off a distinctive smell. It wasn't totally offensive, but took a little getting used to. Bulger hollered for Sonny to get away from the tub—he was poking at the intestines with a stick, watching as it moved and jiggled with each push.

Cullie helped Eli and Jimmy with the scraping of the next hog. Bulger said they'd better learn to do it. It was harder than it looked. This poor ole' pig had more nicks in its hide than a first time shaver had on his chin.

"Did ya hear 'bout that family comin' through from Ohio last week?" Cullie asked.

"Nope," answered Eli and Jimmy at the same time.

"Well, there was this wagon that came through and stopped at the store. A man and his four boys came in and the woman sat on the wagon. Boy, she looked all tired out and wore thin. She didn't look up any time at all as far as I could tell," he continued. "Mr. Jones went over to help the man and the boys scattered all over the store. I couldn't keep an eye on any one of'em," he shook his head and kept scraping. "Them boys was quicker than a flea on a dog. Finally the man picked up some cigars and paid for them and they left. Mr. Jones followed them to the door and shut it. They pulled out and left town right down Main Street. Mr. Jones went back to the counter and I heard a loud, 'I'll be gol-derned!' When I reached the counter, I saw what he was talkin' about. About two good handfuls of candy, three pocketknives, and a box of handkerchiefs were missing. I just looked at Mr. Jones. His face was red and his knuckles had turned white from mashing his fists together so hard. Finally all he could say was 'I never seen anything like it.' That whole bunch was rough as cobs. Yes sir, rough as cobs."

Eli and Jimmy chuckled and before they knew it, the hog was clean and free of hair.

Standing to take a quick break, Jimmy noticed Sonny gathering small black berries from some tall bushes near the spring. He walked over.

"What'cha got there?" he asked Sonny.

Scooping a handful of berries in his mouth, he mumbled, "Sugarberries."

Jimmy picked a few and tried them. Sure enough, they had

a sweet, grainy, sugary taste. He called Eli over and they ate a double handful. They heard the echo of the rifle shot.

Their break was short-lived. Mr. Gore and Bulger had another hog ready to scrape.

The women stayed busy scrubbing table tops with rags and water and trying to stay warm. Their toes felt numb and fingers didn't want to bend. Nevertheless, when Eli and Jimmy dropped the tub of innards beside the spring, the women flocked to it like birds to seed. They cut out the liver, heart, lungs, or 'lights'—Miss Eva, Mr. Sheppard's wife, especially liked the 'lights'; and they carefully clamped off the intestines. Each of the organs was placed in smaller buckets or dishpans and covered with cold spring water to keep fresh. Miss Claudie set back a few intestines and carried the rest to the edge of the woods. She saved the bigger ones and cleaned them to use as casings for sausage. This was a job that nobody wanted, but Miss Claudie usually ended up with. Jimmy looked in her direction when he caught a whiff of what was being dumped. "Whew," he said, wrinkling his nose. "It's hard to believe I eat sausage in those wrappings knowing what comes out of 'em".

Miss Claudie looked up when she heard his complaints and shot him a frown. She decided then that Mrs. Sheppard could clean her own sausage casings.

Jimmy ducked his head and put his eyes back to his job.

What was left in the tub of the hog's innerds was 'trash' and would be taken deeper down in the woods and thrown out for a treat for the local scavengers. Buzzards would circle these woods for days.

While the women separated the good parts of the hog's insides, the men carved the carcass. Hams, shoulders, and ribs were cut out and set aside. Floppy, wobbly belly fat and the hard fat was cut into strips and tossed onto the wooden tables. Hog's feet would be pickled; nothing wasted. By the time the women had the washtubs cleaned out, the men had another hog scalded, scraped, and ready to cut.

Lizzie's and Ginger's job was taking the strips of fat on the table tops and trimming away the skin and cutting the remaining strip of fat into bite-sized chunks. When the grease was fried out, all that was left would be lard and crispy cracklins. Skins would be tossed in about the time the cracklins browned, and cook in the grease making brown, crunchy meat skins. The hard fat was easy to cut, especially in the cold air. But the belly fat was an exasperating job. No matter how Lizzie tried to hold it down to cut away the skin, it moved. It flopped to one side and then to the other; jiggled and wobbled. She hated belly fat.

Every time there was a shot, no matter how hard she tried, she could never get the sound of the .22 and that final sharp pig squeal out of her mind. She cringed and turned sick at each squeal and knew sickening silence would follow the crack of the rifle. After witnessing the first killing, she refused to look toward the 'killing tree' where the men shot the hogs. She, like the others, worked automatically. Killing became like an assembly line; fast and efficient.

Lizzie looked up when she heard loud, howling laughter. Sonny had been turned loose with a knife and was up to his tricks. Ginger, too, looked toward the boisterous noise and saw Jimmy pointing to the side of the wagon. There, staring straight at Eli, were two eyeballs, complete with lashes. "What th'," he said, bending forward to get a better look at the wagon with eyes.

Cullie, Jimmy, and the men were having a great chuckle as Eli picked up a stick and poked at one of the eyes.

"Aw, dang it all, Sonny," he said, tossing the stick to the ground. "You almost had me there."

Sonny laughed as Bulger motioned for them to get back to work. "You can count on that boy to come up with something," he said to Mr. Sheppard. "He's done cut out the hog's eyeballs and stuck'em to the wagon," he shook his head. "If that ain't a sight. Guess we needed the break, though. That trick and little laugh did make me feel better. Gotta remember to get them boys some meat for their time."

Everyone put their knives back to the meat and worked through dinnertime. Eli never caught Sonny in the act, but he'd glance over at the pig eyes and they'd be cock-eyed—one looking east and one looking west. Next time they'd be crossed. Sonny kept him busy watching the eyeballs, and before he knew it, by four-thirty, all six hogs had been 'worked up'. Every one of Miss Claudie's dishpans and tubs were filled. The Sheppards and Gores were leaving with full tubs in their wagons, too.

Cullie rode his horse back to town with Sonny hanging on behind, waving a tired hand as they trotted off. Jimmy rode back on the wagon with Lizzie, Bulger, and Miss Claudie. Eli and Ginger followed. Both wagons were loaded. Lizzie couldn't look when they passed the killing tree. Blood puddled there and was already glazed over with a heavy, dark maroon jelly-like film. She kept her eyes ahead, and when Bulger pulled around, her eyes fell on the pallet where the hogs had been scraped clean. The whole pallet was covered with black and white hair; piled from the ground up through the wooden slats. She turned away, sick of hog meat, and the rest weren't too fond of it at that moment either, but the day of handling pork wasn't over.

As soon as the wagons pulled to a stop at the house, Bulger hopped off and opened the door to the smokehouse. He, with help from Eli and Jimmy, carried the meat inside. The bulky hams and shoulders, ribs and backbone, and head were placed where they could rest and the tubs of fat set on the floor. They'd stay cold tonight and be ready to be ground, rubbed, and cooked the next day.

Lizzie stood on the cold porch beside Jimmy, sad that he was leaving. It was the only time that day that they'd been by themselves.

"Hurry up, Jimmy," called Eli. He and Ginger sat huddled on the wagon seat, Ginger wrapped in a blanket and shivering. Little Man stomped his foot and snorted a stream of steam from his nose that would make any dragon proud.

"I'm comin'," Jimmy called back. "I'll see you tomorrow," he whispered in Lizzie's ear. His breath was warm and she quickly turned and gave him a 'bye kiss. His knees almost buckled.

"I gotta' go," he said, and ran and jumped on the back of the wagon.

Eli laughed, Jimmy reddened—and not from the cold--, and Lizzie shook her finger at Eli. He clapped the reins against Little Man's rump and the wagon rumbled into the coming night.

≈

Bright and early the next morning Eli, Ginger, and Jimmy arrived to help finish the meat. None of them looked like they'd had a good night's rest, and all three looked ready for a hot cup of coffee. Miss Claudie was prepared. She had the coffee hot and a huge skillet of brains and eggs fried up. She'd made gravy to go to with biscuits, too.

She'd been up really early. She'd already taken the tub of large intestines to the well and rinsed them over and over with water. Finally she carried them inside and ran water from the hand pump in the sink through them until she was sure they were good and clean. Part of the larger ones she'd cut and batter and fry in deep fat for Bulger. He loved fried chitlin's, and he knew she must really love him to stink up her kitchen with them—just because he had a chitlin' taste. She left the clean guts in the sink covered with water, but a slight, distinct smell lingered in the room. She hoped the strong coffee would mask it.

When the others came in she had coffee, grits and gravy, brains and eggs, and biscuits ready. Lizzie was up and dressed, eager to see Jimmy. Bulger fed the animals, gathered what eggs were to be had, and milked both cows. Ole' Crip didn't seem to miss any of her babies, but Bulger noticed two others were missing besides the ones he'd killed. He reasoned they'd probably gotten through the fence and wandered off.

If they noticed the bad smell, nobody spoke about it. After a quick breakfast, Bulger set the grinder up on the edge of the table and Eli brought in the meat they'd cut up for sausage. Miss Claudie insisted on cutting up one shoulder and adding to the 'trimmings' from the ribs and backbone to be ground. Lizzie got out the dishpans, sage, salt and pepper, and the hot peppers they'd strung and dried during the summer.

Jimmy turned the handle on the grinder and Lizzie fed in the meat. Out came little squirmy, wormy lines of ground pork that piled up in the dishpan. As soon as one pan filled, Miss Claudie pulled it away and replaced it with another. She sprinkled the spices over the ground meat and Ginger began kneading the meat and spices together. When it was mixed really well, Miss Claudie got an intestine from the dishpan, dried it off, gathered a handful of sausage and began stuffing the intestine. She soon had long trails of sausage-filled lengths. When one was full, she tied off the ends and Eli transferred it to a rod in the smokehouse and hung it there.

When she ran out of casing, she stuffed flour sacks with sausage and mashed the sack flat. Bulger and Eli liked this particular kind of dried sausage. It was more pungent than that in the casings.

Bulger busied himself washing hams, shoulder, ribs, and belly meat and drying it thoroughly. He had several sacks of rock salt that Mr. Pollard got in for him, just for curing. His salt box was ready. Carefully, he poured a thick layer of salt in the bottom of the box and rubbed down the hams with more salt. He lowered the meat on into the box and continued rubbing salt on the joints and slabs of pork and covering them with salt in the box. The last meat was covered and in the second of two boxes when Bulger lowered the lid. That job was finished and the meat would be cured in time for salt-cured ham for Christmas.

He joined Eli in the yard where he had set three washpots up with a fire around them. A fourth held the three hog's heads and Eli covered them with water to let them boil tender.

Together they carried the lard cans filled with cut chunks of fat and dumped them in the empty pots. Soon they were cracking and popping. Eli and Bulger stayed busy stirring each pot with wooden sticks so the meat wouldn't stick to the bottom and scorch. The air filled with the good smell of frying pork. Jack and Bell scratched at the barn door and whimpered to be let out. Eli laughed. "They smell this meat and want a taste of it," he said.

"Don't blame'em none," answered Bulger, "But can't let'em out now. They'd cut up stumps to get at this meat and we can't take the chance of tripping over one of'em running around. If we fell in these pots or got this hot grease on us, we'd be in a fix. Better let'em whine away. We'll let'em out when we're done."

Eli nodded in agreement and kept stirring the pots with his long oak paddle.

Miss Claudie came out and took over stirring one of the pots. "Got the sausage finished up. I tied the hot with a red string and the mild with white so's we can tell what's what. Some's fried up and in the warming oven. Biscuits, too. Go in and try some out when you get a chance. I think Jimmy's on his way out pretty soon," she looked at Bulger and winked. "He's kinda tied up right now."

Bulger and Eli chuckled. "Looks like the cracklin's are cooking up and floating to the top, and the lard's most done," Bulger observed. "Eli, get the skins out'a the smokehouse and put'em in this pot. Miss Claudie, bring a few 'taters and drop'em over here in this one. They'll be mighty tasty with that sausage and biscuit."

Eli gently lowered the meat skins in the hot grease. They popped and sizzled and puffed up. Miss Claudie added clean, washed whole potatoes to one pot. Soon Ginger came out with a dishpan and wire dipper. Bulger dipped crunchy cracklin's and let the grease drip back in the pot before dumping the crispy chunks in the dishpan. He killed the fire under that pot and moved to the pot with the skins and began dipping. Soon that fire was killed and the grease started cooling. The last pot was dipped clean and Miss Claudie separated the potatoes and carried them inside. Ginger and Eli carried the hot cracklin's in, and Bulger killed the last fire. He tested the boiled hog heads for tenderness and saw they'd cooked to pieces. He killed the fire under that pot and covered it over with a piece of tin.

They tried out the new sausage, dug in to the fried potatoes, and sopped everything up with biscuits. By the time they'd finished, the grease was almost cool enough to pour in the lard cans and stored away. After sampling the sausage and finding it fine enough to pull a mule's tail, they rested a bit—all but Miss Claudie. She scooped the hog head from the pot into a big dishpan and set it inside on the table. She picked meat and put it in one pan and discarded bones in another. Her work wasn't finished until she'd picked every piece of meat off the hog heads. She'd make thin strips of pressed meat.

When she had all the meat off the bones, she sprinkled salt, pepper, and some ground hot peppers in and mixed it well.

"Jack and Bell will have a time with these bones," she said. "Bulger, don't forget ya gotta get Beth back home from the Jones's this evenin'," she worried. "I hope she didn't get homesick. Last night was the first night she's spent away."

Lizzie laughed. "I don't think you have to worry none about her getting homesick," she said. "I'll be willing to bet Beth's had a ball."

"Ya got that right," Bulger agreed, getting up from his chair and getting his coat. "Ya'll come on. We need to get that lard poured up so we can let the dogs out. I know ya'll are 'bout sick of fresh meat, but I'll bet they're the ones that are sick---of bein' shut up."

Eli and Jimmy followed Bulger to the yard and filled eight buckets with lard. That gave each two to keep.

Looking at the filled lard buckets, Bulger was reminded that he was almost out of beef tallow. The only good use for that grease was to rub into his boots to make them water proof. If he used any on the harnesses, he'd need more, he reckoned. He raised up and surveyed their day's work. Pretty good job, he decided.

Ginger and Lizzie packed cracklin's in lard buckets and put the lids on tight. They carried them to the smokehouse with the rest of the meat.

Miss Claudie got down her heaviest dishes and turned one bottom side up. She made a ball of meat and pressed it flat on the plate, then put another plate on top. She spread meat and stacked plates until she had two stacks, each about eighteen inches tall with a thin layer of meat between each one. She carefully moved the stacks to her bedroom where she'd covered the top of her sewing machine with a folded sheet and left the meat in its 'press' there to dry. It would dry quickly in the cold bedroom, and be good eating later.

When she returned to the kitchen, Lizzie and Ginger had it all cleaned and everything in its place.

"Well," she said, "It's mighty good to have hog killin' over for another year. Now all we have to do is wait for the meat to cure out, but right now we have plenty of fresh meat to last a while. Lizzie, tomorrow I want you to take a mess to Minshue. With Skipping Rock gone, I bet she could use some. Bulger can take some over to Cullie and Sonny's ma."

Lizzie agreed. "I'd love to go, and Beth can go along. I need to be sure they know about my wedding so they can plan to be there."

Ginger sighed and said, "Am I tired! I thought we'd have time to talk about your wedding a little while I was here, but we've been too busy."

"I guess everything's all set—if you can wear my bridesmaid dress I wore in yours. Beth is wearing the same one she wore." She went to the wall beside her bed and took down the dress. "Here, take it with you." She looked at Miss Claudie. "You can make alterations if they're needed, can't you Miss Claudie?"

She smiled and nodded.

Eli and Jimmy tromped in. "Bulger's on his way to pick up Beth, but I think we need to stay around 'til he gets back." Eli looked at Jimmy. "We walked around behind the barn and think we know where those two other hogs went. We found a few footprints and a bit of blood where they'd been stuck. It was them Panthers, bet'cha anything."

Miss Claudie paled.

"Don't worry now, they're long gone and with that much meat, probably won't be back anytime soon.

Eli and Ginger sat beside the fire with Miss Claudie and Lizzie and Jimmy sat alone at the table. They held hands as they talked.

"I gotta go by the courthouse and fill out the papers for our marriage license," he said. "I'll pick them up on Friday morning when I'm on my way to Eli's before our wedding. I'll have it ready for Preacher Sheets to sign when he does the ceremony.

Lizzie got butterflies in her stomach thinking about the wedding. She shouldn't worry: Miss Claudie had her dress finished and it hung in the bedroom, everything was set. The shower would be the coming Saturday, but it was a little different from most bridal showers. Ginger planned a bigger party. There would be cakes and breads with cheese and ham. Eli had a surprise planned that he knew everyone would love. She could hardly wait!

They heard the jingle of harness before they heard Bulger holler "Whoa!" to let Beth off the wagon. Her footsteps bounded across the porch and the door flew open. "Hey, ya'll,

I'm home!"

She shut the door with a 'bam' and immediately stopped and sniffed the air. "What'cha been cookin' in here?"

Miss Claudie laughed. "Don't bother none 'bout that," she said. "I'll cook something good for you in the morning."

Beth walked over to sit with Lizzie. "I don't think I'll want it if'in it smells as bad as this," she murmured. She sniffed again. "Smells almost as bad as that rabbit tobacco Sonny gave me and Melody to smoke."

Lizzie's head shot up and she looked at Jimmy. "Whaa, what did she just say?" she said in amazement.

Jimmy laughed and started for the door. "Don't worry 'bout that," he said. "If you never done it, you missed a treat!"

While Bulger unhitched Moses, Eli hitched Little Man. He had to hang lanterns on both sides of the wagon to see enough to make their way home. Eli explained to Bulger about the Indian prints and blood behind the barn. Bulger looked worried.

"Gone leave the dogs out at night from now on," he said. "They'll let us know if anybody's sneaking around and I'll have my gun ready. Ain't no thieving nobody gone come 'round here without gettin' a load of buckshot."

Eli noticed his words were strong, but his face showed otherwise. He was worried; and a little scared.

Ginger bundled up and sat between Eli and Jimmy. Miss Claudie called out as they left the yard, "Ya'll be careful, now. We love ya." She stood out in the cold and watched until the tiny yellow lantern orbs disappeared into the darkness.

FORTY-FOUR

The rest of the week flew by. Lizzie could barely sleep and she absentmindedly finished her chores. Beth thought it was funny. She watched as Bulger tore strips from old sheets Miss Claudie had given him. He wound them tightly and made two balls a little larger than a softball, and tucked in the ends. Then he filled a gallon can with kerosene and gently dropped the cloth balls in.

"What'cha doin' with that?" Beth asked.

Bulger chuckled. "This is Eli's surprise for the shower. We'll let the balls soak in the kerosene until Saturday morning and get them out and let'em drain until 'bout night when the fun's almost over. Eli and them Walls boys went back to where we left the hogs' leftovers out in the woods and set a trap, hopin' to catch a buzzard and they did. The Walls boys have it in their barn and have been givin' it a little to eat, but it should be good and hungry by Saturday."

Beth propped one hand on her hips, tilted her head, squinched her eyes, and pursed her lips. "What'cha gone do with a stinky ole' buzzard?" she asked.

Bulger covered the can with the balls soaking inside and laughed out loud. He reached and put his hand on Beth's back and turned her toward the house. "Ya just gotta wait and see, Little Bit." He sniggered all the way to the kitchen.

All day Friday was spent baking and getting ready for the shower. It was to be at Miss Claudie and Bulger's as a matter of convenience. No need to repack the gifts. Lizzie could get them to Jimmy's the following day.

Saturday arrived. Lizzie swept the floor twice and scolded Beth for having Dolly and Patty out. Beth put them away, but pouted about it.

"Just be lucky you're getting to stay for the party at all," Lizzie admonished. "I could send you to spend the night with Melody and you'd miss everything." She said with a final 'swish' of the broom.

Beth flounced out the door, jerking her arms into her coat sleeves as she went.

By midafternoon, wagons began pulling into the yard. There was a suspiciously large crate covered with a tarp sitting in the middle of the Walls boys' wagon.

Lizzie and Beth wore their Sunday dresses and Miss Claudie had a fine table set. Nervousness quickly disappeared as happy voiced drifted inside.

Young couples, and many singles, came running and laughing into the warm kitchen. Jimmy rode along with Eli and Ginger, anxious to see Lizzie. Even with a crowded kitchen and an overflow onto the porch, Jimmy's eyes were only for her.

During the party Lizzie sat near the end of her cot which was covered with bags and boxes. Ginger held a tablet and pencil, ready to record each gift and the person who'd given it so Lizzie could send accurate thank you notes. The boys were shooed out and went to lounge around outside, sitting and warming around a campfire Bulger had set up especially for the event, telling tales, waiting for the festivities inside to finish. Every once in a while, they heard loud "awww's", and "ohhhh's", and knew Lizzie had received a special present. The bed was covered in all sorts of handy and helpful linens, cooking utensils, sewing goods, and odds and ends she and Jimmy would certainly need.

The kitchen door finally opened and Miss Claudie invited the men-folk inside to eat. This was the part they'd been looking forward to! They scrambled up and filed into the kitchen. Eli was surprised to see that Cullie singled out Susan, the oldest Jones girl, and shared his plate with her.

Come to think of it, he hadn't talked to Cullie as often as he had before he and Ginger married. Could something be up? He wondered.

Miss Claudie asked Miss Myline about her plans to move back to Atlanta.

"Yes," Miss Myline agreed. "My long-time beau asked me to marry him and that means returning home. I guess absence really does make the heart grow fonder," she smiled. "We plan a wedding in February. I would marry sooner," she said, dropping her head and looking at her hands, "but Mamma wants the wedding to be extra special, and I want to make this a special time for everyone." She sighed. "I do hate to leave the children," she said looking back at Miss Claudie. "I think the trustees have someone in mind, but are waiting until Christmas break to ask," she paused. "I know whomever they choose will be the one the children need."

Miss Claudie nodded. Bulger wasn't a school board trustee, but was close with the group. She had her suspicions about who might be asked---and she hoped her suspicions proved correct. "Well, we'll surely miss ya. You've done a fine job with the children. Beth just loves ya to death," she said, placing a comforting hand on Miss Myline's arm. "We wish ya the very best. I know you'll be blessed and have a happy life." Then Miss Claudie moved to the table to refill the plates and platters.

The group soon finished off most of the refreshments and the sun was dropping behind the tree line. Bulger called for attention. "Alright, ya'll, everyone outside." And he motioned with his long arms for them to gather in the yard. He nodded his head to the oldest Walls boy and he scooted outside ahead of the others. Miss Claudie handed Bulger a roll of stout string and he pushed it down in his back pocket.

"Come on ya folks," he said to the young folks. "Make a circle here. We're gone toss one of these kerosene balls." He looked at Eli and grinned.

The group got in place, waiting to see what Bulger and Eli had planned. Eyes widened as Bulger picked up one of the soaked balls and lit it. It immediately began glowing and flames seemed to make a slow lick around the cloth, almost dancing above it instead of consuming it. Bulger quickly tossed it to Eli. Wasting no time, Eli barely touched the ball and passed it to Ginger. She almost dropped it, but knowing Eli wasn't burned and ready to keep up the fun, reached out and handled it barely long enough to toss it to Lizzie; then to Jimmy, and on around. Girls squealed and danced as the ball got closer and closer to them. They were brave; they didn't want to be the one to drop the ball and cause the ball to stop its round.

Beth stood beside Bulger. Miss Claudie watched from the porch. She grinned as the glowing ball came closer and closer to Beth and Beth's eyes got wider and wider. Only one more person away--- the ball was tossed to Beth! Bulger reached out to help, but Beth gritted her teeth and stretched her arms to meet the ball. She had it! Deftly, she turned and tossed it to surprised Bulger. He bent and caught it and passed it on.

The game lasted until the ball finally blazed too brightly and got too hot to handle. Bulger rolled it in the dirt and extinguished it.

The boys and girls, happy, began breaking into couples or talking around the now smoldering campfire. Cullie and Susan again, Eli noticed.

"Whoa, now, one more treat," Bulger said as he pulled the string from his pocket. Everyone turned and gathered around him once more.

Eli and Kenneth, one of the Walls's, trotted over to their wagon and uncovered the crate. Inside was the scrawniest, sorriest looking buzzard anyone had ever seen. Eli put on his gloves—buzzard are known to puke on their attackers or whenever they became alarmed---and he wanted to be safe. Their up-chuck was more than unpleasant and left a most awful after smell.

Kenneth held the crate door open and Eli gently removed the buzzard. He carried it over where Bulger had attached the string to the one remaining kerosene ball. "Now, ya'll," he said, carefully tying the other end of the string to the buzzard's leg. "This here will be the grand finale! I'll light this ball and Eli will let this ole' buzzard go. Between getting free of that crate and having this burning ball after him, I'll bet he'll take off. Buzzards catch the wind and he'll circle up high before heading back to his roost. We can watch. It's a purdy sight; that lighted ball floating up and around, higher and higher, like it's moving all by itself. Can't see the buzzard, its dark feathers disappear in the night. You can see the ball until it goes out of sight or if the string gets burned in two we can watch it fall out'a sight. Here we go!"

And as Eli held the terrified buzzard, Bulger lit the ball. "Let'er go!" he shouted.

Eli tossed the buzzard as high as he could, and the bird's huge wings beat the air. The bird lifted, dragging the ball behind. As the bird flew higher, the ball trailed behind, making lovely floating circles and becoming smaller and smaller as the buzzard headed for home. There wasn't a sound in the yard. All eyes were on the glowing orb, beautiful in the clear, cloudless night.

Suddenly the ball began a free-fall toward earth. The girls clasped their hands over their mouths and gasped. Boys pointed and laughed.

"Wonder where it will land?" Bulger mused. "Probably burn itself out 'fore hittin' the ground," he added. He took a deep breath. "That's it," he said as he rubbed his hands together and smiled. "Hope ya'll had a good time, but ya better be gettin' on back home if'n I don't want any of your folks to come huntin' ya."

The girls lined up to give Lizzie a 'bye hug and the boys gathered their horses or mules and got the wagons turned around.

Eli, his curiosity piqued, watched Cullie. Sure enough, he'd brought Susan along with him. Cullie pulled his wagon from the yard, and by the light from the lamps hanging from each side, Eli noticed their heads bent closely toward one another as the horse carried their wagon out of sight.

Jimmy was last to bid Lizzie 'bye. "I'll see you tomorrow. I'll ride in with Eli and Ginger to church." He breathed deeply and held both her hands in his. "Only one more week," he said. "I wish I had more to offer, but we'll do fine. I'll have a buggy bought before the wedding, and can borrow Eli's wagon if need be," he paused and looked longingly at her face, reflecting moonlight and become even more beautiful.

Lizzie smiled. "I love your plans, Jimmy," she said. "Ginger and Eli are gonna to come back for dinner tomorrow; you, too, of course, and we'll load our presents on their wagon. You can take them back to our place when Eli takes you home." She blushed. "But you don't put anything away. That's my job." She smiled and squeezed his hands. "Oh, Jimmy, I'm so happy, I can hardly wait!"

He leaned and gave her a soft kiss on her lips, then on to Eli's wagon and to home. Lizzie retreated up the steps to stand with Beth and Miss Claudie. She noticed Miss Claudie wiping her cheeks and tracks still wet on her face.

That night Bulger's log home was filled with almost as many sleepless people as there were in Hooverville before Eli's family headed out for Georgia.

Lizzie lay and dreamed of Jimmy and what she hoped the rest of her life would be: filled with hope and love. She prayed for blessings, and an abundance pouring out of God's grace to keep them happy, healthy, and prosperous.

Beth, snuggled in the trundle bed Bulger had made for Ginger's stay, settled Dolly and Patty in for the night. She whispered, "You should have seen how brave I was," she said. "I caught a ball that was a'fire! I handed it on to Bulger and got to be with the big folks." She closed her eyes and settled her head on her pillow. "I'm getting' to be a big girl now," she said through a yawn. And as Dolly and Patty watched, Beth's breathing became slow and deep. She began dreaming new dreams; Lizzie's wedding and Jack and Bell chasing raccoons through the woods, bawling and bellowing as the raccoon hid in the hollow of a tree.

Miss Claudie lay quietly beside Bulger. Her thoughts filled with a little sadness; her children were growing up and moving out. Beth was still with them, and a lively one at that, but before they'd know it, she and Bulger would be back to just the two of them again. She sighed and turned to her side, her long gray braid falling across her shoulder. Comin' back full circle, she thought. She closed her eyes and willed sleep to overtake her.

Bulger lay on his back with his arms angled so that his head rested in his elbow on the pillow. He softly chuckled. 'That was one mighty fine party,' he murmured. 'Ain't had that much fun since I was a scrappin' young fella' m'self.' He lifted his head and removed his arm and pulled the covers tighter around his neck. He heard the wind picking up outside and thought of the buzzard, flying and circling to find its way home. He, too, felt the soft stab of loneliness. His and Miss Claudie's birds were flying the coop and all that was left was one little biddy. 'We've been blessed,' he whispered. He kissed Miss Claudie lightly on her forehead. At last he closed his eyes and thanked God for all He had done; given them a family when they'd thought there was no hope.

As he and Miss Claudie drifted off to sleep, Bulger wiggled deeper under the covers. He turned his head toward to window and involuntarily sniffed. The last thing his brain registered just before slumber overtook him for the night was, 'Wonder if'in that's smoke I smell?'

FORTY-FIVE

The first week in December broke cold and windy. Jimmy jumped out of bed and tossed more wood on the low fire in the fireplace and blew on it to get it going. He shook the ashes from the stove's grate and poked up the fire before adding a few sticks of kindling. As soon as the heart pine caught and flamed up, he added more wood and filled the coffee pot with water and coffee grounds. He grabbed his coat and hurried to the make-shift shed to feed his horse. He'd traded one so he could get supplies and more tools he needed to work on the house and farm. The shed was all right for now, and he planned a good, sturdy barn come spring.

He hurried back inside. Soon his kitchen was warm and toasty—in spite of the wind reaching out chilly fingers and trying to push their way inside.

While the coffee came to a boil, Jimmy sat in a chair near the mud-daubbed fireplace. His thoughts fell back to the December days on the train. He remembered the last of November when Lizzie's family left. He wanted to follow, and might have later as December came, except he wasn't sure which way they'd traveled. He reached and picked up a twig from the hearth that had broken off a limb as he tossed it into the fireplace and sat back. December of last year was a hard, lonely time for him; even more than when he'd lost Ma and Pa.

How he'd missed hunting with Eli and the good talks they'd had. He loved sharing meals at Eli's wagon, too. He smiled. And that little Beth. He really missed her laughter and how she managed to wrap herself around everybody's little

Sunrise

finger and get whatever she wanted. But more than anything, he'd missed Lizzy. He'd prayed more than he'd prayed since Pa got sick. He almost got sick himself; with worry about her safety.

He kept remembering: Mr. Denney and the remaining wagons reached Heard County, it seemed, at last. Jimmy had no way of knowing if Lizzie's folks had gotten that far or not. He found his 'perfect spot' just over the Georgia/Alabama line and made his stand in Alabama. It was hard going; chopping trees and getting them stacked---all by himself. He finally had a one-room house complete with fireplace and ladder to the loft. He crossed the Chattahoochee and 'discovered' Franklin. It was there he met Cullie, a mountain of information, and learned that several families he knew from the train had settled nearby—including Eli, Lizzie, and Beth. His heart almost jumped out of his chest, he was so happy! Cullie told him about the awful circumstances that had befallen his friends, and the good news that they'd found a home with a good, loving, Christian family. He could hardly wait to finish his house and get his first crop in. He had a horse and good credit, and for that he was thankful. Then he could search out Lizzie and face her with pride. He hoped she'd be as glad to see him as he would be to see her.

He visited Mr. Rogers from the train, who'd settled outside Franklin and set up the town's only sawmill, and he passed enough slabs to him so that he was able to make a somewhat flat area that covered half of the ceiling of the room-- his house----, and he'd made a ladder to access it. Perhaps it would be a sleeping loft for his and Lizzie's children, he hoped. Only Lizzie hadn't known anything about his plans back then.

Sitting there by the fire, he reached for his Bible and turned and read his morning scriptures. Another habit he'd formed since Pa died. Somehow, his morning reading kept him strong; his mind at ease, and confidence high. He knew "all things are possible for those who love the Lord and are called according to His purpose." Jimmy believed with all his heart that he and Lizzie were meant to be together as part of God's great plan. He thanked and praised Him every day for bringing him this far. He looked forward to spending the rest of his life with Lizzie.

The coffee boiled over, sending wisps of steam off the black iron stove top. Jimmy jumped up and rushed to it and grabbed a rag to move the hot pot off the eye. He left the pot to set a few minutes and let the coffee grounds settle to the bottom; then poured a cup. He had a long trip planned for his morning.

After he finished his coffee and gobbled a slab of bread slathered with butter, he pulled on his coat and started out. It was cold, and he had a way to go. He was going to Franklin and apply for his and Lizzie's marriage license, then on to Eli's. He wanted to be sure he could spend Friday and Saturday nights before the wedding with Eli and Ginger.

He bridled his horse and threw a blanket over his back. The horse was a work horse and plowed and pulled a wagon, so Jimmy didn't have a saddle. Both his and his mount's breath puffed white as they made their way down the road, rode the ferry across the Chattahoochee, and into Franklin.

He pulled up in front of the courthouse and tied his horse. He was so excited! He fairly ran up the steps and to the probate judge's office.

"Hey there, Judge Joseph," he called with a wave of his hand.

"Morning to you, Jimmy. What on earth have you been doing? Out in this cold! Your nose is a red as a June apple," he chuckled.

Jimmy grinned and backed up to the tall pot-bellied stove. His hands and face were freezing. "Need to get a marriage license," he grinned.

"I heard about that, and the kerosene balls you had out at Bulger's too," replied Judge Joseph as he reached in a cabinet and brought out a blank marriage license. "Seems Mr. Todd's woods got burned off the night of the party," he said with a sly look toward Jimmy.

Jimmy's face paled even whiter than his morning breath had been that morning and his throat tightened. "Di, di, di, did we do any harm?" he asked.

Judge Joseph sat and began filling out the license and grinned. "Not really. Mr. Todd planned to burn'em off soon anyway. Keep the underbrush down and briars from growing in." He chuckled. "Bulger hit it lucky on that one. That buzzard flew over the right spot all right." He paused holding his pencil. "Now who do I need to write in these blanks?"

Jimmy breathed a great sigh of relief. Good thing that kerosene ball was almost burned out when it fell—and that it fell in Mr. Todd's woods and not somewhere where it could have really caused damage. He moved to help Judge Joseph fill out his license with his heart finally slowing and his hands and face really, really warm.

≈

It was a busy morning at Miss Claudie's. She rose early and ordered Lizzie and Beth to bundle up. She planned to walk through the pasture to the back side where it met the trees. She'd been watching the broomsage growing there and it had grown almost shoulder high. During the last cold months, it had dried out and the tops had fluffed out. She was on a mission to gather it and make new brooms. She wanted enough for Ginger and Lizzie to have two or three apiece, too.

They crossed through the pass-through in the fence and started across the pasture. Bessie and Bossie were already out of the barn, bags emptied after Bulger finished the milking. They raised their heads and watched the trio pass, but weren't at all interested. They bowed their heads back to break of bits of dried grass and chew.

Miss Claudie reached the broom sage patch and began cutting dry stalks and handing them to Lizzie.

"Don't get them all twisted up, now," she said. "We gotta beat the tops and get all the fuzz off 'fore we can bundle them for brooms." She stayed bent, cutting while she talked. "I'm glad for this, my old'un is wore off to hard nubs."

Lizzie held broomstraw until her arms were full, then Miss Claudie loaded Beth. They ended up with both girls carrying a good load and Miss Claudie had a fair bundle under her arm.

When they reached the yard, Miss Claudie instructed them to put the straw carefully on the ground. "Here's what ya do," she demonstrated. She picked a handful and began swishing and whacking it the ground and the fluff from the tops began to fly.

Before they'd finished cleaning the whole stack, the yard looked as if it had snowed.

Beth, naturally, was full of questions and every time she tried to talk, one of the 'fluffs' landed in her mouth. Miss Claudie and Lizzie laughed while she 'thuffed' and 'spfftted' to spit out the seedy puffs.

Miss Claudie stood back and looked at their work. "Looks mighty good. Beth, run in the house and get that ball of twine from behind the lower cupboard door." With a second thought she added, "Get the scissors, too."

Beth took off and was back quick as a wink.

Miss Claudie grabbed a double handful of clean broomstraw and wrapped one end of twine around it about halfway. She looped the twine so that the end was secure and worked the twine down the straw, winding it tightly. When she reached the end, she pulled the twine in and out of the cut ends of the straw and finished it off with a tight knot. She held the boom up and shook it. The bare straw made a stout handle and the ends stripped of their fluff formed a lovely broom.

"This'un will last a while," she said with satisfaction.

Lizzie proved to be apt at broom-making, but Beth barely got one together. She was proud of it and claimed it for her very own.

"I'll use mine and sweep the kitchen every day," she vowed.

Lizzie looked at Miss Claudie and grinned.

Miss Claudie added. "Here, Lizzie. Here're your three. Next time Eli comes by, we'll send Ginger's to her."

They brushed and shook their skirts free of any fluff hanging on, and tromped inside to warm up and treat themselves to some sweets and hot coffee.

FORTY-SIX

Lizzie stood in Miss Claudie's bedroom wearing Ginger's wedding dress. Miss Claudie had done wonders with it and modified it to fit her exactly. She'd added a few more tucks and puffed out the sleeves making the dress look so different that no one would ever guess it was Ginger's. She'd even made a lacy bouquet for Lizzie to carry since flowers were scarce as hen's teeth this time of year.

"Oh, Miss Claudie," Lizzie exclaimed, twirling around. "You are so talented. You have magic fingers! I love the dress--- and the bouquet."

Beth, sitting on the bed, loved it, too. "You think you will be able to make it fit me one day when I get married?" she asked.

Miss Claudie laughed. "I thought ya weren't gone get married, Little Bit," she said. "Have ya changed your mind?"

Beth squirmed and pulled at a thread on the spread. "Well, I am growing up. I've put Dolly and Patty in a special drawer so they can sleep and rest. I don't have to have them sleep with me anymore." She looked up. "I want to be a bride and wear a beautiful dress and have parties, too."

Lizzie ran and grabbed her in a great hug. "You are growing up. I can tell." She looked at Beth and her eyes softened. "I wish Mamma and Papa could see us now." She stood and smoothed her dress. "You all grown up and here I am in my wedding dress. They would be so proud." She turned and walked to Miss Claudie and gave her a hug, too. "Thank you, Miss Claudie. You've been our mother and we love you so much!"

Miss Claudie was completely taken by surprise. Her eyes filled and she held Lizzie tightly. Her words finally came. "I love all ya'll, too, child. Like my own. God gave ya to us and we're the ones who've been blessed. I am so proud of ya," she pushed Lizzie back and held her at arm's length. "I know ya folks would be proud, too."

Just then a knock came at the door and Ginger called, "You decent?"

Lizzie laughed and Miss Claudie released her hold. "Come on in, I'm just trying on my dress for my final fitting."

Ginger swished in and closed the door behind her. "Oh, Lizzie, it's beautiful," she said. "By this time tomorrow, you'll be an old married woman!"

"And I can hardly wait!" Lizzie replied, clasping her hands with excitement.

Ginger walked across the room and sat with Beth on the bed. "Wait until you hear what Jimmy's been through with the marriage license," she said. "You won't believe what happened."

"We want to hear all of it," Miss Claudie said. "Get this dress off and we'll go to the kitchen. It's cold in here and my old bones can't take much more. Go on, now, Lizzie get your other things on and hurry. I'll have us something warm to drink while the men finish up the chores," and Miss Claudie left the girls to put away the dress.

As they sat around the table and Miss Claudie had coffee poured, she asked, "Now what were ya saying about Jimmy getting into some kind of trouble?"

"No, he didn't get in trouble, but he had a round with some trouble," said Ginger.

"Tell us then," urged Beth.

Ginger sat straighter, always ready to recount a good story. "Yesterday morning Jimmy hitched his horse to the buggy and started to our place. He had his clothes in a bag and checked to be sure he had all the papers he needed for Preacher Sheets to sign. He had the license signed by Judge Joseph and was sure he put it in the inside of his coat pocket. It was really early when he left home, and it was cold, too. A couple of times while he was riding along, he looped the reins around his foot and rubbed his hands together to warm them. They were cold in spite of his gloves," she chuckled. "His old horse, bless his heart, kept on plodding down the road," she perked up. "He knows the way to our place and could get there even if he was blind. Anyway, with Jimmy's jostling his hands and arms, he thought he'd better check on the license. Low and behold," she said, raising her arms and opening her eyes wide, "it was gone! He looked everywhere; on the floor at his feet, under the seat, in the back, but the license was nowhere to be found." She paused to let this sink in.

Beth looked stricken. "But Lizzie can't get married without the marriage license!" she cried.

"I know, I know, calm down," Ginger said, and continued. "Well, he was afraid that if he turned the buggy around he'd miss seeing the paper if it had blown a little off the road, so he tied his horse some bushes next to the road and started backtracking on foot. He was so afraid the paper was gone for good," she said sorrowfully, shaking her head.

"He walked and walked. The horse and buggy was plumb out of sight. He was about to freeze, but he kept on walking and looking behind every bush and between every rock by the road. Finally, he saw something fluttering and ran to check. Sure enough, it was the license. He grabbed it up and he said he even kissed it he was so happy to've found it!"

She smiled and clasped her hands in front. "He ran all the way back to his buggy and by the time he got there, his feet were numb. His fingers didn't want to hold on to the reins, but his horse was ready to go. With one word, that horse took off and all Jimmy had to do was hang on. Good thing, too, after all that walking. Bet he walked over four miles trying to find that paper." She sat back and folded her hands in her lap. "But you know him, he didn't give up, and when he got to the house, he WAS almost froze. Eli went out and put his horse in the barn and Jimmy hugged the stove." She laughed. "Lizzie, you better be good to that boy after all he's been through to see that this wedding goes off without a hitch."

Lizzie sat still. She could imagine how Jimmy felt walking down that dark, cold, lonely road so early in the morning.

Afraid that he'd let her down and lost the license. No, she'd never be anything but good to him. He was so good and caring. She couldn't wait until they were married and safely at his—and her—house.

The next day, Lizzie, Beth, Miss Claudie, and Bulger had a quick breakfast as the sun came up over the barn. It was just like any other sunrise that day, but this day was special. Lizzie hardly ate a bite and rushed to get dressed. Bulger's eyes glistened when he saw Lizzie come into the kitchen wearing her wedding gown.

Beth and Miss Claudie were filled with a wonderful, warm feeling, too, as Lizzie came through the door. It was truly as if Miss Claudie and Bulger were about to give their daughter away in marriage.

Thankfully, the day was clear. Bulger helped the women in the wagon. Miss Claudie had quilts ready and warmed, and they wrapped snugly in them as they rode to the church.

The wedding routine was much the same as Eli's and Ginger's, except because it was cold, Jimmy, Eli the best man, and Ginger the matron of honor, along with the congregation were already seated inside where it was good and warm. Everybody was in place and ready when Bulger pulled the wagon next to the church. No chance for Jimmy to see Lizzie before the ceremony. Miss Claudie gave Lizzie a big, final hug, and hurried inside to her seat. Beth hung back. Lizzie and she shared a special sister moment.

"You be good to Miss Claudie and Bulger," Lizzie admonished. "Miss Claudie needs all the help you can give her. Bulger, too. Remember you're a big girl now, and you must look for chores you can help with; don't wait 'til Miss Claudie asks you." She held Beth tight.

Beth promised, "I will, Lizzie. I love you so much," and she tore away and ran to the church door to gather her basket and get in place.

Bulger led Lizzie to the doorway. He was shivering from the morning cold, but the cold left and he was filled with warmth as Lizzie reached and held his arm. His chin quivered and his eyes filled with happy tears when he heard the beginning notes of the Wedding March. Miss Minnie kept an eye on the doorway and timed her tune perfectly. Bulger and Lizzie started down the aisle behind Beth. Miss Claudie cried; Ginger smiled. Jimmy couldn't speak when he saw her. His head swam and his heart pounded. She was coming to him!

Skipping Rock, sitting near the back of the church, silently slipped and closed the door to keep out the cold as soon as Lizzie and Bulger entered. Preacher Sheets stood waiting, grinning broad as the side of the barn.

Bulger swelled with pride when he uttered, "I do," and handed his 'daughter' to Jimmy. The service was sweet, loving, and tender. They exchanged vows, and then they heard Preacher Sheets say, "You may now kiss your bride!"

And Jimmy did.

Beth covered her mouth with both hands and giggled. Someone in the audience started clapping and before Lizzie and Jimmy could turn and rush out the door, as at Ginger's wedding, the whole church applauded. It was such a happy day!

It was cold out, but the sunshine beamed down and warmed the front of the church and kept the deep chills away. When everyone was outside, Lizzie climbed the steps and turned with her back to the crowd. All the eligible young ladies gathered around closely, waiting for Lizzie to throw her bouquet. She took a breath and tossed her hand-made flowers over her shoulder.

They flew high and all the girls squealed and laughed as they jostled for a better position to catch the bouquet. Down it came—right into Susan's hands. She held the lace close to her chest and looked at Cullie. Cullie blushed from his head to—probably—his toes!

The crowds quickly dissipated and wagons cleared out, eager to carry the happy folks back to their warm homes. Skipping Rock and Bright Star, Minshue, and Warm DayRah stayed long enough to present Lizzie with their gifts: a colorful woven blanket, a new dipping gourd, and a sharp knife with a section of carved deer antler for a handle.

Eli noticed Skipping Rock looked especially chipper. Marriage must agree with him, too.

Lizzie and Jimmy got in his buggy and Bulger handed up heavy rocks, warmed while they sat under the huge pot-belly stove in the church. He'd wrapped them with old burlap bags. "Put a couple of these on the floorboards and keep ya feet on them. Then put the other on either side of ya. They'll help keep ya warm on your trip home," he said. Right behind him, Miss Claudie came and handed the wedding ring quilt up to Lizzie.

"Miss Claudie," she said full of surprise, "When did you ever have time to do this?"

Reaching high to tuck the corners snugly around Lizzie, Miss Claudie explained, "I didn't do it by myself. When ya get home, look around the edges. This is an extra special quilt. All the ladies in the community came to the house while ya visited Ginger and worked on it. They signed their names and all of them said every stitch is filled with love for ya two."

Lizzie leaned down and kissed Miss Claudie quickly. Jimmy pulled his buggy out of the church yard and on the road to his and his bride's house. It would take much of the afternoon for them to get home; snug in the quilt and warmed by the heated rocks.

Beth already sat in the wagon beside Bulger. He helped Miss Claudie up and they followed Lizzie and Jimmy as far as their house. Beth waved to the newlyweds until their wagon disappeared out of sight in the bend of the road.

FORTY-SEVEN

Weeks between Lizzie's wedding and Christmas flew by. All three houses soon filled with Christmas spirit: Bulger, Miss Claudie, and Beth's, Eli and Ginger's, and Jimmy and Lizzie's.

Miss Claudie helped Beth bake cookies and Bulger led the way through cold woods while he and Beth searched for that perfect cedar Christmas tree. It was the first Christmas they'd had a tree in the house for as long as Miss Claudie could remember. It was a little after Christmas just a year before that she and Bulger brought three sad, desolate children into their home. What a year they'd had!

Beth chatted all the way along the trail as Bulger wound through trees and more trees. Suddenly, they came to the top of a rise and there, with morning sun rising behind it, was 'the' tree. It seemed to glow as sunbeams danced around it, framing it with golden radiance. It took Beth's breath away.

"That's it!" she said as she lifted a hand and pointed to the tree.

Bulger walked over and knelt on his knees to get the best chopping angle. In short time, he yelled, "Timber!" and the tree was on its side on the ground.

"Grab the end, Little Bit," he said. "Ya need to get this thing to the house."

Beth ran and hoisted the cut end of the tree, pulling with all her might. It didn't move but an inch. She pulled and grunted; squinted her eyes and bit her tongue, but couldn't move the tree further.

Bulger chuckled.

"Okay, move along," he instructed. "I'll get it. Ya can carry the hatchet, but be careful."

Miss Claudie watched through the kitchen window as Bulger and Beth dragged the tree into the yard. She rushed to open the door. "Ya'll come in and warm up a while 'fore gettin' back out there and settin' the tree up."

Bulger and Beth gratefully came in and warmed by the fire. Miss Claudie had hot coffee for Bulger and warm sweetened milk for Beth. When their fingers and toes returned to normal and their noses weren't red anymore, Beth was ready to get the tree inside.

Bulger found a deep bucket in the barn. He trimmed lower limbs off the tree and stood it in it. Beth held it straight while Bulger shoveled in dirt and packed it tight. Beth let go and the tree stood tall and straight as an arrow. She propped her hands on her hips and grinned. Bulger smiled, too.

Together they pulled and tugged the bucket inside. "My, my," Miss Claudie observed, "that's a mighty fine tree ya'll got there." She pointed to the special place beside the wall cupboard. "Now we gone get it decorated," she said.

Beth could hardly wait. She was so excited to have a real tree for Christmas; all decorated when Lizzie and Eli came.

Miss Claudie set out a huge bowl of red berries she'd collected from Sumac and wild holly bushes and two large threaded needles. She and Beth threaded berries into long strings and Beth arranged them along the cedar limbs. When they finished placing the scarlet chains, Miss Claudie brought out scissors and paper she'd saved from their shopping trips and showed Beth how to fold and cut to make snowflakes, paper dolls, curly circles, lacy ovals, diamond-shapes, and squares. They used colored yarn to hang their creations on the tree. Then Miss Claudie brought out a special box. She looked to Bulger wistfully and gently set it on the table.

"This is something I been saving for a long, long time," she said and glanced to Beth. "Come on over and open it."

Beth moved to the table and lifted the lid. Inside were pine-cone angels, a few short colored candles, and some shiny metal ornaments. She looked at Miss Claudie.

"These were mine when I was a little girl," she offered. "My Mamma and me made most of them," she said as she picked up an angel and held it gently. "I've always hoped that one day Bulger and me would have a little girl or boy, and we could put them on our tree." She looked back at Beth. "And now we have our little girl and we can decorate our tree."

Beth ran and grabbed Miss Claudie around her waist and held her tight. Miss Claudie held Beth close, too.

"Come on, now, let's get this tree finished so we can set back and look at it a while 'fore we go to bed."

Bulger sat in his rocker, puffed on his pipe, and quietly watched as his wife and their little angel decorated their Christmas tree. Again, he thanked God for all His great works.

≈

Eli and Ginger laughed while she chased him along a worn animal trail as they searched for their cedar tree in morning's early birth. Eli took the lead, and the sun slowly rose. He walked swiftly, his hatchet hanging from his belt, tied securely. Every so often he'd hold onto a low limb as he walked along. He'd let it go just as Ginger walked in range, and she'd receive a sharp whack when it hit her and squeal out and run to catch him and return the a smack with her hand. Eventually they walked hand in hand along the trail, laughing and loving the time together, almost forgetting their search for a tree and instead getting lost in their quiet time in the forest.

"I can't wait to give Bulger and Miss Claudie our Christmas present," Ginger said, grasping Eli's hand tighter.

He looked at her and smiled, eyes twinkling, "Me neither."

They wound their way along meandering trails and came to the bank of the Chattahoochee. Eli stopped and dropped Ginger's hand. He gazed over the muddy water and his face softened. "You know," he said, sticking his hands deep in his coat pockets, "I'd come to think this river took everything away from me," he turned to Ginger. "But it didn't. It took a large part of me, but it didn't beat me," he turned back and added. "It didn't beat Lizzie or Beth, either." Ginger moved and wrapped her arms around his waist and rested her head on his shoulder.

He reached and pulled her closer. He continued, "The river carried the old Eli away, just like it did the wagon and ole' Maude, but I've been blessed and made new." The sun peeped through the trees and reflected in the rippling water of the Chattahoochee. "Look," he said, "sunrise. Sunrise is comin'. A new day." He squeezed Ginger more.

The sun moved upward as the pair watched. It broke free of the horizon and they felt warm sunshine on their faces. They were together, quiet and somber, and reflections of their pasts rippled through their minds. At last, Eli reached and lifted Ginger's head and gave her a soft, loving kiss.

"Come on, let's get our tree and get ready for our first Christmas. We gotta get it fixed up and invite Beth to spend a few nights with us."

Ginger smiled and they turned to walk into the forest in the light, searching for their perfect tree.

≈

Jimmy led Lizzie out of the yard and past the crib where his corn was stored. She heard the horse stomp and whinny as they passed the barn, expecting Jimmy to give him an extra handful of hay. She laughed as they entered the shadows of the pine thicket.

"You know where we can find a tree?" she asked.

"Sure," he replied, reaching for her hand. "Come on. I found a good one the other day and can't wait for you to see it. I know it's the perfect one."

Lizzie reached to grasp his hand and be pulled close to his side. Her stride matched his as he led her through tall pines and over soft pine needles. Every once in a while they heard the 'skitter sk-sk-skitter' of an annoyed squirrel as they passed through his domain.

Lizzie's thoughts flew back to another pine thicket near Bulger's. It was there that he and Miss Claudie had buried her parents; in a quiet, lovely place just like this one. She and Beth planted flowers last spring and watched as they bloomed in summer and died with the fall. They would reseed and there would be a scattering of blooms come the new spring. She smiled and looked upward through the green branches. A soft breeze gently passed through the treetops making swishing sounds, whispering to Lizzie. Sunbeams danced between the boughs and bounced off her cheeks. She looked at Jimmy.

"Do you ever wonder how our lives ever got so put together?" she asked.

He grinned and squeezed her hand. "I never wonder about it," he said, "but I wonder AT it." He dropped his head as they continued on. "I'm forever amazed at how we met—the timing was exactly right; I'm amazed at how you ended up just across the river from where I decided to build; I'm amazed at finding you at all." He stopped and wrapped his arms around her waist and pulled her close. He looked into her eyes and she could see her reflection in the blue sea there. He kissed her and she felt warmth from his lips all the way to her toes. She was happy.

He pulled away and blushed. "What would them Panther Clan think, seeing us spooning here in the middle of the woods?" he asked.

Lizzie laughed. "I don't know, and I really don't care," she replied, and gave him a second quick peck. "Come on and show me the tree. I want to get it in the house and our presents around it before bed."

As they made their way to Jimmy's tree, Lizzie's mind returned to her last Christmas. Presents: Eli and her present to Beth, a doll she'd named Patty; the cedar-scented doily they'd made for Mamma, and Pa's sheath for his knife. No presents for Pa and Mamma this year, she thought. But they'd be with us, in our thoughts and in our hearts, and our Christmas will be a special one; one of many special ones to come, she hoped. She walked along, happy and contented with her new husband on their way to get the perfect tree.

≈

Three small families; all preparing for Christmas. Little did Beth realize how special this Christmas would be for her; nor Eli ever think how this Christmas would bring out the 'new' Eli he'd become; or Lizzie realize how true her statement of being watched by the Muscogees really was.

FORTY-EIGHT

Christmas fell on Sunday. It had become a tradition that Eli and Ginger, and Jimmy and Lizzie, meet for breakfast at Bulger's before they traveled to Caney Head's church services. Jimmy and Lizzie were always the last to arrive—they had the longest way to travel. The buggy was a great idea. They made great time in it, much faster than a cumbersome wagon.

Christmas morning Miss Claudie was up early. Beth heard her and jumped out of bed to help make breakfast. Bulger had the animals fed and cows milked by the time the biscuits came out of the oven.

"Looks like a mild Christmas this year, Miss Claudie," Bulger said as he set the milk bucket in the sink and reached for the strainer.

"And a good thing, too," she replied as she automatically handed him a clean pitcher for the strained milk.

Beth couldn't help but notice how the two worked together. Miss Claudie could finish Bulger's sentences; Bulger anticipated Miss Claudie's actions---have her chair waiting, the wood ready for the stove, and water for the kettle without missing a beat. She exhaled. She was so happy.

By the time Beth had the table set, she heard the wagons pulling in the yard. Eli and Ginger were first followed quickly by Jimmy and Lizzie. Ginger and Lizzie made their way to the kitchen, arms filled with gifts, while Jimmy and Eli put Little Man and Jimmy's horse in the barn.

Beth jumped around the room like a fish on a line. "Can

we open our presents now instead of after while?" she asked.

Lizzie laughed, "Not on your life. We're going to church and then back for Christmas dinner—then we'll open our presents."

Beth's face dropped and she moped around to the other side of the table and over to the tree. Presents hidden under wrappings piled all under the beautiful Christmas tree. She took a deep breath and resolved her wait.

Miss Claudie's heart was filled. She looked over the cozy kitchen, so filled with love. Her 'children', chatting and laughing, working together getting ready for breakfast and Sunday worship. They'd have a wonderful time together this day. Christmas service was a special one, her Christmas dinner almost finished-complete with a roasted turkey Eli'd brought in---and then she'd planned a special Christmas treat before present-opening time.

Bulger's blessing that Christmas morning was truly a blessing for them all. He spoke of love, sharing, and miracles. By the time they'd finished breakfast and gotten ready for church, they felt that they'd already been a part of one Christmas message and ready to be filled with another.

Bulger pulled the wagon to the porch and they all clambered on. They went to church as a family. The day would be a day filled with the glory and love of God.

Beth sat in front between Bulger and Miss Claudie. They pulled into the church yard and stopped beside the Jones's wagon. Eli noticed right away that Cullie and Susan had arrived in a two-seater buggy.

Yep, he thought, he'd bet a sack of corn seed there would be another wedding soon.

Preacher Arp spoke eloquently. He told the Christmas story in such a way that Beth could smell the hay and warm animal smells in the stable and see the glow of the star. She heard baby Jesus coo and heard the rustle of covers as Mary held and comforted Him. Too soon, the service was over and they were on their way home.

The women had dinner on the table before the men could get Moses and Little Man settled. When they came stomping in, they only had to wash their hands and find a seat. Turkey and dressing, ham, green beans and mashed potatoes; cornbread and biscuits, sweet potato pie and special—and a seldom treat---sweet tea.

Bulger pushed back from the table and patted his stomach. "Miss Claudie, ya really out done yourself on this dinner. I think I gotta set a spell 'fore exertin' myself any."

Miss Claudie chuckled. "That's fine with me." She turned to the girls and said, "Ya'll get the dishes in the sink. We can get this cleaned up in a jiffy." Then she eyed Beth, "and then we'll open them presents."

Beth jumped up and began quickly scraping bits of food from their plates in a bucket for the barn cats and Lizzie poured hot water in the dishpan in the sink. She washed and Ginger dried. Miss Claudie packed two baskets with leftovers for the couples to take home, and Beth wiped the table clean.

"Now can we open our presents?" Beth begged.

Everyone looked at Bulger expectantly and he shook his head and laughed softly. "Yep, but I think Miss Claudie has something to say before we dig under the tree."

Miss Claudie brought out the Bible---the one from Pa and Mamma's trunk---and handed it to Lizzie. "Lizzie, will ya read the Christmas story aloud for us?" she asked. "Then I want us to sing a verse of 'Silent Night' before we open our gifts."

Eli and Lizzie stared at each other. They couldn't utter a word. Lizzie accepted the Bible and lay it, open, in her lap. She looked at Miss Claudie in wonder. Eli spoke.

He cleared his throat and wiped his nose. "This is unbelievable," he began. "I don't know how you came to this, or where the idea came from, but this is the very same thing we did back in the wagon with Pa and Mamma last Christmas." He reached and held Lizzie's hand. Beth moved and stood beside Lizzie and leaned into her shoulder.

Miss Claudie's eyes met Bulger's. Neither knew what to say. Finally Miss Claudie broke the silence. "I was thinkin' the other night, right 'fore goin' to sleep when somethin' told me to read the Christmas scripture and sing. It was plain as someone talkin' directly to me." She looked back at Lizzie and shrugged. "I don't know where it came from, but it was plain and I knew we had to do this. It's meant to be."

Sweet calmness filled the room, loving and warm. Lizzie's voice recited the beautiful story of the birth of Jesus, and afterward their voices harmonized as they joined hands and sang about the Virgin Mother and Child on that silent, holy night from ages past.

It was quiet only for a moment. Beth was the first to reach under the tree and read the name on the present. "Finally," she murmured, "we can open our presents!"

"Wait!" said Lizzie. "Jimmy and I have something to share first."

Miss Claudie's eyes widened and she looked at Bulger. He shrugged. Eli's and Ginger's faces filled with bewilderment and a little bit of 'uh-oh'. What's this, they wondered.

Lizzie sucked in a breath and continued. "Last week the trustees of the school came by the house. They wanted to speak to Jimmy, and he went out to meet with them." She smiled like a cat that had had her fill of milk. "When he came inside, he said I'd better not get mad at him, but he'd made a decision for me." She paused. "The men were disappointed that Miss Myline was leaving and wanted to know if Jimmy thought it would be all right if I took over teaching at the school." She sat straight and beamed. "I couldn't believe it—here I am, a married woman, and they still chose me! Jimmy gave his blessings and you're looking at the new Heard County teacher!"

Everyone was excited about her opportunity.

Eli rushed over to give her a hug. "I think Heard County is ahead of everyone," he said. "To think, a married schoolmarm! We're leading the way! I'm so proud of you." And the others agreed and congratulated her—and Jimmy, too, for giving his blessing.

"*Now* we can open our presents," Beth began, and reached under the tree.

"Whoa, Little Bit," Eli teased, "Let me and Ginger give our present."

All eyes went to them as they moved closer together and grasped hands. They looked around the room at their family. "You go," Ginger urged.

Eli, eyes sparkling, almost shouted, "Ya'll all get ready, we're having a baby!"

Miss Claudie clapped her hands and Bulger rocked back in his chair. Beth jumped up and down, uttering "Yes, yes!" Lizzie squealed in delight and Jimmy looked like he'd swallowed a whole fish. Eli laughed and slapped him on the back.

"You don't have to follow suit too quick, brother," he teased. "This one's mine—you can wait a while if you'd like."

Jimmy's color slowly returned to his face and he seemed at ease. "Whew, I'm glad it's you and not me—not yet, anyway. Scared me silly to think of being a pa just yet."

Everyone settled down, still giddy with joy when Eli motioned for Beth to pass out the gifts.

"Finally," she said, and their afternoon was filled with giving and receiving special, thoughtful gifts.

≈

That night while everyone snuggled under their covers, each one mirrored the events of the day. They all cherished their very own special memory and kept it locked in his and her heart.

Ginger sighed and moved closer to Eli and fitted her head in the crook of his arm.

Bulger and Miss Claudie lay still and Bulger listened to Miss Claudie's soft whisper as she whispered her nightly prayers and asked for blessings for her family.

In the kitchen, Beth lay in her bed, missing Lizzie. "Just think, Dolly and Patty, I'm getting a real baby. I love you both, but I'm a big girl now, and I'm gonna save you for the baby.' She gently set them on the shelf above her bed. "You can stay there now, but you go back in the drawer in the morning." she whispered. "I can sleep by myself." And she snuggled down under her quilt and closed her eyes.

Across the river, Jimmy pulled the covers around his and Lizzie's necks and settled his head against hers, his arm resting across her middle, ready for night's peaceful rest.

It had been the best Christmas ever.

FORTY-NINE

The week flew by. New Year's Day was there before they knew it. Jimmy had been to town and heard bad news. He hurried home, his heart in his throat, concerned that Lizzie might be in trouble. He reached the house and threw open the door. "Thank goodness," he said, and grabbed Lizzie and held her tight.

"What in the world?" she asked when he finally let go.

He closed the door and sat beside the fire. "Cullie told me that the Indians are cuttin' up again." He said. "They've been burnin' out families and hidin' in caves south of here. More livestock has gone missing; they've got more of a taste for beef now than for deer," he said. He rubbed his hands across his face. "They're getting' bold and I was so afraid they'd come here while I was gone. Don't know if it's true or not, but stories are they've taken some white women. Posses have been out for them, but so far the Clan's been sly enough to not get caught. I won't be leavin' you here by yourself anymore, and I'll take you to school and pick you up every day. No ridin' in by yourself."

Lizzie moved and placed her hands on Jimmy's shoulders. He loved her so much. It hurt her to see him so scared because of his fear of losing her.

"Let me get you some hot coffee," she offered. "You'd better get out and get the horse settled away. I'll have the coffee ready by the time you get back."

Jimmy nodded and went out to the buggy. Lizzie slowly closed the door.

≈

Eli was awakened when he heard Cullie shouting at his door. Ginger was up, too, as soon as she heard his frantic voice.

"The church is on fire, and the woods will go too if we don't get the fire out quick," he huffed.

"Get to Skipping Rock as fast as you can. He's closer to Jimmy since he's in his wife's village," Eli shouted to Cullie. "Tell him to send men and then go get Jimmy. Meet us at the church." Eli quickly hitched Little Man to the wagon. Ginger dressed quickly and got aboard. He slapped the reins and shouted for Little Man to step high. Cullie followed in his buggy only as far as the main road. He turned toward Skipping Rock's village, and Eli headed to Bulger's.

"You stay with Miss Claudie and Beth," he instructed when he hit the main road. Ginger clung to the seat and kept quiet.

≈

Jimmy and Lizzie were awakened by a pounding on the door. Jimmy jumped out of bed and ran to open it. Skipping Rock was standing there, breathing heavily.

"We got to get to the church now," he said. "Eli sent Cullie for me to tell you. The church's been set afire and they need all the help they can get."

Jimmy rushed back and grabbed his clothes. "Get dressed. We gotta go with Skipping Rock," he said to Lizzie. "I'll drop you off to stay with Miss Claudie."

She was dressed before Jimmy got in from the barn. Thankfully the buggy was faster than the cumbersome wagon. Skipping Rock raced ahead on his paint.

≈

Bulger was awakened when their neighbor, Mr. Hull, came by and the dogs set up a howl. Bulger rushed out to see what the ruckus was all about.

Mr. Hull pulled his wagon to a quick halt. "Caney Head's afire! I've sent my boys on with all the buckets we got at our place to the church," he said. "and the oldest to town for help. Get ya buckets and meet us at the fire, I'm gone make a round for some more folks." He removed his cap and wiped his forehead with his arm. "The church is pure heart pine. It's goin' fast, and the fire's spreadin'."

"I'm on my way," Bulger answered.

Miss Claudie stood in the kitchen in her gown. Bulger looked back at her. "Go." was all she said.

"Gone shut them dogs in the barn," he said as he left. "You and Beth stay inside. I'll be back 'fore long." And he was gone.

It was less than ten minutes and Miss Claudie heard a wagon in the yard. She ran to the door expecting Bulger, but it was Eli.

"Keep Ginger here with you," he said as Ginger climbed down. He whipped the wagon around and was out of the yard faster than two shakes of a sheep's tail.

Jimmy and Lizzie made record time in their light buggy. He met Eli on his way out. "I'll be there right behind you!" he shouted.

Eli raised a hand to acknowledge his message and raced on.

Lizzie threw Jimmy a kiss and whispered a prayer from Miss Claudie's porch as his wagon wound its way out of the yard.

≈

Bulger saw the flames dancing in the dark night, high above the treetops, miles before arriving. When he pulled up, the church was engulfed in flames and red-hot fire licked out every window. Men and boys had formed a bucket brigade from the creek to the church, but most of the water was sloshing out before getting to the fire or turning to steam as soon as it hit the flames. Heat was intense. He watched as flames leapt from the church roof to nearby trees and they burst into flames. In disbelief, he saw burning limbs fall and grasses catch and fire began eating its way toward the line of men passing water buckets. He jumped off the wagon and cut pine limbs and began beating the ground; hitting the burning grass over and over to stop its spread. It must not get to the men.

The church fire grew; its deafening roar overpowering; smoke filled the air and the men soaked their handkerchiefs in water, wrung them out, and tied them across their faces so they could breathe.

Bulger fought the fire; tried to kill the flames, but where one died, another birthed. His arms ached, his lungs burned, but he kept slinging his pine bough until the needles on his bough were beaten away. He cut another.

His breath came in gasps.

Eli and Cullie joined the bucket brigade; relieving a couple of men who had been the first to arrive. The church was lost, they knew, but the fire still had to be stopped; every spark extinguished.

Several men, knowing they had the church fire under control, joined Bulger on the ground and began fighting to keep flames out of the wooded area. Bulger's work paid off; the men's water-line was safe. He'd stopped the fire on that side of the inferno; now to protect the woods.

Bulger's shoulders felt as if they were coming apart; his chest pained. His legs felt like rubber. Suddenly, the pain in his chest felt like one of the flames had shot up inside him and was leaping down his arm.

As Jimmy and Skipping Rock pulled up, Eli saw Bulger go down.

"Jimmy!" Eli yelled.

Behind him, Cullie heard Eli's scream and knew something was very wrong. He looked up to see Eli running through the smoke. He dropped his bucket and followed.

Jimmy saw Eli running and shot his eyes forward in the direction of Eli's flight. He saw Bulger's smoke-stained coat and pants on the ground and rushed toward him, Skipping Rock close behind. They all reached Bulger simultaneously and Eli knelt and rolled him onto his back.

Bulger's eyes were pinched shut and his lips ground together in a tight line. Eli heard a long low breath escape and Bulger's face softened. He opened his eyes and looked at Eli. With a shaking hand, Bulger grasped Eli's coat collar and whispered, "Take care of Miss Claudie. Don't leave her and Little Bit by themselves."

Eli, tears flowing, nodded.

Bulger opened his hand and stroked Eli's blackened face, lined with tear tracks through smoke and soot left there. His eyes softened and looked beyond Eli. He smiled a soft smile and his hand fell away.

"No!" Eli yelled, holding to Bulger's coat collar and shaking him. "No, not now! Don't do this, you can't leave, too!"

But Bulger had.

≈

Jack and Bell were pitching a fit to get out. Beth could hear them all the way in the house.

"Now don't ya go out there, Beth," Miss Claudie warned. Beth knew she meant business when she said 'Beth' and not 'Little Bit.' She sat at the table, tapping her feet and drumming her fingers on the table.

Ginger and Miss Claudie sat beside the hearth and Lizzie sat at the table with Beth.

"Don't worry about the dogs, now Beth," Lizzie coaxed. "You know they'd follow Bulger or one of the wagons and get in the way. Maybe even get hurt, too," she said.

Beth huffed, "I know," she said. "But couldn't they at least come in here with us?" she begged. "They don't want to be left out in that old cold barn."

Lizzie looked at Miss Claudie.

"Oh, I guess she can bring them inside," Miss Claudie said and looked out the window. "It's almost sunrise. It will be light soon and the menfolk will be back." She turned to Beth and shook her finger in her direction. "But you'd better get right out there and right back inside, young lady," she warned.

Beth shot up and ran over to give Miss Claudie a big hug. "Thank you, Miss Claudie," she said, and raced out of the room, pulling her arms in her coat as she went.

Lizzie and Ginger laughed to see Beth so glad to be out and get her dogs close by.

The dogs kept barking, an agitated, loud, bark. After two minutes too long, and no Beth or dogs, Lizzie became worried. She went to the door and opened it. As soon as she stepped on the porch, she knew something was dreadfully wrong.

The barn doors were shut tight and the dogs' barking escalated to a frenzy. Lizzie, in the early morning light, saw Beth's footprints in the frosty ground. There were some softer, other prints there as well, and the ground was scuffed up. She looked from the footprints to the barn and back. Then she knew. She whirled around and ran into the kitchen.

"They've got her!" she screamed.

Miss Claudie and Ginger jumped up. Ginger paled and Miss Claudie ran to the door. "What do you mean?" she asked, reaching for Lizzie.

Lizzie grabbed Miss Claudie's hands and cried, "The Panthers, they got Beth."

FIFTY

After waiting an agonizing day for the men to get back, the women heard wagons rumbling into the yard. All three rushed to the porch, worried and anxious, and stood crying and wringing their hands there on the steps. Miss Claudie noticed immediately that Eli sat alone on his wagon seat and felt a cold fear in her belly. Her hands began fluttering like wounded birds.

Jimmy drove his horse and buggy, and Skipping Rock was driving Bulger's wagon with his paint tied behind---Bulger was nowhere to be seen. She looked from one face to the other and read what was written invisibly across each one. She clasped her hands to her face and crumpled down into a limp heap on the top step. Lizzie caught her and eased her down. She looked toward the men driving the wagons. She, too, missed Bulger. She looked to Ginger and saw her stricken face.

Eli pulled his wagon to a stop. Wrapped in a blackened tarp on the back was Bulger's body. Lizzie heard a low, agonizing moan leave Miss Claudie. She held her closer.

Eli got off the wagon as Jimmy, Cullie, and Skipping Rock pulled theirs to a stop. Slowly, Jimmy wrapped his reins around the brake stick and climbed down. The others followed. Jimmy met Eli at the rear of the wagon and helped him lift Bulger's body. Lizzie and Ginger helped Miss Claudie to stand, clinging to them both, hardly able to move her legs. Before they could get Bulger inside, Miss Claudie wailed, "They took Beth."

Skipping Rock stopped still as a hawk in the night. His blood ran cold and his temples throbbed with each heartbeat.

He was the only one who was able to speak. "Is this true?" he asked. "The Panther Clan has Beth?"

Lizzie started sobbing. She could only nod her head. Inside the barn, Jack and Bell went wild.

"Get in the house," Eli commanded. Carrying Bulger between them, Cullie, Skipping Rock, and Jimmy worked their way through the kitchen and dogtrot and gently placed him on the bed. They returned to the kitchen where Miss Claudie sat with her head in her hands, crying her heart out.

Jimmy pulled Lizzie to the side. "Bulger had a heart attack fighting the fire," he explained. "Take care of Miss Claudie, we're going after Beth." He held her and kissed her, then held her a moment longer.

Lizzie, in shock, nodded mutely.

Eli hugged Ginger long and hard and kissed her before joining Skipping Rock on the porch. "Help Lizzie and Miss Claudie," he said as he left.

Cullie spoke, "I'm goin' to town and get as many men as I can. Sheriff Bledsoe will know who to get together. I'll send coroner Buchanan out with Mr. Stutts from the mortuary. He'll have a box already and can come and get the body and get him cleaned and dressed. Mr. Stutts'll take care of it." He added, "We'll meet you at the river," and he was in Jimmy's wagon and gone.

Skipping Rock added, his face hardened more than Eli had ever seen it, "As bad as I hate to say it, I hope we find the Panthers before any of you do. This time there will be no asking for peace. It will be the Indian's judgment and no mercy." He turned, jumped on his paint and whipped him into a run.

Eli and Jimmy were left in the yard. "We have the dogs. Jack and Bell sensed the Indians were close; I remember hearing them barking even before we left." He hit his fist on his thigh. "We were in too big a hurry to notice that anything might be wrong here." Eli turned on his heel. "Probably the same bunch that set fire to the church took Beth. Just wanted to get us out there and away from the house," he added. He stomped the ground and threw up his hands, fists pumping the air. "I'll kill them!"

Jimmy, always calm and thoughtful, assured Eli. "We'll get

Beth back. Let's get leashes for the dogs. I'll bet they can track that bunch and lead us right to her." He looked toward the west. "It's gettin' dark. Better get the lanterns ready."

Eli turned and looked at Jimmy and he could tell his idea clicked. "Com'on," he said, and headed to the barn. "Get those lines and lights ready. The shotguns Bulger keep in the barn too," he added.

Jimmy had Bell on a leash and Eli held Jack's. The dogs put their noses to the ground and jerked their leashes tight as they pulled Jimmy and Eli along. The sun was setting, and the scent on the trail had weakened, evaporated from a day in the soft sun's warmth. The dogs tracked diligently. Jimmy lit a lantern and let the dogs lead them through the woods and down a branch before turning and heading south.

They walked over an hour and quickly covered several miles. The dogs plunged on, pulling and straining on their leashes. The boys had to trot to keep up. Eli thought he'd have to stop and rest, they both were totally exhausted, especially after fighting the fire, when the dogs lifted their heads and began quivering all over.

Ask, and it shall be given you; seek, and ye shall find; knock, and it shall be opened unto you.
Matthew 7: 7-8

"She's close," Jimmy whispered.

"I hope the dogs stay quiet," Eli answered. "Sure as shootin' there's more of'em than there is of us."

"Come on, tie them over here and put out that light," Jimmy said and moved to a nearby tree. They tied the dogs and admonished them to stay quiet. "They seem to know what we mean," he said to Eli, amazed. The dogs sat side-by-side, quietly at attention, waiting for Beth to return to them.

The boys bent down, moving slowly in the direction the dogs indicated. The sun had long slipped behind the tree line. Even in January's late dark coolness, they sweated. They slipped quietly through bushes and crawled on their stomachs through thorns and bushes. They smelled smoke from the Indians' campfire before spying their camp. They couldn't believe what they saw.

Skipping Rock was poised behind a large pine and had already spied Eli and Jimmy. He willed Eli to look his way and they made eye contact. His body language sent a silent message for the men lay low—not to get in his way. He lowered his head and turned toward Beth. She was bound and gagged, placed in front of a tree along with two other white girls, facing the spirited Indians. The girls were partially covered with deerskin. The Panther Clan rallied around a campfire, laughing and rough-housing, ignoring their captives.

Skipping Rock moved closer. Beth saw him from the corner of her eye and started to turn toward him. He motioned quickly for her to remain still. She understood and continued watching the Panthers celebrate.

Eli and Jimmy, enveloped with awe and intrigue, watched as a dozen others who'd come along with Skipping Rock materialized out of the trees. They couldn't believe it. The Indians had been there all the while and he and Jimmy never noticed.

Skipping Rock slipped behind Beth's tree; slowly and silently reached and slid his knife through her ropes. "Stay still," he whispered. He moved to the other two girls and freed them. With lightning speed, he gathered the girls and whisked them to a waiting brave who led them away from the camp and mercifully removed their gags. The Muscogees, so far, hadn't noticed a thing.

Suddenly a cry so harsh and loud rang out that it made hairs on Eli's and Jimmy's necks and arms stand on end. It echoed through the woods and sent sleeping birds flying. The woods exploded. Jack and Bell howled an eerie haunting wail. Skipping Rock barreled into the Muscogee like a bear after a deer: all teeth and claws. Chaos reigned.

Miraculously Beth and the girls materialized beside Eli, and their guide made it clear for Jimmy and him to get out of there---fast. Just as silently as he'd appeared, and without a word, he disappeared. They got to their feet as quickly as they could. Jimmy scooped up one child and Eli the other. He grabbed Beth's hand and they ran to the dogs. Beth jerked free of Eli's hand and ran ahead and untied the dogs. They ran in a gallop.

Behind them, they heard yelling and running; thumping and crying screams. They dared not look back.

≈

They ran for half a mile and had to stop. They were beyond exhaustion. Jimmy and Eli lowered their girls to the ground and dropped to their knees beside them. Beth gathered Jack and Bell and crooned softly to them, rubbing behind their ears and scratching their bellies. They looked like they were grinning at her, so happy to have her safely back.

"I'll never let'cha get locked up in that ole' barn again," she promised, "You found us!"

Eli agreed. "Yep, they did that. They followed your trail right to the camp." He looked at the other two girls. "You okay?" he asked.

They nodded. He noticed they were trying very hard not to cry.

Beth noticed Eli and Jimmy: black, sooty, and smelling of smoke. "Did'ja get the fire put out?" she asked.

Jimmy answered. "We did, but we can't stay around here to tell about it. We need to get to town and get these girls back home. Do'ya know them?"

"Sure," Beth answered. "They go to school with me. This is Jennie," she said, pointing to a lovely little curly haired blonde girl, "and this is Melody, from the store."

"Hey," they both said in unison. They were trying very hard not to cry. They were shaking all over, but were trying so hard to be brave, big girls.

"I'm ready to go home," Melody whimpered.

Jimmy stood and replied, "Well, let's get goin'. We're not too far now. Let me know if you get tired and I'll carry you."

Jennie straightened her shoulders and tossed back her curls. "We can make it now." She said solemnly. "I bet them Indians won't bother us anymore."

Eli took her hand and they started down the road to town. "No, I bet they won't be botherin' anybody from now on," he added surely.

FIFTY-ONE

By the time they got Melody and Jennie home, the posse had returned. Sheriff Bledsoe and Cullie, driving Eli's wagon, stopped off at Jones's store and met Eli and Jimmy.

"All we found out there was a deserted camp and lots of blood," Sheriff Bledsoe reported. "No bodies, no horses, no nothin'. Looks like the troublemakers won't be making any more trouble," he said with a relieved expression. "Only thing is, I hope the Muscogees from down south don't blame us with any of this," he added.

Eli responded, "I have a feeling we won't have to worry none 'bout that," and looked to Jimmy. "I'm glad we got the girls back safe."

Sheriff Bledsoe perked up. "Yes, their folks were beside themselves when they discovered their girls missing. Course, they knew the Panthers had'em, and what went through their minds couldn't be described." He dropped his head. "Never seen such a thankful homecoming. It's a miracle they're still alive. Ya need to tell me how ya'll came up on them."

Jimmy looked tired. "Sure thing, Sheriff, but right now we're dog tired, got a lot to get back to. We'll explain later if that's fine with you. Just want you to know it wasn't us that did it. Give your thanks to our friends in the village. Skipping Rock and his braves are the real heroes."

The sheriff understood; the fire, the loss of Bulger, and searching for Beth and finding two more lost girls. "Sure, get on home and take care of things. We're plain thankful ya got the girls home safe." And he waved them on their way.

Sunrise

Cullie climbed down from Eli's wagon and he, Jimmy, and Beth climbed in. Jack and Bell hopped in the back. "I'm starved," Beth commented as they drove out of town. "Them Indians ain't nothin' like Minshue's friends. Didn't get much dinner and no supper a'tall. Hope Miss Claudie has plenty cooked when we get home." Then she looked at Eli and Jimmy. With a trembling chin, she admitted, "I was really scared. I didn't know what to do, but I knew ya'll were looking for me. Skipping Rock, too. I had to be strong for Jennie and Melody." She gave in to her feelings and the dam broke. "I'm so sorry, Eli. I just wanted the dogs in the house. I'm so glad to be going home."

Eli looked at Jimmy and he knew how much Eli dreaded going home; and explaining to Beth all had happened since she was taken.

FIFTY-TWO

Beth knew immediately something was wrong the minute they pulled in the yard. Bulger's wagon stood empty near the barn. Neither Lizzie, Ginger, nor Miss Claudie stood waiting for them on the porch. Jack and Bell fell on their bellies in the back of the wagon and dropped their heads to their paws. She looked at Eli and Jimmy and they stared straight ahead. She suddenly felt afraid. More afraid than she'd been with the Indians.

Eli pulled his wagon to a stop and Jimmy hopped off and lifted Beth to the ground. "I'll go in with you before we put the horse away," he offered. He looked to the ground, kicked a rock with the toe of his boot, and nodded. They led Beth inside.

They found Miss Claudie slumped in Bulger's rocking chair near the hearth. She looked extra tiny sitting there. She seemed to have aged ten years since morning.

Lizzie and Ginger sat at the table, their eyes swollen from crying. They rose in unison and ran to their husbands. Beth slowly walked to Miss Claudie and placed her hand on the back of the rocker.

"Miss Claudie, I'm here. Don't worry 'bout me anymore. I'm fine," she whispered.

Miss Claudie drew her eyes from the fire and looked into Beth's eyes. "Oh, child," she cried, and drew Beth close and held her tightly.

Beth couldn't hear her cries, but felt Miss Claudie's sobs. "Miss Claudie, it's me, Beth, what's wrong?" She abruptly felt a chill and filled with apprehension. The only sound was the ticking of the mantle clock. She felt sorrow and it was strangling her. Tears stung her eyes.

Miss Claudie pulled away and wiped her face with her handkerchief. "It's Bulger, child, he's gone."

"Gone? Gone where?" she asked.

Lizzie moved and placed her hands on Beth's shoulders and looked into her eyes. "He's gone, Beth. He had a heart attack fighting the fire. Mr. Stutts came and he and Mr. Buchanan carried his body to town. They'll bring him back as soon as they get him cleaned up."

Beth went numb. Pa, Mamma, and now Bulger. It's not fair, she thought. She let the tears come and held on to Lizzie for dear life.

"Let her cry it out," Jimmy said.

There came a knock at the door and Mr. and Mrs. Denney, the Tuggles, Gores, and Walls were there. The men came to sit and the women brought food.

Mr. Walls said, "Ya'll boys need to get cleaned up. Folks'll be coming in the rest of the night to offer comfort. We'll sit here with the women 'til ya get ready."

Lizzie got out the large washpan and filled it with warm water. Eli and Jimmy moved the washpan to the bedroom and Mrs. Gore and Mrs. Tuggle brought soap and towels.

Jimmy and Eli got the greasy soot off their faces and arms and washed their hair. They'd have to make do with some of Bulger's clothes until they could get home for their own.

More neighbors arrived bringing food and prayers.

Miss Claudie bowed her head in appreciation with each gift. The men slid Beth's bed to one side of the room, and the door opened and Mr. Stutts stood there.

"Where should we place the coffin?" he softly asked.

Mr. Walls pointed to the empty spot where Beth's bed had been. "Over here, I think." He moved aside and the men held their hats in their hands as Mr. Stutts and three others brought Bulger's body, resting in a lovely pine box. Mr. Stutts set two pairs of casket legs down, and the men lifted the coffin and set it on top.

"I'll stay tonight 'til midnight," said Mr. Pollard.

Mr. Gore added, "I'll set with ya."

Sheriff Bledsoe and Mr. Jones offered to come in at midnight and sit with the body through morning.

As hungry as they were and as good as the food was, it was hard for the family to get anything down. Even Beth picked at her plate. All they could get down Miss Claudie was a few swallows of coffee. She nibbled on a biscuit. Bedtime came at last. Everyone left except Mr. Pollard and Mr. Gore who took vigil beside Bulger's body.

"Come on, Miss Claudie, let me help you to bed." And Lizzie led her adopted mother silently into the bedroom. "Beth and I are staying with you. Jimmy will stay with Eli and Ginger. They'll be back first thing in the morning."

Miss Claudie let Lizzie dress her in her nightgown and tuck her into bed like a baby. Beth climbed in beside Miss Claudie and snuggled close. Lizzie turned and looked back as she left the room. Miss Claudie's and Beth's arms intertwined as they lay lumped beneath the cover, and both were already sound asleep.

She entered the kitchen and sat at the table with Eli, Jimmy, and Ginger. Eli spoke first.

He rubbed his hand through his hair and shook his head. "I can't believe it," he said. "What now?" he looked up. "We've got some serious decisions to make and make them in a hurry. What we gone do?"

Jimmy spoke up. "I told Mr. Stutts to have a grave ready in the grove where your Pa and Mamma are. We don't have a church anymore, and no graveyard to speak of, so I asked Mr. Stutts have Preacher Sheets say a graveside service there." He looked around. "Hope I wasn't out of line doin' that."

Lizzie touched his arm. "Course you weren't. You're family." She sighed. "I'm glad you thought through this. We sure haven't thought that far ahead and at least the funeral's taken care of. All we need to do is ask who we want to be pall bearers."

They talked a few minutes and decided Miss Claudie would approve Skipping Rock, Mr. Gore, Cullie, Mr. Pollard, Mr. Marshall, and Mr. Jones. Eli and Jimmy would sit with their wives, Beth, and Miss Claudie.

Eli pulled himself up and walked to the coffin. He looked

at Bulger, so peaceful, so serene. At last he let his emotions loose and cried his heart out.

At the table, his sister and wife watched silently, stifling their tears and feeling the emptiness that seeped through the house.

Eli, cried dry, turned and said, "Come on, Ginger. Let's get on home and get some sleep. Jimmy, you and Lizzie come on, too."

"I'm staying with Miss Claudie and Beth," Lizzie said. "You go. I'll have plenty of room in the bed with Miss Claudie and Beth. The way they're huddled together there's half a bed left for me." She rose and added, "If you don't mind, Ginger, bring a fresh set of your clothes for me when you come back in the morning."

Ginger nodded.

Eli moved and embraced Lizzie. "We'll get through this. We've suffered worse."

Lizzie's eyes filled again, but she remained composed. "If you can, try to come up with how we're gone work this out. Miss Claudie and Beth certainly can't stay here alone and do the chores and keep the place up. I'm wore out, and know you are, too, but God has plans for us yet. Pray about it, and seek our answer."

Jimmy hugged her and kissed her lightly as Eli and Ginger opened the door to leave. "We'll do all we can. God is our guide, and He's always in control." He turned and Lizzie watched as her husband closed the door.

She quietly moved to the coffin and said her good-byes to Bulger. The men sat silently and reverently as Lizzie made her peace. She left the room and lay with Beth and Miss Claudie. She was still awake when she heard the sheriff and Mr. Jones come in to replace the two sitting with Bulger. Finally sleep came.

There was enough food for an army in the kitchen. Women from all over the community, even Warm DayRah and Minshue brought food. Mr. Stutts reported that the grave was ready and Preacher Sheets would speak over Bulger's body. 'An honor to do it,' he'd said.

The morning flew by, dinner served but not much eaten,

and it came time to dress and ride to the pine grove for Bulger's funeral.

Miss Claudie was pitiful. She'd seemed to shrink even more and all her spark was burned out. She moved in a daze; hardly speaking and eating nothing. Even Beth couldn't bring her around. The girls helped her onto Eli's wagon and they rode down the road to the serene pine grove. The sun shone and soft white clouds puffed along in the beautiful blue sky. A few birds sang as they passed, and a line of wagons lumbered along behind them—far as Eli could see. Bulger was a well-thought of, respected man, but Eli already knew that.

Mr. Stutts had chairs sitting alongside the grave. Eli helped Miss Claudie down and Ginger and Lizzie helped her to her seat. She sat and stared at the empty hole in the ground.

Bulger's six pall bearers lifted the box from the back of Eli's wagon and carried it to the grave. Wagons pulled in all through the wooded glade and people spilled in. They moved silently and formed a circle around the three graves. Preacher Sheets began.

He spoke of Bulger's honor, his faith, and his love for his family. He told how hard he'd worked to help build up the community and support the efforts of the Creeks in the area. He expressed how much Bulger would be missed, and prayed a beautiful closing prayer. He stepped back and asked Mr. Demmie to lead those gathered there to sing 'Amazing Grace' as a final tribute and benediction. The voices carrying the song still echoed through the treetops as Preacher Sheets made his way to Miss Claudie and her family to offer condolences. A line formed, and those who came to pay their respects followed his example and hugged and shook hands with Bulger's loved ones.

Eli stood as the last handshake was given and invited everyone back to Miss Claudie's. "Follow and join us to take a meal with us. We have plenty of food and it can't go to waste—it's more than we can ever put away." He helped Miss Claudie up, and together they made their way to the wagon and led the processional back home.

The house filled and people spilled onto the porch and into the yard. Eventually laughter was heard as someone told a familiar story about Bulger; something he'd done as a joke or prank. Gradually, the somber mood changed to a lighter-hearted one, and as the folks drifted to their wagons and started home, Eli felt better.

During the ceremony, he'd heard a voice. He knew what must be done. God had worked everything out, just as Jimmy had predicted.

When the last of the food was put away, the kitchen clean, Beth's bed back in place, and lamps lit, Eli gathered everyone around the worn kitchen table once more.

"I think I have a plan," he said. "It came to me during the service, almost as if Bulger told me what we need to do."

They all remained silent, waiting for Eli to continue.

"We know Miss Claudie and Beth can't stay here and run the place." He saw Miss Claudie blanch white and reached for her hand to reassure her. "But that don't mean they have to leave. Think about this: Jimmy and Lizzie's place is across state line and it's small." Looking at Jimmy, he continued. "Jimmy you have a lot to do there yet, and to be honest, I'd like for you and Lizzie to be closer to us. What if you sell your place and move in here?" Then a thought hit him. "You know, I heard Preacher Arp asking 'bout a place for his Uncle Bud and Aunt Della. Your place would be perfect for them!" He noticed Jimmy frown and Lizzie brighten and rushed on. "We could add another bedroom on here with no problem and make a room for Beth in the space above one end of the dogtrot." He noticed Beth's eyes light up at the idea of having her own room. "Miss Claudie can still sleep in her own room in her own bed and ya'll will have the new one. The kitchen is plenty big, even for us when we come by." He sat back to let this idea sink in.

He could tell Jimmy was a little hesitant. He added. "We can both use Moses, along with Little Man and your horse, and Ginger and I will take Bessie's and Bossie's calves, and Bessie, too, to our place. Bessie and Bossie are both bred back and we'll have plenty of milk. We can share the work getting in crops since we'll be close by. What do you say?"

Lizzie grabbed Jimmy's shoulder and shook it. "Please, Jimmy. I know it's what Bulger would have wanted. It makes sense. We can live here and take care of Miss Claudie and Beth. It's like having our place all set up and ready to go. What else could we want?"

Jimmy reached and held Lizzie's hand. He grinned and kissed it. "I say it's a grand idea. I think I'll ask Cullie 'bout buying our place first, though. I think he and Susan will be needin' a place of their own pretty soon, and Cullie can get to town to work easy from our place."

Lizzie grinned and Jimmy added, "If they don't need it, maybe Mr. Bud will." He looked at Eli. "I'll sell only if I put the money we get from our place on the new church building. Maybe I won't feel so guilty 'bout having this place if we do that. I hear a new church is already in the works. The Caswells are giving the land. The new church will be built on the top of the hill about half a mile from where the old one burned."

"That's a wonderful idea," Lizzie said. "What about you, Miss Claudie, what do you think?"

She stared through blurry, swollen eyes. She looked around the table and let her eyes drink in each face. Then she declared in a firm voice, "This day, this time, has ended. Tomorrow, God willing, the sun will rise. Darkness cannot dwell where there is light, and light is coming to cover us anew with the sunrise." She smiled and reached for Beth and Lizzie's hands. She squeezed them hard. "We will watch the sun rise and be bathed in its warmth and brightness. Each sunrise brings us a new day to rejoice and be happy in. Each day is a day the Lord has made and we will be glad in it." Tears ran down her cheeks and dropped to the table. "Cherish the memories we've made." She looked at Ginger. "Bulger is gone, but a baby is coming. Together we will make new memories."

And as night folded over the house, a family was mending and finding peace. They were learning to grow even more in faith. Light from the lamps kept the night's darkness at bay. Sunrise would surely come the next morning and banish all the night's darkness, bringing hope, faith, new and exciting expectations, and gladness. They would carry on and live---fully and joyfully---in the light.

References

www.carrollcountyga.com/page/history

www.native-languages.org   (Muscogee, Creek information and words)

www.accessgeneology.com/native/creeknotes   (Creek Indian tribal traditions)

http://enwikipedia.org/wiki/TreatyofCasseta

http://ensikipedia.org/wiki/muscogee_people

Scriptures taken from the King James version of the *Holy Bible*

Hymn references as written in *The United Methodist Hymnal.* Book of United Methodist Worship. The United Methodist Publishing House. Nashville, Tennessee. 1993

www.Urbandictionary.com/define   (Old southern dialogue: ya all. (ya'll) Used among indigenous populations of the southern continental U.S. Attributed to southern normal cadence. *Used specifically as a preservation of old southern dialect*. True southerners would never say cumbersome 'you all', but instead 'ya all'. Would be 'you all' to those of the uninformed Yankees.

Once Upon a Time the wonder-story Books: A Unit in The Row, Peterson Basic Reading Program; "Why the Bear has a Short Tail". Edited by R.P. Maison; Row, Peterson & Company, Evanston Illinois, 1962/(Indian legend retold from the story.)

Illustration by Greer Harper
– nine-year old granddaughter

Charles Gore and the original
red-boned hounds, Jack and Bell

Recipes From Days Gone By...

Keep on turnin'...

Lola's Canned Vegetable Soup
CGP's paternal Grandmother

1 cup sugar
½ cup salt
1 cup vinegar
2 gallons peeled and chopped tomatoes
2 cups cooked butter beans (or other pea)
16 ears corn, kernels cut off and scalded
2 cups okra
6 large green peppers, diced
Hot peppers to taste, diced
6 medium onions, diced
4 or 5 diced potatoes, boiled until just tender

Boil peppers and onions in water until onions are clear.

In large boiler, add all ingredients. Bring to a boil and boil 10 to 15 minutes, stirring often to prevent scorching. Have jars and lids hot, ladle boiling soup into jars and seal.* vegetables may be adjusted to taste—add more or omit. Makes about 14 quarts.

Miss Minnie's Meal (or Vinegar) Pie
CGP's maternal grandmother

1 stick butter
1 cup sugar
3 eggs
2 Tbsp. corn meal
1 Tsp. vinegar
1 tsp. lemon flavoring (opt)
1 tsp. vanilla

Combine butter and sugar. Cream well. Add all the other ingredients and mix thoroughly. Pour into unbaked 8" pie shell. Bake at 325 for 45 minutes to an hour.

**variation: add ½ cup coconut flakes to mixture before baking.

Grandma Denney's Pound Cake
CGP's paternal great-grandmother

3 cups sifted all-purpose flour
3 cups sugar
6 eggs
2 sticks butter
1 cup sweet milk
½ tsp. baking powder
½ tsp. cream of tartar
½ tsp. salt
1 tsp. vanilla
½ cup Crisco

Sift together dry ingredients. Mix sugar, butter, and Crisco, then eggs, one at a time. Beating each time until fluffy. Add milk and dry ingredients, alternating. Cook in 10 inch spout pan 1 hour at 325.

Fried Squash Blooms
Aunt Della Hanes

12 large squash blooms
Milk
Salt
3 Tbsp. all-purpose flour
2 eggs, separated
oil for deep frying

Rinse thoroughly very fresh, still closed squash blossoms, dry gently, but well. Combine flour and just enough milk to make a smooth, medium-thick paste. Add egg yolks and blend until very smooth. Add salt to taste. Stir in enough additional milk to make a smooth, runny batter. Allow batter to stand for about an hour if time permits.

Beat egg whites until stiff, moist peaks form, fold into batter. Dip blossoms completely in batter, retrieve with a slotted spoon, and deep-fry a few at a time in oil preheated until 350. When golden brown, drain on paper towels. Sprinkle lightly with salt and serve hot.

Dara's Pecan Pie (from Miss Betty Ann Walls)
CGP's Mom

3 cups sugar   heaping Tbsp. flour
Pinch salt
mix well. In another bowl, mix:
1 ½ cups light syrup   1 ½ sticks margarine melted
9 eggs   Tbsp. vanilla
Add dry ingredients
Layer 3 cups (lightly toasted) pecans in bottoms of 3 unbaked pie shells. Pour mixture over pecans and bake 350 for 40 or 45 minutes until set in middle.

Mr. Demmie's Rabbit, Squirrel, Frog Legs or Quail

Thoroughly clean your critter and soak in salt water. Heat 'bout ¼ cup grease in deep black iron skillet. Cut critter into pieces: legs and backbone. Batter in flour, salt and pepper, and drop in grease to fry. Turn to brown on all sides. When meat is browned, pour 1 cup water over meat, cover, and reduce heat. Simmer until meat is tender and gravy has formed. Serve over hot biscuits.

Bill's Dills
CGPs brother-in-law

2 quarts water   1 quart vinegar
2/3 cup canning salt
   --- mix above ingredients and bring to a boil

Have already placed in canning jars: generous sprig of fresh dill, med. clove garlic lightly crushed, jalapeno pepper cut in half, and cucumber strips. (strips work better than circles). Pour boiling liquid over cucumbers. Use knife to rid air bubbles. Seal with hot lids. Let set several weeks for flavor.

Old Timey Chicken Dumplins' - Cheryl

One whole chicken, boiled and deboned. Set meat aside. In large pot, pour 1 ½ quarts water, 2 cups milk, and 1 stick butter or margarine. Add salt and pepper to taste and a can of condensed chicken soup. (may add 2 or 3 small chicken bouillon cubes if no soup). Stir well and heat. *optional: about ¼ tsp. onion flakes

In large bowl sift 5 cups flour. Make a depression in the middle of the flour and add 3/4 cup shortening. Pour 1 ½ cup milk over shortening and work together with hand. Begin pulling in flour when the shortening and milk is mixed. Continue working in flour and kneading it until a large round of dough is formed. Leave it a little sticky.

When the pot begins to boil, drop in bits of the dough until all is used. Reduce heat and cover for 5 minutes until dough is cooked light and fluffy. Add chicken meat and stir LIGHTLY. Serve warm.

Mrs. Tina Hull's Irish Potato Candy

Boil and mash 1 medium Irish potato. Add powdered sugar until the mixture becomes thick enough to roll out - 1/4 in. thick. Spread peanut butter evenly over and roll into a log. Slice into circles and serve.

*leftover mashed potatoes may be used if minimum salt and pepper used)

Aunt Glimmer's Tea Cakes
CGP's paternal great-aunt

3 eggs
1 cup butter
4 cups self-rising flour

2 cups sugar
1 tsp. vanilla

Cream eggs, sugar, vanilla, and butter. Add flour and mix well. Drop by teaspoon full on lightly greased baking sheet. 325 for 10 minutes or until bottoms are brown.

Charles's Brunswick Stew
CGP's daddy

Boil each meat in a separate pot. Reserve Chicken stock.

3 whole chickens 5 pounds beef roast
7 pounds pork shoulder boil until tender and debone. Grind meat.
6 pounds potatoes, and 3 pounds onions- put through grinder and boil in chicken stock until tender.
6 (16 oz.) cans whole kernel corn, sent through a grinder
4 (#10 cans) whole peeled tomatoes sent through grinder

In a large very large pot—a black iron washpot over an outside open fire is best—begin heating the cooked vegetables in chicken stock. Add: 2 bottles Worcestershire sauce, 1 cup yellow mustard, ½ cup lemon juice, 3 tsp. (or 4 depending on taste) hot sauce, ¼ cup sugar, 2 #10 cans ketchup, ½ can Chili sauce, and salt and pepper to taste. Mix well. When thoroughly heated, add ground meat. May need to add more broth, but mixture should be thick. Stir well and simmer 1 to 1 ½ hours or until steady steam rises from the pot. Cool and put in containers to freeze.

Miss Nora's Beet Pickles

Dig beets and cut off tops. Do not cut into the beet root, leave stubble of stems on top. Wash thoroughly. Place whole beets in boiling water and cook until skins begin to pop and beets are tender. Remove with slotted dipper and place in cold water. Peel - peelings should slip right off. Cut off tops and any spots. Slice or quarter each beet and pack in jars.

Mix 2 cups vinegar to 1 cup water and add 2 cups sugar. May add cinnamon and cloves if prefer. Bring the vinegar, water, and sugar to a boil until sugar is dissolved.

Pour liquid over beets and seal with hot lids. Water bath 10 minutes.

*more liquid depending on amount of beets.

Old Timey Creamy Potato Salad
CGP

Peel and dice 5 or 6 potatoes. Boil until tender. Drain and pour into large bowl. Add diced sweet pickles, 2 tsp. vinegar, dash of sugar, mayonnaise, and salt and pepper to taste. Stir until creamy with a few potato chunks. Slice 3 hard-boiled eggs and arrange over the top.

Homemade mayonnaise:
1 egg- room temp   1tsp .(dry) mustard-reg. yellow will do
1 cup salad oil   Tsp. lemon juice or vinegar
1 tsp. salt

Break egg into bowl. Add mustard, salt, and liquid. Add ½ the oil. Whisk until blended well. Continue whisking; add the remaining oil. Makes 1 ¼ cups

Miss Eva's Chicken Dressing

Whole boiled chicken, boned and chopped (or several thighs)
large pan cooked cornbread
2 eggs
chicken broth – 1 can
Condensed chicken soup – 1 can
2 onions, chopped
Poultry seasoning – to taste
salt and pepper to taste
½ stick margarine

Crumble cornbread in large bowl. Add other ingredients. Mix well. May need to add more chicken broth (from boiling) to make the dressing thinner. (needs to be fairly juicy). Bake in 350 oven until lightly browned.